A
TREASURY
OF
VICTORIAN
GHOST
STORIES

Also by the author

A TREASURY OF VICTORIAN DETECTIVE STORIES
SCIENCE FICTION WRITERS

A TREASURY OF VICTORIAN GHOST STORIES

EDITED BY

Everett F. Bleiler

Charles Scribner's Sons
New York

A Note on the Text of This Volume

The stories in this collection have been taken from many different sources, which do not always agree with one another on matters of style. Original punctuation and other stylistic points have been followed exactly. Although obvious typographical errors have been corrected, variant usages have been allowed to stand.

Contents

Contents

A
TREASURY
OF
VICTORIAN
GHOST
STORIES

Introduction

When we classify English literature historically, we usually identify chronological groupings by the name of the reigning sovereign and speak of Elizabethan or Jacobean literature, Georgian or Edwardian. On the whole this system works, for the average British reign since the accession of Queen Elizabeth I has been about twenty-two years, which is long enough for a style to emerge, flower, and die, as each new generation of authors matures. Boundaries of style, too, are vague enough that few authors become trapped in an unsuitable milieu. But if a reign is too long, as occasionally happens, the system fails. Such is the case with Queen Victoria, who ruled from 1837 to 1901. A novel written in 1840 by, say, Theodore Hook, does not have much in common with a novel written around 1900 by Henry James. Yet we call all the fiction in this period "Victorian," perhaps qualifying the word with adjectives like early, middle or high, late or fin de siècle.

In some branches of popular fiction—the detective story, science fiction, and the ghost story—this large lumping together of Victorian is even less satisfactory than in mainstream literature, for popular literature, paradoxically, is more likely to respond to changes in the outside world than is mainstream; yet it is also more likely to continue, by internal momentum, beyond its period of origin. To illustrate this bifurcation: the detective novels of Wilkie Collins or Mary E. Braddon of the 1860s are quite different from the short stories of Arthur Conan Doyle or Arthur Morrison of the 1890s, yet Dick Donovan in the 1890s was still writing a story much like those of the pseudonymous "Waters" in the 1860s. Of the stories in this collection Mrs. Margaret Oliphant's

"The Library Window" really should have been written two decades earlier.

In supernatural fiction, what by accident of longevity we usually lump together as Victorian really should be seen as three literatures which in many ways offer opposing theories of the supernatural and of literary practice. It would be rash to give exact dates for period breaks, beyond saying that the late 1850s and early 1860s, and the late 1880s and early 1890s, seem to be transition zones. And, of course, one must bear a caveat in mind: literary history is a subtraction from a totality and is usually concerned with the avant-garde of each period, rather than with the older, sometimes minor people who are writing in the style of a generation or two earlier. Times may change, but individual authors do not necessarily change.

The early Victorian period is much the weakest of these three divisions as far as supernatural fiction is concerned. Perhaps in reaction to the exuberance of the earlier Romantic period, supernatural fiction is not frequently met between 1840 and 1860, and where it appears, it usually has a secondary property that serves as an apology for its existence. Charles Dickens, for example, wrote most of his supernatural fiction either as semiallegory or as tongue-in-cheek humor. Other historically important authors of the period show much the same attitude. George MacDonald's *Phantastes* (1858) is a very elaborate allegory of Christian faith, told in a wealth of fantastic imagery, while Edward Bulwer-Lytton's *Zanoni* (1842) is so formalized an allegory that most modern editions append to the story a table, prepared by Harriet Martineau, identifying the characters with the abstractions they represent.

In this collection Charles Dickens's "The Ghost in the Bride's Chamber," in addition to displaying typical character grotesques and a tongue-in-cheek ending, is really a morality, like *A Christmas Carol in Prose* (1843) and *The Chimes* (1844), about civilized behavior. Wilkie Collins's "Nine O'Clock!," an early work, is somewhat archaic for its date of writing. It was probably suggested in part by an anonymous story of German origin, anthologized under such titles as "The Fated Hour," "The Fatal Hour," and "The Sisters." In "The Fated Hour," which was first published in English in 1813, there is a preoccupation with time (also with nine o'clock), a supernatural death warning, a hope to circumvent fate, and defeat. In Collins's case the story ties in with the fascination, almost obsession, with fate that characterizes his later novels, particularly *Armadale* (1866). The immediate background of the story mirrors contemporary British interest in French political activities. The sensation and social fiction of Victor Hugo and Eugène Sue were popular in Great Britain, and the latest French revolution was still fresh in mind.

Stories from the middle period of Victoria's reign, perhaps from 1860 or so to 1885 or so, are no longer allegorical or tongue-in-cheek, but resemble the domestic novel of the time. Matters of everyday life are very important. The role of women is significant (whereas in the fiction of the immediately earlier and later periods the stories tend to be male-oriented), but not in a modern, feminist sense. Women are seen as housewives, mothers, platonic sweethearts, or security symbols. Such a focus is not too surprising, since most of this fiction appeared in magazines published for women and written and edited by women. The domesticity of country life can be seen in this collection in Miss Braddon's "At Chrighton Abbey," while Mrs. Henry Wood's "A Curious Experience" displays all the solidarity of life that we usually associate with the middle class in the high Victorian period. Quite different are the fright pattern and unconscious fears projected by Rhoda Broughton's "The Man with the Nose," which although Victorian on the surface is anachronistic underneath. As might be expected from their domestic readership, an important theme in both the "security" story and the "insecurity" story is stability—maintaining it, violating it, or restoring it.

Where supernatural phenomena are concerned, the chief interest of the middle Victorian authors lay in what we would call parapsychology, or the phenomena of psychical research. Indeed, there is a very close correspondence between literary themes of the 1860s and 1870s and what was believed by such Victorians as believed such things. If the ghost stories of this period are compared with the topics studied in the reports of the British Society for Psychical Research, five common interests are to be found: apparitions that announce the recent death of their bodies, prophetic dreams, second sight, haunted houses, and ghosts that are unquiet for one reason or another. Factually, these are the stories and anecdotes, say, of Cousin Euphemia, who saw the swarth of her old lover looking in the window and later learned that he had died in India on that day. Or of, perhaps, Mrs. Dreemer, who dreamed that the "Great Northern" was sinking, and begged her brother not to sail on it. Or of Major Shudderleigh's rented house, where an apparition fumbles at the doors of a locked cabinet, presumably worried about compromising letters hidden inside a drawer. Other ghosts wanted their murderers punished and were willing to go to a great deal of trouble for this purpose.

These were typical situations, represented in this collection by such stories as Miss Braddon's "At Chrighton Abbey," with its portent of tragedy, and Mrs. Henry Wood's "A Curious Experience," where a crime in the past results in a faded haunting. Similar in nature are the ghost in the anonymous "Le Vert Galant" and the symbol of conscience in Mrs. J. H. Riddell's "A Terrible Vengeance."

The ghosts themselves are simple creatures. They live in a fairly concrete form and are purposive: they want justice. They are not really malevolent, and they can be gotten rid of easily. One simply looks to see what they want, and that is the end of them. There seldom are psychological depths or repercussions.

In all these stories, it will be observed, the technical means of presentation involves contrast. The middle Victorians seem to have believed that a ghost story is most effective if it takes place in an everyday setting, and that one ghost or piece of supernaturalism per story is enough for any reasonable person. This is certainly a permissible aesthetic, but it is not necessarily the only one.

The late Victorians took the opposite point of view on almost everything that the middle Victorians held to be firm and established. The writers of the 1890s believed that supernaturalism should be organic, connected with and emerging naturally from its setting, and not something alien. Thus, Count Dracula flits out of a detailed and exotic assemblage of Balkan peasant folkways, travelers' accounts, Rumanian history, decrepit architecture, and the unfamiliar. The early horrors of M. R. James lurk around ancient piles, ready to pounce on the unwary, and are not easily dispelled. The supernatural is something that exists in its own right, subject to its own dynamics and realities, a point of view much closer to that of the Romantic period or of our own time. In this collection Paul Heyse's "Midday Magic" is set on an abnormally hot day, when a young man suffering from physical and mental exhaustion, possibly on the edge of a breakdown, is momentarily psychologically receptive to the remnant of an ancient tragedy. Bernard Capes's "The Vanishing House" and R. Murray Gilchrist's "Witch In-Grain" offer strange environments in which many odd things might happen.

By and large the late Victorians—one must ignore survivals on the sub-culture levels of literature—were much less concerned with paranormal phenomena than with problems of evil, the inexplicable, and the depths of human personality. They were not concerned with the occasional act of violence on the part of a frail mortal, but with evil as a force. Sometimes this evil was externalized and concentrated, as in the portrait in Oscar Wilde's *The Picture of Dorian Gray* (1891); sometimes such evil resulted from a dualistic universe, as in John Meade Falkner's *The Lost Stradivarius* (1895), where evil so balances good that there is a *visio malefica* to parallel the mystical vision of the saints. In the stories of Arthur Machen, ancient evil, forced under-ground both literally and figuratively, has swollen and grown in the dark, and can destroy a mortal foolish or unlucky enough to encounter it. Such supernatural beings, like those of the early stories of M. R. James, are malevolent, a far cry from the symbols of justice that people the middle Victorian ghost stories.

A curious difference between the middle and late Victorian stories lies in the author's relation to the supernaturalism in the stories. In the later works the supernatural often has personal meaning to the writer and is not just a societal symbol or a literary device. Whereas high Victorian writers like Mrs. Oliphant or Mrs. Wood, who accepted a supernatural religion, wrote about ghosts that they did not believe in, in the later period agnostics and atheists like Ambrose Bierce, Gertrude Atherton, and Henry James wrote in supernatural terms about things they took very seriously. Bierce, for example, embodied his horror dreams in his fiction and found a morbid fascination in stories of dis-appearances and the unquiet dead.

Middle Victorian ghost stories tend to be uniform in their ideas and literary techniques, except for those of Le Fanu, but the late Victorian ghost stories, paralleling the enormous explosion of subject matter in the mainstream novel, emerge in a shower of different forms, with many different types of association with the supernatural. There are ghost stories, like the work of Henry James and Gertrude Atherton, that are psychological studies, and ghost stories that are self-analysis, like those of Ambrose Bierce. There are stories that are interwoven with a quest for beauty, such as those of Emma Dawson, incorporating Swinburnian verse. Some stories show cross-fertilization from other genres, like Arthur Quiller-Couch's "The Laird's Luck" (which is related to the contemporary historical adventure novel), and stories that have a proto-Expressionist point like Heyse's "Midday Magic." Many stories, like the works included here of Vincent O'Sullivan, R. Murray Gilchrist, and Emma Dawson, are written in the decorated style of the Aesthetic Movement. Others, like Bierce's, are concerned with matters of form and tone—matters that had little relevance to the middle Victorians, who displayed a classical freezing of form and little interest in experimentation.

II.

The stories in this collection have been chosen, in part, to illustrate developmental patterns in the Victorian period, and to show ap-proaches peculiar to important authors as well as styles widely used during a particular part of the period. A second criterion has been newness to the reader. There would be no point in reprinting the over-familiar nineteenth-century stories that have been standard fare in anthologies for the past seventy years or so. Bulwer-Lytton's "The Haunted and the Haunters" (1859), for example, has been anthologized at least thirty times in the past fifty years, and Dickens's two conventional ghost stories, "To Be Taken with a Grain of Salt" (1865) and "No. 1 Branch Line, The Signalman" (1866), have been reprinted at least twenty times, not even counting special collections of Dickens's works. Similarly the stories of Arthur Machen, M. P. Shiel, and Henry James have been anthologized to death. But there are many stories by authors less well known that may be reprinted without apology.

To my knowledge only two of the stories in the present collection have ever been printed in an American anthology of supernatural fiction (and that long ago), and most of the others have not been reprinted since their first publication. Dickens's "The Ghost in the Bride's Chamber" has escaped all but the fullest editions of his collected works, while Wilkie Collins's "Nine O'Clock!" has never before been reprinted. Bierce's series of stories collectively called "Bodies of the Dead" is almost unknown. They do not appear in *The Collected Works of Ambrose Bierce* nor in the "complete" short story collections. They were first printed in the 1893 edition of *Can Such Things Be?* and last printed in the Neale 1903 edition of the same book. Since then they have dropped out of sight.

Much the most important reason for reprinting the stories in this volume is, of course, neither historical example nor novelty to the reader, but literary quality and enjoyability. Most of all I hope that the reader agrees that these are stories to be read and enjoyed.

E. F. Bleiler

Charles Dickens

Charles John Huffam Dickens (1812–1870) in his major works usually treated the supernatural as a mechanism for a semiallegorical message. Noteworthy, of course, is A Christmas Carol in Prose, in which forces of power browbeat a miser into a reformation. In The Haunted Man and the Ghost's Bargain memory is personified as a spirit, and in The Chimes a horror dream causes a change in character, much as happened to Scrooge. Today we might call these stories narratives of unconscious emergence or dissociated personality fragments.

Another group of supernatural stories is characterized by a tongue-in-cheek approach. The narratives in The Pickwick Papers, if read closely, really offer alcoholic delirium as the explanation for what another author might have left unexplained. The Bagman's uncle was simply drunk.

Yet Dickens also wrote traditional stories in which the fragmentary dead cry out for justice, as in "The Trial for Murder," and stories in which visions can reveal the future, as in "The Signalman."

The following two stories are among Dickens's least-known works. "To Be Read at Dusk" first appeared as a contribution to The Keepsake for 1852, a Christmas annual. It is not included in most editions of Dickens's works, but around 1895 copies of a little pamphlet entitled To Be Read at Dusk began to turn up at rare-book auctions. This pamphlet was eagerly sought by collectors, and was considered one of the rarest of Dickens items until John Carter and Graham Pollard, in their investigation of book forgeries, revealed that the pamphlet was one of a series of falsified editions perpetrated by Thomas Wise around 1890, and back-dated to 1852. The Keepsake printing of 1852, however, is genuine.

7

The untitled story here called "The Ghost in the Bride's Chamber" has also long been neglected. It was one of the results of a journalistic junket undertaken by Dickens and Wilkie Collins. In the summer of 1857 they started a walking tour of Cumberland and Lancashire, sending back their impressions and experiences to Dickens's periodical Household Words, where they were serialized as "The Lazy Tour of Two Idle Apprentices." On one occasion Collins sprained an ankle and the trip was halted for a time at the King's Arms Hotel in Lancaster, where Dickens wrote about the multiple ghost in the bride's chamber.

TO BE READ
AT DUSK

One, two, three, four, five. There were five of them.

Five couriers, sitting on a bench outside the convent on the summit of the Great St. Bernard in Switzerland, looking at the remote heights, stained by the setting sun, as if a mighty quantity of red wine had been broached upon the mountain top, and had not yet had time to sink into the snow.

This is not my simile. It was made for the occasion by the stoutest courier, who was a German. None of the others took any more notice of it than they took of me, sitting on another bench on the other side of the convent door, smoking my cigar, like them, and—also like them—looking at the reddened snow, and at the lonely shed hard by, where the bodies of belated travellers, dug out of it, slowly wither away, knowing no corruption in that cold region.

The wine upon the mountain top soaked in as we looked; the mountain became white; the sky, a very dark blue; the wind rose; and the air turned piercing cold. The five couriers buttoned their rough coats. There being no safer man to imitate in all such proceedings than a courier, I buttoned mine.

The mountain in the sunset had stopped the five couriers in a conversation. It is a sublime sight, likely to stop conversation. The mountain being now out of the sunset, they resumed. Not that I had heard any part of their previous discourse; for indeed, I had not then broken away from the American gentleman, in the travellers' parlour of the convent, who, sitting with his face to the fire, had undertaken to realise to me the whole progress of events which had led to the accumulation by the Honourable Ananias Dodger of one of the largest acquisitions of dollars ever made in our country.

9

"My God!" said the Swiss courier, speaking in French, which I do not hold (as some authors appear to do) to be such an all-sufficient excuse for a naughty word, that I have only to write it in that language to make it innocent; "if you talk of ghosts—"

"But I *don't* talk of ghosts," said the German.

"Of what then?" asked the Swiss.

"If I knew of what then," said the German, "I should probably know a great deal more."

It was a good answer, I thought, and it made me curious. So I moved my position to that corner of my bench which was nearest to them, and leaning my back against the convent wall, heard perfectly, without appearing to attend.

"Thunder and lightning!" said the German, warming, "when a certain man is coming to see you, unexpectedly; and, without his own knowledge, sends some invisible messenger, to put the idea of him into your head all day, what do you call that? When you walk along a crowded street—at Frankfort, Milan, London, Paris—and think that a passing stranger is like your friend Heinrich, and then that another passing stranger is like your friend Heinrich, and so begin to have a strange foreknowledge that presently you'll meet your friend Heinrich —which you do, though you believe him at Trieste—what do you call *that?*"

"It's not uncommon, either," murmured the Swiss and the other three.

"Uncommon!" said the German. "It's as common as cherries in the Black Forest. It's as common as maccaroni at Naples. And Naples reminds me! When the old Marchesa Senzanima shrieks at a card-party on the Chiaja—as I heard and saw her, for it happened in a Bavarian family of mine, and I was overlooking the service that evening—I say, when the old Marchesa starts up at the card-table, white through her rouge, and cries, 'My sister in Spain is dead! I felt her cold touch on my back!—and when that sister *is* dead at the moment—what do you call that?"

"Or when the blood of San Gennaro liquefies at the request of the clergy—as all the world knows that it does regularly once a year, in my native city," said the Neapolitan courier after a pause, with a comical look, "what do you call that?"

"*That!*" cried the German. "Well, I think I know a name for that."

"Miracle?" said the Neapolitan, with the same sly face.

The German merely smoked and laughed; and they all smoked and laughed.

"Bah!" said the German, presently. "I speak of things that really do happen. When I want to see the conjurer, I pay to see a professed one, and have my money's worth. Very strange things do happen without ghosts. Ghosts! Giovanni Baptista, tell your story of the English bride. There's no ghost in that, but something full as strange. Will any man tell me what?"

As there was a silence among them, I glanced around. He whom I took to be Baptista was lighting a fresh cigar. He presently went on to speak. He was a Genoese, as I judged.

"The story of the English bride?" said he. "Basta! one ought not to call so slight a thing a story. Well, it's all one. But it's true. Observe me well, gentlemen, it's true. That which glitters is not always gold: but what I am going to tell, is true."

He repeated this more than once.

Ten years ago, I took my credentials to an English gentleman at Long's Hotel, in Bond Street, London, who was about to travel—it might be for one year, it might be for two. He approved of them; likewise of me. He was pleased to make inquiry. The testimony that he received was favourable. He engaged me by the six months, and my entertainment was generous.

He was young, handsome, very happy. He was enamoured of a fair young English lady, with a sufficient fortune, and they were going to be married. It was the wedding-trip, in short, that we were going to take. For three months' rest in the hot weather (it was early summer then) he had hired an old place on the Riviera, at an easy distance from my city, Genoa, on the road to Nice. Did I know that place? Yes; I told him I knew it well. It was an old palace with great gardens. It was a little bare, and it was a little dark and gloomy, being close surrounded by trees; but it was spacious, ancient, grand, and on the seashore. He said it had been so described to him exactly, and he was well pleased that I knew it. For its being a little bare of furniture, all such places were. For its being a little gloomy, he had hired it principally for the gardens, and he and my mistress would pass the summer weather in their shade.

"So all goes well, Baptista?" said he.

"Indubitably, signore; very well."

We had a travelling chariot for our journey, newly built for us, and in all respects complete. All we had was complete; we wanted for nothing. The marriage took place. They were happy. *I* was happy, seeing all so bright, being so well situated, going to my own city, teaching my language in the rumble to the maid, la bella Carolina, whose heart was gay with laughter: who was young and rosy.

The time flew. But I observed—listen to this, I pray! (and here the courier dropped his voice)—I observed my mistress sometimes brooding in a manner very strange; in a frightened manner; in an un-happy manner; with a cloudy, uncertain alarm upon her. I think that I began to notice this when I was walking up hills by the carriage side, and master had gone on in front. At any rate, I remember that it impressed itself upon my mind one evening in the South of France, when she called to me to call master back; and when he came back, and walked for a long way, talking encouragingly and affectionately to her, with his hand upon the open window, and her in it. Now and then, he laughed in a merry way, as if he were bantering her out of something. By-and-by, she laughed, and then all went well again.

It was curious. I asked la bella Carolina, the pretty little one, Was mistress unwell?—No.—Out of spirits?—No.—Fearful of bad roads, or brigands?—No. And what made it more mysterious was, the pretty little one would not look at me in giving answer, but *would* look at the view.

But one day she told me the secret.

"If you must know," said Carolina, "I find, from what I have over-heard, that mistress is haunted."

"How haunted?"

"By a dream."

"What dream?"

"By a dream of a face. For three nights before her marriage, she saw a face in a dream—always the same face, and only One."

"A terrible face?"

"No. The face of a dark, remarkable-looking man, in black, with black hair and a grey moustache—a handsome man except for a re-served and secret air. Not a face she ever saw, or at all like a face she ever saw. Doing nothing in the dream but looking at her fixedly, out of darkness."

"Does the dream come back?"

"Never. The recollection of it, is all her trouble."

"And why does it trouble her?"

Carolina shook her head.

"That's master's question," said la bella. "She don't know. She wonders why, herself. But I heard her tell him, only last night, that if she was to find a picture of that face in our Italian house (which she is afraid she will) she did not know how she could ever bear it."

Upon my word, I was fearful after this (said the Genoese courier) of our coming to the old palazzo, lest some such ill-starred picture should happen to be there. I knew there were many there; and, as we got nearer and nearer to the place, I wished the whole gallery in the crater of Vesuvius. To mend the matter, it was a stormy dismal evening when we, at last, approached that part of the Riviera. It thundered;

and the thunder of my city and its environs, rolling among the high hills, is very loud. The lizards ran in and out of the chinks in the broken stone wall of the garden, as if they were frightened; the frogs bubbled and croaked their loudest; the sea-wind moaned, and the wet trees dripped; and the lightning—body of San Lorenzo, how it lightened!

We all know what an old palace in or near Genoa is—how time and the sea air have blotted it—how the drapery painted on the outer walls has peeled off in great flakes of plaster—how the lower windows are darkened with rusty bars of iron—how the courtyard is overgrown with grass—how the outer buildings are dilapidated—how the whole pile seems devoted to ruin. Our palazzo was one of the true kind. It had been shut up close for months. Months?—years!—it had an earthy smell, like a tomb. The scent of the orange trees on the broad back terrace, and of the lemons ripening on the wall, and of some shrubs that grew around a broken fountain, had got into the house somehow, and had never been able to get out again. There was, in every room, an aged smell, grown faint with confinement. It pined in all the cupboards and drawers. In the little rooms of communication between great rooms, it was stifling. If you turned a picture—to come back to the pictures—there it still was, clinging to the wall behind the frame, like a sort of bat.

The lattice-blinds were close shut, all over the house. There were two ugly grey old women in the house, to take care of it; one of them with a spindle, who stood winding and mumbling in the door-way, and who would as soon have let in the devil as the air. Master, mistress, la bella Carolina, and I, went all through the palazzo. I went first, though I have named myself last, opening the windows and the lattice-blinds, and shaking down on myself splashes of rain, and scraps of mortar, and now and then a dozing mosquito, or a monstrous, fat, blotchy, Genoese spider.

When I had let the evening light into a room, master, mistress, and la bella Carolina, entered. Then we looked round at all the pictures, and I went forward again into another room. Mistress secretly had great fear of meeting with the likeness of that face—we all had; but there was no such thing. The Madonna and Bambino, San Francisco, San Sebastiano, Venus, Santa Caterina, Angels, Brigands, Friars, Temples at Sunset, Battles, White Horses, Forests, Apostles, Doges, all my old acquaintances many times repeated?—yes. Dark handsome man in black, reserved and secret, with black hair and grey moustache, looking fixedly at mistress out of darkness?—no.

At last we got through all the rooms and all the pictures, and came out into the gardens. They were pretty well kept, being rented by a gardener, and were large and shady. In one place there was a rustic theatre, open to the sky; the stage a green slope; the coulisses, three entrances upon a side, sweet-smelling leafy screens. Mistress moved her bright eyes, even there, as if she looked to see the face come in upon the scene; but all was well.

"Now, Clara," master said, in a low voice, "you see that it is nothing? You are happy."

Mistress was much encouraged. She soon accustomed herself to that grim palazzo, and would sing, and play the harp, and copy the old pictures, and stroll with master under the green trees and vines all day. She was beautiful. He was happy. He would laugh and say to me, mounting his horse for his morning ride before the heat:

"All goes well, Baptista!"

"Yes, signore, thank God, very well."

We kept no company. I took la bella to the Duomo and Annunciata, to the Café, to the Opera, to the village Festa, to the Public Garden, to the Day Theatre, to the Marionetti. The pretty little one was charmed with all she saw. She learnt Italian—heavens! miraculously! Was mistress quite forgetful of that dream? I asked Carolina sometimes. Nearly, said la bella—almost. It was wearing out.

One day master received a letter, and called me.

"Baptista!"

"Signore!"

"A gentleman who is presented to me will dine here to-day. He is called the Signor Dellombra. Let me dine like a prince."

It was an odd name. I did not know that name. But there had been many noblemen and gentlemen pursued by Austria on political suspicions, lately, and some names had changed. Perhaps this was one. Altro! Dellombra was as good a name to me as another.

When the Signor Dellombra came to dinner (said the Genoese courier in the low voice, into which he had subsided once before), I showed him into the reception-room, the great sala of the old palazzo. Master received him with cordiality, and presented him to mistress. As she rose, her face changed, she gave a cry, and fell upon the marble floor.

Then I turned my head to the Signor Dellombra, and saw that he was dressed in black, and had a reserved and secret air, and was a dark remarkable-looking man, with black hair and a grey moustache.

Master raised mistress in his arms, and carried her to her own room, where I sent la bella Carolina straight. La bella told me afterwards that mistress was nearly terrified to death, and that she wandered in her mind about her dream, all night.

Master was vexed and anxious—almost angry, and yet full of solicitude. The Signor Dellombra was a courtly gentleman, and spoke with great respect and sympathy of mistress's being so ill. The African wind had been blowing for some days (they had told him at his hotel of the Maltese Cross), and he knew that it was often hurtful. He hoped the beautiful lady would recover soon. He begged permission to retire, and to renew his visit when he should have the happiness of hearing that she was better. Master would not allow of this, and they dined alone.

He withdrew early. Next day he called at the gate, on horseback, to inquire for mistress. He did so two or three times in that week.

What I observed myself, and what la bella Carolina told me, united to explain to me that master had now set his mind on curing mistress of her fanciful terror. He was all kindness, but he was sensible and firm. He reasoned with her, that to encourage such fancies was to invite melancholy, if not madness. That it rested with herself to be herself. That if she once resisted her strange weakness, so successfully as to receive the Signor Dellombra as an English lady would receive any other guest, it was for ever conquered. To make an end, the signore came again, and mistress received him without marked distress (though with constraint and apprehension still), and the evening passed serenely. Master was so delighted with this change, and so anxious to confirm it, that the Signor Dellombra became a constant guest. He was accomplished in pictures, books, and music; and his society, in any grim palazzo, would have been welcome.

I used to notice, many times, that mistress was not quite recovered. She would cast down her eyes and droop her head, before the Signor Dellombra, or would look at him with a terrified and fascinated glance, as if his presence had some evil influence or power upon her. Turning from her to him, I used to see him in the shaded gardens, or the large half-lighted sala, looking, as I might say, "fixedly upon her out of darkness." But, truly, I had not forgotten la bella Carolina's words describing the face in the dream.

After his second visit I heard master say:

"Now, see, my dear Clara, it's over! Dellombra has come and gone, and your apprehension is broken like glass."

"Will he—will he ever come again?" asked mistress.

"Again? Why, surely, over and over again! Are you cold?" (she shivered).

"No, dear—but—he terrifies me: are you sure that he need come again?"

"The surer for the question, Clara!" replied master, cheerfully.

But he was very hopeful of her complete recovery now, and grew more and more so every day. She was beautiful. He was happy.

"All goes well, Baptista?" he would say to me again.

"Yes, signore, thank God; very well."

We were all (said the Genoese courier, constraining himself to speak a little louder), we were all at Rome for the Carnival. I had been out, all day, with a Sicilian, a friend of mine, and a courier, who was there with an English family. As I returned at night to our hotel, I met the little Carolina, who never stirred from home alone, running distractedly along the Corso.

"Carolina! What's the matter?"

"O Baptista! O, for the Lord's sake! where is my mistress?"

"Mistress, Carolina?"

"Gone since morning—told me, when master went out on his day's journey, not to call her, for she was tired with not resting in the night (having been in pain), and would lie in bed until the evening; then get up refreshed. She is gone!—she is gone! Master has come back, broken down the door, and she is gone! My beautiful, my good, my innocent mistress!"

The pretty little one so cried, and raved, and tore herself that I could not have held her, but for her swooning on my arm as if she had been shot. Master came up—in manner, face, or voice, no more the master that I knew, than I was he. He took me (I laid the little one upon her bed in the hotel, and left her with the chamber-women), in a carriage, furiously through the darkness, across the desolate Campagna. When it was day, and we stopped at a miserable post-house, all the horses had been hired twelve hours ago, and sent away in different directions. Mark me! by the Signor Dellombra, who had passed there in a carriage, with a frightened English lady crouching in one corner.

I never heard (said the Genoese courier, drawing a long breath) that she was ever traced beyond that spot. All I know is, that she vanished into infamous oblivion, with the dreaded face beside her that she had seen in her dream.

"What do you call *that?*" said the German courier, triumphantly. "Ghosts! There are no ghosts *there!* What do you call this, that I am going to tell you? Ghosts! There are no ghosts *here!*"

I took an engagement once (pursued the German courier) with an English gentleman, elderly and a bachelor, to travel through my country, my Fatherland. He was a merchant who traded with my country and knew the language, but who had never been there since he was a boy—as I judge, some sixty years before.

His name was James, and he had a twin-brother John, also a bachelor. Between these brothers there was a great affection. They were in business together, at Goodman's Fields, but they did not live together. Mr. James dwelt in Poland Street, turning out of Oxford Street, London; Mr. John resided by Epping Forest.

Mr. James and I were to start for Germany in about a week. The exact day depended on business. Mr. John came to Poland Street (where I was staying in the house), to pass that week with Mr. James. But he said to his brother on the second day, "I don't feel very well, James. There's not much the matter with me; but I think I am a little gouty. I'll go home and put myself under the care of my old house-keeper, who understands my ways. If I get quite better, I'll come back and see you before you go. If I don't feel well enough to resume my visit where I leave it off, why *you* will come and see *me* before you go." Mr. James, of course, said he would, and they shook hands—both hands, as they always did—and Mr. John ordered out his old-fashioned chariot and rumbled home.

It was on the second night after that—that is to say, the fourth in the week—when I was awoke out of my sound sleep by Mr. James coming into my bedroom in his flannel-gown, with a lighted candle. He sat upon the side of my bed, and looking at me, said:

"Wilhelm, I have reason to think I have got some strange illness upon me."

I then perceived that there was a very unusual expression in his face.

"Wilhelm," said he, "I am not afraid or ashamed to tell you what I might be afraid or ashamed to tell another man. You come from a sensible country, where mysterious things are inquired into and are not settled to have been weighed and measured—or to have been unweighable and unmeasurable—or in either case to have been completely disposed of, for all time—ever so many years ago. I have just now seen the phantom of my brother."

I confess (said the German courier) that it gave me a little tingling of the blood to hear it.

"I have just now seen," Mr. James repeated, looking full at me, that I might see how collected he was, "the phantom of my brother John. I was sitting up in bed, unable to sleep, when it came into my room, in a white dress, and regarding me earnestly, passed up to the end of the room, glanced at some papers on my writing-desk, turned, and, still looking earnestly at me as it passed the bed, went out at the door. Now, I am not in the least mad, and am not in the least disposed to invest that phantom with any external existence out of myself. I think it is a warning to me that I am ill; and I think I had better be bled."

I got out of bed directly (said the German courier) and began to get on my clothes, begging him not to be alarmed, and telling him that I would go myself to the doctor. I was just ready, when we heard a loud knocking and ringing at the street door. My room being an attic at the back, and Mr. James's being the second-floor room in the front, we went down to his room, and put up the window, to see what was the matter.

"Is that Mr. James?" said a man below, falling back to the opposite side of the way to look up.

"It is," said Mr. James, "and you are my brother's man, Robert."

"Yes, Sir. I am sorry to say, Sir, that Mr. John is ill. He is very bad, Sir. It is even feared that he may be lying at the point of death. He wants to see you, Sir. I have a chaise here. Pray come to him. Pray lose no time."

Mr. James and I looked at one another. "Wilhelm," said he, "this is strange. I wish you to come with me!" I helped him to dress, partly there and partly in the chaise; and no grass grew under the horses' iron shoes between Poland Street and the Forest.

Now, mind! (said the German courier) I went with Mr. James into his brother's room, and I saw and heard myself what follows.

His brother lay upon his bed, at the upper end of a long bed-chamber. His old housekeeper was there, and others were there: I think three others were there, if not four, and they had been with him since early in the afternoon. He was in white, like the figure—neces-sarily so, because he had his nightdress on. He looked like the figure—necessarily so, because he looked earnestly at his brother when he saw him come into the room.

But, when his brother reached the bed-side, he slowly raised himself in bed, and looking full upon him, said these words:

"JAMES, YOU HAVE SEEN ME BEFORE, TO-NIGHT—AND YOU KNOW IT!"
And so died!

I waited, when the German courier ceased, to hear something said of this strange story. The silence was unbroken. I looked round, and the five couriers were gone: so noiselessly that the ghostly mountain might have absorbed them into its eternal snows. By this time, I was by no means in a mood to sit alone in that awful scene, with the chill air coming solemnly upon me—or, if I may tell the truth, to sit alone anywhere. So I went back into the convent-parlour, and, finding the American gentleman still disposed to relate the biography of the Honourable Ananias Dodger, heard it all out.

THE GHOST
IN THE
BRIDE'S CHAMBER

When Mr. Goodchild had looked out of the Lancaster Inn-window for two hours on end, with great perseverance, he began to entertain a misgiving that he was growing industrious. He therefore set himself next, to explore the country from the tops of all the steep hills in the neighbourhood.

He came back at dinner-time, red and glowing, to tell Thomas Idle what he had seen. Thomas [who had sprained one ankle because he had exerted himself to go up a mountain when he ought to have known that his proper course of conduct was to stop at the bottom of it, was] on his back reading. [He] listened with great composure, and asked him whether he really had gone up those hills, and bothered himself with those views, and walked all those miles?

"Because I want to know," added Thomas, "what you would say of it, if you were obliged to do it?"

"It would be different, then," said Francis. "It would be work, then; now, it's play."

"Play!" replied Thomas Idle, utterly repudiating the reply. "Play! Here is a man goes systematically tearing himself to pieces, and putting himself through an incessant course of training, as if he were always under articles to fight a match for the champion's belt, and he calls it Play! Play!" exclaimed Thomas Idle, scornfully contemplating his one boot in the air. "You *can't* play. You don't know what it is. You make work of everything."

The bright Goodchild amiably smiled.

"So you do," said Thomas. "I mean it. To me you are an absolutely terrible fellow. You do nothing like another man. Where another fellow would fall into a footbath of action or emotion, you fall into a

mine. Where any other fellow would be a painted butterfly, you are a
fiery dragon. Where another man would stake a sixpence, you stake
your existence. If you were to go up in a balloon, you would make for
Heaven; and if you were to dive into the depths of the earth, nothing
short of the other place would content you. What a fellow you are,
Francis!"

The cheerful Goodchild laughed.

"It's all very well to laugh, but I wonder you don't feel it to be
serious," said Idle. "A man who can do nothing by halves appears to
me to be a fearful man."

"Tom, Tom," returned Goodchild, "if I can do nothing by halves,
and be nothing by halves, it's pretty clear that you must take me as a
whole, and make the best of me."

With this philosophical rejoinder, the airy Goodchild clapped Mr.
Idle on the shoulder in a final manner, and they sat down to dinner.

"By the bye," said Goodchild, "I have been over a lunatic asylum
too, since I have been out."

"He has been," exclaimed Thomas Idle, casting up his eyes, "over a
lunatic asylum! Not content with being as great an Ass as Captain
Barclay in the pedestrian way, he makes a Lunacy Commissioner of
himself—for nothing!"

"An immense place," said Goodchild, "admirable offices, very good
arrangements, very good attendants; altogether a remarkable place."

"And what did you see there?" asked Mr. Idle, adapting Hamlet's
advice to the occasion, and assuming the virtue of interest, though he
had it not.

"The usual thing," said Francis Goodchild, with a sigh. "Long groves
of blighted men-and-women trees; interminable avenues of hopeless
faces; numbers, without the slightest power of really combining for any
earthly purpose; a society of human creatures who have nothing in
common but that they have all lost the power of being humanly social
with one another."

"Take a glass of wine with me," said Thomas Idle, "and let *us* be
social."

"In one gallery, Tom," pursued Francis Goodchild, "which looked
to me about the length of the Long Walk at Windsor, more or less——"

"Probably less," observed Thomas Idle.

"In one gallery, which was otherwise clear of patients (for they were
all out), there was a poor little dark-chinned, meagre man, with a
perplexed brow and a pensive face, stooping low over the matting on
the floor, and picking out with his thumb and forefinger the course of
its fibres. The afternoon sun was slanting in at the large end-window,
and there were cross patches of light and shade all down the vista,

made by the unseen windows and the open doors of the little sleeping cells on either side. In about the centre of the perspective, under an arch, regardless of the pleasant weather, regardless of the solitude, regardless of approaching footsteps was the poor little dark-chinned, meagre man, poring over the matting. 'What are you doing there?' said my conductor, when we came to him. He looked up, and pointed to the matting. 'I wouldn't do that, I think,' said my conductor, kindly; 'if I were you, I would go and read, or I would lie down if I felt tired; but I wouldn't do that.' The patient considered a moment, and vacantly answered, 'No, sir, I won't; I'll—I'll go and read,' and so he lamely shuffled away into one of the little rooms. I turned my head before we had gone many paces. He had already come out again, and was again poring over the matting, and tracking out its fibres with his thumb and forefinger. I stopped to look at him, and it came into my mind, that probably the course of those fibres as they plaited in and out, over and under, was the only course of things in the whole wide world that it was left to him to understand—that his darkening intellect had narrowed down to the small cleft of light which showed him, 'This piece was twisted this way, went in here, passed under, came out there, was carried on away here to the right where I now put my finger on it, and in this progress of events, the thing was made and came to be here.' Then, I wondered whether he looked into the matting, next, to see if it could show him anything of the process through which *he* came to be there, so strangely poring over it. Then, I thought how all of us, GOD help us! in our different ways are poring over our bits of matting, blindly enough, and what confusions and mysteries we make in the pattern. I had a sadder fellow-feeling with the little dark-chinned, meagre man, by that time, and I came away."

Mr. Idle diverting the conversation to grouse, custards, and they were drinking, they were talking, they were dozing; the door was always opened at an unexpected moment, and they looked towards it, and it was clapped-to again, and nobody was to be seen. When this had happened fifty times or so, Mr. Goodchild had said to his companion, jestingly: "I begin to think, Tom, there was something wrong with those six old men."

Night had come again, and they had been writing for two or three hours: writing, in short, a portion of the lazy notes from which these lazy sheets are taken. They had left off writing, and glasses were on the table between them. The house was closed and quiet. Around the head of Thomas Idle, as he lay upon his sofa, hovered light wreaths of fragrant smoke. The temples of Francis Goodchild, as he leaned back in his chair, with his two hands clasped behind his head, and his legs crossed, were similarly decorated.

They had been discussing several idle subjects of speculation, not omitting the strange old men, and were still so occupied, when Mr. Goodchild abruptly changed his attitude to wind up his watch. They were just becoming drowsy enough to be stopped in their talk by any such slight check. Thomas Idle, who was speaking at the moment, paused and said, "How goes it?"

"One," said Goodchild.

As if he had ordered One old man, and the order were promptly executed (truly, all orders were so, in that excellent hotel), the door opened, and One old man stood there.

He did not come in, but stood with the door in his hand.

"One of the six, Tom, at last!" said Mr. Goodchild, in a surprised whisper.—"Sir, your pleasure?"

"Sir, *your* pleasure?" said the One old man.

"I didn't ring."

"The bell did," said the One old man.

He said BELL, in a deep strong way, that would have expressed the church Bell.

"I had the pleasure, I believe, of seeing you, yesterday?" said Goodchild.

"I cannot undertake to say for certain," was the grim reply of the One old man.

"I think you saw me? Did you not?"

"Saw *you?*" said the old man. "O yes, I saw *you*. But, I see many who never see me."

A chilled, slow, earthy, fixed old man. A cadaverous old man of measured speech. An old man who seemed as unable to wink, as if his eyelids had been nailed to his forehead. An old man whose eyes—two spots of fire—had no more motion than if they had been connected with the back of his skull by screws driven through it, and rivetted and bolted outside, among his grey hair.

The night had turned so cold, to Mr. Goodchild's sensations, that he shivered. He remarked lightly, and half apologetically, "I think somebody is walking over my grave."

"No," said the weird old man, "there is no one there."

Mr. Goodchild looked at Idle, but Idle lay with his head enwreathed in smoke.

"No one there?" said Goodchild.

"There is no one at your grave, I assure you," said the old man.

He had come in and shut the door, and he now sat down. He did not bend himself to sit, as other people do, but seemed to sink bolt upright, as if in water, until the chair stopped him.

"My friend, Mr. Idle," said Goodchild, extremely anxious to introduce a third person into the conversation.

"I am," said the old man, without looking at him, "at Mr. Idle's service."

"If you are an old inhabitant of this place," Francis Goodchild resumed:

"Yes."

"Perhaps you can decide a point my friend and I were in doubt upon, this morning. They hang condemned criminals at the Castle, I believe?"

"*I* believe so," said the old man.

"Are their faces turned towards that noble prospect?"

"Your face is turned," replied the old man, "to the Castle wall. When you are tied up, you see its stones expanding and contracting violently, and a similar expansion and contraction seem to take place in your own head and breast. Then, there is a rush of fire and an earthquake, and the Castle springs into the air, and you tumble down a precipice."

His cravat appeared to trouble him. He put his hand to his throat, and moved his neck from side to side. He was an old man of a swollen character of face, and his nose was immovably hitched up on one side, as if by a little hook inserted in that nostril. Mr. Goodchild felt exceedingly uncomfortable, and began to think the night was hot, and not cold.

"A strong description, sir," he observed.

"A strong sensation," the old man rejoined.

Again, Mr. Goodchild looked to Mr. Thomas Idle; but Thomas lay on his back with his face attentively turned towards the One old man, and made no sign. At this time Mr. Goodchild believed that he saw threads of fire stretch from the old man's eyes to his own, and there attach themselves. (Mr. Goodchild writes the present account of his experience, and, with the utmost solemnity, protests that he had the strongest sensation upon him of being forced to look at the old man along those two fiery films, from that moment.)

"I must tell it to you," said the old man, with a ghastly and a stony stare.

"What?" asked Francis Goodchild.

"You know where it took place. Yonder!"

Whether he pointed to the room above, or to the room below, or to any room in that old house, or to a room in some other old house in that old town, Mr. Goodchild was not, nor is, nor ever can be, sure. He was confused by the circumstance that the right forefinger of the One old man seemed to dip itself in one of the threads of fire, light itself, and make a fiery start in the air, as it pointed somewhere. Having pointed somewhere, it went out.

"You know she was a Bride," said the old man.

"I know they still send up Bride-cake," Mr. Goodchild faltered. "This is a very oppressive air."

"She was a Bride," said the old man. "She was a fair, flaxen-haired, large-eyed girl, who had no character, no purpose. A weak, credulous, incapable, helpless nothing. Not like her mother. No, no. It was her father whose character she reflected.

"Her mother had taken care to secure everything to herself, for her own life, when the father of this girl (a child at that time) died— of sheer helplessness; no other disorder—and then He renewed the acquaintance that had once subsisted between the mother and Him. He had been put aside for the flaxen-haired, large-eyed man (or non-entity) with Money. He could overlook that for Money. He wanted compensation in Money.

"So, he returned to the side of that woman the mother, made love to her again, danced attendance on her, and submitted himself to her whims. She wreaked upon him every whim she had, or could invent. He bore it. And the more he bore, the more he wanted compensation in Money, and the more he was resolved to have it.

"But, lo! Before he got it, she cheated him. In one of her imperious states, she froze, and never thawed again. She put her hands to her head one night, uttered a cry, stiffened, lay in that attitude certain hours, and died. And he had got no compensation from her in Money, yet. Blight and Murrain on her! Not a penny.

"He had hated her throughout that second pursuit, and had longed for retaliation on her. He now counterfeited her signature to an instrument, leaving all she had to leave, to her daughter—ten years old then —to whom the property passed absolutely, and appointing himself the daughter's Guardian. When He slid it under the pillow of the bed on which she lay, He bent down in the deaf ear of Death, and whispered: 'Mistress Pride, I have determined a long time that, dead or alive, you must make me compensation in Money.'

"So, now there were only two left. Which two were, He, and the fair flaxen-haired, large-eyed foolish daughter, who afterwards became the Bride.

"He put her to school. In a secret, dark, oppressive, ancient house, he put her to school with a watchful and unscrupulous woman. 'My worthy lady,' he said, 'here is a mind to be formed; will you help me to form it?' She accepted the trust. For which she, too, wanted compensation in Money, and had it.

"The girl was formed in the fear of him, and in the conviction, that there was no escape from him. She was taught, from the first, to regard him as her future husband—the man who must marry her—the destiny that overshadowed her—the appointed certainty that could never be evaded. The poor fool was soft white wax in their hands, and took the impression that they put upon her. It hardened with time. It became a part of herself. Inseparable from herself, and only to be torn away from her, by tearing life away from her.

"Eleven years she had lived in the dark house and its gloomy garden. He was jealous of the very light and air getting to her, and they kept her close. He stopped the wide chimneys, shaded the little windows, left the strong-stemmed ivy to wander where it would over the house-front, the moss to accumulate on the untrimmed fruit-trees in the red-walled garden, the weeds to over-run its green and yellow walks. He surrounded her with images of sorrow and desolation. He caused her to be filled with fears of the place and of the stories that were told of it, and then on pretext of correcting them, to be left in it in solitude, or made to shrink about it in the dark. When her mind was most depressed and fullest of terrors, then, he would come out of one of the hiding-places from which he overlooked her, and present himself as her sole resource.

"Thus, by being from her childhood the one embodiment her life presented to her of power to coërce and power to relieve, power to bind and power to loose, the ascendency over her weakness was secured. She was twenty-one years and twenty-one days old, when he brought her home to the gloomy house, his half-witted, frightened, and submissive Bride of three weeks.

"He had dismissed the governess by that time—what he had left to do, he could best do alone—and they came back, upon a rainy night, to the scene of her long preparation. She turned to him upon the threshold, as the rain was dripping from the porch, and said:

" 'O sir, it is the Death-watch ticking for me!'

" 'Well!' he answered. 'And if it were?'

" 'O sir!' she returned to him, 'look kindly on me, and be merciful to me! I beg your pardon. I will do anything you wish, if you will only forgive me!'

"That had become the poor fool's constant song: 'I beg your pardon,' and 'Forgive me!'

"She was not worth hating; he felt nothing but contempt for her. But, she had long been in the way, and he had long been weary, and the work was near its end, and had to be worked out.

" 'You fool,' he said. 'Go up the stairs!'

"She obeyed very quickly, murmuring, 'I will do anything you wish!' When he came into the Bride's Chamber, having been a little retarded by the heavy fastenings of the great door (for they were alone in the house, and he had arranged that the people who attended on them should come and go in the day), he found her withdrawn to the furthest corner, and there standing pressed against the paneling as if she would have shrunk through it: her flaxen hair all wild about her face, and her large eyes staring at him in vague terror.

" 'What are you afraid of? Come and sit down by me.'

" 'I will do anything you wish. I beg your pardon, sir. Forgive me!' Her monotonous tune as usual.

" 'Ellen, here is a writing that you must write out tomorrow, in your own hand. You may as well be seen by others, busily engaged upon it. When you have written it all fairly, and corrected all mistakes, call in any two people there may be about the house, and sign your name to it before them. Then, put it in your bosom to keep it safe, and when I sit here again to-morrow night, give it to me.'

" 'I will do it all, with the greatest care. I will do anything you wish.'

" 'Don't shake and tremble, then.'

" 'I will try my utmost not to do it—if you will only forgive me!'

"Next day, she sat down at her desk, and did as she had been told. He often passed in and out of the room, to observe her, and always saw her slowly and laboriously writing: repeating to herself the words she copied, in appearance quite mechanically, and without caring or endeavouring to comprehend them, so that she did her task. He saw her follow the directions she had received, in all particulars; and at night, when they were alone again in the same Bride's Chamber, and he drew his chair to the hearth, she timidly approached him from her distant seat, took the paper from her bosom, and gave it into his hand.

"It secured all her possessions to him, in the event of her death. He put her before him, face to face, that he might look at her steadily; and he asked her, in so many plain words, neither fewer nor more, did she know that?

"There were spots of ink upon the bosom of her white dress, and they made her face look whiter and her eyes look larger as she nodded her head. There were spots of ink upon the hand with which she stood before him, nervously plaiting and folding her white skirts.

"He took her by the arm, and looked her, yet more closely and steadily, in the face. 'Now, die! I have done with you.'

"She shrunk, and uttered a low, suppressed cry.

" 'I am not going to kill you. I will not endanger my life for yours. Die!'

"He sat before her in the gloomy Bride's Chamber, day after day, night after night, looking the word at her when he did not utter it. As often as her large unmeaning eyes were raised from the hands in which she rocked her head, to the stern figure, sitting with crossed arms and knitted forehead, in the chair, they read in it, 'Die!' When she dropped asleep in exhaustion, she was called back to shuddering consciousness, by the whisper, 'Die!' When she fell upon her old entreaty to be pardoned, she was answered, 'Die!' When she had out-watched and out-suffered the long night, and the rising sun flamed into the sombre room, she heard it hailed with, 'Another day and not dead?—Die!'

"Shut up in the deserted mansion, aloof from all mankind, and engaged alone in such a struggle without any respite, it came to this—that either he must die, or she. He knew it very well, and concentrated his strength against her feebleness. Hours upon hours he held her by the arm when her arm was black where he held it, and bade her Die!

"It was done, upon a windy morning, before sunrise. He computed the time to be half-past four; but, his forgotten watch had run down, and he could not be sure. She had broken away from him in the night, with loud and sudden cries—the first of that kind to which she had given vent—and he had had to put his hands over her mouth. Since then, she had been quiet in the corner of the paneling where she had sunk down; and he had left her, and had gone back with his folded arms and his knitted forehead to his chair.

"Paler in the pale light, more colourless than ever in the leaden dawn, he saw her coming, trailing herself along the floor towards him—a white wreck of hair, and dress, and wild eyes, pushing itself on by an irresolute and bending hand.

" 'O, forgive me! I will do anything. O, sir, pray tell me I may live!'

" 'Die!'

" 'Are you so resolved? Is there no hope for me?'

" 'Die!'

"Her large eyes strained themselves with wonder and fear; wonder and fear changed to reproach; reproach to blank nothing. It was done. He was not at first so sure it was done, but that the morning sun was hanging jewels in her hair—he saw the diamond, emerald, and ruby, glittering among it in little points, as he stood looking down at her—when he lifted her and laid her on her bed.

"She was soon laid in the ground. And now they were all gone, and he had compensated himself well.

"He had a mind to travel. Not that he meant to waste his Money, for he was a pinching man and liked his Money dearly (liked nothing else, indeed), but, that he had grown tired of the desolate house and wished to turn his back upon it and have done with it. But, the house was worth Money, and Money must not be thrown away. He determined to sell it before he went. That it might look the less wretched and bring a better price, he hired some labourers to work in the over-grown garden; to cut out the dead wood, trim the ivy that drooped in heavy masses over the windows and gables, and clear the walks in which the weeds were growing mid-leg high.

"He worked himself, along with them. He worked later than they did, and, one evening at dusk, was left working alone, with his bill-hook in his hand. One autumn evening, when the Bride was five weeks dead.

" 'It grows too dark to work longer,' he said to himself, 'I must give over for the night.'

"He detested the house, and was loath to enter it. He looked at the dark porch waiting for him like a tomb, and felt that it was an ac-cursed house. Near to the porch, and near to where he stood, was a tree whose branches waved before the old bay-window of the Bride's Chamber, where it had been done. The tree swung suddenly, and made him start. It swung again, although the night was still. Looking up into it, he saw a figure among the branches.

"It was the figure of a young man. The face looked down, as his looked up; the branches cracked and swayed; the figure rapidly de-scended, and slid upon its feet before him. A slender youth of about her age, with long light brown hair.

" 'What thief are you?' he said, seizing the youth by the collar.

"The young man, in shaking himself free, swung him a blow with his arm across the face and throat. They closed, but the young man got from him and stepped back, crying, with great eagerness and hor-ror, 'Don't touch me! I would as lieve be touched by the Devil!'

"He stood still, with his bill-hook in his hand, looking at the young man. For, the young man's look was the counterpart of her last look, and he had not expected ever to see that again.

" 'I am no thief. Even if I were, I would not have a coin of your wealth, if it would buy me the Indies. You murderer!'

" 'What!'

" 'I climbed it,' said the young man, pointing up into the tree, 'for the first time, nigh four years ago. I climbed it, to look at her. I saw her. I spoke to her. I have climbed it, many a time, to watch and listen for her. I was a boy, hidden among its leaves, when from that bay-window she gave me this!'

"He showed a tress of flaxen hair, tied with a mourning ribbon.

" 'Her life,' said the young man, 'was a life of mourning. She gave me this, as a token of it, and a sign that she was dead to every one but you. If I had been older, if I had seen her sooner, I might have saved her from you. But, she was fast in the web when I first climbed the tree, and what could I do then to break it!'

"In saying those words, he burst into a fit of sobbing and crying: weakly at first, then passionately.

" 'Murderer! I climbed the tree on the night when you brought her back. I heard her, from the tree, speak of the Death-watch at the door. I was three times in the tree while you were shut up with her, slowly killing her. I saw her, from the tree, lie dead upon her bed. I have watched you, from the tree, for proofs and traces of your guilt. The manner of it, is a mystery to me yet, but I will pursue you until you have rendered up your life to the hangman. You shall never, until then, be rid of me. I loved her! I can know no relenting towards you. Murderer, I loved her!'

"The youth was bare-headed, his hat having fluttered away in his descent from the tree. He moved towards the gate. He had to pass— Him—to get to it. There was breadth for two old-fashioned carriages abreast; and the youth's abhorrence, openly expressed in every feature of his face and limb of his body, and very hard to bear, had verge enough to keep itself at a distance in. He (by which I mean the other) had not stirred hand or foot, since he had stood still to look at the boy. He faced round, now, to follow him with his eyes. As the back of the bare light-brown head was turned to him, he saw a red curve stretch from his hand to it. He knew, before he threw the bill-hook, where it had alighted—I say, had alighted, and not, would alight; for, to his clear perception the thing was done before he did it. It cleft the head, and it remained there, and the boy lay on his face.

"He buried the body in the night, at the foot of the tree. As soon as it was light in the morning, he worked at turning up all the ground near the tree, and hacking and hewing at the neighbouring bushes and undergrowth. When the labourers came, there was nothing suspicious, and nothing suspected.

"But, he had, in a moment, defeated all his precautions, and destroyed the triumph of the scheme he had so long concerted, and so successfully worked out. He had got rid of the Bride, and had acquired her fortune without endangering his life; but now, for a death by which he had gained nothing, he had evermore to live with a rope around his neck.

"Beyond this, he was chained to the house of gloom and horror, which he could not endure. Being afraid to sell it or to quit it, lest discovery should be made, he was forced to live in it. He hired two old people, man and wife, for his servants; and dwelt in it, and dreaded it. His great difficulty, for a long time, was the garden. Whether he should keep it trim, whether he should suffer it to fall into its former state of neglect, what would be the least likely way of attracting attention to it?

"He took the middle course of gardening, himself, in his evening leisure, and of then calling the old serving-man to help him; but, of never letting him work there alone. And he made himself an arbour over against the tree, where he could sit and see that it was safe.

"As the seasons changed, and the tree changed, his mind perceived dangers that were always changing. In the leafy time, he perceived that the upper boughs were growing into the form of the young man —that they made the shape of him exactly, sitting in a forked branch swinging in the wind. In the time of the falling leaves, he perceived that they came down from the tree, forming tell-tale letters on the path, or that they had a tendency to heap themselves into a church-yard-mound above the grave. In the winter, when the tree was bare, he perceived that the boughs swung at him the ghost of the blow the young man had given, and that they threatened him openly. In the spring, when the sap was mounting in the trunk, he asked himself, were the dried-up particles of blood mounting with it: to make out more obviously this year than last, the leaf-screened figure of the young man, swinging in the wind?

"However, he turned his Money over and over, and still over. He was in the dark trade, the gold-dust trade, and most secret trades that yielded great returns. In ten years, he had turned his Money over, so many times, that the traders and shippers who had dealings with him, absolutely did not lie—for once—when they declared that he had increased his fortune, Twelve Hundred Per Cent.

"He possessed his riches one hundred years ago, when people could be lost easily. He had heard who the youth was, from hearing of the search that was made after him; but, it died away, and the youth was forgotten.

"The annual round of changes in the tree had been repeated ten times since the night of the burial at its foot, when there was a great thunder-storm over this place. It broke at midnight, and raged until morning. The first intelligence he heard from his old serving-man that morning, was, that the tree had been struck by Lightning.

"It had been riven down the stem, in a very surprising manner, and the stem lay in two blighted shafts: one resting against the house, and one against a portion of the old red garden-wall in which its fall had made a gap. The fissure went down the tree to a little above the earth, and there stopped. There was great curiosity to see the tree, and, with most of his former fears revived, he sat in his arbour—grown quite an old man—watching the people who came to see it.

"They quickly began to come, in such dangerous numbers, that he closed his garden-gate and refused to admit any more. But, there were certain men of science who travelled from a distance to examine the tree, and, in an evil hour, he let them in—Blight and Murrain on them, let them in!

"They wanted to dig up the ruin by the roots, and closely examine it, and the earth about it. Never, while he lived! They offered money for it. They! Men of science, whom he could have bought by the gross, with a scratch of his pen! He showed them the garden-gate again, and locked and barred it.

"But they were bent on doing what they wanted to do, and they bribed the old serving-man—a thankless wretch who regularly complained when he received his wages, of being underpaid—and they stole into the garden by night with their lanterns, picks, and shovels, and fell to at the tree. He was lying in a turret-room on the other side of the house (the Bride's Chamber had been unoccupied ever since), but he soon dreamed of picks and shovels, and got up.

"He came to an upper window on that side, whence he could see their lanterns, and them, and the loose earth in a heap which he had himself disturbed and put back, when it was last turned to the air. It was found! They had that minute lighted on it. They were all bending over it. One of them said, 'The skull is fractured;' and another, 'See here the bones;' and another, 'See here the clothes;' and then the first struck in again, and said, 'A rusty bill-hook!'

"He became sensible, next day, that he was already put under a strict watch, and that he could go nowhere without being followed. Before a week was out, he was taken and laid in hold. The circumstances were gradually pieced together against him, with a desperate malignity, and an appalling ingenuity. But, see the justice of men, and how it was extended to him! He was further accused of having poisoned that girl in the Bride's Chamber. He, who had carefully and expressly avoided imperilling a hair of his head for her, and who had seen her die of her own incapacity!

"There was doubt for which of the two murders he should be first tried; but, the real one was chosen, and he was found Guilty, and cast for Death. Bloodthirsty wretches! They would have made him Guilty of anything, so set they were upon having his life.

"His money could do nothing to save him, and he was hanged. *I* am He, and I was hanged at Lancaster Castle with my face to the wall, a hundred years ago!"

At this terrific announcement, Mr. Goodchild tried to rise and cry out. But, the two fiery lines extending from the old man's eyes to his own, kept him down, and he could not utter a sound. His sense of hearing, however, was acute, and he could hear the clock strike Two. No sooner had he heard the clock strike Two, than he saw before him Two old men!

Two.

The eyes of each, connected with his eyes by two films of fire: each, exactly like the other: each, addressing him at precisely one and the same instant: each, gnashing the same teeth in the same head, with the same twitched nostril above them, and the same suffused expression around it. Two old men. Differing in nothing, equally distinct to the sight, the copy no fainter than the original, the second as real as the first.

"At what time," said the Two old men, "did you arrive at the door below?"

"At Six."

"And there were Six old men upon the stairs!"

Mr. Goodchild having wiped the perspiration from his brow, or tried to do it, the Two old men proceeded in one voice, and in the singular number:

"I had been anatomised, but had not yet had my skeleton put together and re-hung on an iron hook, when it began to be whispered that the Bride's Chamber was haunted. It *was* haunted, and I was there.

"*We* were there. She and I were there. I, in the chair upon the hearth; she, a white wreck again, trailing itself towards me on the floor. But, I was the speaker no more, and the one word that she said to me from midnight until dawn was, 'Live!'

"The youth was there, likewise. In the tree outside the window. Coming and going in the moonlight, as the tree bent and gave. He has, ever since, been there, peeping in at me in my torment; revealing to me by snatches, in the pale lights and slatey shadows where he comes and goes, bare-headed—a bill-hook, standing edgewise in his hair.

"In the Bride's Chamber, every night from midnight until dawn— one month in the year excepted, as I am going to tell you—he hides in the tree, and she comes towards me on the floor; always approaching; never coming nearer; always visible as if by moonlight, whether the moon shines or no; always saying, from midnight until dawn, her one word, 'Live!'

"But, in the month wherein I was forced out of this life—this present month of thirty days—the Bride's Chamber is empty and quiet. Not so my old dungeon. Not so the rooms where I was restless and afraid, ten years. Both are fitfully haunted then. At One in the morning, I am what you saw me when the clock struck that hour—One old man. At Two in the morning, I am Two old men. At Three, I am Three. By Twelve at noon, I am Twelve old men, One for every hundred per cent. of old gain. Every one of the Twelve, with Twelve times my old power of suffering and agony. From that hour until Twelve at night, I, Twelve old men in anguish and fearful foreboding, wait for the coming of the executioner. At Twelve at night, I, Twelve old men turned off, swing invisible outside Lancaster Castle, with Twelve faces to the wall!

"When the Bride's Chamber was first haunted, it was known to me that this punishment would never cease, until I could make its nature, and my story, known to two living men together. I waited for the coming of two living men together into the Bride's Chamber, years upon years. It was infused into my knowledge (of the means I am ignorant) that if two living men, with their eyes open, could be in the Bride's Chamber at One in the morning, they would see me sitting in my chair.

"At length, the whispers that the room was spiritually troubled, brought two men to try the adventure. I was scarcely struck upon the hearth at midnight (I come there as if the Lightning blasted me into being), when I heard them ascending the stairs. Next, I saw them enter. One of them was a bold, gay, active man, in the prime of life, some five and forty years of age; the other, a dozen years younger. They brought provisions with them in a basket, and bottles. A young woman accompanied them, with wood and coals for the lighting of the fire. When she had lighted it, the bold, gay, active man accompanied her along the gallery outside the room, to see her safely down the staircase, and came back laughing.

"He locked the door, examined the chamber, put out the contents of the basket on the table before the fire—little recking of me, in my appointed station on the hearth, close to him—and filled the glasses, and ate and drank. His companion did the same, and was as cheerful and confident as he: though he was the leader. When they had supped, they laid pistols on the table, turned to the fire, and began to smoke their pipes of foreign make.

"They had travelled together, and had been much together, and had an abundance of subjects in common. In the midst of their talking and laughing, the younger man made a reference to the leader's being always ready for any adventure; that one, or any other. He replied in these words:

" 'Not quite so, Dick; if I am afraid of nothing else, I am afraid of myself.'

"His companion seeming to grow a little dull, asked him, in what sense? How?

" 'Why, thus,' he returned. 'Here is a Ghost to be disproved. Well! I cannot answer for what my fancy might do if I were alone here, or what tricks my senses might play with me if they had me to themselves. But, in company with another man, and especially with you, Dick, I would consent to outface all the Ghosts that were ever told of in the universe.'

" 'I had not the vanity to suppose that I was of so much importance to-night,' said the other.

" 'Of so much,' rejoined the leader, more seriously than he had spoken yet, 'that I would, for the reason I have given, on no account have undertaken to pass the night here alone.'

"It was within a few minutes of One. The head of the younger man had drooped when he made his last remark, and it drooped lower now.

" 'Keep awake, Dick!' said the leader, gaily. 'The small hours are the worst.'

"He tried, but his head drooped again.

" 'Dick!' urged the leader. 'Keep awake!'

" 'I can't,' he indistinctly muttered. 'I don't know what strange influence is stealing over me. I can't.'

"His companion looked at him with a sudden horror, and I, in my different way, felt a new horror also; for it was on the stroke of One, and I felt that the second watcher was yielding to me, and that the curse was upon me that I must send him to sleep.

" 'Get up and walk, Dick!' cried the leader. 'Try!'

"It was in vain to go behind the slumberer's chair and shake him. One o'clock sounded, and I was present to the elder man, and he stood transfixed before me.

"To him alone, I was obliged to relate my story, without hope of benefit. To him alone, I was an awful phantom making a quite useless confession. I foresee it will ever be the same. The two living men together will never come to release me. When I appear, the senses of one of the two will be locked in sleep; he will neither see nor hear me; my communication will ever be made to a solitary listener, and will ever be unserviceable. Woe! Woe! Woe!"

As the Two old men, with these words, wrung their hands, it shot into Mr. Goodchild's mind that he was in the terrible situation of being virtually alone with the spectre, and that Mr. Idle's immoveability was explained by his having been charmed asleep at One o'clock. In the terror of this sudden discovery which produced an indescribable dread, he struggled so hard to get free from the four fiery threads, that he snapped them, after he had pulled them out to a great width. Being then out of bonds, he caught up Mr. Idle from the sofa and rushed down stairs with him.

"What are you about, Francis?" demanded Mr. Idle. "My bedroom is not down here. What the deuce are you carrying me at all for? I can walk with a stick now. I don't want to be carried. Put me down."

Mr. Goodchild put him down in the old hall, and looked about him wildly.

"What are you doing? Idiotically plunging at your own sex, and rescuing them or perishing in the attempt?" asked Mr. Idle, in a highly petulant state.

"The One old man!" cried Mr. Goodchild, distractedly,—"and the Two old men!"

Mr. Idle deigned no other reply than "The One old woman, I think you mean," as he began hobbling his way back up the staircase, with the assistance of its broad balustrade.

"I assure you, Tom," began Mr. Goodchild, attending at his side, "that since you fell asleep—"

"Come, I like that!" said Thomas Idle, "I haven't closed an eye!"

With the peculiar sensitiveness on the subject of the disgraceful action of going to sleep out of bed, which is the lot of all mankind, Mr. Idle persisted in this declaration. The same peculiar sensitiveness impelled Mr. Goodchild, on being taxed with the same crime, to repudiate it with honourable resentment. The settlement of the question of The One old man and The Two old men was thus presently complicated, and soon made quite impracticable. Mr. Idle said it was all Bridecake, and fragments, newly arranged, of things seen and thought about in the day. Mr. Goodchild said how could that be, when he hadn't been asleep, and what right could Mr. Idle have to say so, who had been asleep? Mr. Idle said he had never been asleep, and never did go to sleep, and that Mr. Goodchild, as a general rule, was always asleep. They consequently parted for the rest of the night, at their bedroom doors, a little ruffled. Mr. Goodchild's last words were, that he had had, in that real and tangible old sitting-room of that real and tangible old Inn (he supposed Mr. Idle denied its existence?), every sensation and experience, the present record of which is now within a line or two of completion; and that he would write it out and print it every word. Mr. Idle returned that he might if he liked—and he did like, and has now done it.

Wilkie Collins

William Wilkie Collins (1824–1889) enjoys a well-deserved reputation as one of the most skilled plotters and devisers of sensationalism in English literature. As T. S. Eliot said of his novel The Haunted Hotel, "There is no contemporary novelist who could not learn something from Collins in the art of interesting and exciting the reader." Collins's two great mystery novels, The Woman in White (1860) and The Moonstone (1868), remain enjoyable classics.

Collins wrote three novels and at least ten short stories that deal with the supernatural. Of the novels, Armadale (1866) is worthy of being classed with his great mysteries; The Haunted Hotel (1878) is on a somewhat lower level; and the third, The Two Destinies (1876), is generally considered a potboiler. In all three novels Collins was intrigued with the concept of fate and its interference in human life. His short stories, on the other hand, are more conventional and are usually concerned with ghosts of one sort or another. The present story, which has not previously appeared in book form, was printed anonymously in Bentley's Miscellany in 1852.

NINE O'CLOCK!

The night of the 30th of June, 1793, is memorable in the prison annals of Paris, as the last night in confinement of the leaders of the famous Girondin party in the first French Revolution. On the morning of the 31st, the twenty-one deputies who represented the department of the Gironde, were guillotined to make way for Robespierre and the Reign of Terror.

With these men fell the last revolutionists of that period who shrank from founding a republic on massacre; who recoiled from substituting for a monarchy of corruption, a monarchy of bloodshed. The elements of their defeat lay as much in themselves, as in the events of their time. They were not, as a party, true to their own convictions; they temporized; they fatally attempted to take a middle course amid the terrible emergencies of a terrible epoch, and they fell—fell before worse men, because those men were in earnest.

Condemned to die, the Girondins submitted nobly to their fate; their great glory was the glory of their deaths. The speech of one of them on hearing his sentence pronounced, was a prophecy of the future, fulfilled to the letter.

"*I* die," he said to the Jacobin judges, the creatures of Robespierre, who tried him. "*I* die at a time when the people have lost their reason; *you* will die on the day when they recover it." Valazé was the only member of the condemned party who displayed a momentary weakness; he stabbed himself on hearing his sentence pronounced. But the blow was not mortal—he died on the scaffold, and died bravely with the rest.

On the night of the 30th the Girondins held their famous banquet in the prison; celebrated, with the ferocious stoicism of the time, their last social meeting before the morning on which they were to die. Other

men, besides the twenty-one, were present at this supper of the condemned. They were prisoners who held Girondin opinions, but whose
names were not illustrious enough for history to preserve. Though
sentenced to confinement they were not sentenced to death. Some of
their number, who had protested most boldly against the condemna-
tion of the deputies, were ordered to witness the execution on the morrow, as a timely example to terrify them into submission. More than
this, Robespierre and his colleagues did not, as yet, venture to attempt:
the Reign of Terror was a cautious reign at starting.

The supper-table of the prison was spread; the guests, twenty-one of
their number stamped already with the seal of death, were congregated
at the last Girondin banquet; toast followed toast; the *Marseillaise* was
sung; the desperate triumph of the feast was rising fast to its climax,
when a new and ominous subject of conversation was started at the
lower end of the table, and spread electrically, almost in a moment, to
the top.

This subject (by whom originated no one knew) was simply a question as to the hour in the morning at which the execution was to take
place. Every one of the prisoners appeared to be in ignorance on this
point; and the gaolers either could not, or would not, enlighten them.
Until the cart for the condemned rolled into the prison-yard, not one
of the Girondins could tell whether he was to be called out to the
guillotine soon after sunrise, or not till near noon.

This uncertainty was made a topic for discussion, or for jesting on
all sides. It was eagerly seized on as a pretext for raising to the highest
pitch the ghastly animation and hilarity of the evening. In some quarters, the recognised hour of former executions was quoted as a prece-
dent sure to be followed by the executioners of the morrow; in others,
it was asserted that Robespierre and his party would purposely depart
from established customs in this, as in previous instances. Dozens of
wild schemes were suggested for guessing the hour by fortune-telling
rules on the cards; bets were offered and accepted among the prisoners
who were not condemned to death, and witnessed in stoical mockery
by the prisoners who were. Jests were exchanged about early rising
and hurried toilets; in short, every man contributed an assertion, a con-
tradiction, or a witticism to keep up the new topic of conversation,
with one solitary exception. That exception was the Girondin, Duprat,
one of the deputies who was sentenced to die by the guillotine.

He was a younger man than the majority of his brethren, and was
personally remarkable by his pale, handsome, melancholy face, and his
reserved yet gentle manners. Throughout the evening, he had spoken
but rarely; there was something of the silence and serenity of a martyr
in his demeanour. That he feared death as little as any of his com-

panions was plainly visible in his bright, steady eye; in his unchanging complexion; in his firm, calm voice, when he occasionally addressed those who happened to be near him. But he was evidently out of place at the banquet; his temperament was reflective, his disposition serious; feasts were at no time a sphere in which he was calculated to shine.

His taciturnity, while the hour of the execution was under discussion, had separated him from most of those with whom he sat, at the lower end of the table. They edged up towards the top, where the conversation was most general and most animated. One of his friends, however, still kept his place by Duprat's side, and thus questioned him anxiously, but in low tones, on the cause of his immovable silence:

"Are you the only man of the company, Duprat, who has neither a guess nor a joke to make about the time of the execution?"

"I never joke, Marigny," was the answer, given with a slight smile which had something of the sarcastic in it; "and as for guessing at the time of the execution, I never guess at things which I *know*."

"Know! You know the hour of the execution! Then why not communicate your knowledge to your friends around you?"

"Because not one of them would believe what I said."

"But, surely, you could prove it. Somebody must have told you."

"Nobody has told me."

"You have seen some private letter, then; or you have managed to get sight of the execution-order; or—"

"Spare your conjectures, Marigny. I have not read, as I have not been told, what is the hour at which we are to die to-morrow."

"Then how on earth can you possibly know it?"

"I do *not* know when the execution will begin, or when it will end. I only know that it will be *going on* at nine o'clock to-morrow morning. Out of the twenty-one who are to suffer death, one will be guillotined exactly at that hour. Whether he will be the first whose head falls, or the last, I cannot tell."

"And pray who may this man be, who is to die exactly at nine o'clock? Of course, prophetically knowing so much, you know that!"

"I *do* know it. I am the man whose death by the guillotine will take place exactly at the hour I have mentioned."

"You said just now, Duprat, that you never joked. Do you expect me to believe that what you have just spoken is spoken in earnest?"

"I repeat that I never joke; and I answer that I expect you to believe me. I know the hour at which my death will take place to-morrow, just as certainly as I know the fact of my own existence to-night."

"But how? My dear friend, can you really lay claim to supernatural intuition, in this eighteenth century of the world, in this renowned Age of Reason?"

"No two men, Marigny, understand that word, supernatural, exactly in the same sense; you and I differ about its meaning, or, in other words, differ about the real distinction between the doubtful and the true. We will not discuss the subject: I wish to be understood, at the outset, as laying claim to no superior intuitions whatever; but I tell you, at the same time, that even in this Age of Reason, I have reason for what I have said. My father and my brother both died at nine o'clock in the morning, and were both warned very strangely of their deaths. I am the last of my family; I was warned last night, as they were warned; and I shall die by the guillotine, as they died in their beds, at the fatal hour of nine."

"But, Duprat, why have I never heard of this before? As your oldest and, I am sure, your dearest friend, I thought you had long since trusted me with all your secrets."

"And you shall know this secret; I only kept it from you till the time when I could be certain that my death would substantiate my words, to the very letter. Come! you are as bad supper-company as I am; let us slip away from the table unperceived, while our friends are all engaged in conversation. Yonder end of the hall is dark and quiet— we can speak there uninterruptedly, for some hours to come."

He led the way from the supper-table, followed by Marigny. Arrived at one of the darkest and most retired corners of the great hall of the prison, Duprat spoke again:

"I believe, Marigny," he said, "that you are one of those who have been ordered by our tyrants to witness my execution, and the execution of my brethren, as a warning spectacle for an enemy to the Jacobin cause?"

"My dear, dear friend! it is too true; I am ordered to witness the butchery which I cannot prevent—our last awful parting will be at the foot of the scaffold. I am among the victims who are spared—merci-lessly spared—for a little while yet."

"Say the martyrs! We die as martyrs, calmly, hopefully, innocently. When I am placed under the guillotine to-morrow morning, listen, my friend, for the striking of the church clocks; listen for the hour while you look your last on me. Until that time, suspend your judgment on the strange chapter of family history which I am now about to relate."

Marigny took his friend's hand, and promised compliance with the request. Duprat then began as follows:

"You knew my brother Alfred, when he was quite a youth, and you knew something of what people flippantly termed, the eccentricities of his character. He was three years my junior; but, from childhood, he showed far less of a child's innate levity and happiness than his elder brother. He was noted for his seriousness and thoughtfulness as a boy; showed little inclination for a boy's usual lessons, and less still for a boy's usual recreations,—in short, he was considered by everybody (my father included) as deficient in intellect; as a vacant dreamer, and an inveterate idler, whom it was hopeless to improve. Our tutor tried to lead him to various studies, and tried in vain. It was the same when the cultivation of his mind was given up, and the cultivation of his body was next attempted. The fencing-master could make nothing of him; and the dancing-master, after the first three lessons, resigned in despair. Seeing that it was useless to set others to teach him, my father made a virtue of necessity, and left him, if he chose, to teach himself.

"To the astonishment of every one, he had not been long consigned to his own guidance, when he was discovered in the library, reading every old treatise on astrology which he could lay his hands on. He had rejected all useful knowledge for the most obsolete of obsolete sciences—the old, abandoned delusion of divination by the stars! My father laughed heartily over the strange study to which this idle son had at last applied himself, but made no attempt to oppose his new caprice, and sarcastically presented him with a telescope on his next birthday. I should remind you here, of what you may perhaps have forgotten, that my father was a philosopher of the Voltaire school, who believed that the summit of human wisdom was to arrive at the power of sneering at all enthusiasms, and doubting of all truths. Apart from his philosophy, he was a kind-hearted, easy man, of quick, rather than of profound intelligence. He could see nothing in my brother's new occupation, but the evidence of a new idleness, a fresh caprice which would be abandoned in a few months. My father was not the man to appreciate those yearnings towards the poetical and the spiritual, which were part of Alfred's temperament, and which gave to his peculiar studies of the stars and their influences, a certain charm altogether unconnected with the more practical attractions of scientific investigation.

"This idle caprice of my brother's, as my father insisted on terming it, had lasted more than a twelvemonth, when there occurred the first of a series of mysterious and—as I consider them—supernatural events, with all of which Alfred was very remarkably connected. I was myself a witness of the strange circumstance, which I am now about to relate to you.

"One day—my brother being then sixteen years of age—I happened to go into my father's study, during his absence, and found Alfred there, standing close to a window, which looked into the garden. I walked up to him, and observed a curious expression of vacancy and rigidity in his face, especially in his eyes. Although I knew him to be subject to what are called fits of absence, I still thought it rather extraordinary that he never moved, and never noticed me when I was close to him. I took his hand, and asked if he was unwell. His flesh felt quite cold; neither my touch nor my voice produced the smallest sensation in him. Almost at the same moment when I noticed this, I happened to be looking accidentally towards the garden. There was my father walking along one of the paths, and there, by his side, walking with him, was *another Alfred!*—Another, yet exactly the same as the Alfred by whose side I was standing, whose hand I still held in mine!

"Thoroughly panic-stricken, I dropped his hand, and uttered a cry of terror. At the loud sound of my voice, the statue-like presence before me immediately began to show signs of animation. I looked round again at the garden. The figure of my brother, which I had beheld there, was gone, and I saw to my horror, that my father was looking for it—looking in all directions for the companion (spectre, or human being?) of his walk!

"When I turned towards Alfred once more, he had (if I may so express it) come to life again, and was asking, with his usual gentleness of manner and kindness of voice, why I was looking so pale? I evaded the question by making some excuse, and in my turn inquired of him, how long he had been in my father's study.

" 'Surely you ought to know best,' he answered with a laugh, 'for you must have been here before me. It is not many minutes ago since I was walking in the garden with—'

"Before he could complete the sentence my father entered the room.

" 'Oh! here you are, Master Alfred,' said he. 'May I ask for what purpose you took it into your wise head to vanish in that extraordinary manner? Why you slipped away from me in an instant, while I was picking a flower! On my word, sir, you're a better player at hide-and-seek than your brother,—*he* would only have run into the shrubbery, *you* have managed to run in here, though how you did it in the time passes my poor comprehension. I was not a moment picking the flower, yet in that moment you were gone!'

"Alfred glanced suddenly and searchingly at me; his face became deadly pale, and, without speaking a word, he hurried from the room.

" 'Can *you* explain this?' said my father, looking very much astonished.

"I hesitated a moment, and then told him what I had seen. He took a pinch of snuff—a favourite habit with him when he was going to be sarcastic, in imitation of Voltaire.

" 'One visionary in a family is enough,' said he; 'I recommend you not to turn yourself into a bad imitation of your brother Alfred! Send your ghost after me, my good boy! I am going back into the garden, and should like to see him again!'

"Ridicule, even much sharper than this, would have had little effect on me. If I was certain of anything in the world, I was certain that I had seen my brother in the study—nay, more, had touched him,—and equally certain that I had seen his double—his exact similitude, in the garden. As far as any man could know that he was in possession of his own senses, I knew myself to be in possession of mine. Left alone to think over what I had beheld, I felt a supernatural terror creeping through me—a terror which increased, when I recollected that, on one or two occasions friends had said they had seen Alfred out of doors, when we all knew him to be at home. These statements, which my father had laughed at, and had taught me to laugh at, either as a trick, or a delusion on the part of others, now recurred to my memory as startling corroborations of what I had just seen myself. The solitude of the study oppressed me in a manner which I cannot describe. I left the apartment to seek Alfred, determined to question him, with all possible caution, on the subject of his strange trance, and his sensations at the moment when I had awakened him from it.

"I found him in his bed-room, still pale, and now very thoughtful. As the first words in reference to the scene in the study passed my lips, he started violently, and entreated me, with very unusual warmth of speech and manner, never to speak to him on that subject again,— never, if I had any love or regard for him! Of course, I complied with his request. The mystery, however, was not destined to end here.

"About two months after the event which I have just related, we had arranged, one evening, to go to the theatre. My father had insisted that Alfred should be of the party, otherwise he would certainly have declined accompanying us; for he had no inclination whatever for public amusements of any kind. However, with his usual docility, he prepared to obey my father's desire, by going up-stairs to put on his evening dress. It was winter-time, so he was obliged to take a candle with him.

"We waited in the drawing-room for his return a very long time, so long, that my father was on the point of sending up-stairs to remind him of the lateness of the hour, when Alfred reappeared without the candle which he had taken with him from the room. The ghastly alteration that had passed over his face—the hideous, death-look that distorted his features I shall never forget,—I shall see it to-morrow on the scaffold!

"Before either my father or I could utter a word, my brother said:— 'I have been taken suddenly ill; but I am better now. Do you still wish me to go to the theatre?'

"‘Certainly not, my dear Alfred,' answered my father; 'we must send for the doctor immediately.'

"‘Pray do not call in the doctor, sir; he would be of no use. I will tell you why, if you will let me speak to you alone.'

"My father, looking seriously alarmed, signed to me to leave the room. For more than half an hour I remained absent, suffering almost unendurable suspense and anxiety on my brother's account. When I was recalled, I observed that Alfred was quite calm, though still deadly pale. My father's manner displayed an agitation which I had never observed in it before. He rose from his chair when I re-entered the room, and left me alone with my brother.

"‘Promise me,' said Alfred, in answer to my entreaties to know what had happened, 'promise that you will not ask me to tell you more than my father has permitted me to tell. It is his desire that I should keep certain things a secret from you.'

"I gave the required promise, but gave it most unwillingly. Alfred then proceeded.

"‘When I left you to go and dress for the theatre, I felt a sense of oppression all over me, which I cannot describe. As soon as I was alone, it seemed as if some part of the life within me was slowly wasting away. I could hardly breathe the air around me, big drops of perspiration burst out on my forehead, and then a feeling of terror seized me which I was utterly unable to control. Some of those strange fancies of seeing my mother's spirit, which used to influence me at the time of her death, came back again to my mind. I ascended the stairs slowly and painfully, not daring to look behind me, for I heard—yes, heard!—something following me. When I had got into my room, and had shut the door, I began to recover my self-possession a little. But the sense of oppression was still as heavy on me as ever, when I approached the wardrobe to get out my clothes. Just as I stretched forth my hand to turn the key, I saw, to my horror, the two doors of the wardrobe opening of themselves, opening slowly and silently. The candle went out at the same moment, and the whole inside of the wardrobe became to me like a great mirror, with a bright light shining in the middle of it. Out of that light there came a figure, the exact counterpart of myself. Over its breast hung an open scroll, and on that I read the warning of my own death, and a revelation of the destinies of my father and his race. Do not ask me what were the words on the scroll, I have given my promise not to tell you. I may only say that, as soon as I had read all, the room grew dark, and the vision disappeared.'

"Forgetful of my promise, I entreated Alfred to repeat to me the words on the scroll. He smiled sadly, and refused to speak on the subject any more. I next sought out my father, and begged him to divulge the secret. Still sceptical to the last, he answered that one diseased imagination in the family was enough, and that he would not permit me to run the risk of being infected by Alfred's mental malady. I passed the whole of that day and the next in a state of agitation and alarm which nothing could tranquillize. The sight I had seen in the study gave a terrible significance to the little that my brother had told me. I was uneasy if he was a moment out of my sight. There was something in his expression,—calm and even cheerful as it was,—which made me dread the worst.

"On the morning of the third day after the occurrence I have just related, I rose very early, after a sleepless night, and went into Alfred's bedroom. He was awake, and welcomed me with more than usual affection and kindness. As I drew a chair to his bedside, he asked me to get pen, ink, and paper, and write down something from his dictation. I obeyed, and found to my terror and distress, that the idea of death was more present to his imagination than ever. He employed me in writing a statement of his wishes in regard to the disposal of all his own little possessions, as keepsakes to be given, after he was no more, to my father, myself, the house-servants, and one or two of his own most intimate friends. Over and over again I entreated him to tell me whether he really believed that his death was near. He invariably replied that I should soon know, and then led the conversation to indifferent topics. As the morning advanced, he asked to see my father, who came, accompanied by the doctor, the latter having been in attendance for the last two days.

"Alfred took my father's hand, and begged his forgiveness of any offence, any disobedience of which he had ever been guilty. Then, reaching out his other hand, and taking mine, as I stood on the opposite side of the bed, he asked what the time was. A clock was placed on the mantel-piece of the room, but not in a position in which he could see it, as he now lay. I turned round to look at the dial, and answered that, it was just on the stroke of nine.

" 'Farewell!' said Alfred, calmly; 'in this world, farewell for ever!'

"The next instant the clock struck. I felt his fingers tremble in mine, then grow quite still. The doctor seized a hand-mirror that lay on the table, and held it over his lips. He was dead—dead, as the last chime of the hour echoed through the awful silence of the room!

"I pass over the first days of our affliction. You, who have suffered the loss of a beloved sister, can well imagine their misery. I pass over these days, and pause for a moment at the time when we could speak with some calmness and resignation on the subject of our bereavement. On the arrival of that period, I ventured, in conversation with my father, to refer to the vision which had been seen by our dear Alfred in his bedroom, and to the prophecy which he described himself as having read upon the supernatural scroll.

"Even yet my father persisted in his scepticism; but now, as it seemed to me, more because he was afraid, than because he was unwilling, to believe. I again recalled to his memory what I myself had seen in the study. I asked him to recollect how certain Alfred had been beforehand, and how fatally right, about the day and hour of his death. Still I could get but one answer; my brother had died of a nervous disorder (the doctor said so); his imagination had been diseased from his childhood; there was only one way of treating the vision which he described himself as having seen, and that was, not to speak of it again between ourselves; never to speak of it at all to our friends.

"We were sitting in the study during this conversation. It was evening. As my father uttered the last words of his reply to me, I saw his eye turn suddenly and uneasily towards the further end of the room. In dead silence, I looked in the same direction, and saw the door opening slowly of itself. The vacant space beyond was filled with a bright, steady glow, which hid all outer objects in the hall, and which I cannot describe to you by likening it to any light that we are accustomed to behold either by day or night. In my terror, I caught my father by the arm, and asked him, in a whisper, whether he did not see something extraordinary in the direction of the doorway?

" 'Yes,' he answered, in tones as low as mine, 'I see, or fancy I see, a strange light. The subject on which we have been speaking has impressed our feelings as it should not. Our nerves are still unstrung by the shock of the bereavement we have suffered: our senses are deluding us. Let us look away towards the garden.'

" 'But the opening of the door, father; remember the opening of the door!'

" 'Ours is not the first door which has accidentally flown open of itself.'

" 'Then why not shut it again?'

" 'Why not, indeed. I will close it at once.' He rose, advanced a few paces, then stopped, and came back to his place. 'It is a warm evening,' he said, avoiding my eyes, which were eagerly fixed on him, 'the room will be all the cooler, if the door is suffered to remain open.'

"His face grew quite pale as he spoke. The light lasted for a few minutes longer, then suddenly disappeared. For the rest of the evening my father's manner was very much altered. He was silent and thoughtful, and complained of a feeling of oppression and languor, which he tried to persuade himself was produced by the heat of the weather. At an unusually early hour he retired to his room.

"The next morning, when I got down stairs, I found, to my astonishment, that the servants were engaged in preparations for the departure of somebody from the house. I made inquiries of one of them who was hurriedly packing a trunk. 'My master, sir, starts for Lyons the first thing this morning,' was the reply. I immediately repaired to my father's room, and found him there with an open letter in his hand, which he was reading. His face, as he looked up at me on my entrance, expressed the most violent emotions of apprehension and despair.

" 'I hardly know whether I am awake or dreaming; whether I am the dupe of a terrible delusion, or the victim of a supernatural reality more terrible still,' he said in low awe-struck tones as I approached him. 'One of the prophecies which Alfred told me in private that he had read upon the scroll, has come true! He predicted the loss of the bulk of my fortune—here is the letter, which informs me that the merchant at Lyons in whose hands my money was placed, has become a bankrupt. Can the occurrence of this ruinous calamity be the chance fulfilment of a mere guess? Or was the doom of my family really revealed to my dead son? I go to Lyons immediately to know the truth: this letter may have been written under false information; it may be the work of an impostor. And yet, Alfred's prediction—I shudder to think of it!'

" 'The light, father!' I exclaimed, 'the light we saw last night in the study!'

" 'Hush! don't speak of it! Alfred said that I should be warned of the truth of the prophecy, and of its immediate fulfilment, by the shining of the same supernatural light that he had seen—I tried to disbelieve what I beheld last night—I hardly know whether I dare believe it even now! This prophecy is not the last: there are others yet to be fulfilled—but let us not speak, let us not think of them! I must start at once for Lyons; I must be on the spot, if this horrible news is true, to save what I can from the wreck. The letter—give me back the letter! —I must go directly!'

"He hurried from the room. I followed him; and, with some difficulty, obtained permission to be the companion of his momentous journey. When we arrived at Lyons, we found that the statement in the letter was true. My father's fortune was gone: a mere pittance, derived from a small estate that had belonged to my mother, was all that was left to us.

"My father's health gave way under this misfortune. He never referred again to Alfred's prediction, and I was afraid to mention the subject; but I saw that it was affecting his mind quite as painfully as the loss of his property. Over, and over again, he checked himself very strangely when he was on the point of speaking to me about my brother. I saw that there was some secret pressing heavily on his mind, which he was afraid to disclose to me. It was useless to ask for his confidence. His temper had become irritable under disaster; perhaps, also, under the dread uncertainties which were now evidently torment-ing him in secret. My situation was a very sad, and a very dreary one, at that time: I had no remembrances of the past that were not mournful and affrighting remembrances; I had no hopes for the future that were not darkened by a vague presentiment of troubles and perils to come; and I was expressly forbidden by my father to say a word about the terrible events which had cast an unnatural gloom over my youthful career, to any of the friends (yourself included) whose counsel and whose sympathy might have guided and sustained me in the day of trial.

"We returned to Paris; sold our house there; and retired to live on the small estate, to which I have referred, as the last possession left us. We had not been many days in our new abode, when my father im-prudently exposed himself to a heavy shower of rain, and suffered, in consequence from a violent attack of cold. This temporary malady was not dreaded by the medical attendant; but it was soon aggravated by a fever, produced as much by the anxiety and distress of mind from which he continued to suffer, as by any other cause. Still the doctor gave hope; but still he grew daily worse—so much worse, that I re-moved my bed into his room, and never quitted him night or day.

"One night I had fallen asleep, overpowered by fatigue and anxiety, when I was awakened by a cry from my father. I instantly trimmed the light, and ran to his side. He was sitting up in bed, with his eyes fixed on the door, which had been left ajar to ventilate the room. I saw nothing in that direction, and asked what was the matter. He mur-mured some expressions of affection towards me, and begged me to sit by his bedside till the morning; but gave no definite answer to my question. Once or twice, I thought he wandered a little; and I observed that he occasionally moved his hand under the pillow, as if searching for something there. However, when the morning came, he appeared to be quite calm and self-possessed. The doctor arrived; and pronouncing him to be better, retired to the dressing-room to write a prescription. The moment his back was turned, my father laid his weak hand on my arm, and whispered faintly:—'Last night I saw the supernatural light again—the second prediction—true, true—my death this time—the same hour as Alfred's—nine—nine o'clock, this morning.' He paused a moment through weakness; then added:—'Take that sealed paper— under the pillow—when I am dead, read it—now go into the dressing-room—my watch is there—I have heard the church clock strike eight; let me see how long it is now till nine—go—go quickly!'

"Horror-stricken, moving and acting like a man in a trance, I silently obeyed him. The doctor was still in the dressing-room: despair made me catch eagerly at any chance of saving my father; I told his medical attendant what I had just heard, and entreated advice and assistance without delay.

" 'He is a little delirious,' said the doctor—'don't be alarmed: we can cheat him out of his dangerous idea, and so perhaps save his life. Where is the watch?' (I produced it)—'See: it is ten minutes to nine. I will put back the hands one hour; that will give good time for a composing draught to operate. There! take him the watch, and let him see the false time with his own eyes. He will be comfortably asleep before the hour hand gets round again to nine.'

"I went back with the watch to my father's bed-side. 'Too slow,' he murmured, as he looked at the dial—'too slow by an hour—the church clock—I counted eight.'

" 'Father! dear father! you are mistaken,' I cried, '*I* counted also: it was only seven.'

" 'Only seven!' he echoed faintly, 'another hour then—another hour to live!' He evidently believed what I had said to him. In spite of the fatal experiences of the past, I now ventured to hope the best from our stratagem, as I resumed my place by his side.

"The doctor came in; but my father never noticed him. He kept his eyes fixed on the watch, which lay between us, on the coverlid. When the minute hand was within a few seconds of indicating the false hour of eight, he looked round at me, murmured very feebly and doubtingly, 'another hour to live!' and then gently closed his eyes. I looked at the watch, and saw that it was just eight o'clock, according to our alteration of the right time. At the same moment, I heard the doctor, whose hand had been on my father's pulse, exclaim, 'My God! it's stopped! He *has* died at nine o'clock!'

"The fatality, which no human stratagem or human science could turn aside, was accomplished! I was alone in the world!

"In the solitude of our little cottage, on the day of my father's burial, I opened the sealed letter, which he had told me to take from the pillow of his death-bed. In preparing to read it, I knew that I was preparing for the knowledge of my own doom; but I neither trembled nor wept. I was beyond all grief: despair such as mine was then, is calm and self-possessed to the last.

"The letter ran thus:—'After your father and your brother have fallen under the fatality that pursues our house, it is right, my dear son, that you should be warned how *you* are included in the last of the predictions which still remains unaccomplished. Know then, that the final lines read by our dear Alfred on the scroll, prophesied that *you* should

die, as *we* have died, at the fatal hour of nine; but by a bloody and
violent death, the day of which was not foretold. My beloved boy!
you know not, you never will know, what I suffered in the possession of
this terrible secret, as the truth of the former prophecies forced itself
more and more plainly on my mind! Even now, as I write, I hope
against all hope; believe vainly and desperately against all experience,
that this last, worst doom may be avoided. Be cautious; be patient;
look well before you at each step of your career. The fatality by which
you are threatened is terrible; but there is a Power above fatality; and
before that Power my spirit and my child's spirit now pray for you.
Remember this when your heart is heavy, and your path through life
grows dark. Remember that the better world is still before you, the
world where we shall all meet! Farewell!'

"When I first read those lines, I read them with the gloomy, immovable resignation of the Eastern fatalists; and that resignation never left
me afterwards. Here, in this prison, I feel it, calm as ever. I bowed
patiently to my doom, when it was only predicted: I bow to it as
patiently now, when it is on the eve of accomplishment. You have
often wondered, my friend, at the tranquil, equable sadness of my
manner: after what I have just told you, can you wonder any longer?

"But let me return for a moment to the past. Though I had no
hope of escaping the fatality which had overtaken my father and my
brother, my life, after my double bereavement, was the existence of all
others which might seem most likely to evade the accomplishment of
my predicted doom. Yourself and one other friend excepted, I saw no
society; my walks were limited to the cottage garden and the neighbouring fields, and my every-day, unvarying occupation was confined
to that hard and resolute course of study, by which alone I could hope
to prevent my mind from dwelling on what I had suffered in the past,
or on what I might still be condemned to suffer in the future. Never
was there a life more quiet and more uneventful than mine!

"You know how I awoke to an ambition, which irresistibly impelled
me to change this mode of existence. News from Paris penetrated even
to my obscure retreat, and disturbed my self-imposed tranquillity. I
heard of the last errors and weaknesses of Louis the Sixteenth; I heard
of the assembling of the States-General; and I knew that the French
Revolution had begun. The tremendous emergencies of that epoch
drew men of all characters from private to public pursuits, and made
politics the necessity rather than the choice of every Frenchman's life.
The great change preparing for the country acted universally on individuals, even to the humblest, and it acted on *me*.

"I was elected a deputy, more for the sake of the name I bore, than on account of any little influence which my acquirements and my character might have exercised in the neighbourhood of my country abode. I removed to Paris, and took my seat in the Chamber, little thinking at that time, of the crime and the bloodshed to which our revolution, so moderate in its beginning, would lead; little thinking that I had taken the first, irretrievable step towards the bloody and the violent death which was lying in store for me.

"Need I go on? You know how warmly I joined the Girondin party; you know how we have been sacrificed; you know what the death is which I and my brethren are to suffer to-morrow. On now ending, I repeat what I said at the beginning:—Judge not of my narrative till you have seen with your own eyes what really takes place in the morning. I have carefully abstained from all comment, I have simply related events as they happened, forbearing to add my own views of their significance, my own ideas on the explanation of which they admit. You may believe us to have been a family of nervous visionaries, witnesses of certain remarkable contingencies; victims of curious, but not impossible chances, which we have fancifully and falsely interpreted into supernatural events. I leave you undisturbed in this conviction (if you really feel it); to-morrow you will think differently; to-morrow you will be an altered man. In the mean time, remember what I now say, as you would remember my dying words: —Last night I saw the supernatural radiance which warned my father and my brother; and which warns *me*, that, whatever the time when the execution begins, whatever the order in which the twenty-one Girondins are chosen for death, I shall be the man who kneels under the guillotine, as the clock strikes nine!"

It was morning. Of the ghastly festivities of the night no sign remained. The prison-hall wore an altered look, as the twenty-one condemned men (followed by those who were ordered to witness their execution) were marched out to the carts appointed to take them from the dungeon to the scaffold.

The sky was cloudless, the sun warm and brilliant, as the Girondin leaders and their companions were drawn slowly through the streets to the place of execution. Duprat and Marigny were placed in separate vehicles: the contrast in their demeanour at that awful moment was strongly marked. The features of the doomed man still preserved their noble and melancholy repose; his glance was steady; his colour never changed. The face of Marigny, on the contrary, displayed the strongest agitation; he was pale even to his lips. The terrible narrative he had heard, the anticipation of the final and appalling proof by which its

truth was now to be tested, had robbed him, for the first time in his
life, of all his self-possession. Duprat had predicted truly; the morrow
had come, and he was an altered man already.

The carts drew up at the foot of the scaffold which was soon to be
stained with the blood of twenty-one human beings. The condemned
deputies mounted it; and ranged themselves at the end opposite the
guillotine. The prisoners who were to behold the execution remained in
their cart. Before Duprat ascended the steps, he took his friend's hand
for the last time: "Farewell!" he said, calmly. "Farewell! I go to my
father, and my brother! Remember my words of last night."

With straining eyes, and bloodless cheeks, Marigny saw Duprat take
his position in the middle row of his companions, who stood in three
ranks of seven each. Then the awful spectacle of the execution began.
After the first seven deputies had suffered there was a pause; the horrible traces of the judicial massacre were being removed. When the
execution proceeded, Duprat was the third taken from the middle rank
of the condemned. As he came forward, and stood for an instant erect
under the guillotine, he looked with a smile on his friend, and repeated
in a clear voice the word, *"Remember!"*—then bowed himself on the
block. The blood stood still at Marigny's heart, as he looked and
listened, during the moment of silence that followed. That moment
past, the church clocks of Paris struck. He dropped down in the cart,
and covered his face with his hands; for through the heavy beat of the
hour he heard the fall of the fatal steel.

"Pray, sir, was it nine or ten that struck just now?" said one of
Marigny's fellow-prisoners to an officer of the guard who stood near
the cart.

The person addressed referred to his watch, and answered—
"NINE O'CLOCK!"

Mrs. Catherine Crowe

Mrs. Catherine Crowe (née Stevens) (c. 1800–1872), a Scottish author who is now almost totally forgotten, was important in certain subcultures of the middle nineteenth century. Her early mystery and detective novel The Adventures of Susan Hopley, or Circumstantial Evidence (1841) was published in many editions, and was pirated extensively in the United States. It served as the basis for the play Susan Hopley that was performed well into the late nineteenth century.

Even more important were Mrs. Crowe's roles as a translator of German psychological and occult works and as a collector of "factual" accounts of supernatural phenomena. She translated Justin Körner's Die Seherin von Prevorst, an important clinical account of a sensitive somnambulist, and her book The Night Side of Nature (1848), partly derived from German sources, was one of the most widely circulated nineteenth-century collections of supernatural anecdotes.

"The Dutch Officer's Story" is taken from Mrs. Crowe's fictional work Ghosts and Family Legends (1848). It is unusual for its period in describing the ghost of an animal; such animal ghosts do not appear in the literature in quantity until well into the twentieth century.

THE
DUTCH OFFICER'S
STORY

"Well, I think nothing can be so cowardly as to be afraid to own the truth," said the pretty Madame de B., an English woman who had married a Dutch officer of distinction.

"Are you really venturing to accuse the General of cowardice?" said Madame L.

"Yes," said Madame de B.; "I want him to tell Mrs. Crowe a ghost story—a thing that he saw himself—and he pooh, poohs it, though he owned it to me before we were married, and since too, saying that he never could have believed such a thing if he had not seen it himself."

While the wife was making this little tirade, the husband looked as if she was accusing him of picking somebody's pocket—il perdait contenance quite. "Now, look at him," she said, "don't you see guilt in his face, Mrs. Crowe!"

"Decidedly," I answered; "so experienced a seeker of ghost stories as myself cannot fail to recognise the symptoms. I always find that when the circumstances are mere hearsay, and happened to nobody knows who, people are very ready to tell it; when it has happened to one of their own family, they are considerably less communicative, and will only tell it under protest: but when they are themselves the parties concerned it is the most difficult thing imaginable to induce them to relate the thing seriously, and with its details. They say they have forgotten it, and don't believe it; and as an evidence of their incredulity they affect to laugh at the whole affair. If the General will tell me the story I will think it quite as decisive a proof of courage as he ever gave in the field."

Betwixt bantering and persuasion, we succeeded in our object, and the General began as follows:—

54

"You know the Belgian Rebellion" (he always called it so) "took place in 1830. It broke out at Brussels on the 28th of August, and we immediately advanced with a considerable force to attack that city; but as the Prince of Orange hoped to bring people to reason without bloodshed, we encamped at Vilvorde, whilst he entered Brussels alone to hold a conference with the armed people. I was a Lieutenant-Colonel then, and commanded the 20th Foot, to which regiment I had been lately appointed.

"We had been three or four days in cantonment, when I heard two of the men, who were digging a little drain at the back of my tent, talking of Jokel Falck, a private in my regiment, who was noted for his extraordinary disposition to somnolence. One of them remarked that he would certainly have got into trouble for being asleep on his post the previous night if it had not been for Mungo. 'I don't know how many times he has saved him,' added he.

"To which the other answered that Mungo was a very valuable friend, and had saved many a man from punishment.

"This was the first time I had ever heard of Mungo, and I rather wondered who it was they alluded to; but the conversation slipped from my mind, and I never thought of asking anybody.

"Shortly after this I was going my rounds, being field-officer of the day, when I saw, by the moonlight, the sentry at one of the outposts stretched upon the ground. I was some way off when I first perceived him; and I only knew what the object was from the situation, and because I saw the glitter of his accoutrements; but almost at the same moment that I discovered him, I observed a large, black Newfoundland dog trotting towards him. The man rose as the dog approached, and had got upon his legs before I reached the spot. This occupied the space of about two minutes—perhaps not so much.

" 'You were asleep at your post,' I said; and turning to the mounted orderly that attended me, I told him to go back and bring a file of the guard to take him prisoner, and to send a sentry to relieve him.

" 'Non, mon Colonel,' said he; and from the way he spoke, I perceived he was intoxicated; 'it's all the fault of that damné Mungo. Il m'a manqué.'

"But I paid no attention to what he said, and rode on, concluding Mungo was some slang term of the men for drink.

"Some evenings after this, I was riding back from my brother's quarters—he was in the 15th, and was stationed about a mile from us—when I remarked the same dog I had seen before trot up to a sentry who, with his legs crossed, was leaning against a wall. The man started, and began walking backwards and forwards on his beat.

I recognised the dog by a large white streak on his side—all the rest of his coat being black.

"When I came up to the man, I saw it was Jọkel Falck, and although I could not have said he was asleep, I strongly suspected that was the fact.

" 'You had better take care of yourself, my man,' said I. 'I have half a mind to have you relieved, and make a prisoner of you. I believe I should have found you asleep on your post if that dog had not roused you.'

"Instead of looking penitent, as was usual on these occasions, I saw a half-smile on the man's face as he saluted me.

" 'Whose dog is that?' I asked my servant, as I rode away.

" 'Je ne sais pas, mon Colonel,' he answered, smiling too.

"On the same evening at mess, I heard one of the subalterns say to the officer who sat next him, 'It's a fact, I assure you, and they call him Mungo.'

" 'That's a new name they've got for Schnapps, isn't it?' I said.

" 'No, sir; it's the name of a dog,' replied the young man, laughing.

" 'A black Newfoundland, with a large white streak on his flank?'

" 'Yes, sir, I believe that is the description,' replied he, tittering still.

" 'I have seen that dog two or three times,' said I. 'I saw him this evening—who does he belong to?'

" 'Well, sir, that is a difficult question,' answered the lad; and I heard his companion say—'To Old Nick, I should think.'

" 'Do you mean to say you've really seen Mungo?' said somebody at the table.

" 'If Mungo is a large Newfoundland—black, with a white streak on its side—I saw him just now. Who does he belong to?'

"By this time the whole mess-table was in a titter, with the exception of one old captain, a man who had been years in the regiment. He was of very humble extraction, and had risen by merit to his present position.

" 'I believe Captain T. is better acquainted with Mungo than anybody present,' answered Major P., with a sneer. 'Perhaps he can tell you who he belongs to.'

"The laughter increased, and I saw there was some joke; but not understanding what it meant, I said to Captain T.—

" 'Does the dog belong to Jokel Falck?'

" 'No, sir,' he replied; 'the dog belongs to nobody now. He once belonged to an officer called Joseph Atveld.'

" 'Belonging to this regiment?'

" 'Yes, sir.'

" 'He is dead, I suppose?'

" 'Yes, sir, he is.'

" 'And the dog has attached himself to the regiment?'

" 'Yes, sir.'

"During this conversation, the suppressed laughter continued, and every eye was fixed on Captain T., who answered me shortly, but with the utmost gravity.

" 'In short,' said the Major, contemptuously, 'according to Captain T., Mungo is the ghost of a deceased dog.'

"This announcement was received with shouts of laughter, in which, I confess, I joined, whilst Captain T. still maintained an unmoved gravity.

" 'It is easier to laugh at such a thing than to believe it, sir,' said he. 'I believe it, because I know it.'

"I smiled, and turned the conversation.

"If anybody at the table except Captain T. had made such an assertion as this, I should have ridiculed them without mercy; but he was an old man, and from the circumstances I have mentioned regarding his origin, we were careful not to offend him; so no more was said about Mungo, and in the hurry of events that followed, I never thought of it again. We marched on to Brussels the next day; and after that, had enough to do till we went to Antwerp, where we were besieged by the French the following year.

"During the siege, I sometimes heard the name of Mungo again; and, one night, when I was visiting the guards and sentries as grand rounds, I caught a glimpse of him, and I felt sure that the man he was approaching when I observed him had been asleep; but he was screened by an angle of the bastion, and by the time I turned the corner, he was moving about.

"This brought to my mind all I had heard about the dog; and as the circumstance was curious, in any point of view, I mentioned what I had seen to Captain T. the next day, saying—

" 'I saw your friend Mungo, last night.'

" 'Did you, sir?' said he. 'It's a strange thing! No doubt, the man was asleep!'

" 'But do you seriously mean to say that you believe this to be a visionary dog, and not a dog of flesh and blood?'

" 'I do, sir. I have been quizzed enough about it; and, once or twice, have nearly got into a quarrel, because people will persist in laughing at what they know nothing about; but as sure as that is a sword you hold in your hand, so sure is that dog a spectre, or ghost —if such a word is applicable to a four-footed beast!'

" 'But, it's impossible!' I said. 'What reason have you for such an extraordinary belief?'

" 'Why, you know, sir, man and boy, I have been in the regiment all my life. I was born in it. My father was pay-sergeant of No. 3 Company when he died; and I have seen Mungo myself, perhaps twenty times, and known, positively, of others seeing him twice as many more.'

" 'Very possibly; but that is no proof that it is not some dog that has attached himself to the regiment.'

" 'But I have seen and heard of the dog for fifty years, sir; and my father before me had seen and heard of him as long!'

" 'Well, certainly, that is extraordinary—if you are sure of it, and that it's the same dog!'

" 'It's a remarkable dog, sir. You won't see another like it with that large white streak on his flank. He won't let one of our sentries be found asleep if he can help it; unless, indeed, the fellow is drunk. He seems to have less care of drunkards, but Mungo has saved many a man from punishment. I was once not a little indebted to him myself. My sister was married out of the regiment, and we had had a bit of a festivity, and drank rather too freely at the wedding, so that when I mounted guard that night—I wasn't to say drunk, but my head was a little gone, or so, and I should have been caught nodding, but Mungo, knowing, I suppose, that I was not an habitual drunkard, woke me just in time.'

" 'How did he wake you?' I asked.

" 'I was roused by a short, sharp bark, that sounded close to my ears. I started, and had just time to catch a glimpse of Mungo before he vanished!'

" 'Is that the way he always wakes the men?'

" 'So they say; and as they wake, he disappears.'

"I recollected now, that on each occasion when I had observed the dog, I had, somehow, lost sight of him in an instant; and, my curiosity being awakened, I asked Captain T. if ours were the only men he took charge of, or whether he showed the same attention to those of other regiments.

" 'Only the 20th, sir; the tradition is, that after the battle of Fontenoy, a large black mastiff was found lying beside a dead officer. Although he had a dreadful wound from a sabre-cut on his flank, and was much exhausted from loss of blood, he would not leave the body; and even after we buried it, he could not be enticed from the spot. The men, interested by the fidelity and attachment of the animal, bound up his wounds, and fed and tended him; and he became the dog of the regiment. It is said that they had taught him to go his rounds before the guards and sentries were visited, and to wake any men that slept. How this may be, I cannot say; but he remained with the regiment till his death, and was buried with all the respect they could show him. Since that he has shown his gratitude in the way I tell you, and of which you have seen some instances.'

" 'I suppose the white streak is the mark of the sabre-cut. I wonder you never fired at him.'

" 'God forbid, sir, I should do such a thing,' said Captain T., looking sharp round at me. 'It's said that a man did so once, and that he never had any luck afterwards; that may be a superstition, but I confess I wouldn't take a good deal to do it.'

"If, as you believe, it's a spectre, it could not be hurt, you know; I imagine ghostly dogs are impervious to bullets.'

" 'No doubt, sir; but I shouldn't like to try the experiment. Besides, it would be useless, as I am convinced already.'

"I pondered a good deal upon this conversation with the old captain. I had never for a moment entertained the idea that such a thing was possible. I should have as much expected to meet the Minotaur or a flying dragon as a ghost of any sort, especially the ghost of a dog; but the evidence here was certainly startling. I had never observed anything like weakness and credulity about T.; moreover, he was a man of known courage, and very much respected in the regiment. In short, so much had his earnestness on the subject staggered me, that I resolved, whenever it was my turn to visit the guards and sentries, that I would carry a pistol with me ready primed and loaded, in order to settle the question. If T. was right there would be an interesting fact established, and no harm done; if, as I could not help suspecting, it was a cunning trick of the men, who had trained this dog to wake them, while they kept up the farce of the spectre, the animal would be well out of the way; since their reliance on him no doubt led them to give way to drowsiness when they would otherwise have struggled against it; indeed, though none of our men had been detected—thanks, perhaps, to Mungo—there had been so much negligence lately in the garrison that the General had issued very severe orders on the subject.

"However, I carried my pistol in vain; I did not happen to fall in with Mungo; and some time afterwards, on hearing the thing alluded to at the mess-table, I mentioned what I had done, adding, 'Mungo is too knowing, I fancy, to run the risk of getting a bullet in him.'

" 'Well,' said Major R., 'I should like to have a shot at him, I confess. If I thought I had any chance of seeing him, I'd certainly try it; but I've never seen him at all.'

" 'Your best chance,' said another, 'is when Jokel Falck is on duty. He is such a sleepy scoundrel, that the men say if it was not for Mungo he'd pass half his time in the guard house.'

" 'If I could catch him, I'd put an ounce of lead into him; that he may rely on.'

" 'Into Jokel Falck, sir,' said one of the subs, laughing.

" 'No, sir,' replied Major R.; 'into Mungo—and I'll do it too.'

" 'Better not, sir,' said Captain T., gravely, provoking thereby a general titter round the table.

"Shortly after this, as I was one night going to my quarters, I saw a mounted orderly ride in and call out a file of the guard to take a prisoner.

" 'What's the matter?' I asked.

" 'One of the sentries asleep on his post, sir; I believe it's Jokel Falck.'

" 'It will be the last time, whoever it is,' I said; 'for the General is determined to shoot the next man that's caught.'

" 'I should have thought Mungo had stood Jokel Falck's friend so often, that he'd never allow him to be caught,' said the adjutant. 'Mungo has neglected his duty.'

" 'No, sir,' said the orderly, gravely. 'Mungo would have waked him, but Major R. shot at him.'

" 'And killed him?' I said.

"The man made no answer, but touched his cap and rode away.

"I heard no more of the affair that night; but the next morning at a very early hour, my servant woke me, saying that Major R. wished to speak to me. I desired he should be admitted, and the moment he entered the room, I saw by his countenance that something serious had occurred; of course I thought the enemy had gained some unexpected advantage during the night, and sat up in bed, inquiring eagerly what had happened.

"To my surprise, he pulled out his pocket-handkerchief and burst into tears. He had married a native of Antwerp, and his wife was in the city at this time. The first thing that occurred to me was that she had met with some accident, and I mentioned her name.

" 'No, no,' he said; 'my son, my boy, my poor Fritz!'

"You know that in our service every officer first enters his regiment as a private soldier, and for a certain space of time does all the duties of that position. The major's son, Fritz, was thus in his noviciate. I concluded he had been killed by a stray shot, and for a minute or two I remained in this persuasion, the Major's speech being choked by his sobs. The first words he uttered were—

" 'Would to God I had taken Captain T.'s advice!'

" 'About what?' I said. 'What has happened to Fritz?'

" 'You know,' said he, 'yesterday I was field officer of the day; and when I was going my rounds last night, I happened to ask my orderly, who was assisting to put on my sash, what men we had told off for the guard. Amongst others, he named Jokel Falck, and remembering the conversation the other day at the mess-table, I took one of my pistols out of the holster, and, after loading it, put it in my pocket. I did not expect to see the dog, for I had never seen him; but as I had no doubt the story of the spectre was some dodge of the men, I determined, if ever I did, to have a shot at him. As I was going through the Place de Meyer, I fell in with the General, who joined me, and we rode on together, talking of the siege. I had forgotten all about the dog, but when we came to the rampart, above the Bastion du Matte, I suddenly saw exactly such an animal as the one described trotting beneath us. I knew there must be a sentry immediately below where we rode, though I could not see him, and I had no doubt that the animal was making towards him; so, without saying a word, I drew out my pistol and fired, at the same moment jumping off my horse, in order to look over the bastion, and get a sight of the man. Without comprehending what I was about, the General did the same, and there we saw the sentry, lying on his face, fast asleep.'

" 'And the body of the dog?' said I.

" 'Nowhere to be seen,' he answered; 'and yet I must have hit him— I fired bang into him. The General says it must have been a delusion, for he was looking exactly in the same direction, and saw no dog at all—but I am certain I saw him, so did the orderly.'

" 'But Fritz?' I said.

" 'It was Fritz—Fritz was the sentry,' said the Major, with a fresh burst of grief. 'The court-martial sits this morning, and my boy will be shot unless interest can be made with the General to grant him a pardon.'

"I rose and dressed myself immediately, but with little hope of success. Poor Fritz being the son of an officer was against him rather than otherwise—it would have been considered an act of favouritism to spare him. He was shot; his poor mother died of a broken heart, and the Major left the service immediately after the surrender of the city."

"And have you ever seen Mungo again?" said I.

"No," he replied; "but I have heard of others seeing him."

"And are you convinced that it was a spectre, and not a dog of flesh and blood?"

"I fancy I was then—but, of course, one can't believe—"

"Oh no," I rejoined; "oh no; never mind facts if they don't fit into our theories."

J. S. Le Fanu

Joseph Sheridan Le Fanu (1814–1873), who is generally considered the finest Victorian author of supernatural fiction, was a native of Dublin, where he spent most of his life. His father was a clergyman in the Church of Ireland, and his ancestry included both French Huguenots and the gifted Sheridan family, Richard Brinsley Sheridan the dramatist being his great-uncle. J. S. Le Fanu attended Trinity College and seemed destined for the law, but his interests proved literary and he became instead a newspaper and periodical proprietor and publisher. For several years he was owner and editor of The Dublin University Magazine, one of the great Victorian periodicals. He also contributed frequently to the better English periodicals. During his lifetime he was renowned for his mystery novels, preeminent among which is Uncle Silas (1864), which has a good claim to be the finest Victorian mystery novel.

Le Fanu's supernatural fiction has been praised by generations of modern critics and literary figures, including Henry James, M. R. James, V. S. Pritchett, and Elizabeth Bowen, among many others. Its strength probably lies in the fact that it was out of step with what his contemporaries were writing. Although Le Fanu's writing tessitura runs from 1838 to 1873, the ideas in his supernatural fiction really belong a generation or two earlier or later. He wrote subtle stories in an age that believed in directness; he told of hauntings that symbolized psychological processes, when most of his contemporaries were writing about steam-like figurations in sheets; and he brought elements of the human psyche out into strange universes. In his better work, like the short novel The Haunted Baronet, he created weird unities among landscape, nature, sin, the human psyche, birds, and animals, all of which were identified symbolically and permeated one another.

WICKED CAPTAIN WALSHAWE, OF WAULING

CHAPTER I

Peg O'Neill Pays the Captain's Debts

A very odd thing happened to my uncle, Mr. Watson, of Haddlestone; and to enable you to understand it, I must begin at the beginning.

In the year 1822, Mr. James Walshawe, more commonly known as Captain Walshawe, died at the age of eighty-one years. The Captain in his early days, and so long as health and strength permitted, was a scamp of the active, intriguing sort; and spent his days and nights in sowing his wild oats, of which he seemed to have an inexhaustible stock. The harvest of this tillage was plentifully interspersed with thorns, nettles, and thistles, which stung the husbandman unpleasantly, and did not enrich him.

Captain Walshawe was very well known in the neighborhood of Wauling, and very generally avoided there. A "captain" by courtesy, for he had never reached that rank in the army list. He had quitted the service in 1766, at the age of twenty-five; immediately previous to which period his debts had grown so troublesome, that he was induced to extricate himself by running away with and marrying an heiress.

Though not so wealthy quite as he had imagined, she proved a very comfortable investment for what remained of his shattered affections; and he lived and enjoyed himself very much in his old way, upon her income, getting into no end of scrapes and scandals, and a good deal of debt and money trouble.

When he married his wife, he was quartered in Ireland, at Clonmel, where was a nunnery, in which, as pensioner, resided Miss O'Neill, or

63

as she was called in the country, Peg O'Neill—the heiress of whom I have spoken.

Her situation was the only ingredient of romance in the affair, for the young lady was decidedly plain, though good-humoured looking, with that style of features which is termed *potato*; and in figure she was a little too plump, and rather short. But she was impressible; and the handsome young English Lieutenant was too much for her monastic tendencies, and she eloped.

In England there are traditions of Irish fortune-hunters, and in Ireland of English. The fact is, it was the vagrant class of each country that chiefly visited the other in old times; and a handsome vagabond, whether at home or abroad, I suppose, made the most of his face, which was also his fortune.

At all events, he carried off the fair one from the sanctuary; and for some sufficient reason, I suppose, they took up their abode at Wauling, in Lancashire.

Here the gallant captain amused himself after his fashion, sometimes running up, of course on business, to London. I believe few wives have ever cried more in a given time than did that poor, dumpy, potato-faced heiress, who got over the nunnery garden wall, and jumped into the handsome Captain's arms, for love.

He spent her income, frightened her out of her wits with oaths and threats, and broke her heart.

Latterly she shut herself up pretty nearly altogether in her room. She had an old, rather grim, Irish servant-woman in attendance upon her. This domestic was tall, lean, and religious, and the Captain knew instinctively she hated him; and he hated her in return, often threatened to put her out of the house, and sometimes even to kick her out of the window. And whenever a wet day confined him to the house, or the stable, and he grew tired of smoking, he would begin to swear and curse at her for a *diddled* old mischief-maker, that could never be easy, and was always troubling the house with her cursed stories, and so forth.

But years passed away, and old Molly Doyle remained still in her original position. Perhaps he thought that there must be somebody there, and that he was not, after all, very likely to change for the better.

CHAPTER II

The Blessed Candle

He tolerated another intrusion, too, and thought himself a paragon of patience and easy good nature for so doing. A Roman Catholic clergyman, in a long black frock, with a low standing collar, and a little white muslin fillet round his neck—tall, sallow, with blue chin, and dark steady eyes—used to glide up and down the stairs, and through the passages; and the Captain sometimes met him in one place and sometimes in another. But by a caprice incident to such tempers he treated this cleric exceptionally, and even with a surly sort of courtesy, though he grumbled about his visits behind his back.

I do not know that he had a great deal of moral courage, and the ecclesiastic looked severe and self-possessed; and somehow he thought he had no good opinion of him, and if a natural occasion were offered, might say extremely unpleasant things, and hard to be answered.

Well the time came at last, when poor Peg O'Neill—in an evil hour Mrs. James Walshawe—must cry, and quake, and pray her last. The doctor came from Penlynden, and was just as vague as usual, but more gloomy, and for about a week came and went oftener. The cleric in the long black frock was also daily there. And at last came that last sacrament in the gates of death, when the sinner is traversing those dread steps that never can be retraced; when the face is turned for ever from life, and we see a receding shape, and hear a voice already irrevocably in the land of spirits.

So the poor lady died; and some people said the Captain "felt it very much." I don't think he did. But he was not very well just then, and looked the part of mourner and penitent to admiration—being seedy and sick. He drank a great deal of brandy and water that night, and called in Farmer Dobbs, for want of better company, to drink with him; and told him all his grievances, and how happy he and "the poor lady up-stairs" might have been, had it not been for liars, and pick-thanks, and tale-bearers, and the like, who came between them—meaning Molly Doyle—whom, as he waxed eloquent over his liquor, he came at last to curse and rail at by name, with more than his accustomed freedom. And he described his own natural character and amiability in such moving terms, that he wept maudlin tears of sensibility over his theme; and when Dobbs was gone, drank some more grog, and took to railing and cursing again by himself; and then mounted the stairs unsteadily, to see "what the devil Doyle and the other —— old witches were about in poor Peg's room."

When he pushed open the door, he found some half-dozen crones, chiefly Irish, from the neighbouring town of Hackleton, sitting over tea and snuff, etc., with candles lighted round the corpse, which was arrayed in a strangely cut robe of brown serge. She had secretly belonged to some order—I think the Carmelite, but I am not certain —and wore the habit in her coffin.

"What the d—— are you doing with my wife?" cried the Captain, rather thickly. "How dare you dress her up in this —— trumpery, you—you cheating old witch; and what's that candle doing in her hand?"

I think he was a little startled, for the spectacle was grisly enough. The dead lady was arrayed in this strange brown robe, and in her rigid fingers, as in a socket, with the large wooden beads and cross wound round it, burned a wax candle, shedding its white light over the sharp features of the corpse. Moll Doyle was not to be put down by the Captain, whom she hated, and accordingly, in her phrase, "he got as good as he gave." And the Captain's wrath waxed fiercer, and he chucked the wax taper from the dead hand, and was on the point of flinging it at the old serving-woman's head.

"The holy candle, you sinner!" cried she.

"I've a mind to make you eat it, you beast," cried the Captain.

But I think he had not known before what it was, for he subsided a little sulkily, and he stuffed his hand with the candle (quite extinct by this time) into his pocket, and said he—

"You know devilish well you had no business going on with y-y-your d—— witch-craft about my poor wife, without my leave— you do—and you'll please take off that d—— brown pinafore, and get her decently into her coffin, and I'll pitch your devil's waxlight into the sink."

And the Captain stalked out of the room.

"An' now her poor sowl's in prison, you wretch, be the mains o' ye; an' may yer own be shut into the wick o' that same candle, till it's burned out, ye savage."

"I'd have you ducked for a witch, for two-pence," roared the Captain up the staircase, with his hand on the banisters, standing on the lobby. But the door of the chamber of death clapped angrily, and he went down to the parlour, where he examined the holy candle for a while, with a tipsy gravity, and then with something of that reverential feeling for the symbolic, which is not uncommon in rakes and scamps, he thoughtfully locked it up in a press, where were accumulated all sorts of obsolete rubbish—soiled packs of cards, disused tobacco pipes, broken powder flasks, his military sword, and a dusky bundle of the "Flash Songster," and other questionable literature.

He did not trouble the dead lady's room any more. Being a volatile man it is probable that more cheerful plans and occupations began to entertain his fancy.

CHAPTER III

My Uncle Watson Visits Wauling

So the poor lady was buried decently, and Captain Walshawe reigned alone for many years at Wauling. He was too shrewd and too experienced by this time to run violently down the steep hill that leads to ruin. So there was a method in his madness; and after a widowed career of more than forty years, he, too, died at last with some guineas in his purse.

Forty years and upwards is a great *edax rerum*, and a wonderful chemical power. It acted forcibly upon the gay Captain Walshawe. Gout supervened, and was no more conducive to temper than to enjoyment, and made his elegant hands lumpy at all the small joints, and turned them slowly into crippled claws. He grew stout when his exercise was interfered with, and ultimately almost corpulent. He suffered from what Mr. Holloway calls "bad legs," and was wheeled about in a great leathern-backed chair, and his infirmities went on accumulating with his years.

I am sorry to say, I never heard that he repented, or turned his thoughts seriously to the future. On the contrary, his talk grew fouler, and his fun ran upon his favourite sins, and his temper waxed more truculent. But he did not sink into dotage. Considering his bodily infirmities, his energies and his malignities, which were many and active, were marvellously little abated by time. So he went on to the close. When his temper was stirred, he cursed and swore in a way that made decent people tremble. It was a word and a blow with him; the latter, luckily, not very sure now. But he would seize his crutch and make a swoop or a pound at the offender, or shy his medicine-bottle, or his tumbler, at his head.

It was a peculiarity of Captain Walshawe, that he, by this time, hated nearly everybody. My uncle, Mr. Watson, of Haddlestone, was cousin to the Captain, and his heir-at-law. But my uncle had lent him money on mortgage of his estates, and there had been a treaty to sell, and terms and a price were agreed upon, in "articles" which the lawyers said were still in force.

I think the ill-conditioned Captain bore him a grudge for being richer than he, and would have liked to do him an ill turn. But it did not lie in his way; at least while he was living.

My uncle Watson was a Methodist, and what they call a "class-leader"; and, on the whole, a very good man. He was now near fifty—grave, as beseemed his profession—somewhat dry—and a little severe, perhaps—but a just man.

A letter from the Penlynden doctor reached him at Haddlestone, announcing the death of the wicked old Captain; and suggesting his attendance at the funeral, and the expediency of his being on the spot to look after things at Wauling. The reasonableness of this striking my good uncle, he made his journey to the old house in Lancashire incontinently, and reached it in time for the funeral.

My uncle, whose traditions of the Captain were derived from his mother, who remembered him in his slim, handsome youth—in shorts, cocked-hat and lace, was amazed at the bulk of the coffin which contained his mortal remains; but the lid being already screwed down, he did not see the face of the bloated old sinner.

CHAPTER IV

In the Parlour

What I relate, I had from the lips of my uncle, who was a truthful man, and not prone to fancies.

The day turning out awfully rainy and tempestuous, he persuaded the doctor and the attorney to remain for the night at Wauling.

There was no will—the attorney was sure of that; for the Captain's enmities were perpetually shifting, and he could never quite make up his mind, as to how best to give effect to a malignity whose direction was constantly being modified. He had had instructions for drawing a will a dozen times over. But the process had always been arrested by the intending testator.

Search being made, no will was found. The papers, indeed, were all right, with one important exception: the leases were nowhere to be seen. There were special circumstances connected with several of the principal tenancies on the estate—unnecessary here to detail—which rendered the loss of these documents one of very serious moment, and even of very obvious danger.

My uncle, therefore, searched strenuously. The attorney was at his elbow, and the doctor helped with a suggestion now and then. The old serving-man seemed an honest deaf creature, and really knew nothing.

My uncle Watson was very much perturbed. He fancied—but this possibly was only fancy—that he had detected for a moment a queer look in the attorney's face; and from that instant it became fixed in his mind that he knew all about the leases. Mr. Watson expounded that evening in the parlour to the doctor, the attorney, and the deaf servant. Ananias and Sapphira figured in the foreground; and the awful nature of fraud and theft, of tampering in anywise with the plain rule of honesty in matters pertaining to estates, etc., were pointedly dwelt upon; and then came a long and strenuous prayer, in which he entreated with fervour and aplomb that the hard heart of the sinner who had abstracted the leases might be softened or broken in such a way as to lead to their restitution; or that, if he continued reserved and contumacious, it might at least be the will of Heaven to bring him to public justice and the documents to light. The fact is, that he was praying all this time at the attorney.

When these religious exercises were over, the visitors retired to their rooms, and my Uncle Watson wrote two or three pressing letters by the fire. When his task was done, it had grown late; the candles were flaring in their sockets, and all in bed, and, I suppose, asleep, but he.

The fire was nearly out, he chilly, and the flame of the candles throbbing strangely in their sockets, shed alternate glare and shadow round the old wainscoted room and its quaint furniture. Outside were all the wild thunder and piping of the storm; and the rattling of distant windows sounded through the passages, and down the stairs, like angry people astir in the house.

My Uncle Watson belonged to a sect who by no means rejected the supernatural, and whose founder, on the contrary, has sanctioned ghosts in the most emphatic way. He was glad therefore to remember, that in prosecuting his search that day, he had seen some six inches of wax candle in the press in the parlor; for he had no fancy to be overtaken by darkness in his present situation. He had no time to lose; and taking the bunch of keys—of which he was now master—he soon fitted the lock, and secured the candle—a treasure in his circumstances; and lighting it, he stuffed it into the socket of one of the expiring candles, and extinguishing the other, he looked round the room in the steady light reassured. At the same moment, an unusual violent gust of the storm blew a handful of gravel against the parlour window, with a sharp rattle that startled him in the midst of the roar and hubbub; and the flame of the candle itself was agitated by the air.

CHAPTER V

The Bed-Chamber

My uncle walked up to bed, guarding his candle with his hand, for the lobby windows were rattling furiously, and he disliked the idea of being left in the dark more than ever.

His bedroom was comfortable, though old-fashioned. He shut and bolted the door. There was a tall looking-glass opposite the foot of his four-poster, on the dressing-table between the windows. He tried to make the curtains meet, but they would not draw; and like many a gentleman in a like perplexity, he did not possess a pin, nor was there one in the huge pincushion beneath the glass.

He turned the face of the mirror away therefore, so that its back was presented to the bed, pulled the curtains together, and placed a chair against them, to prevent their falling open again. There was a good fire, and a reinforcement of round coal and wood inside the fender. So he piled it up to ensure a cheerful blaze through the night, and placing a little black mahogany table, with the legs of a satyr, beside the bed, and his candle upon it, he got between the sheets, and laid his red night-capped head upon his pillow, and disposed himself to sleep.

The first thing that made him uncomfortable was the sound at the foot of his bed, quite distinct in a momentary lull of the storm. It was only the gentle rustle and rush of the curtains, which fell open again; and as his eyes opened, he saw them resuming their perpendicular dependence, and sat up in his bed almost expecting to see something uncanny in the aperture.

There was nothing, however, but the dressing-table, and other dark furniture, and the window-curtains faintly undulating in the violence of the storm. He did not care to get up, therefore—the fire being bright and cheery—to replace the curtains by a chair, in the position in which he had left them, anticipating possibly a new recurrence of the relapse which had startled him from his incipient doze.

So he got to sleep in a little while again, but he was disturbed by a sound, as he fancied, at the table on which stood the candle. He could not say what it was, only that he wakened with a start, and lying so in some amaze, he did distinctly hear a sound which startled him a good deal, though there was nothing necessarily supernatural in it. He described it as resembling what would occur if you fancied a thinnish table-leaf, with a convex warp in it, depressed the reverse way, and suddenly with a spring recovering its natural convexity. It was a loud, sudden thump, which made the heavy candlestick jump, and there was an end, except that my uncle did not get again into a doze for ten minutes at least.

The next time he awoke, it was in that odd, serene way that sometimes occurs. We open our eyes, we know not why, quite placidly, and are on the instant wide awake. He had had a nap of some duration this time, for his candle-flame was fluttering and flaring, *in articulo*, in the silver socket. But the fire was still bright and cheery; so he popped the extinguisher on the socket, and almost at the same time there came a tap at his door, and a sort of crescendo "hush-sh-sh!" Once more my uncle was sitting up, scared and perturbed, in his bed. He recollected, however, that he had bolted his door; and such inveterate materialists are we in the midst of our spiritualism, that this reassured him, and he breathed a deep sigh, and began to grow tranquil. But after a rest of a minute or two, there came a louder and sharper knock at his door; so that instinctively he called out, "Who's there?" in a loud, stern key. There was no sort of response, however. The nervous effect of the start subsided; and I think my uncle must have remembered how constantly, especially on a stormy night, these creaks or cracks which simulate all manner of goblin noises, make themselves naturally audible.

CHAPTER VI

The Extinguisher Is Lifted

After a while, then, he lay down with his back turned toward that side of the bed at which was the door, and his face toward the table on which stood the massive old candlestick, capped with its extinguisher, and in that position he closed his eyes. But sleep would not revisit them. All kinds of queer fancies began to trouble him—some of them I remember.

He felt the point of a finger, he averred, pressed most distinctly on the tip of his great toe, as if a living hand were between his sheets, and making a sort of signal of attention or silence. Then again he felt something as large as a rat make a sudden bounce in the middle of his bolster, just under his head. Then a voice said "Oh!" very gently, close at the back of his head. All these things he felt certain of, and yet investigation led to nothing. He felt odd little cramps stealing now and then about him; and then, on a sudden, the middle finger of his right hand was plucked backwards, with a light playful jerk that frightened him awfully.

Meanwhile the storm kept singing, and howling, and ha-ha-hooing hoarsely among the limbs of the old trees and the chimney-pots; and

my Uncle Watson, although he prayed and meditated as was his wont
when he lay awake, felt his heart throb excitedly, and sometimes
thought he was beset with evil spirits, and at others that he was in the
early stage of a fever.

He resolutely kept his eyes closed, however, and, like St. Paul's
shipwrecked companions, wished for the day. At last another little doze
seems to have stolen upon his senses, for he awoke quietly and completely as before—opening his eyes all at once, and seeing everything
as if he had not slept for a moment.

The fire was still blazing redly—nothing uncertain in the light—the
massive silver candlestick, topped with its tall extinguisher, stood on
the centre of the black mahogany table as before; and, looking by what
seemed a sort of accident to the apex of this, he beheld something
which made him quite misdoubt the evidence of his eyes.

He saw the extinguisher lifted by a tiny hand, from beneath, and a
small human face, no bigger than a thumb-nail, with nicely propor-
tioned features, peep from beneath it. In this Lilliputian countenance
was such a ghastly consternation as horrified my uncle unspeakably.
Out came a little foot then and there, and a pair of wee legs, in short
silk stockings and buckled shoes, then the rest of the figure; and, with
the arms holding about the socket, the little legs stretched and stretched,
hanging about the stem of the candlestick till the feet reached the base,
and so down the satyr-like leg of the table, till they reached the floor,
extending elastically, and strangely enlarging in all proportions as they
approached the ground, where the feet and buckles were those of a
well-shaped, full grown man, and the figure tapering upward until it
dwindled to its original fairy dimensions at the top, like an object seen
in some strangely curved mirror.

Standing upon the floor he expanded, my amazed uncle could not tell
how, into his proper proportions; and stood pretty nearly in profile at
the bedside, a handsome and elegantly shaped young man, in a bygone
military costume, with a small laced, three-cocked hat and plume on
his head, but looking like a man going to be hanged—in unspeakable
despair.

He stepped lightly to the hearth, and turned for a few seconds very
dejectedly with his back toward the bed and the mantel-piece, and he
saw the hilt of his rapier glittering in the firelight; and then walking
across the room he placed himself at the dressing-table, visible through
the divided curtains at the foot of the bed. The fire was blazing still so
brightly that my uncle saw him as distinctly as if half a dozen candles
were burning.

CHAPTER VII

The Visitation Culminates

The looking-glass was an old-fashioned piece of furniture, and had a drawer beneath it. My uncle had searched it carefully for the papers in the daytime; but the silent figure pulled the drawer quite out, pressed a spring at the side, disclosing a false receptacle behind it, and from this he drew a parcel of papers tied together with pink tape.

All this time my uncle was staring at him in a horrified state, neither winking nor breathing, and the apparition had not once given the smallest intimation of consciousness that a living person was in the same room. But now, for the first time, it turned its livid stare full upon my uncle with a hateful smile of significance, lifting up the little parcel of papers between his slender finger and thumb. Then he made a long, cunning wink at him, and seemed to blow out one of his cheeks in a burlesque grimace, which, but for the horrific circumstances, would have been ludicrous. My uncle could not tell whether this was really an intentional distortion or only one of those horrid ripples and deflections which were constantly disturbing the proportions of the figure, as if it were seen through some unequal and perverting medium.

The figure now approached the bed, seeming to grow exhausted and malignant as it did so. My uncle's terror nearly culminated at this point, for he believed it was drawing near him with an evil purpose. But it was not so; for the soldier, over whom twenty years seemed to have passed in his brief transit to the dressing-table and back again, threw himself into a great high-backed arm-chair of stuffed leather at the far side of the fire, and placed his heels on the fender. His feet and legs seemed indistinctly to swell, and swathings showed themselves round them, and they grew into something enormous, and the upper figure swayed and shaped itself into corresponding proportions, a great mass of corpulence, with a cadaverous and malignant face, and the furrows of a great old age, and colourless glassy eyes; and with these changes, which came indefinitely but rapidly as those of a sunset cloud, the fine regimentals faded away, and a loose, gray, woollen drapery, somehow, was there in its stead; and all seemed to be stained and rotten, for swarms of worms seemed creeping in and out, while the figure grew paler and paler, till my uncle, who liked his pipe, and employed the simile naturally, said the whole effigy grew to the colour of tobacco ashes, and the clusters of worms into little wriggling knots of sparks such as we see running over the residuum of a burnt sheet of paper. And so with the strong draught caused by the fire, and the current of air from the window, which was rattling in the storm, the feet seemed to be drawn into the fire-place, and the whole figure, light as ashes, floated away with them, and disappeared with a whisk up the capacious old chimney.

It seemed to my uncle that the fire suddenly darkened and the air grew icy cold, and there came an awful roar and riot of tempest, which shook the old house from top to base, and sounded like the yelling of a blood-thirsty mob on receiving a new and long-expected victim.

Good Uncle Watson used to say, "I have been in many situations of fear and danger in the course of my life, but never did I pray with so much agony before or since; for then, as now, it was clear beyond a cavil that I had actually beheld the phantom of an evil spirit."

CONCLUSION

Now there are two curious circumstances to be observed in this relation of my uncle's, who was, as I have said, a perfectly veracious man.

First—The wax candle which he took from the press in the parlour and burnt at his bedside on that horrible night was unquestionably, according to the testimony of the old deaf servant, who had been fifty years at Wauling, that identical piece of "holy candle" which had stood in the fingers of the poor lady's corpse, and concerning which the old Irish crone, long since dead, had delivered the curious curse I have mentioned against the Captain.

Secondly—Behind the drawer under the looking-glass, he did actually discover a second but secret drawer, in which were concealed the identical papers which he had suspected the attorney of having made away with. There were circumstances, too, afterwards disclosed which convinced my uncle that the old man had deposited them there preparatory to burning them, which he had nearly made up his mind to do.

Now, a very remarkable ingredient in this tale of my Uncle Watson was this, that so far as my father, who had never seen Captain Walshawe in the course of his life, could gather, the phantom had exhibited a horrible and grotesque, but unmistakeable resemblance to that defunct scamp in the various stages of his long life.

Wauling was sold in the year 1837, and the old house shortly after pulled down, and a new one built nearer to the river. I often wonder whether it was rumoured to be haunted, and, if so, what stories were current about it. It was a commodious and stanch old house, and withal rather handsome; and its demolition was certainly suspicious.

Mrs. Henry Wood

Mrs. Henry Wood (née Ellen Price) (1814–1887) was second only to Miss Braddon as a purveyor of thrills to the women's magazines. Her most famous work was East Lynne (1861), which appeared in many editions in Great Britain and America. Today East Lynne is still of interest for an ingenious detective situation in one of its two subplots; the Victorians cherished it for the other subplot, the experiences of a runaway wife who returns in disguise to nurse her dying child. In an abridged version East Lynne was a mainstay of the Victorian stage, and it is still occasionally performed, although perhaps not with complete seriousness.

While Mrs. Wood worked primarily in sensation fiction and the domestic novel, she ventured into the ghost story on several occasions. Her most famous work in this area is the long novel The Shadow of Ashlydyat (1863), which is concerned with a family curse, spectral shadows, death omens, and crimes. Most of her shorter supernatural fiction appeared in the Johnny Ludlow stories, which were printed anonymously in the Argosy, a periodical that she edited. A couple of these stories are rationalized, but some remain full ghost stories.

In her concept of the supernatural Mrs. Wood was typical of her period. Her stories are usually domestic in setting, and her ghosts are symbols of justice. "A Curious Experience" (1874) is exceptional in its understatement of phenomena and in the pointlessness of the haunting.

A
CURIOUS EXPERIENCE

What I am about to tell of took place during the last year of John Whitney's life, now many years ago. We could never account for it, or understand it: but it occurred (at least, so far as our experience of it went) just as I relate it.

It was not the custom for schools to give a long holiday at Easter then: one week at most. Dr. Frost allowed us from the Thursday in Passion week, to the following Thursday; and many of the boys spent it at school.

Easter was late that year, and the weather lovely. On the Wednesday in Easter week, the Squire and Mrs. Todhetley drove over to spend the day at Whitney Hall, Tod and I being with them. Sir John and Lady Whitney were beginning to be anxious about John's health—their eldest son. He had been ailing since the previous Christmas, and he seemed to grow thinner and weaker. It was so perceptible when he got home from school this Easter, that Sir John put himself into a flurry (he was just like the Squire in that and in many another way), and sent an express to Worcester for Henry Carden, asking him to bring Dr. Hastings with him. They came. John wanted care, they said, and they could not discover any specific disease at present. As to his returning to school, they both thought that question might be left with the boy himself. John told them he should prefer to go back, and laughed a little at this fuss being made over him: he should soon be all right, he said; people were apt to lose strength more or less in the spring. He was sixteen then, a slender, upright boy, with a delicate, thoughtful face, dreamy, grey-blue eyes and brown hair, and he was even gentle, sweet-tempered, and considerate. Sir John related to the Squire what the doctors had said, avowing that he could not "make much out of it."

In the afternoon, when we were out-of-doors on the lawn in the hot sunshine, listening to the birds singing and the cuckoo calling, Featherston came in, the local doctor, who saw John nearly every day. He was a tall, grey, hard-worked man, with a face of care. After talking a few moments with John and his mother, he turned to the rest of us on the grass. The Squire and Sir John were sitting on a garden bench, some wine and lemonade on a little table between them. Featherston shook hands.

"Will you take some?" asked Sir John.

"I don't mind a glass of lemonade with a dash of sherry in it," answered Featherstone, lifting his hat to rub his brow. "I have been walking beyond Goose Brook and back, and upon my word it is as hot as midsummer."

"Ay, it is," assented Sir John. "Help yourself, doctor."

He filled a tumbler with what he wanted, brought it over to the opposite bench, and sat down by Mrs. Todhetley. John and his mother were at the other end of it; I sat on the arm. The rest of them, with Helen and Anna, had gone strolling away; to the North Pole, for all we knew.

"John still says he shall go back to school," began Lady Whitney, to Featherston.

"Ay; to-morrow's the day, isn't it, John? Black Thursday, some of you boys call it."

"I like school," said John.

"Almost a pity, though," continued Featherston, looking up and about him. "To be out at will all day in this soft air, under the blue skies and the sunbeams, might be of more benefit to you, Master John, than being cooped up in a close school-room."

"You hear, John!" cried Lady Whitney. "I wish you would persuade him to take a longer rest at home, Mr. Featherston!"

Mr. Featherston stooped for his tumbler, which he had lodged on the smooth grass, and took another drink before replying. "If you and John would follow my advice, Lady Whitney, I'd give it."

"Yes?" cried she, all eagerness.

"Take John somewhere for a fortnight, and let him go back to school at the end," said the surgeon. "That would do him good."

"Why, of course it would," called out Sir John, who had been listening. "And I say it shall be done. John, my boy, you and your mother shall go to the seaside—to Aberystwith."

"Well, I don't think I should quite say that, Sir John," said Featherston again. "The seaside would be all very well in this warm weather; but it may not last, it may change to cold and frost. I should suggest one of the inland watering-places, as they are called: where there's a Spa, and a Pump Room, and a Parade, and lots of gay company. It would be lively for him, and a thorough change."

"What a nice idea!" cried Lady Whitney, who was the most unsophisticated woman in the world. "Such as Pumpwater."

"Such as Pumpwater: the very place," agreed Featherston. "Well, were I you, my lady, I would try it for a couple of weeks. Let John take a companion with him; one of his schoolfellows. Here's Johnny Ludlow: he might do."

"I'd rather have Johnny Ludlow than any one," said John.

Remarking that his time was up, for a patient waited for him, and that he must leave us to settle the question, Featherston took his departure. But it appeared to be settled already.

"Johnny can go," spoke up the Squire. "The loss of a fortnight's lessons is not much, compared with doing a little service to a friend. Charming spots are those inland watering-places, and Pumpwater is about the best of them all."

"We must take lodgings," said Lady Whitney presently, when they had done expatiating upon the gauds and glories of Pumpwater. "To stay at an hotel would be so noisy; and expensive besides."

"I know of some,"cried Mrs. Todhetley, in sudden thought. "If you could get into Miss Gay's rooms, you would be well off. Do you remember them?"—turning to the Squire. "We stayed at her house on our way from ———— "

"Why, bless me, to be sure I do," he interrupted. "Somebody had given us Miss Gay's address, and we drove straight to it to see if she had rooms at liberty; she had, and took us in at once. We were so comfortable there that we stayed at Pumpwater three days instead of two."

It was hastily decided that Mrs. Todhetley should write to Miss Gay, and she went indoors to do so. All being well, Lady Whitney meant to start on Saturday.

Miss Gay's answer came punctually, reaching Whitney Hall on Friday morning. It was addressed to Mrs. Todhetley, but Lady Whitney, as had been arranged, opened it. Miss Gay wrote that she should be much pleased to receive Lady Whitney. Her house, as it chanced, was then quite empty; a family, who had been with her six weeks, had just left: so Lady Whitney might take her choice of the rooms, which she would keep vacant until Saturday. In conclusion, she begged Mrs. Todhetley to notice that her address was changed. The old house was too small to accommodate the many kind friends who patronized her, and she had moved into a larger house, superior to the other and in the best position.

Thus all things seemed to move smoothly for our expedition; and we departed by train on the Saturday morning for Pumpwater.

It was a handsome house, standing in the high-road, between the parade and the principal street, and rather different from the houses on each side it, inasmuch as that it was detached and had a narrow slip of gravelled ground in front. In fact, it looked too large and handsome for a lodging-house; and Lady Whitney, regarding it from the fly which had brought us from the station, wondered whether the driver had made a mistake. It was built of red-brick, with white stone facings; the door, set in a pillared portico, stood in the middle, and three rooms, each with a bay-window, lay one above another on both sides.

But in a moment we saw it was all right. A slight, fair woman, in a slate silk gown, came out and announced herself as Miss Gay. She had a mild, pleasant voice, and a mild, pleasant face, with light falling curls, the fashion then for every one, and she wore a lace cap, trimmed with pink. I took to her and to her face at once.

"I am glad to be here," said Lady Whitney, cordially, in answer to Miss Gay's welcome. "Is there any one who can help with the luggage? We have not brought either man or maid-servant."

"Oh dear, yes, my lady. Please let me show you indoors, and then leave all to me. Susannah! Oh, here you are, Susannah! Where's Charity?—my cousin and chief help-mate, my lady."

A tall, dark person, about Miss Gay's own age, which might be forty, wearing brown ribbon in her hair and a purple bow at her throat, dropped a curtsy to Lady Whitney. This was Susannah. She looked strong-minded and capable. Charity, who came running up the kitchen-stairs, was a smiling young woman-servant, with a coarse apron tied round her, and red arms bared to the elbow.

There were four sitting-rooms on the ground-floor: two in front, with their large bay-windows; two at the back, looking out upon some bright, semi-public gardens.

"A delightful house!" exclaimed Lady Whitney to Miss Gay, after she had looked about a little. "I will take one of these front-rooms for our sitting-room," she added, entering, haphazard, the one on the right of the entrance-hall, and putting down her bag and parasol. "This one, I think, Miss Gay."

"Very good, my lady. And will you now be pleased to walk up-stairs and fix upon the bedrooms."

Lady Whitney seemed to fancy the front of the house. "This room shall be my son's; and I should like to have the opposite one for myself," she said, rather hesitatingly, knowing they must be the two best chambers of all. "Can I?"

Miss Gay seemed quite willing. We were in the room over our sitting-room on the right of the house looking to the front. The objection, if it could be called one, came from Susannah.

"You can have the other room, certainly, my lady; but I think the young gentleman would find this one noisy, with all the carriages and carts that pass by, night and morning. The back-rooms are much more quiet."

"But I like noise," put in John; "it seems like company to me. If I could do as I would, I'd never sleep in the country."

"One of the back-rooms is very lively, sir; it has a view of the turning to the Pump Room," persisted Susannah, a sort of suppressed eagerness in her tone; and it struck me that she did not want John to have this front-chamber. "I think you would like it best."

"No," said John, turning round from the window, out of which he had been looking, "I will have this. I shall like to watch the shops down that turning opposite, and the people who go into them."

No more was said. John took this chamber, which was over our sitting-room, Lady Whitney had the other front-chamber, and I had a very good one at the back of John's. And thus we settled down.

Pumpwater is a nice place, as you would know if I gave its proper name, bright and gay, and our house was in the best of situations. The principal street, with its handsome shops, lay to our right; the Parade, leading to the Spa and Pump Room, to our left, and company and carriages were continually passing by. We visited some of the shops and took a look at the Pump Room.

In the evening, when tea was over, Miss Gay came in to speak of the breakfast. Lady Whitney asked her to sit down for a little chat. She wanted to ask about the churches.

"What a very nice house this is!" again observed Lady Whitney presently: for the more she saw of it, the better she found it. "You must pay a high rent for it, Miss Gay."

"Not so high as your ladyship might think," was the answer; "not high at all for what it is. I paid sixty pounds for the little house I used to be in, and I pay only seventy for this."

"Only seventy!" echoed Lady Whitney, in surprise. "How is it you get it so cheaply?"

A waggonette, full of people, was passing just then; Miss Gay seemed to want to watch it by before she answered. We were sitting in the dusk with the blinds up.

"For one thing, it had been standing empty for some time, and I suppose Mr. Bone, the agent, was glad to have my offer," replied Miss Gay, who seemed to be as fond of talking as any one else is, once set on. "It had belonged to a good old family, my lady, but they got embarrassed and put it up for sale some six or seven years ago. A Mr. Calson bought it. He had come to Pumpwater about that time from foreign lands; and he and his wife settled down in the house. A puny, weakly little woman she was, who seemed to get weaklier instead of stronger, and in a year or two she died. After her death her husband grew ill; he went away for change of air, and died in London; and the house was left to a little nephew living over in Australia."

"And has the house been vacant ever since?" asked John.

"No, sir. At first it was let furnished, then unfurnished. But it had been vacant some little time when I applied to Mr. Bone. I concluded he thought it better to let it at a low rent than for it to stand empty."

"It must cost you incessant care and trouble, Miss Gay, to conduct a house like this—when you are full," remarked Lady Whitney.

"It does," she answered. "One's work seems never done—and I cannot, at that, give satisfaction to all. Ah, my lady, what a difference there is in people!—you would never think it. Some are so kind and considerate to me, so anxious not to give trouble unduly, and so satisfied with all I do that it is a pleasure to serve them: while others make gratuitous work and trouble from morning till night, and treat me as if I were just a dog under their feet. Of course when we are full I have another servant in, two sometimes."

"Even that must leave a great deal for yourself to do and see to."

"The back is always fitted to the burden," sighed Miss Gay. "My father was a farmer in this county, as his ancestors had been before him, farming his three hundred acres of land, and looked upon as a man of substance. My mother made the butter, saw to the poultry, and superintended her household generally: and we children helped her. Farmers' daughters then did not spend their days in playing the piano and doing fancy work, or expect to be waited upon like ladies born."

"They do now, though," said Lady Whitney.

"So I was ready to turn my hand to anything when hard times came—not that I had thought I should have to do it," continued Miss Gay. "But my father's means dwindled down. Prosperity gave way to adversity. Crops failed; the stock died off; two of my brothers fell into trouble and it cost a mint of money to extricate them. Altogether, when father died, but little of his savings remained to us. Mother took a house in the town here, to let lodgings, and I came with her. She is dead, my lady, and I am left."

The silent tears were running down poor Miss Gay's cheeks.

"It is a life of struggle, I am sure," spoke Lady Whitney, gently. "And not deserved, Miss Gay."

"But there's another life to come," spoke John, in a half-whisper, turning to Miss Gay from the large bay-window. "None of us will be overworked *there*."

Miss Gay stealthily wiped her cheeks. "I do not repine," she said, humbly. "I have been enabled to rub on and keep my head above water, and to provide little comforts for mother in her need; and I gratefully thank God for it."

The bells of the churches, ringing out at eight o'clock, called us up in the morning. Lady Whitney was downstairs, first, I next. Susannah, who waited upon us, had brought up the breakfast. John followed me in.

"I hope you have slept well, my boy," said Lady Whitney, kissing him. "I have."

"So have I," I put in.

"Then you and the mother make up for me, Johnny," he said; "for I have not slept at all."

"Oh, John!" exclaimed his mother.

"Not a wink all night long," added John. "I can't think what was the matter with me."

Susannah, then stooping to take the sugar-basin out of the side-board, rose, turned sharply round and fixed her eyes on John. So curious an expression was on her face that I could but notice it.

"Do you not think it was the noise, sir?" she said to him. "I knew that room would be too noisy for you."

"Why, the room was as quiet as possible," he answered. "A few carriages rolled by last night—and I liked to hear them; but that was all over before midnight; and I have heard none this morning."

"Well, sir, I'm sure you would be more comfortable in a back-room," contended Susannah.

"It was a strange bed," said John. "I shall sleep all the sounder to-night."

Breakfast was half over when John found he had left his watch up-stairs, on the drawers. I went to fetch it.

The door was open, and I stepped to the drawers, which stood just inside. Miss Gay and Susannah were making the bed and talking, too busy to see or hear me. A lot of things lay on the white cloth, and at first I could not see the watch.

"He declares he had not slept at all; *not at all*," Susannah was saying with emphasis. "If you had only seconded me yesterday, Harriet, they need not have had this room. But you never made a word of objection; you gave in at once."

"Well, I saw no reason to make it," said Miss Gay, mildly. "If I were to give in to your fancies, Susannah, I might as well shut up the room. Visitors must get used to it."

The watch had been partly hidden under one of John's neckties. I caught it up and decamped.

We went to church after breakfast. The first hymn sung was that one beginning, "Brief life."

> "Brief life is here our portion;
>   Brief sorrow, short-lived care:
> The life that knows no ending,
>   The tearless life, is *there*."

As the verses went on, John touched my elbow: "Miss Gay," he whispered; his eyelashes moist with the melody of the music. I have often thought since that we might have seen by these very moods of John—his thoughts bent upon heaven more than upon earth—that his life was swiftly passing.

There's not much to tell of that Sunday. We dined in the middle of the day; John fell asleep after dinner; and in the evening we attended church again. And I think every one was ready for bed when bedtime came. I know I was.

Therefore it was all the more surprising when, the next morning, John said he had again not slept.

"What, not at all!" exclaimed his mother.

"No, not at all. As I went to bed, so I got up—sleepless."

"I never heard of such a thing!" cried Lady Whitney. "Perhaps, John, you were too tired to sleep?"

"Something of that sort," he answered. "I felt both tired and sleepy when I got into bed; particularly so. But I had no sleep: not a wink. I could not lie still, either; I was frightfully restless all night; just as I was the night before. I suppose it can't be the bed?"

"Is the bed not comfortable?" asked his mother.

"It seems as comfortable a bed as can be when I first lie down in it. And then I grow restless and uneasy."

"It must be the restlessness of extreme fatigue," said Lady Whitney. "I fear the journey was rather too much for you, my dear."

"Oh, I shall be all right as soon as I can sleep, mamma."

We had a surprise that morning. John and I were standing before a tart-shop, our eyes glued to the window, when a voice behind us called out, "Don't they look nice, boys!" Turning round, there stood Henry Carden of Worcester, arm-in-arm with a little white-haired gentleman. Lady Whitney, in at the fish-monger's next door, came out while he was shaking hands with us.

"Dear me!—is it you?" she cried to Mr. Carden.

"Ay," said he in his pleasant manner, "here am I at Pumpwater! Come all this way to spend a couple of days with my old friend: Dr. Tambourine," added the surgeon, introducing him to Lady Whitney. Any way, that was the name she understood him to say. John thought he said Tamarind, and I Carrafin. The street was noisy.

The doctor seemed to be chatty and courteous, a gentleman of the old school. He said his wife should do herself the honour of calling upon Lady Whitney if agreeable; Lady Whitney replied that it would be. He and Mr. Carden, who would be starting for Worcester by train that afternoon, walked with us up the Parade to the Pump Room. How a chance meeting like this in a strange place makes one feel at home in it!

The name turned out to be Parafin. Mrs. Parafin called early in the afternoon, on her way to some entertainment at the Pump Room: a chatty, pleasant woman, younger than her husband. He had retired from practice, and they lived in a white villa outside the town.

And what with looking at the shops, and parading up and down the public walks, and the entertainment at the Pump Room, to which we went with Mrs. Parafin, and all the rest of it, we felt uncommonly sleepy when night came, and were beginning to regard Pumpwater as a sort of Eden.

"Johnny, have you slept?"

I was brushing my hair at the glass, under the morning sun, when John Whitney, half-dressed, and pale and languid, opened my door and thus accosted me.

"Yes; like a top. Why? Is anything the matter, John?"

"See here," said he, sinking into the easy-chair by the fire-place, "it is an odd thing, but I have again not slept. I *can't* sleep."

I put my back against the dressing-table and stood looking down at him, brush in hand. Not slept again! It *was* an odd thing.

"But what can be the reason, John?"

"I am beginning to think it must be the room."

"How can it be the room?"

"I don't know. There's nothing the matter with the room that I can see; it seems well-ventilated; the chimney's not stopped up. Yet this is the third night that I cannot get to sleep in it."

"But *why* can you not get to sleep?" I persisted.

"I say I don't know why. Each night I have been as sleepy as possible; last night I could hardly undress I was so sleepy; but no sooner am I in bed than sleep goes right away from me. Not only that: I grow terribly restless."

Weighing the problem this way and that, an idea struck me.

"John, do you think it is nervousness?"

"How can it be? I never was nervous in my life."

"I mean this: not sleeping the first night, you may have got nervous about it the second and third."

He shook his head. "I have been nothing of the kind, Johnny. But look here: I hardly see what I am to do. I cannot go on like this without sleep; yet, if I tell the mother again, she'll say the air of the place does not suit me and run away from it—"

"Suppose we change rooms to-night, John?" I interrupted. "I can't think but you would sleep here. If you do not, why, it must be the air of Pumpwater, and the sooner you are out of it the better."

"You wouldn't mind changing rooms for one night?" he said, wistfully.

"Mind! Why, I shall be the gainer. Yours is the better room of the two."

At that it was settled; nothing to be said to any one about the bargain. We did not want to be kidnapped out of Pumpwater—and Lady Whitney had promised us a night at the theatre.

Two or three more acquaintances were made, or found out, that day. Old Lady Scott heard of us, and came to call on Lady Whitney; they used to be intimate. She introduced some people at the Pump Room. Altogether, it seemed that we should not lack society.

Night came; and John and I went upstairs together. He undressed in his own room, and I in mine; and then we made the exchange. I saw him into my bed and wished him a good-night.

"Good-night, Johnny," he answered. "I hope you will sleep."

"Little doubt of that, John. I always sleep when I have nothing to trouble me. A very good-night to *you*."

I had nothing to trouble me, and I was as sleepy as could be; and yet, I did not and could not sleep. I lay quiet as usual after getting into bed, yielding to the expected sleep, and I shut my eyes and never thought but it was coming.

Instead of that, came restlessness. A strange restlessness quite foreign to me, persistent and unaccountable. I tossed and turned from side to side, and I had not had a wink of sleep at day dawn, nor any symptom of it. Was I growing nervous? Had I let the feeling creep over me that I had suggested to John? No; not that I was aware of. What could it be?

Unrefreshed and weary, I got up at the usual hour, and stole silently into the other room. John was in a deep sleep, his calm face lying still upon the pillow. Though I made no noise, my presence awoke him.

"Oh, Johnny!" he exclaimed, "I have had *such* a night."

"Bad?"

"No; *good*. I went to sleep at once and never woke till now. It has done me a world of good. And you?"

"I? Oh well, I don't think I slept quite as well as I did here; it was a strange bed," I answered carelessly.

The next night the same plan was carried out, he taking my bed; I his. And again John slept through it, while I *did not sleep at all*. I said nothing about it: John Whitney's comfort was of more import-ance than mine.

The third night came. This night we had been to the theatre, and had laughed ourselves hoarse, and been altogether delighted. No sooner was I in bed, and feeling dead asleep, than the door slowly opened and in came Lady Whitney, a candle in one hand, a wineglass in the other.

"John, my dear," she began, "your tonic was forgotten this evening. I think you had better take it now. Featherston said, you know— Good gracious!" she broke off. "Why, it is Johnny!"

I could hardly speak for laughing, her face presented such a picture of astonishment. Sitting up in bed, I told her all; there was no help for it: that we had exchanged beds, John not having been able to sleep in this one.

"And do you sleep well in it?" she asked.

"No, not yet. But I feel very sleepy to-night, dear Lady Whitney."

"Well, you are a good lad, Johnny, to do this for him; and to say nothing about it," she concluded, as she went away with the candle and the tonic.

Dead sleepy though I was, I could not get to sleep. It would be simply useless to try to describe my sensations. Each succeeding night they had been more marked. A strange, discomforting restlessness per-vaded me; a feeling of uneasiness, I could not tell why or wherefore. I saw nothing uncanny, I heard nothing; nevertheless, I felt just as though some uncanny presence was in the room, imparting a sense of semi-terror. Once or twice, when I nearly dozed off from sheer weari-ness, I started up in real terror, wide awake again, my hair and face damp with a nameless fear.

I told this at breakfast, in answer to Lady Whitney's questions: John confessed that precisely the same sensations had attacked him the three nights he lay in the bed. Lady Whitney declared she never heard the like; and she kept looking at us alternately, as if doubting what could be the matter with us, or whether we had taken scarlet-fever.

On this morning, Friday, a letter came from Sir John, saying that Featherston was coming to Pumpwater. Anxious on the score of his son, he was sending Featherston to see him, and take back a report. "I think he would stay a couple of days if you made it convenient to entertain him, and it would be a little holiday for the poor hard-worked man," wrote Sir John, who was just as kind-hearted as his wife.

"To be sure I will," said Lady Whitney. "He shall have that room; I dare say he won't say he cannot sleep in it: it will be more comfortable for him than getting a bed at an hotel. Susannah shall put a small bed into the back-room for Johnny. And when Featherston is gone, I will take the room myself. I am not like you two silly boys—afraid of lying awake."

Mr. Featherston arrived late that evening, with his grey face of care and his thin frame. He said he could hardly recall the time when he had had as much as two days' holiday, and thanked Lady Whitney for receiving him. That night John and I occupied the back-room, having conducted Featherston in state to the front, with two candles; and both of us slept excellently well.

At breakfast Featherston began talking about the air. He had always believed Pumpwater to have a rather soporific air, but supposed he must be mistaken. Any way, it had kept him awake; and it was not a little that did that for him.

"Did you not sleep well?" asked Lady Whitney.

"I did not sleep at all; did not get a wink of it all night long. Never mind," he added with a good-natured laugh, "I shall sleep all the sounder to-night."

But he did not. The next morning (Sunday) he looked grave and tired, and ate his breakfast almost in silence. When we had finished, he said he should like, with Lady Whitney's permission, to speak to the landlady. Miss Gay came in at once: in a light fresh print gown and black silk apron.

"Ma'am," began Weatherston, politely, "something is wrong with that bedroom overhead. What is it?"

"Something wrong, sir?" repeated Miss Gay, her meek face flushing. "Wrong in what way, sir?"

"I don't know," answered Featherston; "I thought perhaps you could tell me: any way, it ought to be seen to. It is something that scares away sleep. I give you my word, ma'am, I never had two such restless nights in succession in all my life. Two such *strange* nights. It was not only that sleep would not come near me; that's nothing uncommon you may say; but I lay in a state of uneasy, indescribable restlessness. I have examined the room again this morning, and I can see nothing to induce it, yet a cause there must undoubtedly be. The paper is not made of arsenic, I suppose?"

"The paper is pale pink, sir," observed Miss Gay. "I fancy it is the green papers that have arsenic in them."

"Ay; well. I think there must be poison behind the paper; in the paste, say," went on Featherston. "Or perhaps another paper underneath has arsenic in it?"

Miss Gay shook her head, as she stood with her hand on the back of a chair. Lady Whitney had asked her to sit down, but she declined. "When I came into the house six months ago, that room was re-papered, and I saw that the walls were thoroughly scraped. If you think there's anything—anything in the room that prevents people sleeping, and—and could point out what it is, I'm sure, sir, I should be glad to remedy it," said Miss Gay, with uncomfortable hesitation.

But this was just what Featherston, for all he was a doctor, could not point out. That something was amiss with the room, he felt convinced, but he had not discovered what it was, or how it could be remedied.

"After lying in torment half the night, I got up and lighted my candle," said he. "I examined the room and opened the window to let the cool breeze blow in. I could find nothing likely to keep me awake, no stuffed-up chimney, no accumulation of dust, and I shut the window and got into bed again. I was pretty cool by that time and reckoned I should sleep. Not a bit of it, ma'am. I lay more restless than ever, with the same unaccountable feeling of discomfort and depression upon me. Just as I had felt the night before."

"I am very sorry, sir," sighed Miss Gay, taking her hand from the chair to depart. "If the room is close, or anything of that—"

"But it is not close, ma'am. I don't know what it is. And I'm sure I hope you will be able to find it out, and get it remedied," concluded Featherston as she withdrew.

We then told him of our experience, John's and mine. It amazed him. "What an extraordinary thing!" he exclaimed. "One would think the room was haunted."

"Do you believe in haunted rooms, sir?" asked John.

"Well, I suppose such things are," he answered. "Folks say so. If haunted houses exist, why not haunted rooms?"

"It must lie in the Pumpwater air," said Lady Whitney, who was too practical to give in to haunted regions; "and I am very sorry you should have had your two nights' rest spoilt by it, Mr. Featherston. I will take the room myself: nothing keeps me awake."

"Did you ever see a ghost, sir?" asked John.

"No, never. But I know those who have seen them; and I cannot disbelieve what they say. One such story in particular is often in my mind; it was a very strange one."

"Won't you tell it us, Mr. Featherston?"

The doctor only laughed in answer. But after we came out of church, when he was sitting with me and John on the Parade, he told it. And I wish I had space to relate it here.

He left Pumpwater in the afternoon, and Lady Whitney had the room prepared for her use at once, John moving into hers. So that I had mine to myself again, and the little bed was taken out of it.

The next day was Monday. When Lady Whitney came down in the morning the first thing she told us was, that she had not slept. All the curious symptoms of restless disturbance, of inward agitation, which we had experienced, had visited her.

"I will not give in, my dears," she said, bravely. "It may be, you know, that what I had heard against the room took all sleep out of me, though I was not conscious of it; so I shall keep to it. I must say it is a most comfortable bed."

She "kept" to the room until the Wednesday; three nights in all; getting no sleep. Then she gave in. Occasionally during the third night, when she was dropping asleep from exhaustion, she was startled up from it in sudden terror: terror of she knew not what. Just as it had been with me and with John. On the Wednesday morning she told Susannah that they must give her the back-room opposite mine, and we would abandon that front-room altogether.

"It is just as though there were a ghost in the room," she said to Susannah.

"Perhaps there is, my lady," was Susannah's cool reply.

On the Friday evening Dr. and Mrs. Parafin came in to tea. Our visit would end on the morrow. The old doctor held John before him in the lamplight, and decided that he looked better—that the stay had done him good.

"I am sure it has," assented Lady Whitney. "Just at first I feared he was going backward: but that must have been owing to the sleepless nights."

"Sleepless nights!" echoed the doctor, in a curious tone.

"For the first three nights of our stay here, he never slept; *never slept at all*. After that—"

"Which room did he occupy?" interrupted the doctor, breathlessly. "Not the one over this?"

"Yes, it was. Why? Do you know anything against it?" questioned Lady Whitney, for she saw Dr. and Mrs. Parafin exchange glances.

"Only this: that I have heard of other people who were unable to sleep in that room," he answered.

"But what can be amiss with the room, Dr. Parafin?"

"Ah," said he, "there you go beyond me. It is, I believe, a fact, a singular fact, that there is something or other in the room which prevents people from sleeping. Friends of ours who lived in the house before Miss Gay took it, ended by shutting the room up."

"Is it haunted, sir?" I asked. "Mr. Featherston thought it might be."

He looked at me and smiled, shaking his head. Mrs. Parafin nodded hers, as much as to say *It is*.

"No one has been able to get any sleep in that room since the Calsons lived here," said Mrs. Parafin, dropping her voice.

"How very strange!" cried Lady Whitney. "One might think murder had been done in it."

Mrs. Parafin coughed significantly. "The wife died in it," she said. "Some people thought her husband had—had—had at least hastened her death—"

"Hush, Matty!" interposed the doctor, warningly. "It was all rumour, all talk. Nothing was proved—or attempted to be."

"Perhaps there existed no proof," returned Mrs. Parafin. "And if there had—who was there to take it up? She was in her grave, poor woman, and he was left flourishing, master of himself and every one about him. Any way, Thomas, be that as it may, you cannot deny that the room has been like a haunted room since."

Dr. Parafin laughed lightly, objecting to be serious; men are more cautious than women. "I cannot deny that people find themselves unable to sleep in the room; I never heard that it was 'haunted' in any other way," he added, to Lady Whitney. "But there—let us change the subject; we can neither alter the fact nor understand it."

After they left us, Lady Whitney said she should like to ask Miss Gay what her experience of the room had been. But Miss Gay had stepped out to a neighbour's, and Susannah stayed to talk in her place. She could tell us more about it, she said, than Miss Gay.

"I warned my cousin she would do well not to take this house," began Susannah, accepting the chair to which Lady Whitney pointed. "But it is a beautiful house for letting, as you see, my lady, and that and the low rent tempted her. Besides, she did not believe the rumour about the room; she does not believe it fully yet, though it is beginning to worry her: she thinks the inability to sleep must lie in the people themselves."

"It has been an uncanny room since old Calson's wife died in it, has it not, Susannah?" said John, as if in jest. "I suppose he did not murder her?"

"*I think he did*," whispered Susannah.

The answer sounded so ghostly that it struck us all into silence.

Susannah resumed. "Nobody *knew*: but one or two suspected. The wife was a poor, timid, gentle creature, worshipping the very ground her husband trod on, yet always in awe of him. She lay in the room, sick, for many many months before she died. Old Sarah—"

"What was her illness?" interrupted Lady Whitney.

"My lady, that is more than I can tell you; more, I fancy, than any one could have told. Old Sarah would often say to me that she did not believe there was any great sickness, only he made it out there was, and persuaded his wife so. He could just wind her round his little finger. The person who attended on her was one Astrea, quite a heathenish name I used to think, and a heathenish woman too; she was copper-coloured, and came with them from abroad. Sarah was in the kitchen, and there was only a man besides. I lived housekeeper at that time with an old lady on the Parade, and I looked in here from time to time to ask after the mistress. Once I was invited by Mr. Calson upstairs to see her: she lay in the room over this; the one that nobody can now sleep in. She looked so pitiful!—her poor, pale, patient face down deep in the pillow. Was she better, I asked; and what was it that ailed her. She thought it was not much beside weakness, she answered, and that she felt a constant nausea; and she was waiting for the warm weather: her dear husband assured her she would be better when that came."

"Was he kind to her, Susannah?"

"He seemed to be, Master Johnny; very kind and attentive indeed. He would sit by the hour together in her room, and give her her medicine, and feed her when she grew too weak to feed herself, and sit up at night with her. A doctor came to see her occasionally; it was said he could not find much the matter with her but debility, and that she seemed to be wasting away. Well, she died, my lady; died quietly in that room; and Calson ordered a grand funeral."

"So did Jonas Chuzzlewit," breathed John.

"Whispers got afloat when she was under ground—not before—that there had been something wrong about her death; that she had not come by it fairly, or by the illness either," continued Susannah. "But they were not spoken openly; under the rose, as may be said; and they died away. Mr. Calson continued to live in the house as before; but he became soon ill. Real sickness, his was, my lady, whatever his wife's might have been. His illness was chiefly on the nerves; he grew frightfully thin; and the setting-in of some grave inward complaint was suspected: so if he did act in any ill manner to his wife it seemed he would not reap long benefit from it. All the medical men in Pumpwater were called to him in succession; but they could not cure him. He kept growing thinner and thinner till he was like a walking shadow. At last he shut up his house and went to London for advice; and there he died, fourteen months after the death of his wife."

"How long was the house kept shut up?" asked Lady Whitney, as Susannah paused.

"About two years, my lady. All his property was willed away to the little son of his brother, who lived over in Australia. Tardy instructions came from thence to Mr. Jermy the lawyer to let the house furnished, and Mr. Jermy put it into the hands of Bone the house agent. A family took it, but they did not stay: then another family took it, and they did not stay. Each party went to Bone and told him that something was the matter with one of the rooms and nobody could sleep in it. After that, the furniture was sold off, and some people took the house by the year. They did not remain in it six months. Some other people took it then, and they stayed the year, but it was known that they shut up that room. Then the house stayed empty. My cousin, wanting a better house than the one she was in, cast many a longing eye towards it; finding it did not let, she went to Bone and asked him what the rent would be. Seventy pounds to her, he said; and she took it. Of course she had heard about the room, but she did not believe it; she thought, as Mr. Featherston said the other morning, that something must be wrong with the paper, and she had the walls scraped and cleaned and a fresh paper put on."

"And since then—have your lodgers found anything amiss with the room?" questioned Lady Whitney.

"I am bound to say they have, my lady. It has been the same story with them all—not able to get to sleep in it. One gentleman, an old post-captain, after trying it a few nights, went right away from Pump-water, swearing at the air. But the most singular experience we have had was that of two little girls. They were kept in that room for two nights, and each night they cried and screamed all night long, calling out that they were frightened. Their mother could not account for it; they were not at all timid children, she said, and such a thing had never happened with them before. Altogether, taking one thing with another, I fear, my lady, that something *is* wrong with the room. Miss Gay sees it now: but she is not superstitious, and she asks *what* it can be."

Well, that was Susannah's tale: and we carried it away with us on the morrow.

Sir John Whitney found his son looking all the better for his visit to Pumpwater. Temporarily he was so. Temporarily only; not materially: for John died before the year was out.

Have I heard anything of the room since, you would like to ask. Yes, a little. Some eighteen months later, I was halting at Pumpwater for a few hours with the Squire, and ran to the house to see Miss Gay. But the house was empty. A black board stood in front with big white letters on it TO BE LET. Miss Gay had moved into another house facing the Parade.

"It was of no use my trying to stay in it," she said to me, shaking her head. "I moved into the room myself, Master Johnny, after you and my Lady Whitney left, and I am free to confess that I could not sleep. I had Susannah in, and she could not sleep; and, in short, we had to go out of it again. So I shut the room up, sir, until the year had expired, and then I gave up the house. It has not been let since, and people say it is falling into decay."

"Was anything ever *seen* in the room, Miss Gay?"

"Nothing," she answered, "or heard either; nothing whatever. The room is as nice a room as could be wished for in all respects, light, large, cheerful, and airy; and yet nobody can get to sleep in it. I shall never understand it, sir."

I'm sure I never shall. It remains one of those curious experiences that cannot be solved in this world. But it is none the less true.

Anonymous

LE VERT GALANT

During the long vacation, in the summer of 186–, I started on a walking tour through Normandy and the northern part of France. For long I had been planning this scheme, and delighted I was when at length I stood on "the other side of the water," burning with desire to commence immediately my travels and adventures. For many weeks I journeyed in the usual routine so well-known to pedestrians, and on which I shall therefore not enlarge; for nothing worthy of note occurred until the story I am about to relate, which is certainly out of the common.

One summer's evening, having been walking all day, I was not sorry when, looking down from the hill I had just reached, I discovered through the deepening twilight, at about the distance of a mile, the quaint-looking village of H—— in the valley beneath me. The *entourage* was picturesque in the extreme; and behind the village, making a dark background, rose a sombre-looking pine-wood.

I put my best foot foremost; though, to say the honest truth, there was not much to choose between the two, for I was very weary; and thankful I was when I found myself walking up the quaint paved street, on the look-out for the best inn. Yes, there it stood—that must be it— rather aloof from its neighbours, with its gable-ends and old-fashioned colouring, and the sign-board over the door. "Le Vert Galant" it called itself; and a picture of "Le Galant," dressed in a green coat, rather in the Henri-IV. style, hung over the door, and grinned down on me with a stern welcome.

I entered and asked if I could have a night's lodging there. I was met by the landlady, a handsome and still young-looking woman, her dress betokening her a widow. She courteously invited me in, and, showing me into a room up one pair of stairs, informed me that Nanette, the waiting-maid, should come and announce to me when my supper was *servi*.

I unpacked my knapsack and performed my hasty toilette, thoroughly enjoying the transition from my thick walking-boots to my slippers. Then I gazed out of the window. It looked upon a large old-fashioned garden, thick with flowers, whose drowsy incense filled the air with sweetness. I was charmed with my window, surrounded as it was with ivy; and fully did I sympathise and share in the feelings of any owl who had as charming an ivy-bush as mine. Running down close to my window was a pipe or *goutière*, which caught all the rain-water in a barrel below. "Hurrah!" said I to myself, "soft water into the bargain." In one corner of the garden stood an old-fashioned pump, looking rather green and mouldy, as if it thought itself quite neglected. I was thus musing and thinking how impossible it would be to render adequately the gorgeous colours of the flowers below me on paper (for I was a dabbler in colours myself, and managed to spoil a good deal of paper), when Nanette, tapping briskly at my door, announced my *soupé*. I descended into the comfortable kitchen; for madame, like a sensible woman, surmised I should prefer the snug warm room to a cold cheerless parlour, which could not be warmed in a moment.

I discussed my supper with considerable pleasure, madame again showing her good sense by leaving me quiet until I had taken off the edge of my appetite; and, my meal over, she pointed to a stool in the chimney-corner, saying that if it was not too hot for me, I should find it comfortable; adding also that "c'était permis de fumer dans la cuisine." Charming woman! What more could the heart of man wish for? She seated herself opposite to me with her knitting, and began telling me (while I smoked) about the village, the people who lived in it, and finally of herself; how she had been left early a widow, with one daughter, by name "Justine." Ah, so pretty! but very ailing and weak at present. She continued thus chatting until I rose to go to bed, when she lighted me upstairs, and bade me good-night.

I suppose I must have been overtired by my long walk; anyhow sleep refused to "steep my senses in forgetfulness;" so I got up, and

with a sort of vague attraction I walked to the window. I have already
said that my room looked out into an old-fashioned garden, with a
wall running round it, and, instead of a path of gravel or sand, there
was a narrow red-brick alley or *trottoir*. I peeped out of my ivy-
surrounded window. There was not a leaf stirring. The garden looked
white and cold in the glistening moonlight. All still, I thought to
myself; no life. All the world, save myself, peacefully sleeping. No,
that was not quite the case; for, looking beyond the ivy into the
garden below, I saw the figure of a young girl, in the old Normandy
dress—high cap and sabots. She was pumping slowly, slowly at the old
pump before mentioned, which stood in the corner—so mechanically
that she appeared to me to be a part of a piece of machinery. I only
saw her back. She was entirely in the shadow of the wall, except when
her long arms rose with the handle, and flashed white and gleaming
for a moment in the moonlight. There was a sort of fascination about
her. I *could* not help watching her; but what struck me as odd was,
that though she pumped and the water ran into the trough below, I
could not hear the slightest noise. I gazed again; my artistic eye took it
all in, and I thought (not without half a shudder) what a pretty picture
she would make, standing there, with the moon above, casting long
shadows—still and quiet—upon every object in the garden. I looked
for the shadow of the pump—there it was, and the handle working up
and down across a bed of roses; but apparently it was working of its
own accord. I looked for the girl; there she stood, working in the same
mechanical way, but *she had no shadow*.

A horrible dread of something supernatural now came over me. I
stared at her again, when, just at that moment, I was conscious of a
stir in the ivy around my window, and then, with a swift sliding movement (the ivy gently sighing in response), I saw a dark object swing
itself down the *goutière* or pipe, close to my window, and land below,
beside the black tarred barrel. Looking down, I saw a fine strong
young man rise and walk, heedless of the garden-beds, straight towards
the pump. On getting within a few paces of the girl (she still continu-
ing her unearthly pumping) he raised his hat, a sort of *chapeau brigand*,
and I discerned in the ever-varying moonlight a clear-cut handsome
profile, slightly bent in salutation. He replaced his hat and held out his
hand. No word of greeting passed either of their lips. For the first
time *she* turned, and O, what a wan weird face gleamed on his! She
took his offered hand, and so they walked down the red brick-path—
her sabots (the first sound I had heard) making a hollow click-clack
along the *trottoir*. They reached the old green door in the wall, which,
responsive to his pull, groaned itself open. She passed through. He half

turned and looked back at the old house, then he followed her, and the old door shut again with a resounding bang.

Having partially recovered myself after this horrible and ghostly scene, which seemed to freeze the marrow of my bones, I went to bed, and passed a most disturbed night, mixed up with dreams of pumps and sabots, and I was thankful when morning broke, and I rose.

I packed up my knapsack, and then called Nanette, intending to order my breakfast and get away from this inn, whose very atmosphere now made me shudder; but first I must question Nanette, and get out of her the true story—for story I felt sure there was—of the haunted inn.

Nanette appeared, looking extremely coquettish in a small cap and cherry-coloured bows, and cheerfully hoped monsieur had slept well, and what would he have for his breakfast. I hardly answered her; going straight to the point, I said,

"Nanette, is that pump in the corner of the garden ever used?"

Her countenance fell as she replied,

"But very rarely, monsieur; why?"

"Does your mistress keep any other maid but yourself?"

"Mais non."

I could not help noticing her face of growing alarm.

"Then," I said calmly, "who was that girl I saw last night pumping there with a high cap and sabots?"

Nanette started forward, and caught me by the arm.

"Dites donc que vous ne l'avez pas vu?" said she.

Hardly had the words escaped her lips, when through the house there rang a piercing wailing shriek, and a voice from a neighbouring room cried, "Nanette, Nanette, je meurs!"

Nanette stood stock-still listening, with her lips parted, her arm raised; then exclaiming, "Ciel! c'est accompli déjà!" rushed out of the room. I could not help following her. On the landing she met madame; Nanette made but one step to her, and whispered (but I caught the whisper), "Il l'a vu," indicating me by an expressive thumb pointed over her shoulder.

"Qui?" said madame.

"Susanne."

Madame, on hearing this reply, sat down on the top step of the stairs, and gave herself over to what I thought premature and unnecessary grief, interspersed with ejaculations of "O, mon enfant, que le bon Dieu te prenne aux cieux!"

Meanwhile I had followed Nanette into a room along the passage, and on entering I saw a young girl half sitting, half lying, in bed, struggling to catch her failing breath; the window was thrown wide open, and the scent of those spell-stricken flowers streaming up through it.

I plainly saw she was dying fast. I looked at her again; the face seemed strangely familiar to me—and yet where could I have seen her?

Just then madame entered; the young girl raised herself, and said feebly, "Chère mère, adieu, je pars!" She held up her face to be kissed, and I caught her upturned side face. The likeness flashed upon me like a thunderbolt. She was the living image of that ghostly figure in the *chapeau brigand* that I had watched in the garden the night before.

Justine (for she it was who lay a-dying) whispered, "Pray for me —pray!"

Madame, in an agony, looked at me, and in a strangled voice, said:

"Say just one little prayer for my poor child—for me; I lose my head."

I came near the bed, close to Justine, and repeated an old French prayer which fortunately at that moment came into my head. Hardly was it over when Justine raised herself in bed, with eyes straining at something beyond mortal ken, and, as if in answer to some unheard call, said, "Je viens!" fell back and died.

Was it *only* imagination? or did I really at that moment hear, through the open window, the sound of a hollow footfall in a sabot— click-clack all down the *trottoir*—and then the garden-door bang? I think not.

I was so overwhelmed by all these strange occurrences, that, after leaving poor Justine's room, I sallied forth to stroll by the river and collect my scattered senses. I thought it all over—the strange appari- tions of the previous night, Nanette's face of horror at my mention of them, and subsequently Justine's sudden death. Yes, I must get to the bottom of all this before leaving the village, which I fixed to do that afternoon; so I returned and had an interview with madame, who was very kind, though heartbroken at Justine's death. She said it was no good concealing from me the story that overshadowed the inn, and as I was soon going, perhaps I should like to hear it. On my acquiescing at once, she led the way into the kitchen, and sitting down, she related the narrative, of which this is the epitome.

It appears that Le Vert Galant had for some generations belonged to the same family, and had always been handed down from father to son; eventually madame's husband had come into possession thereof. But it was of one of his ancestors that I would speak, who lived in this inn, and rejoiced in a large family of both sons and daughters. One of the former fell very much in love with a pretty girl living in the village; but the match was disapproved by all the parents, so that the lovers had to meet clandestinely.

When this girl—Susanne by name—could slip away unobserved, she used to give the sign, before agreed upon between the two, of running into the old garden of the inn and pumping; on hearing which welcome sound, Jacques, a strong able-bodied young man, would swing himself down from his window by the *goutière*, and so, unperceived, they used to wander into the adjoining pine-wood.

But one evening, the tryst having been accomplished as usual, they sallied forth, and once in the sheltering pine-wood, Susanne turned round on her lover and upbraided him bitterly with a decrease of affection for her, and then the usual lovers' quarrel ensued. Swift angry words passed on both sides, till Jacques, goaded almost to madness by her reproaches, and being also of a very hasty temper, drew out his knife, and without a moment's hesitation stabbed her to the heart. No sooner was the deed done than O, how bitterly was it repented of! He threw himself on the ground by her side, and by every endearing name strove to recall that life which his own hand had taken; but all of no avail. Then he began to think of the consequences: what would become of him? what would his parents say? He rose and wandered miles and miles, pursued by revengeful phantoms, all the creation of his own overwrought brain, till finally, coming to the edge of a dangerous precipice, he recklessly flung himself over, and thus ended his own miserable existence.

But as surely as any of his family die, so surely is the event foreshadowed by the ghostly appearance of his murdered Susanne in the garden, bidding her lover to the well-known tryst; and his spirit answering her summons, they react together the horrible tragedy which time cannot obliterate or years efface.

That afternoon, with many expressions of sympathy, I took my leave of madame and of the village of H——, mentally resolving that, should fortune at any future time conduct my steps thither, I would avoid that old haunted inn—Le Vert Galant.

Mary E. Braddon

Mary Elizabeth Braddon (*1835–1915*), the wife of the publisher John Maxwell, was the most popular woman novelist of the nineteenth century. A very facile and productive writer, she was the mainstay of her husband's publishing program and a frequent contributor to the periodicals of the day. She wrote sensation novels, domestic fiction, social novels, adventure stories, mysteries, and ghost stories. Her most famous work was Lady Audley's Secret (*1861–62*), the story of a beautiful bigamist who pushed her first husband down a well. The sensation novel par excellence of the century, it was published in many editions and was also turned into a very popular play. Despite the fact that Miss Braddon wrote best sellers, her work was highly regarded by many critics and leading novelists of her time. As William Thackeray said, "If I could plot as well as Miss Braddon, I would be the greatest novelist in the English language."

Most of Miss Braddon's short stories were published anonymously or pseudonymously, and her bibliography is not settled, even though some of her work records have recently become accessible. As far as is known, she wrote nine supernatural short stories. Her themes are traditional—apparitions that reveal crimes, prophetic visions, dreams with supernatural content—but her development of these motifs is always individual. In "At Chrighton Abbey," which first appeared anonymously in Belgravia in *1871*, the picture of holiday life at a county estate is filled with interesting detail.

AT
CHRIGHTON ABBEY

The Chrightons were very great people in that part of the country
where my childhood and youth were spent. To speak of Squire
Chrighton was to speak of a power in that remote western region of
England. Chrighton Abbey had belonged to the family ever since the
reign of Stephen, and there was a curious old wing and a cloistered
quadrangle still remaining of the original edifice, and in excellent
preservation. The rooms at this end of the house were low, and somewhat darksome and gloomy, it is true; but, though rarely used, they
were perfectly habitable, and were of service on great occasions when
the Abbey was crowded with guests.

The central portion of the Abbey had been rebuilt in the reign of
Elizabeth, and was of noble and palatial proportions. The southern
wing, and a long music-room with eight tall narrow windows added on
to it, were as modern as the time of Anne. Altogether, the Abbey was a
very splendid mansion, and one of the chief glories of our county.

All the land in Chrighton parish, and for a long way beyond its
boundaries, belonged to the great Squire. The parish church was within
the park walls, and the living in the Squire's gift—not a very valuable
benefice, but a useful thing to bestow upon a younger son's younger
son, once in a way, or sometimes on a tutor or dependent of the
wealthy house.

I was a Chrighton, and my father, a distant cousin of the reigning
Squire, had been rector of Chrighton parish. His death left me utterly
unprovided for, and I was fain to go out into the bleak unknown world,
and earn my living in a position of dependence—a dreadful thing for
a Chrighton to be obliged to do.

Out of respect for the traditions and prejudices of my race, I made it my business to seek employment abroad, where the degradation of one solitary Chrighton was not so likely to inflict shame upon the ancient house to which I belonged. Happily for myself I had been carefully educated, and had industriously cultivated the usual modern accomplishments in the calm retirement of the Vicarage. I was so fortunate as to obtain a situation at Vienna, in a German family of high rank; and here I remained seven years, laying aside year by year, a considerable portion of my liberal salary. When my pupils had grown up, my kind mistress procured me a still more profitable position at St. Petersburg, where I remained five more years, at the end of which time I yielded to a yearning that had been long growing upon me—an ardent desire to see my dear old country home once more.

I had no very near relations in England. My mother had died some years before my father; my only brother was far away, in the Indian Civil Service; sister I had none. But I was a Chrighton, and I loved the soil from which I had sprung. I was sure, moreover, of a warm welcome from friends who had loved and honored my father and mother, and I was still farther encouraged to treat myself to this holiday by the very cordial letters I had from time to time received from the Squire's wife, a noble warm-hearted woman, who fully approved the independent course I had taken, and who had ever shown herself my friend.

In all her letters for some time past, Mrs. Chrighton begged that, whenever I felt myself justified in coming home, I would pay a long visit to the Abbey.

"I wish you could come at Christmas," she wrote, in the autumn of the year of which I am speaking. "We shall be very gay, and I expect all kinds of pleasant people at the Abbey. Edward is to be married early in the spring—much to his father's satisfaction, for the match is a good and appropriate one. His *fiancée* is to be among our guests. She is a very beautiful girl; perhaps I should say handsome rather than beautiful. Julia Tremaine, one of the Tremaines of Old Court, near Hayswell—a very old family, as I daresay you remember. She has several brothers and sisters, and will have little, perhaps nothing, from her father; but she has a considerable fortune left her by an aunt, and is thought quite an heiress in the county—not, of course, that this latter fact had any influence with Edward. He fell in love with her at an assize ball in his usual impulsive fashion, and proposed to her in something less than a fortnight. It is, I hope and believe, a thorough love match on both sides."

After this followed a cordial repetition of the invitation to myself. I was to go straight to the Abbey when I went to England, and was to take up my abode there as long as ever I pleased.

This letter decided me. The wish to look on the dear scenes of my happy childhood had grown almost into a pain. I was free to take a holiday, without detriment to my prospects. So, early in December, regardless of the bleak dreary weather, I turned my face homewards, and made the long journey from St. Petersburg to London, under the kind escort of Major Manson, a Queen's Messenger, who was a friend of my late employer, the Baron Fruydorff, and whose courtesy had been enlisted for me by that gentleman.

I was three-and-thirty years of age. Youth was quite gone; beauty I had never possessed; and I was content to think of myself as a confirmed old maid, a quiet spectator of life's great drama, disturbed by no feverish desire for an active part in the play. I had a disposition to which this kind of passive existence is easy. There was no wasting fire in my veins. Simple duties, rare and simple pleasures, filled up my sum of life. The dear ones who had given a special charm and brightness to my existence were gone. Nothing could recall *them*, and without them actual happiness seemed impossible to me. Everything had a subdued and neutral tint; life at its best was calm and colorless, like a gray sunless day in early autumn, serene but joyless.

The old Abbey was in its glory when I arrived there, at about nine o'clock on a clear starlit night. A light frost whitened the broad sweep of grass that stretched away from the long stone terrace in front of the house, to a semi-circle of grand old oaks and beeches. From the music-room at the end of the southern wing, to the heavily framed gothic windows of the old rooms on the north, there shone one blaze of light. The scene reminded me of some weird palace in a German legend; and I half expected to see the lights fade out all in a moment, and the long stone façade wrapped in sudden darkness.

The old butler, whom I remembered from my very infancy, and who did not seem to have grown a day older during my twelve years' exile, came out of the dining-room as the footman opened the hall-door for me, and gave me cordial welcome, nay, insisted upon helping to bring in my portmanteau with his own hands, an act of unusual condescension, the full force of which was felt by his subordinates.

"It's a real treat to see your pleasant face once more, Miss Sarah," said this faithful retainer, as he assisted me to take off my traveling cloak, and took my dressing-bag from my hand. "You look a trifle older than when you used to live at the Vicarage twelve years ago, but you're looking uncommon well for all that; and, lord love your heart, miss, how pleased they all will be to see you! Missus told me with her own lips about your coming. You'd like to take off your bonnet before you go to the drawing-room, I daresay. The house is full of company. Call Mrs. Marjorum, James, will you?"

The footman disappeared into the back regions, and presently re-appeared with Mrs. Marjorum, a portly dame, who, like Truefold, the butler, had been a fixture at the Abbey in the time of the present Squire's father. From her I received the same cordial greeting, and by her I was led off up staircases and along corridors, till I wondered where I was being taken.

We arrived at last at a very comfortable room—a square tapestried chamber, with a low ceiling supported by a great oaken beam. The room looked cheery enough, with a bright fire roaring in the wide chimney; but it had a somewhat ancient aspect, which the super-stitiously inclined might have associated with possible ghosts.

I was fortunately of a matter-of-fact disposition, utterly skeptical upon the ghost subject; and the old-fashioned appearance of the room took my fancy.

"We are in King Stephen's wing, are we not, Mrs. Marjorum?" I asked; "This room seems quite strange to me. I doubt if I have ever been in it before."

"Very likely not, miss. Yes, this is the old wing. Your window looks out into the old stable-yard, where the kennel used to be in the time of our Squire's grandfather, when the Abbey was even a finer place than it is now, I've heard say. We are so full of company this winter, you see, miss, that we are obliged to make use of all these rooms. You'll have no need to feel lonesome. There's Captain and Mrs. Cranwick in the next room to this, and the two Miss Newports in the blue room opposite."

"My dear, good Marjorum, I like my quarters excessively; and I quite enjoy the idea of sleeping in a room that was extant in the time of Stephen, when the Abbey really was an abbey. I daresay some grave old monk has worn these boards with his devout knees."

The old woman stared dubiously, with the air of a person who had small sympathy with monkish times, and begged to be excused for leaving me, she had so much on her hands just now.

There was coffee to be sent in; and she doubted if the still-room maid would manage matters properly, if she, Mrs. Marjorum, were not at hand to see that things were right.

"You've only to ring your bell, miss, and Susan will attend to you. She's used to help waiting on our young ladies sometimes, and she's very handy. Missus has given particular orders that she should be always at your service."

"Mrs. Chrighton is very kind; but I assure you, Marjorum, I don't require the help of a maid once in a month. I am accustomed to do everything for myself. There, run along, Mrs. Marjorum, and see after your coffee; and I'll be down in the drawing-room in ten minutes. Are there many people there, by-the-bye?"

"A good many. There's Miss Tremaine, and her mamma and younger sister; of course you've heard all about the marriage—such a handsome young lady—rather too proud for my liking; but the Tremaines always were a proud family, and this one's an heiress. Mr. Edward is so fond of her—thinks the ground is scarcely good enough for her to walk upon, I do believe; and somehow I can't help wishing he'd chosen some one else—some one who would have thought more of him, and who would not take all his attentions in such a cool off-hand way. But of course is isn't my business to say such things, and I wouldn't venture upon it to any one but you, Miss Sarah."

She told me that I would find dinner ready for me in the breakfast-room, and then bustled off, leaving me to my toilet.

This ceremony I performed as rapidly as I could, admiring the perfect comfort of my chamber as I dressed. Every modern appliance had been added to the sombre and ponderous furniture of an age gone by, and the combination produced a very pleasant effect. Perfume-bottles of ruby-colored Bohemian glass, china brush-trays and ring-stands brightened the massive oak dressing-table; a low, luxurious chintz-covered easy chair, of the Victorian era, stood before the hearth; a dear little writing-table of polished maple, was placed conveniently near it; and in the background the tapestried walls loomed duskily, as they had done hundreds of years before my time.

I had no leisure for dreamy musings on the past, however, provocative though the chamber might be of such thoughts. I arranged my hair in its usual simple fashion, and put on a dark gray silk dress, trimmed with some fine old black lace that had been given to me by the Baroness—an unobtrusive demi-toilette, adapted to any occasion. I tied a massive gold cross, an ornament that had belonged to my dear mother, round my neck with a scarlet ribbon; and my costume was complete. One glance at the looking-glass convinced me that there was nothing dowdy in my appearance; and then I hurried along the corridor and down the staircase to the hall, where Truefold received me and conducted me to the breakfast-room, in which an excellent dinner awaited me.

I did not waste much time over this repast, although I had eaten nothing all day; for I was anxious to make my way to the drawing-room. Just as I had finished, the door opened, and Mrs. Chrighton sailed in, looking superb in a dark-green velvet dress richly trimmed with old point lace. She had been a beauty in her youth, and, as a matron, was still remarkably handsome. She had, above all, a charm of expression which to me was rarer and more delightful than her beauty of feature and complexion.

She put her arms round me, and kissed me affectionately.

"I have only this moment been told of your arrival, my dear Sarah," she said, "and I find you have been in the house half an hour. What must you have thought of me!"

"What can I think of you, except that you are all goodness, my dear Fanny? I did not expect you to leave your guests to receive me, and am really sorry that you have done so. I need no ceremony to convince me of your kindness."

"But, my dear child, it is not a question of ceremony. I have been looking forward so anxiously to your coming, and I should not have liked to see you for the first time before all those people. Give me another kiss, that's a darling. Welcome to Chrighton. Remember, Sarah, this house is always to be your home, whenever you have need of one."

"My dear kind cousin! And you are not ashamed of me who have eaten the bread of strangers?"

"Ashamed of you! No, my love; I admire your industry and spirit. And now come to the drawing-room. The girls will be so pleased to see you."

"And I to see them. They were quite little things when I went away, romping in the hay-fields in their short white frocks; and now, I suppose, they are handsome young women."

"They are very nice-looking; not as handsome as their brother. Edward is really a magnificent young man. I do not think my maternal pride is guilty of any gross exaggeration when I say that."

"And Miss Tremaine?" I said; "I am very curious to see her."

I fancied a faint shadow came over my cousin's face as I mentioned this name.

"Miss Tremaine—yes—you cannot fail to admire her," she said rather thoughtfully.

She drew my hand through her arm and led me to the drawing-room; a very large room, with a fireplace at each end, brilliantly lighted to-night, and containing about twenty people, scattered about in little groups, and all seeming to be talking and laughing merrily. Mrs. Chrighton took me straight to one of the fireplaces, beside which two girls were sitting on a low sofa, while a young man of something more than six feet high stood near them, with his arm resting on the broad marble slab of the mantel-piece. A glance told me that this young man with the dark eyes and crisp waving brown hair, was Edward Chrighton. His likeness to his mother was in itself enough to tell me who he was; but I remembered the boyish face and bright eyes which had so often looked up to mine in the days when the heir of the Abbey was one of the most juvenile scholars at Eton.

The lady seated nearest Edward Chrighton attracted my chief attention; for I felt sure that this lady was Miss Tremaine. She was tall and slim, and carried her head and neck with a stately air, which struck me more than anything in that first glance. Yes, she was handsome, undeniably handsome; and my cousin had been right when she said I could not fail to admire her; but to me the dazzlingly fair face with its perfect features, the marked aquiline nose, the short upper lip expressive of unmitigated pride, the full cold blue eyes, pencilled brows, and aureole of pale golden hair, were the very reverse of sympathetic. That Miss Tremaine must needs be universally admired, it was impossible to doubt; but I could not understand how any man could fall in love with such a woman.

She was dressed in white muslin, and her only ornament was a superb diamond locket, heart-shaped, tied round her long white throat with a broad black ribbon. Her hair, of which she seemed to have a great quantity, was arranged in a massive coronet of plaits, which surmounted the small head as proudly as an imperial crown.

To this young lady, Mrs. Chrighton introduced me.

"I have another cousin to present to you, Julia," she said smiling— "Miss Sarah Chrighton, just arrived from St. Petersburg."

"From St. Petersburg? What an awful journey! How do you do, Miss Chrighton? It was really very courageous of you to come so far. Did you travel alone?"

"No; I had a companion as far as London, and a very kind one. I came on to the Abbey by myself."

The young lady had given me her hand with rather a languid air. I thought I saw the cold blue eyes surveying me curiously from head to foot, and it seemed to me as if I could read the condemnatory summing-up—"A frump, and a poor relation"—in Miss Tremaine's face.

I had not much time to think about her just now; for Edward Chrighton suddenly seized both my hands, and gave me so hearty and loving a welcome, that he almost brought the tears "up from my heart into my eyes."

Two pretty girls in blue crape, came running forward from different parts of the room, and gayly saluted me as "Cousin Sarah;" and the three surrounded me in a little cluster, and assailed me with a string of questions—whether I remembered this, and whether I had forgotten that, the battle in the hayfield, the charity-school tea-party in the vicarage orchard, our picnics in Hawsley Combe, our botanical and entomological excursions on Chorwell common, and all the simple pleasures of their childhood and my youth. While this catechism was going on, Miss Tremaine watched us with a disdainful expression, which she evidently did not care to hide.

"I should not have thought you capable of such Arcadian simplicity, Mr. Chrighton," she said. "Pray continue your recollections. These juvenile experiences are most interesting."

"I don't expect you to be interested in them, Julia," Edward answered, with a tone that sounded rather too bitter for a lover. "I know what a contempt you have for trifling rustic pleasures. Were you ever a child yourself, I wonder, by the way? I don't believe you ever ran after a butterfly in your life."

Her speech put an end to our talk of the past, somehow. I saw that Edward was vexed, and that all the pleasant memories of his boyhood had fled before that cold, scornful face. A young lady in pink, who had been sitting next Julia Tremaine, vacated the sofa, and Edward slipped into her place, and devoted himself for the rest of the evening to his betrothed. I glanced at his bright expressive face, now and then, as he talked to her, and could not help wondering what charm he could discover in one who seemed to be so unworthy of him.

It was midnight when I went back to my room in the north wing, thoroughly happy in the cordial welcome that had been given me. I rose early next morning—for early rising had long been habitual to me—and, drawing back the damask-curtain that sheltered my window, looked out at the scene below.

I saw a stable-yard, a spacious quadrangle, surrounded by the closed doors of stables and dog-kennels: low, massive buildings of gray stone, with the ivy creeping over them here and there, and with an ancient moss-grown look, that gave them a weird kind of interest in my eyes. This range of stabling must have been disused for a long time, I fancied. The stables now in use were a pile of handsome red-brick buildings at the other extremity of the house, to the rear of the music-room, and forming a striking feature in the back view of the Abbey.

I had often heard how the present Squire's grandfather had kept a pack of hounds, which had been sold immediately after his death; and I knew that my cousin, the present Mr. Chrighton, had been more than once requested to follow his ancestor's good example; for there were no hounds now within twenty miles of the Abbey, though it was a fine country for fox-hunting.

George Chrighton, however—the reigning lord of the Abbey—was not a hunting man. He had, indeed, a secret horror of the sport; for more than one scion of the house had perished untimely in the hunting-field. The family had not been altogether a lucky one, in spite of its wealth and prosperity. It was not often that the goodly heritage had descended to the eldest son. Death in some form or other—on too many occasions a violent death—had come between the heir and his inheritance. And when I pondered on the dark pages in the story of the house, I used to wonder whether my cousin Fanny was ever troubled by morbid forebodings about her only and fondly-loved son.

Was there a ghost as Chrighton—that spectral visitant without which the state and splendor of a grand old house seem scarcely complete? Yes, I had heard vague hints of some shadowy presence that had been seen on rare occasions within the precincts of the Abbey; but I had never been able to ascertain what shape it bore.

Those whom I questioned, were prompt to assure me that they had seen nothing. They had heard stories, of the past—foolish legends, most likely, not worth listening to. Once, when I had spoken of the subject to my cousin George, he told me angrily never again to let him hear any allusion to *that* folly from my lips.

That December passed merrily. The old house was full of really pleasant people, and the brief winter days were spent in one unbroken round of amusement and gayety. To me the old familiar English country-house life was a perpetual delight—to feel myself amongst kindred, an unceasing pleasure. I could not have believed myself capable of being so completely happy.

I saw a great deal of my cousin Edward, and I think he contrived to make Miss Tremaine understand that, to please him, she must be gracious to me. She certainly took some pains to make herself agreeable to me; and I discovered that, in spite of that proud disdainful temper, which she so rarely took the trouble to conceal, she was really anxious to gratify her lover.

Their courtship was not altogether a halcyon period. They had frequent quarrels, the details of which Edward's sisters Sophy and Agnes delighted to discuss with me. It was the struggle of two proud spirits for mastery; but my cousin Edward's pride was of the nobler kind—the lofty scorn of all things mean—a pride that does not ill-become a generous nature. To me he seemed all that was admirable, and I was never tired of hearing his mother praise him. I think my cousin Fanny knew this, and that she used to confide in me as fully as if I had been her sister.

"I daresay you can see I am not quite so fond as I should wish to be of Julia Tremaine," she said to me one day; "but I am very glad that my son is going to marry. My husband's has not been a fortunate family, you know, Sarah. The eldest sons have been wild and unlucky for generations past; and when Edward was a boy I used to have many a bitter hour, dreading what the future might bring forth. Thank God he has been, and is, all that I can wish. He has never given me an hour's anxiety by any act of his. Yet I am not the less glad of his marriage. The heirs of Chrighton who have come to an untimely end have all died unmarried. There was Hugh Chrighton, in the reign of George the Second, who was killed in a duel; John, who broke his back in the hunting-field thirty years later; Theodore, shot accidentally by a school-fellow at Eton; Jasper, whose yacht went down in the Mediterranean forty years ago. An awful list, is it not, Sarah? I shall feel as if my son were safer somehow when he is married. It will seem as if he has escaped the ban that has fallen on so many of our house. He will have greater reason to be careful of his life when he is a married man."

I agreed with Mrs. Chrighton; but could not help wishing that Edward had chosen any other woman than the cold handsome Julia. I could not fancy his future life happy with such a mate.

Christmas came by and by—a real old English Christmas—frost and snow without, warmth and revelry within; skating on the great pond in the park, and sledging on the ice-bound high-roads, by day; private theatricals, charades, and amateur concerts, by night. I was surprised to find that Miss Tremaine refused to take any active part in these evening amusements. She preferred to sit among the elders as a spectator, and had the air and bearing of a princess for whose diversion all our enter-tainments had been planned. She seemed to think that she fulfilled her mission by sitting still and looking handsome. No desire to show off appeared to enter her mind. Her intense pride left no room for vanity. Yet I knew that she could have distinguished herself as a musician if she had chosen to do so; for I had heard her sing and play in Mrs. Chrighton's morning-room, when only Edward, his sisters, and myself were present; and I knew that both as a vocalist and a pianist she excelled all our guests.

The two girls and I had many a happy morning and afternoon, going from cottage to cottage in a pony-carriage laden with Mrs. Chrighton's gifts to the poor of her parish. There was no public formal distribution of blanketing and coals, but the wants of all were amply provided for in a quiet friendly way. Agnes and Sophy, aided by an indefatigable maid, the Rector's daughter, and one or two other young ladies, had been at work for the last three months making smart warm frocks and useful under-garments for the children of the cottagers; so that on Christmas morning every child in the parish was arrayed in a complete set of new garments. Mrs. Chrighton had an admirable faculty of knowing precisely what was wanted in every household; and our pony carriage used to convey a varied collection of goods, every parcel directed in the firm free hand of the châtelaine of the Abbey.

Edward used sometimes to drive us on these expeditions, and I found that he was eminently popular among the poor of Chrighton parish. He had such a pleasant airy way of talking to them, a manner which set them at their ease at once. He never forgot their names or relationships, or wants or ailments; had a packet of exactly the kind of tobacco each man liked best always ready in his coat-pockets; and was full of jokes, which may not have been particularly witty, but which used to make the small low-roofed chambers ring with hearty laughter.

Miss Tremaine coolly declined any share in the pleasant duties.

"I don't like poor people," she said. "I daresay it sounds very dreadful, but it's just as well to confess my iniquity at once. I never can get on with them, or they with me. I am not *simpatica*, I suppose. And then I cannot endure their stifling rooms. The close faint odor of their houses gives me a fever. And again, what is the use of visiting them? It is only an inducement to them to become hypocrites. Surely it is better to arrange on a sheet of paper what it is just and fair for them to have—blankets, and coals, and groceries, and money, and wine, and so on—and let them receive the things from some trustworthy servant. In that case, there need be no cringing on one side, and no endurance on the other."

"But, you see, Julia, there are some kinds of people to whom that sort of thing is not a question of endurance," Edward answered, his face flushing indignantly. "People who like to share in the pleasure they give—who like to see the poor careworn faces lighted up with sudden joy—who like to make these sons of the soil feel that there is some friendly link between themselves and their masters—some point of union between the cottage and the great house. There is my mother, for instance: all these duties which you think so tiresome are to her an unfailing delight. There will be a change, I'm afraid, Julia, when you are mistress of the Abbey."

"You have not made me that yet," she answered; "and there is plenty of time for you to change your mind, if you do not think me suited for the position. I do not pretend to be like your mother. It is better that I should not affect any feminine virtues which I do not possess."

After this Edward insisted on driving our pony-carriage almost every day, leaving Miss Tremaine to find her own amusement; and I think this conversation was the beginning of an estrangement between them, which became more serious than any of their previous quarrels had been.

Miss Tremaine did not care for sledging, or skating, or billiard-playing. She had none of the "fast" tendencies which have become so common lately. She used to sit in one particular bow-window of the drawing-room all the morning, working a screen in berlin-wool and beads, assisted and attended by her younger sister Laura, who was a kind of slave to her—a very colorless young lady in mind, capable of no such thing as an original opinion, and in person a pale replica of her sister.

Had there been less company in the house, the breach between Edward Chrighton and his betrothed must have become notorious; but with a house so full of people, all bent on enjoying themselves, I doubt if it was noticed. On all public occasions my cousin showed himself attentive and apparently devoted to Miss Tremaine. It was only I and his sisters who knew the real state of affairs.

I was surprised, after the young lady's total repudiation of all benevolent sentiments, when she beckoned me aside one morning, and slipped a little purse of gold—twenty sovereigns—into my hand.

"I shall be very much obliged if you will distribute that among your cottagers to-day, Miss Chrighton," she said. "Of course I should like to give them something; it's only the trouble of talking to them that I shrink from; and you are just the person for an almoner. Don't mention my little commission to any one, please."

"Of course I may tell Edward," I said; for I was anxious that he should know his betrothed was not as hard-hearted as she had appeared.

"To him least of all," she answered eagerly. "You know that our ideas vary on that point. He would think I gave the money to please him. Not a word, pray, Miss Chrighton." I submitted, and distributed my sovereigns quietly, with the most careful exercise of my judgment. So Christmas came and passed. It was the day after the great anniversary—a very quiet day for the guests and family at the Abbey, but a grand occasion for the servants, who were to have their annual ball in the evening—a ball to which all the humbler class of tenantry were invited. The frost had broken up suddenly, and it was a thorough wet day—a depressing kind of day for any one whose spirits are liable to be affected by the weather, as mine are. I felt out of spirits for the first time since my arrival at the Abbey.

No one else appeared to feel the same influence. The elder ladies sat in a wide semi-circle round one of the fireplaces in the drawing-room; a group of merry girls and dashing young men chatted gayly before the other. From the billiard-room there came the frequent clash of balls, and cheery peals of stentorian laughter. I sat in one of the deep windows, half hidden by the curtains, reading a novel—one of a boxful that came from town every month.

If the picture within was bright and cheerful, the prospect was dreary enough without. The fairy forest of snow-wreathed trees, the white valleys and undulating banks of snow, had vanished, and the rain dripped slowly and sullenly upon a darksome expanse of sodden grass, and a dismal background of leafless timber. The merry sound of the sledge bells no longer enlivened the air; all was silence and gloom.

Edward Chrighton was not amongst the billiard-players; he was pacing the drawing-room to and fro from end to end, with an air that was at once moody and restless.

"Thank heaven, the frost has broken up at last!" he exclaimed, stopping in front of the window where I sat.

He had spoken to himself, quite unaware of my close neighborhood. Unpromising as his aspect was just then, I ventured to accost him.

"What bad taste, to prefer such weather as this to frost and snow!" I answered. "The park looked enchanting yesterday—a real scene from fairyland. And only look at it to-day!"

"Oh, yes, of course, from an artistic point of view, the snow was better. The place does look something like the great dismal swamp to-day; but I am thinking of hunting, and that confounded frost made a day's sport impossible. We are in for a spell of mild weather now, I think!"

"But you are not going to hunt, are you, Edward?"

"Indeed I am, my gentle cousin, in spite of that frightened look in your amiable countenance."

"I thought there were no hounds hereabouts."

"Nor are there; but there is as fine a pack as any in the country— the Daleborough hounds—five-and-twenty miles away."

"And you are going five-and-twenty miles for the sake of a day's run?"

"I would travel forty, fifty, a hundred miles for that same diversion. But I am not going for a single day this time; I am going over to Sir Francis Wycherly's place—young Frank Wycherly and I were sworn chums at Christchurch—for three or four days. I am due to-day, but I scarcely cared to travel by cross-country roads in such rain as this. However, if the floodgates of the sky are loosened for a new deluge, I must go to-morrow."

"What a headstrong young man!" I exclaimed. "And what will Miss Tremaine say to this desertion?" I asked in a lower voice.

"Miss Tremaine can say whatever she pleases. She had it in her power to make me forget the pleasures of the chase, if she had chosen, though we had been in the heart of the shires, and the welkin ringing with the baying of hounds."

"Oh, I begin to understand. This hunting engagement is not of long standing."

"No; I began to find myself bored here a few days ago, and wrote to Frank to offer myself for two or three days at Wycherly. I received a most cordial answer by return, and am booked till the end of this week."

"You have not forgotten the ball on the first?"

"Oh, no; to do that would be to vex my mother, and to offer a slight to our guests. I shall be here for the first, come what may."

Come what may! so lightly spoken. The time came when I had bitter occasion to remember those words.

"I'm afraid you will vex your mother by going at all," I said. "You know what a horror both she and your father have of hunting."

"A most un-country-gentleman-like aversion on my father's part. But he is a dear old book-worm, seldom happy out of his library. Yes, I admit they both have a dislike to hunting in the abstract; but they know I am a pretty good rider, and that it would need a bigger country than I shall find about Wycherly to floor me. You need not feel nervous, my dear Sarah; I am not going to give papa and mamma the smallest ground for uneasiness."

"You will take your own horses, I suppose?"

"That goes without saying. No man who has cattle of his own cares to mount another man's horses. I shall take Pepperbox and the Druid."

"Pepperbox has a queer temper, I have heard your sisters say."

"My sisters expect a horse to be a kind of overgrown baa-lamb. Everything splendid in horseflesh and womankind is prone to that slight defect, an ugly temper. There is Miss Tremaine, for instance."

"I shall take Miss Tremaine's part. I believe it is you who are in the wrong in the matter of this estrangement, Edward."

"Do you? Well, wrong or right, my cousin, until the fair Julia comes to me with sweet looks and gentle words, we can never be what we have been."

"You will return from your hunting expedition in a softer mood," I answered; "that is to say, if you persist in going. But I hope and believe you will change your mind."

"Such a change is not within the limits of possibility, Sarah. I am fixed as Fate."

He strolled away, humming some gay hunting-song as he went. I was alone with Mrs. Chrighton later in the afternoon, and she spoke to me about this intended visit to Wycherly.

"Edward has set his heart upon it evidently," she said regretfully, "and his father and I have always made a point of avoiding anything that could seem like domestic tyranny. Our dear boy is such a good son, that it would be very hard if we came between him and his pleasures. You know what a morbid horror my husband has of the dangers of the hunting-field, and perhaps I am almost as weak-minded. But in spite of this we have never interfered with Edward's enjoyment of a sport which he is passionately fond of; and hitherto, thank God! he has escaped without a scratch. Yet I have had many a bitter hour, I can assure you, my dear, when my son has been away in Leicestershire hunting four days a week."

"He rides well, I suppose."

"Superbly. He has a great reputation among the sportsmen of our neighborhood. I daresay when he is master of the Abbey he will start a pack of hounds, and revive the old days of his great-grandfather, Meredith Chrighton."

"I fancy the hounds were kenneled in the stable-yard below my bed-room window in those days, were they not, Fanny?"

"Yes," Mrs. Chrighton answered, gravely; and I wondered at the sudden shadow that fell upon her face.

I went up to my room earlier than usual that afternoon, and I had a clear hour to spare before it would be time to dress for the seven o'clock dinner. This leisure hour I intended to devote to letter-writing; but on arriving in my room I found myself in a very idle frame of mind, and instead of opening my desk, I seated myself in the low easy-chair before the fire, and fell into a reverie.

How long I had been sitting there I scarcely know; I had been half-meditating, half dozing, mixing broken snatches of thought with brief glimpses of dreaming, when I was startled into wakefulness by a sound that was strange to me.

It was a huntsman's horn—a few low plaintive notes on a huntsman's horn—notes which had a strange far-away sound, that was more un-earthly than anything my ears had ever heard. I thought of the music in *Der Freischutz;* but the weirdest snatch of melody Weber ever wrote had not so ghastly a sound as these few simple notes conveyed to my ear.

I stood transfixed, listening to that awful music. It had grown dusk, my fire was almost out, and the room in shadow. As I listened, a light flashed suddenly on the wall before me. The light was as unearthly as the sound—a light that never shone from earth or sky.

I ran to the window; for this ghastly shimmer flashed through the window upon the opposite wall. The great gates of the stable-yard were open, and men in scarlet coats were riding in, a pack of hounds crowding in before them, obedient to the huntsman's whip. The whole scene was dimly visible by the declining light of the winter evening and the weird gleams of the lantern carried by one of the men. It was this lantern which had shone upon the tapestried wall. I saw the stable-doors opened one after another; gentlemen and grooms alighting from their horses; the dogs driven into their kennel; helpers hurrying to and fro; and that strange wan lantern-light glimmering here and there in the gathering dusk. But there was no sound from the horse's hoof or of human voices—not one yelp or cry from the hounds. Since those faint far-away sounds of the horn had died out in the distance, the ghastly silence had been unbroken.

I stood at my window quite calmly, and watched while the group of men and animals in the yard below noiselessly dispersed. There was nothing supernatural in the manner of their disappearance. The figures did not vanish or melt into empty air. One by one I saw the horses led into their separate quarters; one by one the redcoats strolled out of the gates, and the grooms departed, some one way, some another. The scene but for its noiselessness, was natural enough; and had I been a stranger in the house, I might have fancied that those figures were real—those stables in full occupation.

But I knew that stable-yard and all its range of building to have been disused for more than half a century. Could I believe that, without an hour's warning, the long-deserted quadrangle could be filled—the empty stalls tenanted?

Had some hunting-party from the neighborhood sought shelter here, glad to escape the pitiless rain? That was not possible, I thought. I was an utter unbeliever in all ghostly things—ready to credit any possibility rather than suppose that I had been looking upon shadows. And yet the noiselessness, the awful sound of that horn—the strange unearthly gleam of that lantern! Little superstitious as I might be, a cold sweat stood out upon my forehead, and I trembled in every limb.

For some minutes I stood by the window, statue-like, staring blankly into the empty quadrangle. Then I roused myself suddenly, and ran softly down stairs by a back staircase leading to the servants' quarters, determined to solve the mystery somehow or other. The way to Mrs. Marjorum's room was familiar to me from old experience, and it was thither that I bent my steps, determined to ask the housekeeper the meaning of what I had seen. I had a lurking conviction that it would be well for me not to mention that scene to any member of the family till I had taken counsel with some one who knew the secrets of Chrighton Abbey.

I heard the sound of merry voices and laughter as I passed the kitchen and servants' hall. Men and maids were all busy in the pleasant labor of decorating their rooms for the evening's festival. They were putting the last touches to garlands of holly and laurel, ivy and fir, as I passed the open doors; and in both rooms I saw tables laid for a substantial tea. The housekeeper's room was in a retired nook at the end of a long passage—a charming old room panelled with dark oak, and full of capacious cupboards, which in my childhood I had looked upon as storehouses of inexhaustible treasures in the way of preserves and other confectionery. It was a shady old room, with a wide old-fashioned fireplace, cool in summer, when the hearth was adorned with a great jar of roses and lavender; and warm in winter, when the logs burnt merrily all day long.

I opened the door softly, and went in. Mrs. Marjorum was dozing in a high-backed arm-chair by the glowing hearth dressed in her state gown of gray watered silk, and with a cap that was a perfect garden of roses. She opened her eyes as I approached her and stared at me with a puzzled look for the first moment or so.

"Why, is that you, Miss Sarah?" she exclaimed; "and looking as pale as a ghost, I can see, even by this fire-light! Let me just light a candle, and then I'll get you some sal volatile. Sit down in my arm-chair, miss; why, I declare you're all of a tremble!"

She put me into her easy-chair before I could resist, and lighted the two candles which stood ready upon her table, while I was trying to speak. My lips were dry, and it seemed at first as if my voice was gone.

"Never mind the sal volatile, Marjorum," I said at last. "I am not ill: I've been startled, that's all; and I've come to ask you for an explanation of the business that frightened me."

"What business, Miss Sarah?"

"You must have heard something of it yourself, surely. Didn't you hear a horn just now, a huntsman's horn?"

"A horn! Lord no, Miss Sarah. What ever could have put such a fancy into your head?"

I saw that Mrs. Marjorum's ruddy cheeks had suddenly lost their color, that she was now almost as pale as I could have been myself.

"It was no fancy," I said; "I heard the sound, and saw the people. A hunting-party has just taken shelter in the north quadrangle. Dogs and horses, and gentlemen and servants."

"What were they like, Miss Sarah?" the housekeeper asked in a strange voice.

"I can hardly tell you that. I could see that they wore red coats; and I could scarcely see more than that. Yes, I did get a glimpse of one of the gentlemen by the light of the lantern. A tall man, with gray hair and whiskers, and a stoop in his shoulders. I noticed that he wore a short-waisted coat with a very high collar—a coat that looked a hundred years old."

"The old Squire!" muttered Mrs. Marjorum under her breath; and then turning to me, she said with a cheery resolute air, "You've been dreaming, Miss Sarah, that's just what it is. You've dropped off in your chair before the fire, and had a dream, that's it."

"No, Marjorum, it was no dream. The horn woke me, and I stood at my window and saw the dogs and huntsmen come in."

"Do you know, Miss Sarah, that the gates of the north quadrangle have been locked and barred for the last forty years, and that no one ever goes in there except through the house?"

"The gates may have been opened this evening to give shelter to strangers," I said.

"Not when the only keys that will open them hang yonder in my cupboard, miss," said the housekeeper pointing to a corner of the room.

"But I tell you, Marjorum, these people came into the quadrangle; the horses and dogs are in the stables and kennels at this moment. I'll go and ask Mr. Chrighton, or my cousin Fanny, or Edward, all about it, since you won't tell me the truth."

I said this with a purpose, and it answered. Mrs. Marjorum caught me eagerly by the wrist.

"No, miss, don't do that; for pity's sake don't do that; don't breathe a word to missus or master."

"But why not?"

"Because you've seen that which always brings misfortune and sorrow to this house, Miss Sarah. You've seen the dead."

"What do you mean?" I gasped, awed in spite of myself.

"I daresay you've heard say that there's been *something* seen at times at the Abbey—many years apart, thank God; for it never came that trouble didn't come after it."

"Yes," I answered hurriedly; "but I could never get any one to tell me what it was that haunted this place."

"No, miss. Those that know have kept the secret. But you have seen it all to-night. There's no use in trying to hide it from you any longer. You have seen the old Squire, Meredith Chrighton, whose eldest son was killed by a fall in the hunting-field, brought home dead one December night, an hour after his father and the rest of the party had come safe home to the Abbey. The old gentleman had missed his son in the field, but had thought nothing of that, fancying that master John had had enough of the day's sport, and had turned his horse's head homewards. He was found by a laboring-man, poor lad, lying in a ditch with his back broken, and his horse beside him staked. The old Squire never held his head up after that day, and never rode to hounds again, though he was passionately fond of hunting. Dogs and horses were sold, and the north quadrangle has been empty from that day."

"How long is it since this kind of thing has been seen?"

"A long time, miss. I was a slip of a girl when it last happened. It was in the winter-time—this very night—the night Squire Meredith's son was killed; and the house was full of company, just as it is now. There was a wild young Oxford gentleman sleeping in your room at that time, and he saw the hunting-party come into the quadrangle; and what did he do but throw his window wide open, and give them the view-hallo as loud as ever he could. He had only arrived the day before, and knew nothing about the neighborhood; so at dinner he began to ask where were his friends the sportsmen, and to hope he should be allowed to have a run with the Abbey hounds next day. It was in the time of our master's father; and his lady at the head of the table turned as white as a sheet when she heard this talk. She had good reason, poor soul. Before the week was out her husband was lying dead. He was struck with a fit of apoplexy, and never spoke or knew any one afterwards."

"An awful coincidence," I said; "but it may have been only a coincidence."

"I've heard other stories, miss—heard them from those that wouldn't deceive—all proving the same thing: that the appearance of the old Squire and his pack is a warning of death to this house."

"I cannot believe these things," I exclaimed; "I *cannot* believe them. Does Mr. Edward know anything about this?"

"No, miss. His father and mother have been most careful that it should be kept from him."

"I think he is too strong-minded to be much affected by the fact," I said.

"And you'll not say anything about what you've seen to my master or my mistress, will you, Miss Sarah?" pleaded the faithful old servant. "The knowledge of it would be sure to make them nervous and unhappy. And if evil is to come upon this house, it isn't in human power to prevent its coming."

"God forbid that there is any evil at hand!" I answered. "I am no believer in visions or omens. After all, I would sooner fancy that I was dreaming—dreaming with my eyes open as I stood at the window—than that I beheld the shadows of the dead."

Mrs. Marjorum sighed, and said nothing. I could see that she believed firmly in the phantom hunt.

I went back to my room to dress for dinner. However rationally I might try to think of what I had seen, its effect upon my mind and nerves was not the less powerful. I could think of nothing else; and a strange morbid dread of coming misery weighed me down like an actual burden.

There was a very cheerful party in the drawing-room when I went downstairs, and at dinner the talk and laughter were unceasing; but I could see that my cousin Fanny's face was a little graver than usual, and I had no doubt she was thinking of her son's intended visit to Wycherly.

At the thought of this a sudden terror flashed upon me. How if the shadows I had seen that evening were ominous of danger to him—to

Edward, the heir and only son of the house? My heart grew cold as I thought of this, and yet in the next moment I despised myself for such weakness.

"It is natural enough for an old servant to believe in such things," I said to myself; "but for me—an educated woman of the world— preposterous folly."

And yet from that moment I began to puzzle myself in the endeavor to devise some means by which Edward's journey might be prevented. Of my own influence I knew that I was powerless to hinder his departure by so much as an hour; but I fancied that Julia Tremaine could persuade him to any sacrifice of his inclination, if she could only humble her pride so far as to entreat it. I determined to appeal to her in the course of the evening.

We were very merry all that evening. The servants and their guests danced in the great hall, while we sat in the gallery above, and in little groups upon the staircase, watching their diversions. I think this arrangement afforded excellent opportunities for flirtation, and that the younger members of our party made good use of their chances— with one exception: Edward Chrighton and his affianced contrived to keep far away from each other all the evening.

While all was going on noisily in the hall below, I managed to get Miss Tremaine apart from the others in the embrasure of a painted window on the stairs, where there was a wide open seat. Seated here side by side, I described to her, under a promise of secrecy, the scene which I had witnessed that afternoon, and my conversation with Mrs. Marjorum.

"But, good gracious me, Miss Chrighton!" the young lady exclaimed, lifting her pencilled eyebrows with unconcealed disdain, "you don't mean to tell me that you believe in such nonsense—ghosts and omens, and old woman's folly like that!"

"I assure you, Miss Tremaine, it is most difficult for me to believe in the supernatural," I answered earnestly; "but that which I saw this evening was something more than human. The thought of it has made me very unhappy; and I cannot help connecting it somehow with my cousin Edward's visit to Wycherly. If I had the power to prevent his going, I would do it at any cost; but I have not. You alone have influence enough for that. For Heaven's sake use it! do anything to hinder his hunting with the Daleborough hounds."

"You would have me humiliate myself by asking him to forego his pleasure, and that after his conduct to me during the last week?"

"I confess that he had done much to offend you. But you love him, Miss Tremaine, though you are too proud to let your love be seen; I am certain that you do love him. For pity's sake speak to him; do not let him hazard his life, when a few words from you may prevent the danger."

"I don't believe he would give up this visit to please me," she answered; "and I shall certainly not put it in his power to humiliate me by a refusal. Besides, all this fear of yours is such utter nonsense. As if nobody had ever hunted before. My brothers hunt four times a week every winter, and not one of them has ever been the worse for it yet."

I did not give up the attempt lightly. I pleaded with this proud obstinate girl for a long time, as long as I could induce her to listen to me; but it was all in vain. She stuck to her text—no one should persuade her to degrade herself by asking a favor of Edward Chrighton. He had chosen to hold himself aloof from her, and she would show him that she could live without him. When she left Chrighton Abbey, they would part as strangers.

So the night closed, and at breakfast next morning I heard that Edward had started for Wycherly soon after daybreak. His absence made, for me at least, a sad blank in our circle. For one other also, I think! for Miss Tremaine's fair proud face was very pale, though she tried to seem gayer than usual, and exerted herself in quite an unaccustomed manner in her endeavor to be agreeable to every one.

The days passed slowly for me after my cousin's departure. There was a weight upon my mind, a vague anxiety, which I struggled in vain to shake off. The house, full as it was of pleasant people, seemed to me to have become dull and dreary now that Edward was gone. The place where he had sat appeared always vacant to my eyes, though another filled it, and there was no gap on either side of the long dinner-table. Light-hearted young men still made the billiard-room resonant with their laughter; merry girls flirted as gayly as ever, undisturbed in the smallest degree by the absence of the heir of the house. Yet for me all was changed. A morbid fancy had taken complete possession of me. I found myself continually brooding over the housekeeper's words; those words which had told me that the shadows I had seen boded death and sorrow to the house of Chrighton.

My cousins, Sophy and Agnes, were no more concerned about their brother's welfare than were their guests. They were full of excitement about the new-year's ball, which was to be a very grand affair. Every one of importance within fifty miles was to be present, every nook and corner of the Abbey would be filled with visitors coming from a great distance, while others were to be billeted upon the better class of tenantry round about. Altogether the organization of this affair was no small business; and Mrs. Chrighton's mornings were broken by discussions with the housekeeper, messages from the cook, interviews with the head-gardener on the subject of floral decorations, and other details, which all alike demanded the attention of the châtelaine herself. With these duties, and with the claims of her numerous guests, my cousin Fanny's time was so fully occupied, that she had little leisure to indulge in anxious feelings about her son, whatever secret uneasiness may have been lurking in her maternal heart. As for the master of the Abbey, he spent so much of his time in the library, where, under the pretext of business with his bailiff, he read Greek, that it was not easy for any one to discover what he did feel. Once, and once only, I heard him speak of his son, in a tone that betrayed an intense eagerness for his return.

The girls were to have new dresses from a French milliner in Wigmore street; and as the great event drew near, bulky packages of millinery were continually arriving, and feminine consultations and expositions of finery were being held all day long in bedrooms and dressing-rooms with closed doors. Thus, with a mind always troubled by the same dark shapeless foreboding, I was perpetually being called upon to give an opinion about pink tulle and lilies of the valley, or maize silk and apple blossoms.

New-year's morning came at last, after an interval of abnormal length, as it seemed to me. It was a bright clear day, an almost spring-like sunshine lighting up the leafless landscape. The great dining-room was noisy with congratulations and good wishes as we assembled for breakfast on this first morning of a new year, after having seen the old one out cheerily the night before; but Edward had not yet returned, and I missed him sadly. Some touch of sympathy drew me to the side of Julia Tremaine on this particular morning. I had watched her very often during the last few days, and I had seen that her cheek grew paler every day. To-day her eyes had the dull heavy look that betokens a sleepless night. Yes, I was sure that she was unhappy—that the proud relentless nature suffered bitterly.

"He must be home to-day," I said to her in a low voice, as she sat in stately silence before an untasted breakfast.

"Who must?" she answered, turning towards me with a cold distant look.

"My cousin Edward. You know he promised to be back in time for the ball."

"I know nothing of Mr. Chrighton's intended movements," she said, in her haughtiest tone; "but of course it is only natural that he should be here to-night. He would scarcely care to insult half the county by his absence, however little he may value those now staying in his father's house."

"But you know that there is one here whom he does value better than any one else in the world, Miss Tremaine," I answered, anxious to soothe this proud girl.

"I know nothing of the kind. But why do you speak so solemnly about his return? He will come, of course. There is no reason he should not come."

She spoke in a rapid manner that was strange to her, and looked at me with a sharp inquiring glance, that touched me somehow, it was so unlike herself—it revealed to me so keen an anxiety.

"No, there is no reasonable cause for anything like uneasiness," I said; "but you remember what I told you the other night. That has preyed upon my mind, and it will be an unspeakable relief to me when I see my cousin safe at home."

"I am sorry that you should indulge in such weakness, Miss Chrighton."

That was all she said; but when I saw her in the drawing-room after breakfast, she had established herself in a window that commanded a view of the long winding drive leading to the front of the Abbey. From this point she could not fail to see any one approaching the house. She sat there all day; every one else was more or less busy with arrangements for the evening, or at any rate occupied with an appearance of business; but Julia Tremaine kept her place by the window, pleading a headache as an excuse for sitting still, with a book in her hand, all day, yet obstinately refusing to go to her room and lie down, when her mother entreated her to do so.

"You will be fit for nothing to-night, Julia," Mrs. Tremaine said, almost angrily; "you have been looking ill for ever so long, and to-day you are as pale as a ghost."

I knew that she was watching for *him;* and I pitied her with all my heart, as the day wore itself out, and he did not come.

We dined earlier than usual, played a game or two of billiards after dinner, made a tour of inspection through the bright rooms, lit with wax-candles only, and odorous with exotics; and then came a long interregnum devoted to the arts and mysteries of the toilet; while maids flitted to and fro laden with frilled muslin petticoats from the laundry, and a faint smell of singed hair pervaded the corridors. At ten o'clock the band were tuning their violins, and pretty girls and elegant-looking men were coming slowly down the broad oak staircase, as the roll of fast-coming wheels sounded louder without, and stentorian voices announced the best people in the county.

I have no need to dwell upon the details of that evening's festival. It was very much like other balls—a brilliant success, a night of splendor and enchantment for those whose hearts were light and happy, and who could abandon themselves utterly to the pleasure of the moment; a far-away picture of fair faces and bright-hued dresses, a wearisome kaleidoscopic procession of form and color for those whose minds were weighed down with the burden of a hidden care.

For me the music had no melody, the dazzling scene no charm. Hour after hour went by; supper was over, and the waltzers were enjoying those latest dances which always seem the most delightful, and yet Edward Chrighton had not appeared amongst us.

There had been innumerable inquiries about him, and Mrs. Chrighton had apologized for his absence as best she might. Poor soul, I well knew that his non-return was now a source of poignant anxiety to her, although she greeted all her guests with the same gracious smile, and was able to talk gayly and well upon every subject. Once, when she was sitting alone for a few minutes, watching the dancers, I saw the smile fade from her face, and a look of anguish come over it. I ventured to approach her at this moment, and never shall I forget the look which she turned towards me.

"My son, Sarah!" she said, in a low voice—"something has happened to my son!"

I did my best to comfort her; but my own heart was growing heavier and heavier, and my attempt was a very poor one.

Julia Tremaine had danced a little at the beginning of the evening, to keep up appearances, I believe, in order that no one might suppose that she was distressed by her lover's absence; but after the first two or three dances she pronounced herself tired, and withdrew to a seat among the matrons. She was looking very lovely in spite of her extreme pallor, dressed in white tulle, a perfect cloud of airy puffings, and with a wreath of ivy-leaves and diamonds crowning her pale golden hair.

The night waned, the dancers were revolving in the last waltz, when I happened to look toward the doorway at the end of the room. I was startled by seeing a man standing there, with his hat in his hand, not in evening costume; a man with a pale anxious-looking face, peering cautiously into the room. My first thought was of evil; but in the next moment the man had disappeared, and I saw no more of him.

I lingered by my cousin Fanny's side till the rooms were empty. Even Sophy and Aggy had gone off to their own apartments, their airy dresses sadly dilapidated by a night's vigorous dancing. There were only Mr. and Mrs. Chrighton and myself in the long suite of rooms, where the flowers were drooping and the wax-lights dying out one by one in the silver sconces against the walls.

"I think the evening went off very well," Fanny said, looking rather anxiously at her husband, who was stretching himself and yawning with an air of intense relief.

"Yes, the affair went off well enough. But Edward has committed a terrible breach of manners by not being here. Upon my word, the young men of the present day think of nothing but their own pleasures. I suppose that something especially attractive was going on at Wycherly to-day, and he couldn't tear himself away."

"It is so unlike him to break his word," Mrs. Chrighton answered. "You are not alarmed, Frederick? You don't think that anything has happened—any accident?"

"What should happen? Ned is one of the best riders in the county. I don't think there's any fear of his coming to grief."

"He might be ill."

"Not he. He's a young Hercules. And if it were possible for him to be ill—which it is not—we should have had a message from Wycherly."

The words were scarcely spoken when Truefold the butler stood by his master's side, with a solemn anxious face.

"There is a—a person who wishes to see you, sir," he said in a low voice, "alone."

Low as the words were, both Fanny and myself heard them.

"Some one from Wycherly?" she exclaimed. "Let him come here."

"But, madam, the person most particularly wished to see master alone. —Shall I show him into the library, sir? The lights are not out there."

"Then it *is* some one from Wycherly," said my cousin, seizing my wrist with a hand that was icy cold. "Didn't I tell you so, Sarah? Something has happened to my son. Let the person come here, Truefold, here; I insist upon it."

The tone of command was quite strange in a wife who was always deferential to her husband, in a mistress who was ever gentle to her servants.

"Let it be so, Truefold," said Mr. Chrighton. "Whatever ill news has come to us we will hear together."

He put his arm round his wife's waist. Both were pale as marble, both stood in stony stillness waiting for the blow that was to fall upon them.

The stranger, the man I had seen in the doorway, came in. He was curate of Wycherly church, and chaplain to Sir Francis Wycherly; a grave middle-aged man. He told what he had to tell with all kindness, with all the usual forms of consolation which Christianity and an experience of sorrow could suggest. Vain words, wasted trouble. The blow must fall, and earthly consolation was unable to lighten it by a feather's weight.

There had been a steeplechase at Wycherly—an amateur affair with gentlemen riders—on that bright new-year's day, and Edward

Chrighton had been persuaded to ride his favorite hunter Pepper-box. There would be plenty of time for him to return to Chrighton after the races. He had consented; and his horse was winning easily, when, at the last fence, a double one, with water beyond, Pepperbox baulked his leap, and went over head-foremost, flinging his rider over a hedge into a field close beside the course, where there was a heavy stone roller. Upon this stone roller Edward Chrighton had fallen, his head receiving the full force of the concussion. All was told. It was while the curate was relating the fatal catastrophe that I looked round suddenly, and saw Julia Tremaine standing behind the speaker. She had heard all; she uttered no cry, but stood calm and motionless, wait-ing for the end.

I know not how that night ended: there seemed an awful calm upon us all. A carriage was got ready, and Mr. and Mrs. Chrighton started for Wycherly to look upon their dead son. He had died while they were carrying him from the course to Sir Francis's house. I went with Julia Tremaine to her room, and sat with her while the winter morning dawned slowly upon us—a bitter dawning.

I have little more to tell. Life goes on, though hearts are broken. Upon Chrighton Abbey there came a dreary time of desolation. The master of the house lived in his library, shut from the outer world, buried almost as completely as a hermit in his cell. I have heard that Julia Tremaine was never known to smile after that day. She is still unmarried, and lives entirely at her father's country house; proud and reserved in her conduct to her equals, but a very angel of mercy and compassion amongst the poor of the neighborhood. Yes; this haughty girl, who once declared herself unable to endure the hovels of the poor, is now a Sister of Charity in all but the robe. So does a great sorrow change the current of a woman's life.

I have seen my cousin Fanny many times since that awful new-year's night; for I have always the same welcome at the Abbey. I have seen her calm and cheerful, doing her duty, smiling upon her daughter's children, the honored mistress of a great household; but I know that the mainspring of life is broken, that for her there hath passed a glory from the earth, and that upon all the pleasures and joys of this world she looks with a solemn calm of one for whom all things are dark with the shadow of a great sorrow.

Rhoda Broughton

Rhoda Broughton (1840–1920), born in Denbigh, Wales, was one of the more notorious writers of the second half of the nineteenth century, not for her life, which was irreproachable (if a sharp tongue and disregard for social amenities are not subjects for reproach), but for the subject matter of her fiction. She usually wrote about young women and their adjustment to life, and she revealed that they had bodies, desires, and passions. It was not that she was a prurient novelist, but that she stepped over the contemporary boundaries of what was considered acceptable in parlor fiction.

The niece of J. S. Le Fanu, who published her first novel in his Dublin Review, *she found literature an easy and profitable career. Her novels sold well, and if the puritanical disliked them, critics rated them fairly high, especially her later work. Her best-known works were* Cometh Up as a Flower *(1867),* Not Wisely but Too Well *(1867), and* Belinda *(1883), a roman à clef of Oxford society. At her best she was a fine craftsman with an excellent ear for conversation and a style of great vivacity. It was her custom to write her fiction in the present tense.*

Miss Broughton did not write much supernatural fiction. Her volume Tales for Christmas Eve *(1873) contained four ghost stories reprinted from earlier periodical sources. To these can be added another short story, "Betty's Visions." In four of these stories her subject matter was conventional—ghosts, dreams, second sight—but the fifth, "The Man with the Nose," is different. For the Victorian reader, the man was Death. For us he is almost a classic Freudian symbol—fascination, rapport, transfer, ambivalence about marriage, the nose, and all.*

THE MAN
WITH THE NOSE

[The details of this little story are, of course, imaginary, but the main incidents are, to the best of my belief, facts. They happened twenty, or more than twenty years ago.]

CHAPTER I.

"Let us get a map and see what places look pleasantest?" says she.

"As for that," reply I, "on a map most places look equally pleasant."

"Never mind; get one!"

I obey.

"Do you like the seaside?" asks Elizabeth, lifting her little brown head and her small happy white face from the English sea-coast along which her forefinger is slowly travelling.

"Since you ask me, distinctly *no*," reply I, for once venturing to have a decided opinion of my own, which during the last few weeks of imbecility I can be hardly said to have had. "I broke my last wooden spade five and twenty years ago. I have but a poor opinion of cockles— sandy red-nosed things, are not they? and the air always makes me bilious."

"Then we certainly will not go there," says Elizabeth, laughing. "A bilious bridegroom! alliterative but horrible! None of our friends show the least eagerness to lend us their country house."

"Oh that God would put it into the hearts of men to take their wives straight home, as their fathers did!" say I with a cross groan.

"It is evident, therefore, that we must go somewhere," returns she, not heeding the aspiration contained in my last speech, making her forefinger resume its employment, and reaching Torquay.

"I suppose so," say I, with a sort of sigh; "for once in our lives we must resign ourselves to having the finger of derision pointed at us by waiters and landlords."

"You shall leave your new portmanteau at home, and I will leave all my best clothes, and nobody will guess that we are bride and bridegroom; they will think that we have been married—oh, ever since the world began" (opening her eyes very wide).

I shake my head. "With an old portmanteau and in rags we shall still have the mark of the beast upon us."

"Do you mind much? do you hate being ridiculous?" asks Elizabeth, meekly, rather depressed by my view of the case; "because if so, let us go somewhere out of the way, where there will be very few people to laugh at us."

"On the contrary," return I, stoutly, "we will betake ourselves to some spot where such as we do chiefly congregate—where we shall be swallowed up and lost in the multitude of our fellow-sinners." A pause devoted to reflection. "What do you say to Killarney?" say I cheerfully.

"There are a great many fleas there, I believe," replies Elizabeth, slowly; "flea-bites make large lumps on me; you would not like me if I were covered with large lumps."

At the hideous ideal picture thus presented to me by my little beloved I relapse into inarticulate idiocy; emerging from which by-and-by, I suggest "The Lakes?" My arm is round her, and I feel her supple body shiver though it is mid July and the bees are booming about in the still and sleepy noon garden outside.

"Oh—no—no—not *there!*"

"Why such emphasis?" I ask gaily; "more fleas? At this rate, and with this *sine quâ non*, our choice will grow limited."

"Something dreadful happened to me there," she says, with another shudder. "But indeed I did not think there was any harm in it—I never thought anything would come of it."

"What the devil was it?" cry I, in a jealous heat and hurry; "what the mischief *did* you do, and why have not you told me about it before?"

"I did not *do* much," she answers meekly, seeking for my hand, and when found kissing it in timid deprecation of my wrath; "but I was ill—very ill—there; I had a nervous fever. I was in a bed hung with a chintz with a red and green fern-leaf pattern on it. I have always hated red and green fern-leaf chintzes ever since."

"It would be possible to avoid the obnoxious bed, would not it?" say I, laughing a little. "Where does it lie? Windermere? Ulleswater? Wastwater? Where?"

"We were at Ulleswater," she says, speaking rapidly, while a hot colour grows on her small white cheeks—"Papa, mamma, and I; and there came a mesmeriser to Penrith, and we went to see him—everybody did—and he asked leave to mesmerise me—he said I should be such a good medium—and—and—I did not know what it was like. I thought it would be quite good fun—and—and—I let him."

She is trembling exceedingly; even the loving pressure of my arms cannot abate her shivering.

"Well?"

"And after that I do not remember anything—I believe I did all sorts of extraordinary things that he told me—sang and danced, and made a fool of myself—but when I came home I was very ill, very—I lay in bed for five whole weeks, and—and was off my head, and said odd and wicked things that you would not have expected me to say—that dreadful bed! shall I ever forget it?"

"We will *not* go to the Lakes," I say, decisively, "and we will not talk any more about mesmerism."

"That is right," she says, with a sigh of relief, "I try to think about it as little as possible; but sometimes, in the dead black of the night, when God seems a long way off, and the devil near, it comes back to me so strongly—I feel, do not you know, as if he were *there* somewhere in the room, and I *must* get up and follow him."

"Why should not we go abroad?" suggest I, abruptly turning the conversation.

"Why, indeed?" cries Elizabeth, recovering her gaiety, while her pretty blue eyes begin to dance. "How stupid of us not to have thought of it before; only *abroad* is a big word. *What* abroad?"

"We must be content with something short of Central Africa," I say, gravely, "as I think our one hundred and fifty pounds would hardly take us that far."

"Wherever we go, we must buy a dialogue book," suggests my little bride-elect, "and I will learn some phrases before we start."

"As for that, the Anglo-Saxon tongue takes one pretty well round the world," reply I, with a feeling of complacent British swagger, putting my hands in my breeches pockets.

"Do you fancy the Rhine?" says Elizabeth, with a rather timid suggestion; "I know it is the fashion to run it down nowadays, and call it a cocktail river; but—but—after all it cannot be so *very* contemptible, or Byron could not have said such noble things about it."

> " 'The castled crag of Drachenfels
>   Frowns o'er the wide and winding Rhine,
> Whose breast of waters broadly swells
>   Between the banks which bear the vine,' "

say I, spouting. "After all, that proves nothing, for Byron could have made a silk purse out of a sow's ear."

"The Rhine will not do then?" says she resignedly, suppressing a sigh.

"On the contrary, it will do admirably: it *is* a cocktail river, and I do not care who says it is not," reply I, with illiberal positiveness; "but everybody should be able to say so from their own experience, and not from hearsay: the Rhine let it be, by all means."

So the Rhine it is.

CHAPTER II.

I have got over it; we have both got over it, tolerably, creditably; but after all, it is a much severer ordeal for a man than a woman, who, with a bouquet to occupy her hands, and a veil to gently shroud her features, need merely be prettily passive. I am alluding, I need hardly say, to the religious ceremony of marriage, which I flatter myself I have gone through with a stiff sheepishness not unworthy of my country. It is a three-days-old event now, and we are getting used to belonging to one another, though Elizabeth still takes off her ring twenty times a day to admire its bright thickness; still laughs when she hears herself called "Madame." Three days ago, we kissed all our friends, and left them to make themselves ill on our cake, and criticise our bridal behaviour, and now we are at Brussels, she and I, feeling oddly, joyfully free from any chaperone. We have been mildly sight-seeing—very mildly most people would say, but we have resolved not to take our pleasure with the railway speed of Americans, or the hasty sadness of our fellow Britons. Slowly and gaily we have been taking ours. To-day we have been to visit Wiertz's pictures. Have you ever seen them, oh reader? They are known to comparatively few people, but if you have a taste for the unearthly terrible—if you wish to sup full of horrors, hasten thither, we have been peering through the appointed peep-hole at the horrible cholera picture—the man buried alive by mistake, pushing up the lid of his coffin, and stretching a ghastly face and livid hands out of his winding sheet towards you, while awful grey-blue coffins are piled around, and noisome toads and giant spiders crawl damply about. On first seeing it, I have reproached myself for bringing one of so nervous a temperament as Elizabeth to see so haunting and hideous a spectacle; but she is less impressed than I expected—less impressed than I myself am.

"He is very lucky to be able to get his lid up," she says, with a half-laugh; "we should find it hard work to burst our brass nails, should not we? When you bury me, dear, fasten me down very slightly, in case there may be some mistake."

And now all the long and quiet July evening we have been prowling together about the streets. Brussels is the town of towns for *flâner*-ing —have been flattening our noses against the shop windows, and making each other imaginary presents. Elizabeth has not confined herself to imagination, however; she has made me buy her a little bonnet with feathers—"in order to look married," as she says, and the result is such a delicious picture of a child playing at being grown up, having prac- tised a theft on its mother's wardrobe, that for the last two hours I have been in a foolish ecstacy of love and laughter over her and it. We are at the "Bellevue," and have a fine suite of rooms, *au premier*, evi- dently specially devoted to the English, to the gratification of whose well-known loyalty the Prince and Princess of Wales are simpering from the walls. Is there any one in the three kingdoms who knows his own face as well as he knows the faces of Albert Victor and Alexandra? The long evening has at last slidden into night—night far advanced— night melting into earliest day. All Brussels is asleep. One moment ago I also was asleep, soundly as any log. What is it that has made me take this sudden, headlong plunge out of sleep into wakefulness? Who is it that is clutching at and calling upon me? What is it that is making me struggle mistily up into a sitting posture, and try to revive my sleep-numbed senses? A summer night is never wholly dark; by the half light that steals through the closed *persiennes* and open windows I see my wife standing beside my bed; the extremity of terror on her face, and her fingers digging themselves with painful tenacity into my arm.

"Tighter, tighter!" she is crying, wildly. "What are you thinking of? You are letting me go!"

"Good heavens!" say I, rubbing my eyes, while my muddy brain grows a trifle clearer. "What is it? What has happened? Have you had a nightmare?"

"You saw him," she says, with a sort of sobbing breathlessness; "you know you did! You saw him as well as I."

"I!" cry I, incredulously—"not I! Till this second I have been fast asleep. *I* saw nothing."

"You did!" she cries, passionately. "You know you did. Why do you deny it? You were as frightened as I."

"As I live," I answer, solemnly, "I know no more than the dead what you are talking about; till you woke me by calling and catching hold of me, I was as sound asleep as the seven sleepers."

"Is it possible that it can have been a *dream*?" she says, with a long sigh, for a moment loosing my arm, and covering her face with her hands. "But no—in a dream I should have been somewhere else, but I was here—*here*—on that bed, and he stood *there*," pointing with her forefinger, "just *there*, between the foot of it and the window!"

She stops, panting.

"It is all that brute Wiertz," say I, in a fury. "I wish I had been buried alive myself before I had been fool enough to take you to see his beastly daubs."

"Light a candle," she says, in the same breathless way, her teeth chattering with fright. "Let us make sure he is not hidden somewhere in the room."

"How could he be?" say I, striking a match; "the door is locked."

"He might have got in by the balcony," she answers, still trembling violently.

"He would have had to have cut a very large hole in the *persiennes*," say I, half mockingly. "See, they are intact, and well fastened on the inside."

She sinks into an arm-chair, and pushes her loose soft hair from her white face.

"It *was* a dream then, I suppose?"

She is silent for a moment or two, while I bring her a glass of water, and throw a dressing-gown round her cold and shrinking form.

"Now tell me, my little one," I say coaxingly, sitting down at her feet, "what it was—what you thought you saw?"

"*Thought* I saw!" echoes she, with indignant emphasis, sitting upright, while her eyes sparkle feverishly. "I am as certain that I saw him standing there as I am that I see that candle burning—that I see this chair—that I see you."

"*Him*! but who is *him*?"

She falls forward on my neck, and buries her face in my shoulder.

"That—dreadful—man!" she says, while her whole body is one tremor.

"*What* dreadful man?" cry I impatiently.

She is silent.

"Who was he?"

"I do not know."

"Did you ever see him before?"

"Oh, no—no, never! I hope to God I may never see him again!"

"What was he like?"

"Come closer to me," she says, laying hold of my hand with her small and chilly fingers; "stay *quite* near me, and I will tell you,"— after a pause—"he had a *nose*!"

"My dear soul," cry I, bursting out into a loud laugh in the silence of the night, "do not most people have noses? Would not he have been much more dreadful if he had had *none*?"

"But it was *such* a nose!" she says, with perfect trembling gravity.

"A bottle nose?" suggest I, still cackling.

"For heaven's sake, don't laugh!" she says nervously; "if you had seen his face, you would have been as little disposed to laugh as I."

"But his nose?" return I, suppressing my merriment, "what kind of nose was it? See, I am as grave as a judge."

"It was very prominent," she answers, in a sort of awe-struck half-whisper, "and very sharply chiselled; the nostrils very much cut out." A little pause. "His eyebrows were one straight black line across his face, and under them his eyes burnt like dull coals of fire, that shone and yet did not shine; they looked like dead eyes, sunken, half extinguished, and yet sinister."

"And what did he do?" asked I, impressed, despite myself, by her passionate earnestness; "when did you first see him?"

"I was asleep," she said—"at least, I thought so—and suddenly I opened my eyes, and he was *there—there*"—pointing again with trembling finger—"between the window and the bed."

"What was he doing? Was he walking about?"

"He was standing as still as stone—I never saw any live thing so still—*looking* at me; he never called or beckoned, or moved a finger, but his eyes *commanded* me to come to him, as the eyes of the mesmeriser at Penrith did." She stops, breathing heavily. I can hear her heart's loud and rapid beats.

"And you?" I say, pressing her more closely to my side, and smoothing her troubled hair.

"I *hated* it," she cries, excitedly; I loathed it—abhorred it. I was ice-cold with fear and horror, but—I *felt* myself going to him."

"Yes?"

"And then I shrieked out to you, and you came running, and caught fast hold of me, and held me tight at first—quite tight—but presently I felt your hold slacken—slacken—and though I *longed* to stay with you, though I was *mad* with fright, yet I felt myself pulling strongly away from you—going to him; and he—he stood there always looking —looking—and then I gave one last loud shriek, and I suppose I awoke —and it was a dream!"

"I never heard of a clearer case of nightmare," say I, stoutly; "that vile Wiertz! I should like to see his whole *Musée* burnt by the hands of the hangman to-morrow."

She shakes her head. "It had nothing to say to Wiertz; what it meant I do not know, but—"

"It meant nothing," I answer, reassuringly, "except that for the future we will go and see none but good and pleasant sights, and steer clear of charnel-house fancies."

CHAPTER III.

Elizabeth is now in a position to decide whether the Rhine is a cocktail river or no, for she is on it, and so am I. We are sitting, with an awning over our heads, and little wooden stools under our feet. Elizabeth has a small sailor's hat and blue ribbon on her head. The river breeze has blown it rather awry; has tangled her plenteous hair; has made a faint pink stain on her pale cheeks. It is some fête day, and the boat is crowded. Tables, countless camp stools, volumes of black smoke pouring from the funnel, as we steam along. "Nothing to the Caledonian Canal!" cries a burly Scotchman in leggings, speaking with loud authority, and surveying with an air of contempt the eternal vine-clad slopes, that sound so well, and look so *sticky* in reality. "Cannot hold a candle to it!" A rival bride and bridegroom opposite, sitting together like love-birds under an umbrella, looking into each other's eyes instead of at the Rhine scenery.

"They might as well have stayed at home, might not they?" says my wife, with a little air of superiority. "Come, we are not so bad as that, are we?"

A storm comes on: hailstones beat slantwise and reach us—stone and sting us right under our awning. Everybody rushes down below, and takes the opportunity to feed ravenously. There are few actions more disgusting than eating *can* be made. A handsome girl close to us —her immaturity evidenced by the two long tails of black hair down her back—is thrusting her knife halfway down her throat.

"Come on deck again," says Elizabeth, disgusted and frightened at this last sight. "The hail was much better than this!"

So we returned to our camp stools, and sit alone under one mackintosh in the lashing storm, with happy hearts and empty stomachs.

"Is not this better than any luncheon?" asks Elizabeth, triumphantly, while the rain-drops hang on her long and curled lashes.

"Infinitely better," reply I, madly struggling with the umbrella to prevent its being blown inside out, and gallantly ignoring a species of gnawing sensation at my entrails.

The squall clears off by-and-by, and we go steaming, steaming on past the unnumbered little villages by the water's edge with church spires and pointed roofs, past the countless rocks with their little pert castles perched on the top of them, past the tall, stiff poplar rows. The church bells are ringing gaily as we go by. A nightingale is singing from a wood. The black eagle of Prussia droops on the stream behind us, swish-swish through the dull green water. A fat woman who is interested in it, leans over the back of the boat, and by some happy effect of crinoline, displays to her fellow-passengers two yards of thick white cotton legs. She is, fortunately for herself, unconscious of her generosity.

The day steals on; at every stopping place more people come on. There is hardly elbow room; and, what is worse, almost everybody is drunk. Rocks, castles, villages, poplars, slide by, while the paddles churn always the water, and the evening draws greyly on. At Bingen a party of big blue Prussian soldiers, very drunk, "glorious" as Tam o' Shanter, come and establish themselves close to us. They call for Lager Beer; talk at the tip-top of their strong voices; two of them begin to spar; all seem inclined to sing. Elizabeth is frightened. We are two hours late in arriving at Biebrich. It is half an hour more before we can get ourselves and our luggage into a carriage and set off along the winding road to Wiesbaden. "The night is chilly, but not dark." There is only a little shabby bit of a moon, but it shines as hard as it can. Elizabeth is quite worn out, her tired head droops in uneasy sleep on my shoulder. Once she wakes up with a start.

"Are you sure that it meant nothing?" she asks, looking me eagerly in my face; "do people often have such dreams?"

"Often, often," I answer, reassuringly.

"I am always afraid of falling asleep now," she says, trying to sit upright and keep her heavy eyes open, "for fear of seeing him standing there again. Tell me, do you think I shall? Is there any chance, any probability of it?"

"None, none!"

We reach Wiesbaden at last, and give up to the Hôtel des Quatre Saisons. By this time it is full midnight. Two or three men are standing about the door. Morris, the maid, has got out—so have I, and I am holding out my hand to Elizabeth when I hear her give one piercing scream, and see her with ash-white face and starting eyes point with her fore-finger—

"There he is!—there!—there!"

I look in the direction indicated, and just catch a glimpse of a tall figure standing half in the shadow of the night, half in the gas-light from the hotel. I have not time for more than one cursory glance, as I am interrupted by a cry from the bystanders, and turning quickly round, am just in time to catch my wife, who falls in utter insensibility into my arms. We carry her into a room on the ground floor; it is small, noisy, and hot, but it is the nearest at hand. In about an hour she re-opens her eyes. A strong shudder makes her quiver from head to foot.

"Where is he?" she says, in a terrified whisper, as her senses come slowly back. "He is somewhere about—somewhere near. I feel that he is!"

"My dearest child, there is no one here but Morris and me," I answer soothingly. "Look for yourself. See."

I take one of the candles and light up each corner of the room in succession.

"You saw him!" she says, in trembling hurry, sitting up and clenching her hands together. "I know you did—I pointed him out to you—you *cannot* say that it was a dream *this* time."

"I saw two or three ordinary-looking men as we drove up," I answer, in a commonplace, matter-of-fact tone. "I did not notice anything remarkable about any of them; you know, the fact is, darling, that you have had nothing to eat all day, nothing but a biscuit, and you are over-wrought, and fancy things."

"Fancy!" echoes she, with strong irritation. "How you talk! Was I ever one to fancy things! I tell you that as sure as I sit here—as sure as you stand there—I saw him—*him*—the man I saw in my dream, if it was a dream. There was not a hair's breadth of difference between them —and he was looking at me—looking—"

She breaks off into hysterical sobbing.

"My dear child!" say I, thoroughly alarmed, and yet half angry, "for God's sake do not work yourself up into a fever: wait till to-morrow, and we will find out who he is, and all about him; you your-self will laugh when we discover that he is some harmless bagman."

"Why not *now*?" she says, nervously; "why cannot you find out *now—this minute*?"

"Impossible! Everybody is in bed! Wait till to-morrow, and all will be cleared up."

The morrow comes, and I go about the hotel, inquiring. The house is so full, and the data I have to go upon are so small, that for some time I have great difficulty in making it understood to whom I am alluding. At length one waiter seems to comprehend.

"A tall and dark gentleman, with a pronounced and very peculiar nose? Yes; there has been such a one, certainly, in the hotel, but he left at 'grand matin' this morning; he remained only one night."

"And his name?"

The garçon shakes his head. "That is unknown, monsieur; he did not inscribe it in the visitors' book."

"What countryman was he?"

Another shake of the head. "He spoke German, but it was with a foreign accent."

"Whither did he go?"

That also is unknown. Nor can I arrive at any more facts about him.

CHAPTER IV.

A fortnight has passed; we have been hither and thither; now we are at Lucerne. Peopled with better inhabitants, Lucerne might well do for Heaven. It is drawing towards eventide, and Elizabeth and I are sitting hand in hand on a quiet bench, under the shady linden trees, on a high hill up above the lake. There is nobody to see us, so we sit peaceably hand in hand. Up by the still and solemn monastery we came, with its small and narrow windows, calculated to hinder the holy fathers from promenading curious eyes on the world, the flesh, and the devil, tripping past them in blue gauze veils: below us grass and green trees, houses with high-pitched roofs, little dormer-windows, and shutters yet greener than the grass; below us the lake in its rippleless peace, calm, quiet, motionless as Bethesda's pool before the coming of the troubling angel.

"I said it was too good to last," say I, doggedly, "did not I, only yesterday? Perfect peace, perfect sympathy, perfect freedom from nagging worries—when did such a state of things last more than two days?"

Elizabeth's eyes are idly fixed on a little steamer, with a stripe of red along its side, and a tiny puff of smoke from its funnel, gliding along and cutting a narrow white track on Lucerne's sleepy surface.

"This is the fifth false alarm of the gout having gone to his stomach within the last two years," continue I resentfully. "I declare to Heaven, that if it has not really gone there this time, I'll cut the whole concern."

Let no one cast up their eyes in horror, imagining that it is my father to whom I am thus alluding; it is only a great-uncle by marriage, in consideration of whose wealth and vague promises I have dawdled professionless through twenty-eight years of my life.

"You *must* not go," says Elizabeth, giving my hand an imploring squeeze. "The man in the Bible said, 'I have married a wife, and therefore I cannot come;' why should it be a less valid excuse nowadays?"

"If I recollect rightly, it was considered rather a poor one even then," reply I, dryly.

Elizabeth is unable to contradict this; she therefore only lifts two pouted lips (Monsieur Taine objects to the redness of English women's mouths, but I do not) to be kissed, and says, "Stay." I am good enough to comply with her unspoken request, though I remain firm with regard to her spoken one.

"My dearest child," I say, with an air of worldly experience and superior wisdom, "kisses are very good things—in fact, there are few better—but one cannot live upon them."

"Let us try," she says coaxingly.

"I wonder which would get tired first?" I say, laughing. But she only goes on pleading, "Stay, stay."

"How *can* I stay?" I cry impatiently; "you talk as if I *wanted* to go! Do you think it is any pleasanter to me to leave you than to you to be left? But you know his disposition, his rancorous resentment of fancied neglects. For the sake of two days' indulgence, must I throw away what will keep us in ease and plenty to the end of our days?"

"I do not care for plenty," she says, with a little petulant gesture. "I do not see that rich people are any happier than poor ones. Look at the St. Clairs; they have £40,000 a year, and she is a miserable woman, perfectly miserable, because her face gets red after dinner."

"There will be no fear of *our* faces getting red after dinner," say I, grimly, "for we shall have no dinner for them to get red after."

A pause. My eyes stray away to the mountains. Pilatus on the right, with his jagged peak and slender snow-chains about his harsh neck; hill after hill rising silent, eternal, like guardian spirits standing hand in hand around their child, the lake. As I look, suddenly they have all flushed, as at some noblest thought, and over all their sullen faces streams an ineffable rosy joy—a solemn and wonderful effulgence, such as Israel saw reflected from the features of the Eternal in their prophet's transfigured eyes. The unutterable peace and stainless beauty of earth and sky seemed to lie softly on my soul. "Would God I could stay! Would God all life could be like this!" I say, devoutly, and the aspiration has the reverent earnestness of a prayer.

"Why do you say, '*Would God!*'" she cries passionately, "when it lies with yourself? Oh my dear love," gently sliding her hand through my arm, and lifting wetly-beseeching eyes to my face, "I do not know why I insist upon it so much—I cannot tell you myself—I dare say I seem selfish and unreasonable—but I feel as if your going now would be the end of all things—as if—" She breaks off suddenly.

"My child," say I, thoroughly distressed, but still determined to have my own way, "you talk as if I were going for ever and a day; in a week, at the outside, I shall be back, and then you will thank me for the very thing for which you now think me so hard and disobliging."

"Shall I?" she answers, mournfully. "Well, I hope so."

"You will not be alone, either; you will have Morris."

"Yes."

"And every day you will write me a long letter, telling me every single thing that you do, say, and think."

"Yes."

She answers me gently and obediently; but I can see that she is still utterly unreconciled to the idea of my absence.

"What is it that you are afraid of?" I ask, becoming rather irritated. "What do you suppose will happen to you?"

She does not answer; only a large tear falls on my hand, which she hastily wipes away with her pocket handkerchief, as if afraid of exciting my wrath.

"Can you give me any good reason why I *should* stay?" I ask, dictatorially.

"None—none—only—stay—stay!"

But I am resolved *not* to stay. Early the next morning I set off.

CHAPTER V.

This time it is not a false alarm; this time it really has gone to his stomach, and, declining to be dislodged thence, kills him. My return is therefore retarded until after the funeral and the reading of the will. The latter is so satisfactory, and my time is so fully occupied with a multiplicity of attendant business, that I have no leisure to regret the delay. I write to Elizabeth, but receive no letters from her. This surprises and makes me rather angry, but does not alarm me. "If she had been ill, if anything had happened, Morris would have written. She never was great at writing, poor little soul. What dear little babyish notes she used to send me during our engagement! Perhaps she wishes to punish me for my disobedience to her wishes. Well, *now* she will see who was in the right." I am drawing near her now; I am walking up from the railway station at Lucerne. I am very joyful as I march along under an umbrella, in the grand broad shining of the summer afternoon. I think with pensive passion of the last glimpse I had of my beloved—her small and wistful face looking out from among the thick fair fleece of her long hair—winking away her tears and blowing kisses to me. It is a new sensation to me to have anyone looking tearfully wistful over my departure. I draw near the great glaring Schweizerhof, with its colonnaded tourist-crowded porch; here are all the pomegranates as I left them, in their green tubs, with their scarlet blossoms, and the dusty oleanders in a row. I look up at our windows: nobody is looking out from them; they are open, and the curtains are alternately swelled out and drawn in by the softly-playful wind. I run quickly upstairs and burst noisily into the sitting-room. Empty, perfectly empty! I open the adjoining door into the bedroom, crying "Elizabeth! Elizabeth!" but I receive no answer. Empty too. A feeling of indignation creeps over me as I think, "Knowing the time of my return, she might have managed to be indoors." I have returned to the silent sitting-room, where the only noise is the wind still playing hide-and-seek with the curtains. As I look vacantly round my eye catches sight of a letter lying on the table. I pick it up mechanically and look at the address. Good heavens! what can this mean? It is my own, that I sent her two days ago, unopened, with the seal unbroken. Does she carry her resentment so far as not even to open my letters? I spring at the bell and violently ring it. It is answered by the waiter who has always specially attended us.

"Is madame gone out?"

The man opens his mouth and stares at me.

"Madame! Is monsieur then not aware that madame is no longer at the hotel?"

"*What?*"

"On the same day as monsieur, madame departed."

"*Departed!* Good God! what are you talking about?"

"A few hours after monsieur's departure—I will not be positive as to the exact time, but it must have been between one and two o'clock as the midday *table d'hôte* was in progress—a gentleman came and asked for madame—"

"Yes—be quick."

"I demanded whether I should take up his card, but he said 'No,' that was unnecessary, as he was perfectly well known to madame; and, in fact, a short time afterwards, without saying anything to anyone, she departed with him."

"And did not return in the evening?"

"No, monsieur; madame has not returned since that day."

I clench my hands in an agony of rage and grief. "So this is it! With that pure child-face, with that divine ignorance—only three weeks married—this is the trick she has played me!" I am recalled to myself by a compassionate suggestion from the garçon.

"Perhaps it was the brother of madame."

Elizabeth has no brother, but the remark brings back to me the necessity of self-command. "Very probably," I answer, speaking with infinite difficulty. "What sort of looking gentleman was he?"

"He was a very tall and dark gentleman with a most peculiar nose—not quite like any nose that I ever saw before—and most singular eyes. Never have I seen a gentleman who at all resembled him."

I sink into a chair, while a cold shudder creeps over me as I think of my poor child's dream—of her fainting fit at Wiesbaden—of her unconquerable dread of and aversion from my departure. And this happened twelve days ago! I catch up my hat, and prepare to rush like a madman in pursuit.

"How did they go?" I ask incoherently; "by train?—driving?—walking?"

"They went in a carriage."

"What direction did they take? Whither did they go?"

He shakes his head. "It is not known."

"It *must* be known," I cry, driven to frenzy by every second's delay. "Of course the driver could tell; where is he?—where can I find him?"

"He did not belong to Lucerne, neither did the carriage; the gentleman brought them with him."

"But madame's maid," say I, a gleam of hope flashing across my mind; "did she go with her?"

"No, monsieur, she is still here; she was as much surprised as monsieur at madame's departure."

"Send her at once," I cry eagerly; but when she comes I find that she can throw no light on the matter. She weeps noisily and says many irrelevant things, but I can obtain no information from her beyond the fact that she was unaware of her mistress's departure until long after it had taken place, when, surprised at not being rung for at the usual time, she had gone to her room and found it empty, and on inquiring in the hotel, had heard of her sudden departure; that, expecting her to return at night, she had sat up waiting for her till two o'clock in the morning, but that, as I knew, she had not returned, neither had anything since been heard of her.

Not all my inquiries, not all my cross-questionings of the whole staff of the hotel, of the visitors, of the railway officials, of nearly all the inhabitants of Lucerne and its environs, procure me a jot more knowledge. On the next few weeks I look back as on a hellish and insane dream. I can neither eat nor sleep; I am unable to remain one moment quiet; my whole existence, my nights and my days, are spent in seeking, seeking. Everything that human despair and frenzied love can do is done by me. I advertise, I communicate with the police, I employ detectives; but that fatal twelve days' start for ever baffles me. Only on one occasion do I obtain one tittle of information. In a village a few miles from Lucerne the peasants, on the day in question, saw a carriage driving rapidly through their little street. It was closed, but through the windows they could see the occupants—a dark gentleman, with the peculiar physiognomy which has been so often described, and on the opposite seat a lady lying apparently in a state of utter insensibility. But even this leads to nothing.

Oh, reader, these things happened twenty years ago; since then I have searched sea and land, but never have I seen my little Elizabeth again.

Julian Hawthorne

Julian Hawthorne (*1846–1934*) was the son of Nathaniel Hawthorne, and throughout most of his life he was under the blighting shadow of his father's genius. His education was irregular, what with his father's educational theories, family travels, and general rebelliousness. In his young manhood he followed engineering as a career, but when this failed, he turned to writing, where his facility and gift for sensationalism made him a valued contributor to the periodicals. He wrote many short stories, novels, essays, and critical works, much of which, as he frankly admitted, was hackwork and is now deservedly forgotten. In his later life, as can be seen even in his fiction, he became obsessed with get-rich-quick schemes, particularly in mining and land development, and after an unfortunate venture with Canadian mining stock he was tried for fraudulent use of the mails and was imprisoned for several months in the federal penitentiary at Atlanta. On his release he returned to literature.

Although Julian Hawthorne did not inherit his father's genius and wrote for the moment, some of his work has permanent value. His study Nathaniel Hawthorne and His Wife (*1884*) is a basic document, while his editions of Nathaniel Hawthorne's "Elixir of Life" manuscripts were useful until recently superseded by more scholarly editions. As for his fiction, his contemporaries and many modern critics agree that the short novel Archibald Malmaison (*1884*), a psychological horror story about fugues of memory, is his best work. He also wrote many stories in the area where occultism, science fiction, and supernatural fiction overlap. Many of these stories still have not been reprinted since their original appearance in periodicals.

KEN'S MYSTERY

One cool October evening—it was the last day of the month, and un-usually cool for the time of year—I made up my mind to go and spend an hour or two with my friend Keningale. Keningale was an artist (as well as a musical amateur and poet), and had a very delightful studio built onto his house, in which he was wont to sit of an evening. The studio had a cavernous fire-place, designed in imitation of the old-fashioned fire-places of Elizabethan manor-houses, and in it, when the temperature out-doors warranted, he would build up a cheerful fire of dry logs. It would suit me particularly well, I thought, to go and have a quiet pipe and chat in front of that fire with my friend.

I had not had such a chat for a very long time—not, in fact, since Keningale (or Ken, as his friends called him) had returned from his visit to Europe the year before. He went abroad, as he affirmed at the time, "for purposes of study," whereat we all smiled, for Ken, as far as we knew him, was more likely to do anything else than to study. He was a young fellow of buoyant temperament, lively and social in his habits, of a brilliant and versatile mind, and possessing an income of twelve or fifteen thousand dollars a year; he could sing, play, scribble, and paint very cleverly, and some of his heads and figure-pieces were really well done, considering that he never had any regular training in art; but he was not a worker. Personally he was fine-looking, of good height and figure, active, healthy, and with a remarkably fine brow, and clear, full-gazing eye. Nobody was surprised at his going to Europe, nobody expected him to do anything there except amuse himself, and few anticipated that he would be soon again seen in New York. He was one of the sort that find Europe agree with them. Off he went, therefore; and in the course of a few months the rumor reached us that he was engaged to a handsome and wealthy New York

girl whom he had met in London. This was nearly all we did hear
of him until, not very long afterward, he turned up again on Fifth
Avenue, to every one's astonishment; made no satisfactory answer to
those who wanted to know how he happened to tire so soon of the
Old World; while, as to the reported engagement, he cut short all
allusion to that in so peremptory a manner as to show that it was not
a permissible topic of conversation with him. It was surmised that the
lady had jilted him; but, on the other hand, she herself returned home
not a great while after, and, though she had plenty of opportunities,
she has never married to this day.

Be the rights of that matter what they may, it was soon remarked
that Ken was no longer the careless and merry fellow he used to be; on
the contrary, he appeared grave, moody, averse from general society,
and habitually taciturn and undemonstrative even in the company of
his most intimate friends. Evidently something had happened to him,
or he had done something. What? Had he committed a murder? or
joined the Nihilists? or was his unsuccessful love affair at the bottom
of it? Some declared that the cloud was only temporary, and would
soon pass away. Nevertheless, up to the period of which I am writing,
it had not passed away, but had rather gathered additional gloom, and
threatened to become permanent.

Meanwhile I had met him twice or thrice at the club, at the opera,
or in the street, but had as yet had no opportunity of regularly re-
newing my acquaintance with him. We had been on a footing of
more than common intimacy in the old days, and I was not disposed to
think that he would refuse to renew the former relations now. But
what I had heard and myself seen of his changed condition imparted
a stimulating tinge of suspense or curiosity to the pleasure with which
I looked forward to the prospects of this evening. His house stood at
a distance of two or three miles beyond the general range of habita-
tions in New York at this time, and as I walked briskly along in the
clear twilight air I had leisure to go over in my mind all that I had
known of Ken and had divined of his character. After all, had there
not always been something in his nature—deep down, and held in
abeyance by the activity of his animal spirits—but something strange
and separate, and capable of developing under suitable conditions into
—into what? As I asked myself this question I arrived at his door; and
it was with a feeling of relief that I felt the next moment the cordial
grasp of his hand, and his voice bidding me welcome in a tone that
indicated unaffected gratification at my presence. He drew me at once
into the studio, relieved me of my hat and cane, and then put his hand
on my shoulder.

"I am glad to see you," he repeated, with singular earnestness—"glad to see you and to feel you; and to-night of all nights in the year."

"Why to-night especially?"

"Oh, never mind. It's just as well, too, you didn't let me know beforehand you were coming; the unreadiness is all, to paraphrase the poet. Now, with you to help me, I can drink a glass of whisky and water and take a bit draw of the pipe. This would have been a grim night for me if I'd been left to myself."

"In such a lap of luxury as this, too!" said I, looking round at the glowing fire-place, the low, luxurious chairs, and all the rich and sumptuous fittings of the room. "I should have thought a condemned murderer might make himself comfortable here."

"Perhaps; but that's not exactly my category at present. But have you forgotten what night this is? This November-eve, when, as tradition asserts, the dead arise and walk about, and fairies, goblins, and spiritual beings of all kinds have more freedom and power than on any other day of the year. One can see you've never been in Ireland."

"I wasn't aware till now that you had been there, either."

"Yes, I have been in Ireland. Yes—" He paused, sighed, and fell into a reverie, from which, however, he soon roused himself by an effort, and went to a cabinet in a corner of the room for the liquor and tobacco. While he was thus employed I sauntered about the studio, taking note of the various beauties, grotesquenesses, and curiosities that it contained. Many things were there to repay study and arouse admiration; for Ken was a good collector, having excellent taste as well as means to back it. But, upon the whole, nothing interested me more than some studies of a female head, roughly done in oils, and, judging from the sequestered positions in which I found them, not intended by the artist for exhibition or criticism. There were three or four of these studies, all of the same face, but in different poses and costumes. In one the head was enveloped in a dark hood, overshadowing and partly concealing the features; in another she seemed to be peering duskily through a latticed casement, lit by a faint moonlight; a third showed her splendidly attired in evening costume, with jewels in her hair and ears, and sparkling on her snowy bosom. The expressions were as various as the poses; now it was demure penetration, now a subtle inviting glance, now burning passion, and again a look of elfish and elusive mockery. In whatever phase, the countenance possessed a singular and poignant fascination, not of beauty merely, though that was very striking, but of character and quality likewise.

"Did you find this model abroad?" I inquired at length. "She has evidently inspired you, and I don't wonder at it."

Ken, who had been mixing the punch, and had not noticed my movements, now looked up, and said: "I didn't mean those to be seen. They
don't satisfy me, and I am going to destroy them; but I couldn't rest
till I'd made some attempts to reproduce— What was it you asked?
Abroad? Yes—or no. They were all painted here within the last six
weeks."

"Whether they satisfy you or not, they are by far the best things of
yours I have ever seen."

"Well, let them alone, and tell me what you think of this beverage.
To my thinking, it goes to the right spot. It owes its existence to your
coming here. I can't drink alone, and those portraits are not company,
though, for aught I know, she might have come out of the canvas to-
night and sat down in that chair." Then, seeing my inquiring look, he
added, with a hasty laugh, "It's November-eve, you know, when anything may happen, provided it's strange enough. Well, here's to ourselves."

We each swallowed a deep draught of the smoking and aromatic
liquor, and set down our glasses with approval. The punch was excellent. Ken now opened a box of cigars, and we seated ourselves before
the fire-place.

"All we need now," I remarked, after a short silence, "is a little
music. By-the-by, Ken, have you still got the banjo I gave you before
you went abroad?"

He paused so long before replying that I supposed he had not heard
my question. "I have got it," he said, at length, "but it will never make
any more music."

"Got broken, eh? Can't it be mended? It was a fine instrument."

"It's not broken, but it's past mending. You shall see for yourself."

He arose as he spoke, and going to another part of the studio, opened
a black oak coffer, and took out of it a long object wrapped up in a
piece of faded yellow silk. He handed it to me, and when I had un-
wrapped it, there appeared a thing that might once have been a
banjo, but had little resemblance to one now. It bore every sign of
extreme age. The wood of the handle was honey-combed with the
gnawing of worms, and dusty with dry-rot. The parchment head was
green with mold, and hung in shriveled tatters. The hoop, which was of
solid silver, was so blackened and tarnished that it looked like dilapidated iron. The strings were gone, and most of the tuning-screws had
dropped out of their decayed sockets. Altogether it had the appearance of having been made before the Flood, and been forgotten in the
forecastle of Noah's Ark ever since.

"It is a curious relic, certainly," I said. "Where did you come across
it? I had no idea that the banjo was invented so long ago as this. It

certainly can't be less than two hundred years old, and may be much older than that."

Ken smiled gloomily. "You are quite right," he said; "it is at least two hundred years old, and yet it is the very same banjo that you gave me a year ago."

"Hardly," I returned, smiling in my turn, "since that was made to my order with a view to presenting it to you."

"I know that; but the two hundred years have passed since then. Yes; it is absurd and impossible, I know, but nothing is truer. That banjo, which was made last year, existed in the sixteenth century, and has been rotting ever since. Stay. Give it to me a moment, and I'll convince you. You recollect that your name and mine, with the date, were engraved on the silver hoop?"

"Yes; and there was a private mark of my own there, also."

"Very well," said Ken, who had been rubbing a place on the hoop with a corner of the yellow silk wrapper; "look at that."

I took the decrepit instrument from him, and examined the spot which he had rubbed. It was incredible, sure enough; but there were the names and the date precisely as I had caused them to be engraved; and there, moreover, was my own private mark, which I had idly made with an old etching point not more than eighteen months before. After convincing myself that there was no mistake, I laid the banjo across my knees, and stared at my friend in bewilderment. He sat smoking with a kind of grim composure, his eyes fixed upon the blazing logs.

"I'm mystified, I confess," said I. "Come; what is the joke? What method have you discovered of producing the decay of centuries on this unfortunate banjo in a few months? And why did you do it? I have heard of an elixir to counteract the effects of time, but your recipe seems to work the other way—to make time rush forward at two hundred times his usual rate, in one place, while he jogs on at his usual gait elsewhere. Unfold your mystery, magician. Seriously, Ken, how on earth did the thing happen?"

"I know no more about it than you do," was his reply. "Either you and I and all the rest of the living world are insane, or else there has been wrought a miracle strange as any in tradition. How can I explain it? It is a common saying—a common experience, if you will—that we may, on certain trying or tremendous occasions, live years in one moment. But that's a mental experience, not a physical one, and one that applies, at all events, only to human beings, not to senseless things of wood and metal. You imagine the thing is some trick or jugglery. If it be, I don't know the secret of it. There's no chemical appliance that I ever heard of that will get a piece of solid wood into that condition in a few months, or a few years. And it wasn't done in a few years, or a few months either. A year ago to-day at this very hour that banjo was as sound as when it left the maker's hands, and twenty-four hours afterward—I'm telling you the simple truth—it was as you see it now."

The gravity and earnestness with which Ken made this astounding statement were evidently not assumed. He believed every word that he uttered. I knew not what to think. Of course my friend might be insane, though he betrayed none of the ordinary symptoms of mania; but, however that might be, there was the banjo, a witness whose silent testimony there was no gainsaying. The more I meditated on the matter the more inconceivable did it appear. Two hundred years—twenty-four hours; these were the terms of the proposed equation. Ken and the banjo both affirmed that the equation had been made; all worldly knowledge and experience affirmed it to be impossible. What was the explanation? What is time? What is life? I felt myself beginning to doubt the reality of all things. And so this was the mystery which my friend had been brooding over since his return from abroad. No wonder it had changed him. More to be wondered at was it that it had not changed him more.

"Can you tell me the whole story?" I demanded at length.

Ken quaffed another draught from his glass of whisky and water and rubbed his hand through his thick brown beard. "I have never spoken to any one of it heretofore," he said, "and I had never meant to speak of it. But I'll try and give you some idea of what it was. You know me better than any one else; you'll understand the thing as far as it can ever be understood, and perhaps I may be relieved of some of the oppression it has caused me. For it is rather a ghastly memory to grapple with alone, I can tell you."

Hereupon, without further preface, Ken related the following tale. He was, I may observe in passing, a naturally fine narrator. There were deep, lingering tones in his voice, and he could strikingly enhance the comic or pathetic effect of a sentence by dwelling here and there upon some syllable. His features were equally susceptible of humorous and of solemn expressions, and his eyes were in form and hue wonderfully adapted to showing great varieties of emotion. Their mournful aspect was extremely earnest and affecting; and when Ken was giving utterance to some mysterious passage of the tale they had a doubtful, melancholy, exploring look which appealed irresistibly to the imagination. But the interest of his story was too pressing to allow of noticing these incidental embellishments at the time, though they doubtless had their influence upon me all the same.

"I left New York on an Inman Line steamer, you remember," began

Ken, "and landed at Havre. I went the usual round of sight-seeing on the Continent, and got round to London in July, at the height of the season. I had good introductions, and met any number of agreeable and famous people. Among others was a young lady, a countrywoman of my own—you know whom I mean—who interested me very much, and before her family left London she and I were engaged. We parted there for the time, because she had the Continental trip still to make, while I wanted to take the opportunity to visit the north of England and Ireland. I landed at Dublin about the 1st of October, and, zigzagging about the country, I found myself in County Cork about two weeks later.

"There is in that region some of the most lovely scenery that human eyes ever rested on, and it seems to be less known to tourists than many places of infinitely less picturesque value. A lonely region too: during my rambles I met not a single stranger like myself, and few enough natives. It seems incredible that so beautiful a country should be so deserted. After walking a dozen Irish miles you come across a group of two or three one-roomed cottages, and, like as not, one or more of these will have the roof off and the walls in ruins. The few peasants whom one sees, however, are affable and hospitable, especially when they hear you are from that terrestrial heaven whither most of their friends and relatives have gone before them. They seem simply and primitive enough at first sight, and yet they are as strange and incomprehensible a race as any in the world. They are as superstitious, as credulous of marvels, fairies, magicians, and omens, as the men whom St. Patrick preached to, and at the same time they are shrewd, skeptical, sensible, and bottomless liars. Upon the whole, I met with no nation on my travels whose company I enjoyed so much, or who inspired me with so much kindliness, curiosity, and repugnance.

"At length I got to a place on the sea-coast, which I will not further specify than to say that it is not many miles from Ballymacheen, on the south shore. I have seen Venice and Naples, I have driven along the Cornice Road, I have spent a month at our own Mount Desert, and I say that all of them together are not so beautiful as this glowing, deep-hued, soft-gleaming, silvery-lighted, ancient harbor and town, with the tall hills crowding round it and the black cliffs and headlands planting their iron feet in the blue, transparent sea. It is a very old place, and has had a history which it has outlived ages since. It may once have had two or three thousand inhabitants; it has scarce five or six hundred to-day. Half the houses are in ruins or have disappeared; many of the remainder are standing empty. All the people are poor, most of them abjectly so; they saunter about with bare feet and uncovered heads, the women in quaint black or dark-blue cloaks, the men in such anomalous attire as only an Irishman knows how to get together, the children half naked. The only comfortable-looking people are the monks and the priests, and the soldiers in the fort. For there is a fort there, constructed on the huge ruins of one which may have done duty in the reign of Edward the Black Prince, or earlier, in whose mossy embrasures are mounted a couple of cannon, which occasionally sent a practice-shot or two at the cliff on the other side of the harbor. The garrison consists of a dozen men and three or four officers and non-commissioned officers. I suppose they are relieved occasionally, but those I saw seemed to have become component parts of their surroundings.

"I put up at a wonderful little old inn, the only one in the place, and took my meals in a dining-saloon fifteen feet by nine, with a portrait of George I (a print varnished to preserve it) hanging over the mantel-piece. On the second evening after dinner a young gentleman came in—the dining-saloon being public property of course—and ordered some bread and cheese and a bottle of Dublin stout. We presently fell into talk; he turned out to be an officer from the fort, Lieutenant O'Connor, and a fine young specimen of the Irish soldier he was. After telling me all he knew about the town, the surrounding country, his friends, and himself, he intimated a readiness to sympathize with whatever tale I might choose to pour into his ear; and I had pleasure in trying to rival his own outspokenness. We became excellent friends; we had up a half-pint of Kinahan's whisky, and the lieutenant expressed himself in terms of high praise of my countrymen, my country, and my own particular cigars. When it became time for him to depart I accompanied him—for there was a splendid moon abroad— and bade him farewell at the fort entrance, having promised to come over the next day and make the acquaintance of the other fellows. 'And mind your eye, now, going back, my dear boy,' he called out, as I turned my face homeward. 'Faith, 'tis a spooky place, that graveyard, and you'll as likely meet the black woman there as anywhere else!'

"The graveyard was a forlorn and barren spot on the hill-side, just the hither side of the fort: thirty or forty rough head-stones, few of which retained any semblance of the perpendicular, while many were so shattered and decayed as to seem nothing more than irregular natural projections from the ground. Who the black woman might be I knew not, and did not stay to inquire. I had never been subject to ghostly apprehensions, and as a matter of fact, though the path I had to follow was in places very bad going, not to mention a hap-hazard scramble over a ruined bridge that covered a deep-lying brook, I reached my inn without any adventure whatever.

"The next day I kept my appointment at the fort, and found no reason to regret it; and my friendly sentiments were abundantly re-ciprocated, thanks more especially, perhaps, to the success of my banjo, which I carried with me, and which was as novel as it was popular with those who listened to it. The chief personages in the social circle be-sides my friend the lieutenant were Major Molloy, who was in com-mand, a racy and juicy old campaigner, with a face like a sunset, and the surgeon, Dr. Dudeen, a long, dry, humorous genius, with a wealth of anecdotical and traditional lore at his command that I have never seen surpassed. We had a jolly time of it, and it was the precursor of many more like it. The remains of October slipped away rapidly, and I was obliged to remember that I was a traveler in Europe, and not a resident in Ireland. The major, the surgeon, and the lieutenant all protested cordially against my proposed departure, but, as there was no help for it, they arranged a farewell dinner to take place in the fort on All-halloween.

"I wish you could have been at that dinner with me! It was the essence of Irish good-fellowship. Dr. Dudeen was in great force; the major was better than the best of Lever's novels; the lieutenant was overflowing with hearty good-humor, merry chaff, and sentimental rhapsodies anent this or the other pretty girl of the neighborhood. For my part I made the banjo ring as it had never rung before, and the others joined in the chorus with a mellow strength of lungs such as you don't often hear outside of Ireland. Among the stories that Dr. Dudeen regaled us with was one about the Kern of Querin and his wife, Ethelind Fionguala—which being interpreted signifies 'the white-shouldered.' The lady, it appears, was originally betrothed to one O'Connor (here the lieutenant smacked his lips), but was stolen away on the wedding night by a party of vampires, who, it would seem, were at that period a prominent feature among the troubles of Ireland. But as they were bearing her along—she being unconscious—to that supper where she was not to eat but to be eaten, the young Kern of Querin, who happened to be out duck-shooting, met the party, and emptied his gun at it. The vampires fled, and the Kern carried the fair lady, still in a state of insensibility, to his house. 'And by the same token, Mr. Keningale,' observed the doctor, knocking the ashes out of his pipe, 've're after passing that very house on your way here. The one with the dark archway underneath it, and the big mullioned window at the corner, ye recollect, hanging over the street as I might say—'

" 'Go 'long wid the house, Dr. Dudeen, dear,' interrupted the lieutenant; 'sure can't you see we're all dying to know what happened to sweet Miss Fionguala, God be good to her, when I was after getting her safe up-stairs—'

" 'Faith, then, I can tell ye that myself, Mr. O'Connor,' exclaimed the major, imparting a rotary motion to the remnants of whisky in his tumbler. ' 'Tis a question to be solved on general principles, as Colonel O'Halloran said that time he was asked what he'd do if he'd been the Dook o' Wellington, and the Prussians hadn't come up in the nick o' time at Waterloo. 'Faith,' says the colonel, 'I'll tell ye—'

" 'Arrah, then, major, why would ye be interruptin' the doctor, and Mr. Keningale there lettin' his glass stay empty till he hears— The Lord save us! the bottle's empty!'

"In the excitement consequent upon this discovery, the thread of the doctor's story was lost; and before it could be recovered the evening had advanced so far that I felt obliged to withdraw. It took some time to make my proposition heard and comprehended; and a still longer time to put it in execution; so that it was fully midnight before I found myself standing in the cool pure air outside the fort, with the farewells of my boon companions ringing in my ears.

"Considering that it had been rather a wet evening in-doors, I was in a remarkably good state of preservation, and I therefore ascribed it rather to the roughness of the road than to the smoothness of the liquor, when, after advancing a few rods, I stumbled and fell. As I picked myself up I fancied I had heard a laugh, and supposed that the lieutenant, who had accompanied me to the gate, was making merry over my mishap; but on looking round I saw that the gate was closed and no one was visible. The laugh, moreover, had seemed to be close at hand, and to be even pitched in a key that was rather feminine than masculine. Of course I must have been deceived; nobody was near me: my imagination had played me a trick, or else there was more truth than poetry in the tradition that Halloween is the carnival-time of dis-embodied spirits. It did not occur to me at the time that a stumble is held by the superstitious Irish to be an evil omen, and had I remembered it it would only have been to laugh at it. At all events, I was physically none the worse for my fall, and I resumed my way immediately.

"But the path was singularly difficult to find, or rather the path I was following did not seem to be the right one. I did not recognize it; I could have sworn (except I knew the contrary) that I had never seen it before. The moon had risen, though her light was yet obscured by clouds, but neither my immediate surroundings nor the general aspect of the region appeared familiar. Dark, silent hill-sides mounted up on either hand, and the road, for the most part, plunged downward, as if to conduct me into the bowels of the earth. The place was alive with strange echoes, so that at times I seemed to be walking through the midst of muttering voices and mysterious whispers, and a wild, faint sound of laughter seemed ever and anon to reverberate among the passes of the hills. Currents of colder air sighing up through narrow defiles and dark crevices touched my face as with airy fingers. A certain feeling of anxiety and insecurity began to take possession of me, though there was no definable cause for it, unless that I might be belated in getting home. With the perverse instinct of those who are lost I hastened my steps, but was impelled now and then to glance back over my shoulder, with a sensation of being pursued. But no living creature was in sight. The moon, however, had now risen higher, and the clouds that were drifting slowly across the sky flung into the naked valley dusky shadows, which occasionally assumed shapes that looked like the vague semblance of gigantic human forms.

"How long I had been hurrying onward I know not, when, with a kind of suddenness, I found myself approaching a graveyard. It was situated on the spur of a hill, and there was no fence around it, nor anything to protect it from the incursions of passers-by. There was something in the general appearance of this spot that made me half fancy I had seen it before; and I should have taken it to be the same that I had often noticed on my way to the fort, but that the latter was only a few hundred yards distant therefrom, whereas I must have traversed several miles at least. As I drew near, moreover, I observed that the head-stones did not appear so ancient and decayed as those of the other. But what chiefly attracted my attention was the figure that was leaning or half sitting upon one of the largest of the upright slabs near the road. It was a female figure draped in black, and a closer inspection —for I was soon within a few yards of her—showed that she wore the calla, or long hooded cloak, the most common as well as the most ancient garment of Irish women, and doubtless of Spanish origin.

"I was a trifle startled by this apparition, so unexpected as it was, and so strange did it seem that any human creature should be at that hour of the night in so desolate and sinister a place. Involuntarily I paused as I came opposite her, and gazed at her intently. But the moonlight fell behind her, and the deep hood of her cloak so completely shadowed her face that I was unable to discern anything but the sparkle of a pair of eyes, which appeared to be returning my gaze with much vivacity.

" 'You seem to be at home here,' I said, at length. 'Can you tell me where I am?'

"Hereupon the mysterious personage broke into a light laugh, which, though in itself musical and agreeable, was of a timbre and intonation that caused my heart to beat rather faster than my late pedestrian exertions warranted; for it was the identical laugh (or so my imagination persuaded me) that had echoed in my ears as I arose from my tumble an hour or two ago. For the rest, it was the laugh of a young woman, and presumably of a pretty one; and yet it had a wild, airy, mocking quality, that seemed hardly human at all, or not, at any rate, characteristic of a being of affections and limitations like unto ours. But this impression of mine was fostered, no doubt, by the unusual and uncanny circumstances of the occasion.

"'Sure, sir,' said she, 'you're at the grave of Ethelind Fionguala.'

"As she spoke she rose to her feet, and pointed to the inscription on the stone. I bent forward, and was able, without much difficulty, to decipher the name, and a date which indicated that the occupant of the grave must have entered the disembodied state between two and three centuries ago.

"'And who are you?' was my next question.

"'I'm called Elsie,' she replied. 'But where would your honor be going November-eve?'

"I mentioned my destination, and asked her whether she could direct me thither.

"'Indeed, then, 'tis there I'm going myself,' Elsie replied; 'and if your honor'll follow me, and play me a tune on the pretty instrument, 'tisn't long we'll be on the road.'

"She pointed to the banjo which I carried wrapped up under my arm. How she knew that it was a musical instrument I could not imagine; possibly, I thought, she may have seen me playing on it as I strolled about the environs of the town. Be that as it may, I offered no opposition to the bargain, and further intimated that I would reward her more substantially on our arrival. At that she laughed again, and made a peculiar gesture with her hand above her head. I uncovered my banjo, swept my fingers across the strings, and struck into a fantastic dance-measure, to the music of which we proceeded along the path, Elsie slightly in advance, her feet keeping time to the airy measure. In fact, she trod so lightly, with an elastic, undulating movement, that with a little more it seemed as if she might float onward like a spirit. The extreme whiteness of her feet attracted my eye, and I was surprised to find that instead of being bare, as I had supposed, these were incased in white satin slippers quaintly embroidered with gold thread.

"'Elsie,' said I, lengthening my steps so as to come up with her, 'where do you live, and what do you do for a living?'

"'Sure, I live by myself,' she answered; 'and if you'd be after knowing how, you must come and see for yourself.'

"'Are you in the habit of walking over the hills at night in shoes like that?'

"'And why would I not?' she asked, in her turn. 'And where did your honor get the pretty gold ring on your finger?'

"The ring, which was of no great intrinsic value, had struck my eye in an old curiosity-shop in Cork. It was an antique of very old-fashioned design, and might have belonged (as the vender assured me was the case) to one of the early kings or queens of Ireland.

" 'Do you like it?' said I.

" 'Will your honor be after making a present of it to Elsie?' she returned, with an insinuating tone and turn of the head.

" 'Maybe I will, Elsie, on one condition. I am an artist; I make pictures of people. If you will promise to come to my studio and let me paint your portrait, I'll give you the ring, and some money besides.'

" 'And will you give me the ring now?' said Elsie.

" 'Yes, if you'll promise.'

" 'And will you play the music to me?' she continued.

" 'As much as you like.'

" 'But maybe I'll not be handsome enough for ye,' said she, with a glance of her eyes beneath the dark hood.

" 'I'll take the risk of that,' I answered, laughing, 'though, all the same, I don't mind taking a peep beforehand to remember you by.' So saying, I put forth a hand to draw back the concealing hood. But Elsie eluded me, I scarce know how, and laughed a third time, with the same airy, mocking cadence.

" 'Give me the ring first, and then you shall see me,' she said, coaxingly.

" 'Stretch out your hand, then,' returned I, removing the ring from my finger. 'When we are better acquainted, Elsie, you won't be so suspicious.'

"She held out a slender, delicate hand, on the forefinger of which I slipped the ring. As I did so, the folds of her cloak fell a little apart, affording me a glimpse of a white shoulder and of a dress that seemed in that deceptive semi-darkness to be wrought of rich and costly material; and I caught, too, or so I fancied, the frosty sparkle of precious stones.

" 'Arrah, mind where ye tread!' said Elsie, in a sudden, sharp tone.

"I looked round, and became aware for the first time that we were standing near the middle of a ruined bridge which spanned a rapid stream that flowed at a considerable depth below. The parapet of the bridge on one side was broken down, and I must have been, in fact, in imminent danger of stepping over into empty air. I made my way cautiously across the decaying structure; but, when I turned to assist Elsie, she was nowhere to be seen.

"What had become of the girl? I called, but no answer came. I gazed about on every side, but no trace of her was visible. Unless she had plunged into the narrow abyss at my feet, there was no place where she could have concealed herself—none at least that I could discover. She had vanished, nevertheless; and since her disappearance must have been premeditated, I finally came to the conclusion that it was useless to attempt to find her. She would present herself again in her own good time, or not at all. She had given me the slip very cleverly, and I must make the best of it. The adventure was perhaps worth the ring.

"On resuming my way, I was not a little relieved to find that I once more knew where I was. The bridge that I had just crossed was none other than the one I mentioned some time back; I was within a mile of the town, and my way lay clear before me. The moon, moreover, had now quite dispersed the clouds, and shone down with exquisite brilliance. Whatever her other failings, Elsie had been a trustworthy guide; she had brought me out of the depth of elf-land into the material world again. It had been a singular adventure, certainly, and I mused over it with a sense of mysterious pleasure as I sauntered along, humming snatches of airs, and accompanying myself on the strings. Hark! what light step was that behind me? It sounded like Elsie's; but no, Elsie was not there. The same impression or hallucination, however, recurred several times before I reached the outskirts of the town— the tread of an airy foot behind or beside my own. The fancy did not make me nervous; on the contrary, I was pleased with the notion of being thus haunted, and gave myself up to a romantic and genial vein of reverie.

"After passing one or two roofless and moss-grown cottages, I entered the narrow and rambling street which leads through the town. This street a short distance down widens a little, as if to afford the way-farer space to observe a remarkable old house that stands on the northern side. The house was built of stone, and in a noble style of architecture; it reminded me somewhat of certain palaces of the old Italian nobility that I had seen on the Continent, and it may very probably have been built by one of the Italian or Spanish immigrants of the sixteenth or seventeenth century. The molding of the projecting windows and arched doorway was richly carved, and upon the front of the building was an escutcheon wrought in high relief, though I could not make out the purport of the device. The moonlight falling upon this picturesque pile enhanced all its beauties, and at the same time made it seem like a vision that might dissolve away when the light ceased to shine. I must often have seen the house before, and yet I retained no definite recollection of it; I had never until now examined it with my eyes open, so to speak. Leaning against the wall on the opposite side of the street, I contemplated it for a long while at my leisure. The window at the corner was really a very fine and massive affair. It projected over the pavement below, throwing a heavy shadow aslant;

the frames of the diamond-paned lattices were heavily mullioned. How often in past ages had that lattice been pushed open by some fair hand, revealing the charming countenances of his high-born mistress! Those were brave days. They had passed away long since. The great house had stood empty for who could tell how many years; only bats and vermin were its inhabitants. Where now were those who had built it? and who were they? Probably the very name of them was forgotten.

"As I continued to stare upward, however, a conjecture presented itself to my mind which rapidly ripened into a conviction. Was not this the house that Dr. Dudeen had described that very evening as having been formerly the abode of the Kern of Querin and his mysterious bride? There was the projecting window, the arched doorway. Yes, beyond a doubt this was the very house. I emitted a low exclamation of renewed interest and pleasure, and my speculations took a still more imaginative, but also a more definite turn.

"What had been the fate of that lovely lady after the Kern had brought her home insensible in his arms? Did she recover, and were they married and made happy ever after; or had the sequel been a tragic one? I remembered to have read that the victims of vampires generally became vampires themselves. Then my thoughts went back to that grave on the hill-side. Surely that was unconsecrated ground. Why had they buried her there? Ethelind of the white shoulder! Ah! why had not I lived in those days; or why might not some magic cause them to live again for me? Then would I seek this street at midnight, and standing here beneath her window, I would lightly touch the strings of my bandore until the casement opened cautiously and she looked down. A sweet vision indeed! And who prevented my realizing it? Only a matter of a couple of centuries or so. And was time, then, at which poets and philosophers sneer, so rigid and real a matter that a little faith and imagination might not overcome it? At all events, I had my banjo, the bandore's legitimate and lineal descendant, and the memory of Fionguala should have the love-ditty.

"Hereupon, having returned the instrument, I launched forth into an old Spanish love-song, which I had met with in some moldy library during my travels, and had set to music of my own. I sang low, for the deserted street re-echoed the lightest sound, and what I sang must reach only my lady's ears. The words were warm with the fire of the ancient Spanish chivalry, and I threw into their expression all the passion of the lovers of romance. Surely Fionguala, the white-shouldered, would hear, and awaken from her sleep of centuries, and come to the latticed casement and look down! Hist! see yonder! What light—what shadow is that that seems to flit from room to room within the abandoned house, and now approaches the mullioned window? Are my eyes dazzled by the play of the moonlight, or does the casement move—does it open? Nay, this is no delusion; there is no error of the senses here. There is simply a woman, young, beautiful, and richly attired, bending forward from the window, and silently beckoning me to approach.

"Too much amazed to be conscious of amazement, I advanced until I stood directly beneath the casement, and the lady's face, as she stooped toward me, was not more than twice a man's height from my own. She smiled and kissed her finger-tips; something white fluttered in her hand, then fell through the air to the ground at my feet. The next moment she had withdrawn, and I heard the lattice close.

"I picked up what she had let fall; it was a delicate lace handkerchief, tied to the handle of an elaborately wrought bronze key. It was evidently the key of the house, and invited me to enter. I loosened it from the handkerchief, which bore a faint, delicious perfume, like the aroma of flowers in an ancient garden, and turned to the arched doorway. I felt no misgiving, and scarcely any sense of strangeness. All was as I had wished it to be, and as it should be; the mediæval age was alive once more, and as for myself, I almost felt the velvet cloak hanging from my shoulder and the long rapier dangling at my belt. Standing in front of the door I thrust the key into the lock, turned it, and felt the bolt yield. The next instant the door was opened, apparently from within; I stepped across the threshold, the door closed again, and I was alone in the house, and in darkness.

"Not alone, however! As I extended my hand to grope my way it was met by another hand, soft, slender, and cold, which insinuated itself gently into mine and drew me forward. Forward I went, nothing loath; the darkness was impenetrable, but I could hear the light rustle of a dress close to me, and the same delicious perfume that had emanated from the handkerchief enriched the air that I breathed, while the little hand that clasped and was clasped by my own alternately tightened and half relaxed the hold of its soft cold fingers. In this manner, and treading lightly, we traversed what I presumed to be a long, irregular passageway, and ascended a staircase. Then another corridor, until finally we paused, a door opened, emitting a flood of soft light, into which we entered, still hand in hand. The darkness and the doubt were at an end.

"The room was of imposing dimensions, and was furnished and decorated in a style of antique splendor. The walls were draped with mellow hues of tapestry; clusters of candles burned in polished silver sconces, and were reflected and multiplied in tall mirrors placed in the four corners of the room. The heavy beams of the dark oaken ceiling crossed each other in squares, and were laboriously carved; the curtains and the drapery of the chairs were of heavy-figured damask. At one end of the room was a broad ottoman, and in front of it a table, on which was set forth, in massive silver dishes, a sumptuous repast, with wines in crystal beakers. At the side was a vast and deep fire-place, with space enough on the broad hearth to burn whole trunks of trees. No fire, however, was there, but only a great heap of dead embers; and the room, for all its magnificence, was cold—cold as a tomb, or as my lady's hand—and it sent a subtle chill creeping to my heart.

"But my lady! how fair she was! I gave but a passing glance at the room; my eyes and my thoughts were all for her. She was dressed in white, like a bride; diamonds sparkled in her dark hair and on her snowy bosom; her lovely face and slender lips were pale, and all the paler for the dusky glow of her eyes. She gazed at me with a strange, elusive smile; and yet there was, in her aspect and bearing, something familiar in the midst of strangeness, like the burden of a song heard long ago and recalled among other conditions and surroundings. It seemed to me that something in me recognized her and knew her, had known her always. She was the woman of whom I had dreamed, whom I had beheld in visions, whose voice and face had haunted me from boyhood up. Whether we had ever met before, as human beings meet, I knew not; perhaps I had been blindly seeking her all over the world, and she had been awaiting me in this splendid room, sitting by those dead embers until all the warmth had gone out of her blood, only to be restored by the heat with which my love might supply her.

" 'I thought you had forgotten me,' she said, nodding as if in answer to my thought. 'The night was so late—our one night of the year! How my heart rejoiced when I heard your dear voice singing the song I know so well! Kiss me—my lips are cold!'

"Cold indeed they were—cold as the lips of death. But the warmth of my own seemed to revive them. They were now tinged with a faint color, and in her cheeks also appeared a delicate shade of pink. She drew fuller breath, as one who recovers from a long lethargy. Was it my life that was feeding her? I was ready to give her all. She drew me to the table and pointed to the viands and the wine.

" 'Eat and drink,' she said. 'You have traveled far, and you need food.'

" 'Will you eat and drink with me?' said I, pouring out the wine.

" 'You are the only nourishment I want,' was her answer. 'This wine is thin and cold. Give me wine as red as your blood and as warm, and I will drain a goblet to the dregs.'

"At these words, I know not why, a slight shiver passed through me. She seemed to gain vitality and strength at every instant, but the chill of the great room struck into me more and more.

"She broke into a fantastic flow of spirits, clapping her hands, and dancing about me like a child. Who was she? And was I myself, or was she mocking me when she implied that we had belonged to each other of old? At length she stood still before me, crossing her hands over her breast. I saw upon the forefinger of her right hand the gleam of an antique ring.

" 'Where did you get that ring?' I demanded.

"She shook her head and laughed. 'Have you been faithful?' she asked. 'It is my ring; it is the ring that unites us; it is the ring you gave when you loved me first. It is the ring of the Kern—the fairy ring, and I am your Ethelind—Ethelind Fionguala.'

" 'So be it,' I said, casting aside all doubt and fear, and yielding myself wholly to the spell of her inscrutable eyes and wooing lips. 'You are mine, and I am yours, and let us be happy while the hours last.'

" 'You are mine, and I am yours,' she repeated, nodding her head with an elfish smile. 'Come and sit beside me, and sing that sweet song again that you sang to me so long ago. Ah, now I shall live a hundred years.'

"We seated ourselves on the ottoman, and while she nestled luxuriously among the cushions, I took my banjo and sang to her. The song and the music resounded through the lofty room, and came back in throbbing echoes. And before me as I sang I saw the face and form of Ethelind Fionguala, in her jeweled bridal dress, gazing at me with burning eyes. She was pale no longer, but ruddy and warm, and life was like a flame within her. It was I who had become cold and bloodless, yet with the last life that was in me I would have sung to her of love that can never die. But at length my eyes grew dim, the room seemed to darken, the form of Ethelind alternately brightened and waxed indistinct, like the last flickerings of a fire; I swayed toward her, and felt myself lapsing into unconsciousness, with my head resting on her white shoulder."

Here Keningale paused a few moments in his story, flung a fresh log upon the fire, and then continued:

"I awoke, I know not how long afterward. I was in a vast, empty room in a ruined building. Rotten shreds of drapery depended from the walls, and heavy festoons of spiders' webs gray with dust covered the windows, which were destitute of glass or sash; they had been boarded up with rough planks which had themselves become rotten with age, and admitted through their holes and crevices pallid rays of light and chilly draughts of air. A bat, disturbed by these rays or by my own movement, detached himself from his hold on a remnant of moldy tapestry near me, and after circling dizzily around my head, wheeled the flickering noiselessness of his flight into a darker corner. As I arose unsteadily from the heap of miscellaneous rubbish on which I had been lying, something which had been resting across my knees fell to the floor with a rattle. I picked it up, and found it to be my banjo—as you see it now.

"Well, that is all I have to tell. My health was seriously impaired; all the blood seemed to have been drawn out of my veins; I was pale and haggard, and the chill— Ah, that chill," murmured Keningale, drawing nearer to the fire, and spreading out his hands to catch the warmth —"I shall never get over it; I shall carry it to my grave."

Mrs. J. H. Riddell

Mrs. J. H. Riddell (née Charlotte Eliza Lawson Cowan) (1832–1906) was born near Belfast, but spent most of her adult life in and around London. A professional author who wrote to support an ineffectual husband and pay his debts, she was known during her lifetime as the Novelist of the City, because of her novels set in the City of London. In such works as George Geith of Fen Court *(1864) she was among the first to show the romance of business matters. She was also a popular domestic novelist who wrote many works about the struggles of youth against hardship; these novels are exceptional in their realistic detail, although Victorian in certain values. Her work in this area has been compared to the early work of George Bernard Shaw.*

As a writer of supernatural fiction, Mrs. Riddell is regarded as second only to J. S. Le Fanu among the high Victorians. Her ghost stories were often the feature work in the Christmas annuals of the period. In addition to fourteen identified short stories (much of her work was done anonymously, and no record was kept), she wrote four successful supernatural novels, a noteworthy feat, since the traditional ghost novel is one of the most difficult forms to write well.

Mrs. Riddell's ghosts were mostly unquiet beings in search of the peace that justice will bring to them, but the stories in which they appeared were not thrillers. For Mrs. Riddell the ghost story was a mechanism for exploring a moral problem and a means for stating the evanescence of human life and the permanence of eternal values.

A TERRIBLE
VENGEANCE

CHAPTER ONE

Very Strange

Round Dockett Point and over Dumsey Deep the water-lilies were blooming as luxuriantly as though the silver Thames had been the blue Mummel Lake.

It was time for them. The hawthorn had long ceased to scent the air; the wild roses had shed their delicate leaves; the buttercups and carda-moms and dog-daisies that had dotted the meadows were garnered into hay. The world in early August needed a fresh and special beauty, and here it was floating in its matchless green bark on the bosom of the waters.

If those fair flowers, like their German sisters, ever at nightfall as-sumed mortal form, who was there to tell of such vagaries? Even when the moon is at her full there are few who care to cross Chertsey Mead, or face the lonely Stabbery.

Hard would it be, indeed, so near life, railways, civilization, and London, to find a more lonely stretch of country, when twilight visits the landscape and darkness comes brooding down over the Surrey and Middlesex shores, than the path which winds along the river from Shepperton Lock to Chertsey Bridge. At high noon for months to-gether it is desolate beyond description—silent, save for the rippling and sobbing of the currents, the wash of the stream, the swaying of the osiers, the trembling of an aspen, the rustle of the withies, or the noise made by a bird, or rat, or stoat, startled by the sound of unwonted footsteps. In the warm summer nights also, when tired holiday-makers are sleeping soundly, when men stretched on the green sward outside their white tents are smoking, and talking, and planning excursions for the morrow; when in country houses young people are playing and singing, dancing or walking up and down terraces over-looking well-kept lawns, where the evening air is laden with delicious perfumes—there falls on that almost uninhabited mile or two of riverside a stillness which may be felt, which the belated traveller is loth to disturb even by the dip of his oars as he drifts down with the current past objects that seem to him unreal as fragments of a dream.

It had been a wet summer—a bad summer for the hotels. There had been some fine days, but not many together. The weather could not be depended upon. It was not a season in which young ladies were to be met about the reaches of the Upper Thames, disporting themselves in marvellous dresses, and more marvellous headgear, unfurling brilliant parasols, canoeing in appropriate attire, giving life and colour to the streets of old-world villages, and causing many of their inhabitants to consider what a very strange sort of town it must be in which such extraordinarily-robed persons habitually reside.

Nothing of the sort was to be seen that summer, even as high as Hampton. Excursions were limited to one day; there were few tents, few people camping-out, not many staying at the hotels; yet it was, perhaps for that reason, an enjoyable summer to those who were not afraid of a little, or rather a great deal, of rain, who liked a village inn all the better for not being crowded, and who were not heart-broken because their women-folk for once found it impossible to accompany them.

Unless a man boldly decides to outrage the proprieties and decencies of life, and go off by himself to take his pleasure selfishly alone, there is in a fine summer no door of escape open to him. There was a time—a happy time—when a husband was not expected to sign away his holi-days in the marriage articles. But what boots it to talk of that remote past now? Everything is against the father of a family at present. Un-less the weather help him, what friend has he? and the weather does not often in these latter days prove a friend.

In that summer, however, with which this story deals, the stars in their courses fought for many an oppressed paterfamilias. Any curious inquirer might then have walked ankle-deep in mud from Penton Hook to East Molesey, and not met a man, harnessed like a beast of burden, towing all his belongings up stream, or beheld him rowing against wind and tide as though he were a galley-slave chained to the oar, striving all the while to look as though enjoying the fun.

Materfamilias found it too wet to patronize the Thames. Her dear little children also were conspicuous by their absence. Charming young ladies were rarely to be seen—indeed, the skies were so treacherous that it would have been a mere tempting of Providence to risk a pretty dress on the water; for which sufficient reasons furnished houses remained unlet, and lodgings were left empty; taverns and hotels welcomed visitors instead of treating them scurvily; and the river, with its green banks and its leafy aits, its white swans, its water-lilies, its purple loosestrife, its reeds, its rushes, its weeping willows, its quiet backwaters, was delightful.

One evening two men stood just outside the door of the Ship, Lower Halliford, looking idly at the water, as it flowed by more rapidly than is usually the case in August. Both were dressed in suits of serviceable dark grey tweed; both wore round hats; both evidently belonged to that class which resembles the flowers of the field but in the one respect that it toils not, neither does it spin; both looked intensely bored; both were of rather a good appearance.

The elder, who was about thirty, had dark hair, sleepy brown eyes, and a straight capable nose; a heavy moustache almost concealed his mouth, but his chin was firm and well cut. About him there was an indescribable something calculated to excite attention, but nothing in his expression to attract or repel. No one looking at him could have said offhand, "I think that is a pleasant fellow," or "I am sure that man could make himself confoundedly disagreeable."

His face revealed as little as the covers of a book. It might contain interesting matter, or there might be nothing underneath save the merest commonplace. So far as it conveyed an idea at all, it was that of indolence. Every movement of his body suggested laziness; but it would have been extremely hard to say how far that laziness went. Mental energy and physical inactivity walk oftener hand in hand than the world suspects, and mental energy can on occasion make an indolent man active, while mere brute strength can never confer intellect on one who lacks brains.

In every respect the younger stranger was the opposite of his companion. Fair, blue-eyed, light-haired, with soft moustache and tenderly cared-for whiskers, he looked exactly what he was—a very shallow, kindly, good fellow, who did not trouble himself with searching into the depths of things, who took the world as it was, who did not go out to meet trouble, who loved his species, women included, in an honest way; who liked amusement, athletic sports of all sorts—dancing, riding, rowing, shooting; who had not one regret, save that hours in a Government office were so confoundedly long, "eating the best part out of a day, by Jove;" no cause for discontent, save that he had very little money, and into whose mind it had on the afternoon in question been forcibly borne that his friend was a trifle heavy—"carries too many guns," he considered—"and not exactly the man to enjoy a modest dinner at Lower Halliford."

For which cause, perhaps, he felt rather relieved when his friend refused to partake of any meal.

"I wish you could have stayed," said the younger, with that earnest and not quite insincere hospitality people always assume when they feel a departing guest is not to be overpersuaded to stay.

"So do I," replied the other. "I should have liked to stop with *you*, and I should have liked to stay here. There is a sleepy dullness about the place which exactly suits my present mood, but I must get back to town. I promised Travers to look in at his chambers this evening, and to-morrow as I told you, I am due in Norfolk."

"What will you do, then, till train-time? There is nothing up from here till nearly seven. Come on the river for an hour with me."

"Thank you, no. I think I will walk over to Staines."

"Staines! Why Staines in heaven's name?"

Because I am in the humour for a walk—a long, lonely walk; because a demon has taken possession of me I wish to exorcise; because there are plenty of trains from Staines; because I am weary of the Thames Valley line, and any other reason you like. I can give you none better than I have done."

"At least let me row you part of the way."

"Again thank you, no. The eccentricities of the Thames are not new to me. With the best intentions, you would land me at Laleham when I should be on my (rail) way to London. My dear Dick, step into that boat your soul has been hankering after for the past half-hour, and leave me to return to town according to my own fancy."

"I don't half like this," said genial Dick. "Ah! here comes a pretty girl—look."

Thus entreated, the elder man turned his head and saw a young girl, accompanied by a young man, coming along the road, which leads from Walton Lane to Shepperton.

She was very pretty, of the sparkling order of beauty, with dark eyes, rather heavy eye-brows, dark thick hair, a ravishing fringe, a delicious hat, a coquettish dress, and shoes which by pretty gestures she seemed to be explaining to her companion were many—very many—sizes too large for her. Spite of her beauty, spite of her dress, spite of her shoes so much too large for her, it needed but a glance from one conversant with subtle social distinctions to tell that she was not quite her "young man's" equal.

For, in the parlance of Betsy Jane, as her "young man" she evidently regarded him, and as her young man he regarded himself. There could be no doubt about the matter. He was over head and ears in love with her; he was ready to quarrel—indeed, had quarreled with father, mother, sister, brother on her account. He loved her unreasonably—he loved her miserably, distractedly; except at odd intervals, he was not in the least happy with her. She flouted, she tormented, she maddened him; but then, after having driven him to the verge of distraction, she would repent sweetly, and make up for all previous shortcomings by a few brief minutes of tender affection. If quarreling be really the renewal of love, theirs had been renewed once a day at all events, and frequently much oftener.

Yes, she was a pretty girl, a bewitching girl, an arrant flirt, a scarcely well-behaved coquette; for as she passed the two friends she threw a glance at them, one arch, piquant, inviting glance, of which many would instantly have availed themselves, venturing the consequences certain to be dealt out by her companion, who, catching the look, drew closer to her side, not too well pleased, apparently. Spite of a little opposition, he drew her hand through his arm, and walked on with an air of possession infinitely amusing to onlookers, and plainly distasteful to his lady-love.

"A clear case of spoons," remarked the younger of the two visitors, looking after the pair.

"Poor devil!" said the other compassionately.

His friend laughed, and observed mockingly paraphrasing a very different speech,—

"But for the grace of God, there goes Paul Murray."

"You may strike out the 'but,'" replied the person so addressed, "for that is the very road Paul Murray is going, and soon."

"You are not serious!" asked the other doubtfully.

"Am I not? I am though, though not with such a vixen as I dare swear that little baggage is. I told you I was due to-morrow in Norfolk. But see, they are turning back; let us go inside."

"All right," agreed the other, following his companion into the hall. "This is a great surprise to me, Murray: I never imagined you were engaged."

"I am not engaged yet, though no doubt I shall soon be," answered the reluctant lover. "My grandmother and the lady's father have arranged the match. The lady does not object, I believe, and who am I, Savill, that I should refuse good looks, a good fortune, and a good temper?"

"You do not speak as though you liked the proposed bride, nevertheless," said Mr. Savill dubiously.

"I do not dislike her, I only hate having to marry her. Can't you understand that a man wants to pick a wife for himself—that the one girl he fancies seems worth ten thousand of a girl anybody else fancies?

But I am so situated— Hang it, Dick! what are you staring at that dark-eyed witch for?"

"Because it is so funny. She is making him take a boat at the steps, and he does not want to do it. Kindly observe his face."

"What is his face to me?" retorted Mr. Murray savagely.

"Not much, I daresay, but it is a good deal to him. It is black as thunder, and hers is not much lighter. What a neat ankle, and how you like to show it, my dear. Well, there is no harm in a pretty ankle or a pretty foot either, and you have both. One would not wish one's wife to have a hoof like an elephant. What sort of feet has your destined maiden, Paul?"

"I never noticed."

"That looks deucedly bad," said the younger man, shaking his head.

"I know, however, she has a pure, sweet face," observed Mr. Murray gloomily.

"No one could truthfully make the same statement about our young friend's little lady," remarked Mr. Savill, still gazing at the girl, who was seating herself in the stern. "A termagant, I'll be bound, if ever there was one. Wishes to go up stream, no doubt because he wishes to go down. Any caprice about the Norfolk 'fair'?"

"Not much, I think. She is good, Dick—too good for me," replied the other, sauntering out again.

"That is what we always say about the things we do not know. And so your grandmother has made up the match?"

"Yes: there is money, and the old lady loves money. She says she wants to see me settled—talks of buying me an estate. She will have to do something, because I am sure the stern parent on the other side would not allow his daughter to marry on expectations. The one drop of comfort in the arrangement is that my aged relative will have to come down, and pretty smartly too. I would wed Hecate, to end this state of bondage, which I have not courage to flee from myself. Dick, how I envy you who have no dead person's shoes to wait for!"

"You need not envy me," returned Dick, with conviction, "a poor unlucky devil chained to a desk. There is scarce a day of my life I fail to curse the service, the office, and Fate—"

"Curse no more, then," said the other; "rather go down on your knees and thank Heaven you have, without any merit of your own, a provision for life. I wish Fate or anybody had coached me into the Civil Service—apprenticed me to a trade—sent me to sea—made me enlist, instead of leaving me at the mercy of an old lady who knows neither justice nor reason—who won't let me do anything for myself, and won't do anything for me—who ought to have been dead long ago, but who never means to die—"

"And who often gives you in one cheque as much as the whole of my annual salary," added the other quietly.

"But you know you will have your yearly salary as long as you live. I never know whether I shall have another cheque."

"It won't do, my friend," answered Dick Savill; "you feel quite certain you can get money when you want it."

"I feel certain of no such thing," was the reply. "If I once offended her—" he stopped, and then went on: "And perhaps when I have spent twenty years in trying to humour such caprices as surely woman never had before, I shall wake one morning to find she has left every penny to the Asylum for Idiots."

"Why do you not pluck up courage, and strike out some line for yourself?"

"Too late, Dick, too late. Ten years ago I might have tried to make a fortune for myself, but I can't do that now. As I have waited so long, I must wait a little longer. At thirty a man can't take pick in hand and try to clear a road to fortune."

"Then you had better marry the Norfolk young lady."

"I am steadily determined to do so. I am going down with the firm intention of asking her."

"And do you think she will have you?"

"I think so. I feel sure she will. And she is a nice girl—the sort I would like for a wife, if she had not been thrust upon me."

Mr. Savill stood silent for a moment, with his hands plunged deep in his pockets.

"Then when I see you next?" he said tentatively.

"I shall be engaged, most likely—possibly even married," finished the other, with as much hurry as his manner was capable of. "And now jump into your boat, and I will go on my way to—Staines—"

"I wish you would change your mind, and have some dinner."

"I can't; it is impossible. You see I have so many things to do and to think of. Good-bye, Dick. Don't upset yourself—go down stream, and don't get into mischief with those dark eyes you admired so much just now."

"Make your mind easy about that," returned the other, colouring, however, a little as he spoke. "Good-bye, Murray. I wish you well through the campaign." And so, after a hearty hand-shake, they parted, one to walk away from Halliford, and past Shepperton Church, and across Shepperton Range, and the other, of course, to row up stream, through Shepperton Lock, and on past Dockett Point.

In the grey of the summer's dawn, Mr. Murray awoke next morning from a terrible dream. He had kept his appointment with Mr. Travers and a select party, played heavily, drank deeply, and reached

home between one and two, not much the better for his trip to Lower
Halliford, his walk, and his carouse.

Champagne, followed by neat brandy, is not perhaps the best thing
to insure a quiet night's rest; but Mr. Murray had often enjoyed sound
repose after similar libations; and it was, therefore, all the more unpleasant that in the grey dawn he should wake suddenly from a
dream, in which he thought some one was trying to crush his head with
a heavy weight.

Even when he had struggled from sleep, it seemed to him that a wet
dead hand lay across his eyes, and pressed them so hard he could not
move the lids. Under the weight he lay powerless, while a damp, ice-
cold hand felt burning into his brain, if such a contradictory expression
may be permitted.

The perspiration was pouring from him; he felt the drops falling
on his throat, and trickling down his neck; he might have been lying in
a bath, instead of on his own bed, and it was with a cry of horror he at
last flung the hand aside, and, sitting up, looked around the room, into
which the twilight of morning was mysteriously stealing.

Then, trembling in every limb, he lay down again, and fell into
another sleep, from which he did not awake till aroused by broad daylight and his valet.

"You told me to call you in good time, sir," said the man.

"Ah, yes, so I did," yawned Mr. Murray. "What a bore! I will get up
directly. You can go, Davis. I will ring if I want you."

Davis was standing, as his master spoke, looking down at the floor.
"Yes, sir," he answered, after the fashion of a man who has something
on his mind,—and went.

He had not, however, got to the bottom of the first flight when peal
after peal summoned him back.

Mr. Murray was out of bed, and in the middle of the room, the
ghastly pallor of his face brought into full prominence by the crimson
dressing-gown he had thrown round him on rising.

"What is that?" he asked. "What in the world is that, Davis?" and
he pointed to the carpet, which was covered, Mrs. Murray being an
old-fashioned lady, with strips of white drugget.

"I am sure I do not know, sir," answered Davis. "I noticed it the
moment I came into the room. Looks as if some one with wet feet had
been walking round and round the bed."

It certainly did. Round and round, to and fro, backwards and forwards, the feet seemed to have gone and come, leaving a distinct mark
wherever they pressed.

"The print is that of a rare small foot, too," observed Davis, who
really seemed half stupefied with astonishment.

"But who would have dared—" began Mr. Murray.

"No one in this house," declared Davis stoutly. "It is not the mark of a boy or woman inside these doors;" and then the master and the man looked at each other for an instant with grave suspicion.

But for that second they kept their eyes thus occupied; then, as by common consent, they dropped their glances to the floor. "My God!" exclaimed Davis. "Where have the footprints gone?"

He might well ask. The drugget, but a moment before wet and stained by the passage and repassage of those small restless feet, was now smooth and white, as when first sent forth from the bleach-green. On its polished surface there could not be discerned a speck or mark.

CHAPTER TWO

Where Is Lucy?

In the valley of the Thames early hours are the rule. There the days have an unaccountable way of lengthening themselves out which makes it prudent, as well as pleasant, to utilize all the night in preparing for a longer morrow.

For this reason, when eleven o'clock p.m. strikes, it usually finds Church Street, Walton, as quiet as its adjacent graveyard, which lies still and solemn under the shadow of the old grey tower hard by that ancient vicarage which contains so beautiful a staircase.

About the time when Mr. Travers' friends were beginning their evening, when talk had abated and play was suggested, the silence of Church Street was broken and many a sleeper aroused by a continuous knocking at the door of a house as venerable as any in that part of Walton. Rap—rap—rap—rap awoke the echoes of the old-world village street, and at length brought to the window a young man, who, flinging up the sash, inquired,—

"Who is there?"

"Where is Lucy? What have you done with my girl?" answered a strained woman's voice from out the darkness of that summer night.

"Lucy?" repeated the young man; "is not she at home?"

"No; I have never set eyes on her since you went out together."

"Why, we parted hours ago. Wait a moment, Mrs. Heath; I will be down directly."

No need to tell the poor woman to "wait." She stood on the step, crying softly and wringing her hands till the door opened, and the same young fellow who with the pretty girl had taken boat opposite the Ship Hotel bade her "Come in."

Awakened from some pleasant dream, spite of all the trouble and hurry of that unexpected summons, there still shone the light of a reflected sunshine in his eyes and the flush of happy sleep on his cheek. He scarcely understood yet what had happened, but when he saw Mrs. Heath's tear-stained face, comprehension came to him, and he said abruptly,—

"Do you mean that she has never returned home?"

"Never!"

They were in the parlour by this time, and looking at each other by the light of one poor candle which he had set down on the table.

"Why, I left her," he said, "I left her long before seven."

"Where?"

"Just beyond Dockett Point. She would not let me row her back. I do not know what was the matter with her, but nothing I did seemed right."

"Had you any quarrel?" asked Mrs. Heath anxiously.

"Yes, we had; we were quarreling all the time—at least she was with me; and at last she made me put her ashore, which I did sorely against my will."

"What had you done to my girl, then?"

"I prayed of her to marry me—no great insult, surely, but she took it as one. I would rather not talk of what she answered. Where can she be? Do you think she can have gone to her aunt's?"

"If so, she will be back by the last train. Let us get home as fast as possible. I never thought of that. Poor child! she will go out of her mind if she finds nobody to let her in. You will come with me. O, if she is not there, what shall I do—what ever shall I do?"

The young man had taken his hat, and was holding the door open for Mrs. Heath to pass out.

"You must try not to fret yourself," he said gently, yet with a strange repression in his voice. "Very likely she may stay at her aunt's all night."

"And leave me in misery, not knowing where she is? Oh, Mr. Grantley, I could never believe that."

Mr. Grantley's heart was very hot within him; but he could not tell the poor mother he believed that when Lucy's temper was up she would think of no human being but herself.

"Won't you take my arm, Mrs. Heath?" he asked with tender pity. After all, though everything was over between him and Lucy, her mother could not be held accountable for their quarrel; and he had loved the girl with all the romantic fervour of love's young dream.

"I can walk faster without it, thank you," Mrs. Heath answered.

"But Mr. Grantley, whatever you and Lucy fell out over, you'll forget it, won't you? It isn't in you to be hard on anybody, and she's only a spoiled child. I never had but the one, and I humoured her too much; and if she is wayward, it is all my own fault—all my own."

"In case she does not return by this train," said the young man, wisely ignoring Mrs. Heath's inquiry, "had I not better telegraph to her aunt directly the office opens?"

"I will be on my way to London long before that," was the reply. "But what makes you think she won't come? Surely you don't imagine she has done anything rash?"

"What do you mean by rash?" he asked evasively.

"Made away with herself."

"*That!*" he exclaimed. "No, I feel very sure she has done nothing of the sort."

"But she might have felt sorry when you left her—vexed for having angered you—heartbroken when she saw you leave her."

"Believe me, she was not vexed or sorry or heartbroken; she was only glad to know she had done with me," he answered bitterly.

"What has come to you, Mr. Grantley?" said Mrs. Heath, in wonder. "I never heard you speak the same before."

"Perhaps not; I never felt the same before. It is best to be plain with you," he went on. "All is at an end between us; and that is what your daughter has long been trying for."

"How can you say that, and she so fond of you?"

"She has not been fond of me for many a day. The man she wants to marry is not a poor fellow like myself, but one who can give her carriages and horses, and a fine house, and as much dress as she cares to buy."

"But where could she ever find a husband able to do that?"

"I do not know, Mrs. Heath. All I do know is that she considers I am no match for her; and now my eyes are opened, I see she was not a wife for me. We should never have known a day's happiness."

It was too dark to see his face, but his changed voice and words and manner told Lucy's mother the kindly lad, who a couple of years before came courting her pretty daughter, and offended all his friends for her sake, was gone away for ever. It was a man who walked by her side—who had eaten of the fruit of the tree, and had learned to be as a god, knowing good from evil.

"Well, well," she said brokenly, "you are the best judge, I suppose; but O, my child, my child!"

She was so blinded with tears she stumbled, and must have fallen had he not caught and prevented her. Then he drew her hand within his arm, and said,—

"I am so grieved for you. I never received anything but kindness from you."

"And indeed," she sobbed, "you never were anything except good to me. I always knew we couldn't be considered your equals, and I often had my doubts whether it was right to let you come backwards and forwards as I did, parting you from all belonging to you. But I thought, when your mother saw Lucy's pretty face—for it is pretty, Mr. Grantley—"

"There never was a prettier," assented the young man, though, now his eyes were opened, he knew Lucy's beauty would scarcely have recommended her to any sensible woman.

"I hoped she might take to her, and I'd never have intruded. And I was so proud and happy, and fond of you—I was indeed; and I used to consider how, when you came down, I could have some little thing you fancied. But that's all over now. And I don't blame you; only my heart is sore and troubled about my foolish girl."

They were on Walton Bridge by this time, and the night air blew cold and raw down the river, and made Mrs. Heath shiver.

"I wonder where Lucy is," she murmured, "and what she'd think if she knew her mother was walking through the night in an agony about her? Where was it you said you left her?"

"Between Dockett Point and Chertsey. I shouldn't have left her had she not insisted on my doing so."

"Isn't that the train?" asked Mrs. Heath, stopping suddenly short and listening intently.

"Yes; it is just leaving Sunbury Station. Do not hurry; we have plenty of time."

They had: they were at Lucy's home, one of the small houses situated between Battlecreese Hill and the Red Lion in Lower Halliford before a single passenger came along The Green, or out of Nannygoat Lane.

"My heart misgives me that she has not come down," said Mrs. Heath.

"Shall I go up to meet her?" asked the young man; and almost before the mother feverishly assented, he was striding through the summer night to Shepperton Station, where he found the lights extinguished and every door closed.

CHAPTER THREE

Poor Mrs. Heath

By noon the next day every one in Shepperton and Lower Halliford knew Lucy Heath was "missing."

Her mother had been up to Putney, but Lucy was not with her aunt, who lived not very far from the Bridge on the Fulham side, and who, having married a fruiterer and worked up a very good business, was inclined to take such bustling and practical views of life and its concerns as rather dismayed her sister-in-law, who had spent so many years in the remote country, and then so many other years in quiet Shepperton, that Mrs. Pointer's talk flurried her almost as much as the noise of London, which often maddens middle-aged and elderly folk happily unaccustomed to its roar.

Girt about with a checked apron which lovingly enfolded a goodly portion of her comfortable figure, Mrs. Pointer received her early visitor with the sportive remark, "Why, it's never Martha Heath! Come along in; a sight of you is good for sore eyes."

But Mrs. Heath repelled all such humorous observations, and chilled those suggestions of hospitality the Pointers were never backward in making by asking in a low choked voice,—

"Is Lucy here?"

"Lor! whatever put such a funny notion into your head?"

"Ah! I see she is," trying to smile. "After all, she spent the night with you."

"Did what?" exclaimed Mrs. Pointer. "Spent the night—was that what you said? No, nor the day either, for this year nearly. Why, for the last four months she hasn't set foot across that doorstep, unless it might be to buy some cherries, or pears, or apples, or grapes, or such-like, and then she came in with more air than any lady; and after paying her money and getting her goods went out again, just as if I hadn't been her father's sister and Pointer my husband. But there! for any sake, woman, don't look like that! Come into the parlour and tell me what is wrong. You never mean she has gone away and left you?"

Poor Mrs. Heath was perfectly incapable at that moment of saying what she did mean. Seated on a stool, and holding fast by the edge of the counter for fear of falling, the shop and its contents, the early busses, the people going along the pavement, the tradesmen's carts, the private carriages, were, as in some terrible nightmare, gyrating before her eyes. She could not speak, she could scarcely think, until that wild whirligig came to a stand. For a minute or two even Mrs. Pointer seemed multiplied by fifty; while her checked apron, the bananas suspended from hooks, the baskets of fruit, the pine-apples, the melons, the tomatoes, and the cob-nuts appeared and disappeared, only to re-appear and disappear like the riders in a maddening giddy-go-round.

"Give me a drop of water," she said at last; and when the water was brought she drank a little and poured some on her handkerchief and dabbed her face, and finally suffered herself to be escorted into the par-lour, where she told her tale, interrupted by many sobs. It would have been unchristian in Mrs. Pointer to exult; but it was only human to remember she had remarked to Pointer, in that terrible spirit of prophecy bestowed for some inscrutable reason on dear friends and close rela-tions, she knew some such trouble must befall her sister-in-law.

"You made an idol of that girl, Martha," she went on, "and now it is coming home to you. I am sure it was only last August as ever was that Pointer— But here he is, and he will talk to you himself."

Which Mr. Pointer did, being very fond of the sound of his own foolish voice. He stated how bad a thing it was for people to be above their station or to bring children up above that rank of life in which it had pleased God to place them. He quoted many pleasing saws uttered by his father and grandfather; remarked that as folks sowed they were bound to reap; reminded Mrs. Heath they had the word of Scripture for the fact—than, which, parenthetically, no fact could be truer, as he knew—that a man might not gather grapes from thorns or even figs from thistles. Further he went on to observe generally—the observa-tion having a particular reference to Lucy—that it did not do to judge things by their looks. Over and over again salesmen had tried to "shove off a lot of foreign fruit on him, but he wasn't a young bird to be taken in by that chaff." No; what he looked to was quality; it was what his customers expected from him, and what he could honestly declare his customers got. He was a plain man, and he thought honesty was the best policy. So as Mrs. Heath had seen fit to come to them in her trouble he would tell her what he thought, without beating about the bush. He believed Lucy had "gone off."

"But where?" asked poor Mrs. Heath.

"That I am not wise enough to say; but you'll find she's gone off. Girls in her station don't sport chains and bracelets and brooches for nothing—"

"But they did not cost many shillings," interposed the mother.

"She might tell you that," observed Mrs. Pointer, with a world of meaning.

"To say nothing," went on Mr. Pointer, "of grey gloves she could not abear to be touched. One day she walked in when I was behind the counter, and, not knowing she had been raised to the peerage, I shook hands with her as a matter of course; but when I saw the young lady look at her glove as if I had dirtied it, I said 'O, I beg your pardon, miss'—jocularly, you know. 'They soil so easily,' she lisped."

"I haven't patience with such ways!" interpolated Mrs. Pointer, without any lisp at all. "Yes, it's hard for you, Martha, but you may depend Pointer's right. Indeed, I expected how it would be long ago. Young women who are walking in the straight road don't dress as Lucy dressed, or dare their innocent little cousins to call them by their Christian names in the street. Since the Spring, and long before, Pointer and me has been sure Lucy was up to no good."

"And you held your tongues and never said a word to me!" retorted Mrs. Heath, goaded and driven to desperation.

"Much use it would have been saying any word to you," answered Mrs. Pointer. "When you told me about young Grantley, and I bid you be careful, how did you take my advice? Why, you blared out at me, went on as if I knew nothing and had never been anywhere. What I told you then, though, I tell you now: young Grantleys, the sons of rectors and the grandsons of colonels, don't come after farmer's daughters with any honest purpose."

"Yet young Grantley asked her last evening to fix a day for their marriage," said Mrs. Heath, with a little triumph.

"O, I daresay!" scoffed Mrs. Pointer.

"Talk is cheap," observed Mr. Pointer.

"Some folks have more of it than money," supplemented his wife.

"They have been, as I understand, keeping company for some time now," said the fruiterer, with what he deemed a telling and judicial calmness. "So if he asked her to name the day, why did she not name it?"

"I do not know. I have never seen her since."

"O, then you had only his word about the matter," summed up Mr. Pointer. "Just as I thought—just as I thought."

"What did you think?" inquired the poor troubled mother.

"Why, that she has gone off with this Mr. Grantley."

"Ah, you don't know Mr. Grantley, or you wouldn't say such a thing."

"It is true," observed Mr. Pointer, "that I do not know the gentleman, and, I may add, I do not want to know him; but speaking as a person acquainted with the world—"

"I'll be getting home," interrupted Mrs. Heath. "Most likely my girl is there waiting for me, and a fine laugh she will have against her poor old mother for being in such a taking. Yes, Lucy will have the breakfast ready. No, thank you; I'll not wait to take anything. There will be a train back presently; and besides, to tell you the truth, food would choke me till I sit down again with my girl, and then I won't be able to eat for joy."

Husband and wife looked at each other as Mrs. Heath spoke, and for the moment a deep pity pierced the hard crust of their worldly egotism.

"Wait a minute," cried Mrs. Pointer, "and I'll put on my bonnet and go with you."

"No," interrupted Mr. Pointer, instantly seizing his wife's idea, and appropriating it as his own. "I am the proper person to see this affair out. There is not much doing, and if there were, I would leave everything to obtain justice for your niece. After all, however wrong she may have gone, she is your niece, Maria."

With which exceedingly nasty remark, which held a whole volume of unpleasant meaning as to what Mrs. Pointer might expect from that relationship in the future, Mr. Pointer took Mrs. Heath by the arm, and piloted her out into the street, and finally to Lower Halliford, where the missing Lucy was not, and where no tidings of her had come.

CHAPTER FOUR

Mr. Gage on Portents

About the time when poor distraught Mrs. Heath, having managed to elude the vigilance of that cleverest of men, Maria Pointer's husband, had run out of her small house, and was enlisting the sympathies of gossip-loving Shepperton in Lucy's disappearance, Mr. Paul Murray arrived at Liverpool Street Station, where his luggage and his valet awaited him.

"Get tickets, Davis," he said; "I have run it rather close;" and he walked towards Smith's stall, while his man went into the booking-office.

As he was about to descend the stairs, Davis became aware of a very singular fact. Looking down the steps, he saw precisely the same marks that had amazed him so short a time previously, being printed hurriedly off by a pair of invisible feet, which ran to the bottom and then flew as if in the wildest haste to the spot where Mr. Murray stood.

"I am not dreaming, am I?" thought the man; and he shut his eyes and opened them again.

The footprints were all gone!

At that moment his master turned from the bookstall and proceeded towards the train. A porter opened the door of a smoking carriage, but Murray shook his head and passed on. Mr. Davis, once more looking to the ground, saw that those feet belonging to no mortal body were still following. There were not very many passengers, and it was quite plain to him that wherever his master went, the quick, wet prints went too. Even on the step of the compartment Mr. Murray eventually selected the man beheld a mark, as though some one had sprung in after him. He secured the door, and then walked away, to find a place for himself, marvelling in a dazed state of mind what it all meant; indeed, he felt so much dazed that, after he had found a seat to his mind, he did not immediately notice an old acquaintance in the opposite corner, who affably inquired,—

"And how is Mr. Davis?"

Thus addressed, Mr. Davis started from his reverie, and exclaimed, "Why, bless my soul, Gage, who'd have thought of seeing you here?" after which exchange of courtesies the pair shook hands gravely and settled down to converse.

Mr. Davis explained that he was going down with his governor to Norwich; and Mr. Gage stated that he and the old general had been staying at Thorpe, and were on their way to Lowestoft. Mr. Gage and his old general had also just returned from paying a round of visits in the West of England. "Pleasant enough, but slow," finished the gentleman's gentleman. "After all, in the season or out of it, there is no place like London."

With this opinion Mr. Davis quite agreed, and said he only wished he had never to leave it, adding,—

"We have not been away before for a long time; and we should not be going where we are now bound if we had not to humour some fancy of our grandmother's."

"Deuced rough on a man having to humour a grandmother's fancy," remarked Mr. Gage.

"No female ought to be left the control of money," said Mr. Davis with conviction. "See what the consequences have been in this case—Mrs. Murray outlived her son, who had to ask for every shilling he wanted, and she is so tough she may see the last of her grandson."

"That is very likely," agreed the other. "He looks awfully bad."

"You saw him just now, I suppose?"

"No; but I saw him last night at Chertsey station, and I could but notice the change in his appearance."

For a minute Mr. Davis remained silent. "Chertsey Station!" What could his master have been doing at Chertsey? That was a question he would have to put to himself again, and answer for himself at some convenient time; meanwhile he only answered,—

"Yes, I observe an alteration in him myself. Anything fresh in the paper?"

"No," answered Mr. Gage, handing his friend over the *Daily News*—the print he affected: "everything is as dull as ditchwater."

For many a mile Davis read or affected to read; then he laid the paper aside, and after passing his case, well filled with a tithe levied on Mr. Murray's finest cigars, to Gage, began solemnly,—

"I am going to ask you a curious question, Robert, as from man to man."

"Ask on," said Mr. Gage, striking a match.

"Do you believe in warnings?"

The old General's gentleman burst out laughing. He was so tickled that he let his match drop from his fingers unapplied.

"I am afraid most of us have to believe in them, whether we like it or not," he answered, when he could speak. "Has there been some little difference between you and your governor, then?"

"You mistake," was the reply. "I did not mean warnings in the sense of notice, but warnings as warnings, you understand."

"Bother me if I do! Yes, now I take you. Do I believe in 'coming events casting shadows before,' as some one puts it? Has any shadow of a coming event been cast across you?"

"No, nor across anybody, so far as I know; but I've been thinking the matter over lately, and wondering if there can be any truth in such notions."

"What notions?"

"Why, that there are signs and suchlike sent when trouble is coming to any one."

"You may depend it is right enough that signs and tokens are sent. Almost every good family has its special warning: one has its mouse, another its black dog, a third its white bird, a fourth its drummer-boy, and so on. There is no getting over facts, even if you don't understand them."

"Well, it is very hard to believe."

"There wouldn't be much merit in believing if everything were as plain as a pikestaff. You know what the Scotch minister said to his boy: 'The very devils believe and tremble.' You wouldn't be worse than a devil, would you?"

"Has any sign ever appeared to you?" asked Davis.

"Not exactly; but lots of people have told me they have to them; for instance, old Seal, who drove the Dowager Countess of Ongar till the day of her death, used to make our hair stand on end talking about phantom carriages that drove away one after another from the door of Hainault House, and wakened every soul on the premises, night after night till the old Earl died. It took twelve clergymen to lay the spirit."

"I wonder one wasn't enough!" ejaculated Davis.

"There may have been twelve spirits, for all I know," returned Gage, rather puzzled by this view of the question; "but anyhow, there were twelve clergymen, with the bishop in his lawn sleeves chief among them. And I once lived with a young lady's-maid, who told me when she was a girl she made her home with her father's parents. On a winter's night, after everybody else had gone to bed, she sat up to make some girdle-bread—that is a sort of bread people in Ireland, where she came from, bake over the fire on a round iron plate; with plenty of butter it is not bad eating. Well, as I was saying, she was quite alone; she had taken all the bread off, and was setting it up on edge to cool, supporting one piece against the other, two and two, when on the table where she was putting the cakes she saw one drop of blood fall, and then another, and then another, like the beginning of a shower.

"She looked to the ceiling, but could see nothing, and still the drops kept on falling slowly, slowly; and then she knew something had gone wrong with one dear to her; and she put a shawl over her head, and without saying a word to anybody, went through the loneliness and darkness of night all by herself to her father's."

"She must have been a courageous girl," remarked Mr. Davis.

"She was, and I liked her well. But to the point. When she reached her destination she found her youngest brother dead. Now what do you make of that?"

"It's strange, but I suppose he would have died all the same if she had not seen the blood-drops, and I can't see any good seeing them did her. If she had reached her father's in time to bid brother good-bye, there would have been some sense in such a sign. As it is, it seems to me a lot of trouble thrown away."

Mr. Gage shook his head.

"What a sceptic you are, Davis! But there! London makes sceptics of the best of us. If you had spent a winter, as I did once, in the Highlands of Scotland, or heard the Banshee wailing for the General's nephew in the county of Mayo, you wouldn't have asked what was the use of second sight or Banshees. You would just have stood and trembled as I did many and many a time."

"I might," said Davis doubtfully, wondering what his friend would have thought of those wet little footprints. "Hillo, here's Peterborough! Hadn't we better stretch our legs? and a glass of something would be acceptable."

Of that glass, however, Mr. Davis was not destined to partake.

"If one of you is Murray's man," said the guard as they jumped out, "he wants you."

"I'll be back in a minute," observed Mr. Murray's man to his friend, and hastened off.

But he was not back in a minute; on the contrary, he never returned at all.

CHAPTER FIVE
Kiss Me

The first glance in his master's face filled Davis with a vague alarm. Gage's talk had produced an effect quite out of proportion to its merit, and a cold terror struck to the valet's heart as he thought there might, spite of his lofty scepticism, be something after all in the mouse, and the bird, and the drummer-boy, in the black dog, and the phantom carriages, and the spirits it required the united exertions of twelve clergymen (with the bishop in lawn sleeves among them) to lay; in Highland second sight and Irish Banshees; and in little feet paddling round and about a man's bed and following wherever he went. What awful disaster could those footprints portend? Would the train be smashed up? Did any river lie before them? and if so, was the sign vouchsafed as a warning that they were likely to die by drowning? All these thoughts, and many more, passed through Davis' mind as he stood looking at his master's pallid face and waiting for him to speak.

"I wish you to come in here," said Mr. Murray after a pause, and with a manifest effort. "I am not quite well."

"Can I get you anything, sir?" asked the valet. "Will you not wait and go by another train?"

"No; I shall be better presently; only I do not like being alone."

Davis opened the door and entered the compartment. As he did so, he could not refrain from glancing at the floor, to see if those strange footsteps had been running races there.

"What are you looking for?" asked Mr. Murray irritably. "Have you dropped anything?"

"No, sir; O, no! I was only considering where I should be most out of the way."

"There," answered his master, indicating a seat next the window, and at the same time moving to one on the further side of the carriage. "Let no one get in; say I am ill—mad; that I have scarlet fever—the plague—what you please." And with this wide permission Mr. Murray laid his legs across the opposite cushion, wrapped one rug round his shoulders and another round his body, turned his head aside, and went to sleep or seemed to do so.

"If he is going to die, I hope it will be considered in my wages, but I am afraid it won't. Perhaps it is the old lady; but that would be too good fortune," reflected Davis; and then he fell "a-thinkynge, a-thinkynge," principally of Gage's many suggestions and those mysterious footprints, for which he kept at intervals furtively looking. But they did not appear; and at last the valet, worn out with vain conjections, dropped into a pleasant doze, from which he did not awake till they were nearing Norwich.

"We will go to an hotel till I find out what Mrs. Murray's plans are," said that lady's grandson when he found himself on the platform; and as if they had been only waiting this piece of information, two small invisible feet instantly skipped out of the compartment they had just vacated, and walked after Mr. Murray, leaving visible marks at every step.

"Great heavens! what is the meaning of this?" mentally asked Davis, surprised by fright after twenty prayerless and scheming years into an exclamation which almost did duty for a prayer. For a moment he felt sick with terror; then clutching his courage with the energy of desperation, he remembered that though wet footprints might mean death and destruction to the Murrays, his own ancestral annals held no record of such a portent.

Neither did the Murrays', so far as he was aware, but then he was aware of very little about that family. If the Irish girl Gage spoke of was informed by drops of blood that her brother lay dead, why should not Mr. Murray be made aware, through the token of these pattering footsteps, that he would very soon succeed to a large fortune?

Then any little extra attention Mr. Davis showed his master *now* would be remembered in his wages.

It was certainly unpleasant to know these damp feet had come down from London, and were going to the hotel with them; but "needs must" with a certain driver, and if portents and signs and warnings were made worth his while, Mr. Davis conceived there might be advantages connected with them.

Accordingly, when addressing Mr. Murray, his valet's voice assumed a more deferential tone than ever, and his manner became so respectfully tender, that onlookers rashly imagined the ideal master and the faithful servant of fiction had at last come in the flesh to Norwich. Davis' conduct was, indeed, perfect: devoted without being intrusive, he smoothed away all obstacles which could be smoothed, and even, by dint of a judicious two minutes alone with the doctor for whom he sent, managed the introduction of a useful sedative in some medicine, which the label stated was to be taken every four hours.

He saw to Mr. Murray's rooms and Mr. Murray's light repast, and then he waited on Mr. Murray's grandmother, and managed that lady so adroitly, she at length forgave the offender for having caught a chill.

"Your master is always doing foolish things," she said. "It would have been much better had he remained even for a day or two in London rather than risk being laid up. However, you must nurse him carefully, and try to get him well enough to dine at Losdale Court on Monday. Fortunately to-morrow is Sunday, and he can take complete rest. Now Davis, remember I trust to you."

"I will do my best, ma'am," Davis said humbly, and went back to tell his master the interview had gone off without any disaster.

Then, after partaking of some mild refreshment, he repaired to bed in a dressing-room opening off Mr. Murray's apartment, so that he might be within call and close at hand to administer those doses which were to be taken at intervals of four hours.

"I feel better to-night," said Mr. Murray last thing.

"It is this beautiful air, sir," answered Davis, who knew it was the sedative. "I hope you will be quite well in the morning."

But spite of the air, in the grey dawn Mr. Murray had again a dreadful dream—a worse dream than that which laid its heavy hand on him· in London. He thought he was by the riverside beyond Dockett Point—beyond where the water-lilies grow. To his right was a little grove of old and twisted willows guarding a dell strewed in dry seasons with the leaves of many autumns, but, in his dream, wet and sodden by reason of heavy rain. There in June wild roses bloomed; there in winter hips and haws shone ruddy against the snow. To his left flowed a turbid river—turbid with floods that had troubled its peace. On the other bank lay a stagnant length of Surrey, while close at hand the Middlesex portion of Chertsey Mead stretched in a hopeless flat on to the bridge, just visible in the early twilight of a summer's evening that had followed after a dull lowering day.

From out of the gathering gloom there advanced walking perilously near to Dumsey Deep, a solitary female figure, who, when they met, said, "So you've come at last;" after which night seemed to close around him, silence for a space to lay its hands upon him.

About the same time Davis was seeing visions also. He had lain long awake, trying to evolve order out of the day's chaos, but in vain. The stillness fretted him; the idea that even then those mysterious feet might in the darkness be printing their impress about his master's bed irritated his brain. Twice he got up to give that medicine ordered to be taken every four hours, but finding on each occasion Mr. Murray sleeping quietly, he forbore to arouse him.

He heard hour after hour chime, and it was not till the first hint of dawn that he fell into a deep slumber. Then he dreamt about the subject nearest his heart—a public house.

He thought he had saved or gained enough to buy a roadside inn on which he had long cast eyes of affectionate regard—not in London, but not too far out: a delightful inn, where holiday-makers always stopped for refreshment, and sometimes for the day; an inn with a pretty old-fashioned garden filled with fruit trees and vegetables, with a grass-plot around which were erected little arbours, where people could have tea or stronger stimulants; a skittle-ground, where men could soon make themselves very thirsty; and many other advantages tedious to mention. He had the purchase-money in his pocket, and, having paid a deposit, was proceeding to settle the affair, merely diverging from his way to call on a young widow he meant to make Mrs. Davis—a charming woman, who having stood behind a bar before, seemed the very person to make the Wheatsheaf a triumphant success. He was talking to her sensibly, when suddenly she amazed him by saying, in a sharp, hurried voice, "Kiss me, kiss me, kiss me!" three times over.

The request seemed so strange that he stood astounded, and then awoke to hear the same words repeated.

"Kiss me, kiss me, kiss me!" some one said distinctly in Mr. Murray's room, the door of which stood open, and then all was quiet.

Only half awake, Davis sprang from his bed and walked across the floor, conceiving, so far as his brain was in a state to conceive anything, that his senses were playing him some trick.

"You won't?" said the voice again, in a tone which rooted him to the spot where he stood; "and yet, as we are never to meet again, you might *kiss me once*," the voice added caressingly, "*only once more.*"

"Who the deuce has he got with him now?" thought Davis; but almost before the question was shaped in his mind there came a choked, gasping cry of "Unloose me, tigress, devil!" followed by a sound of desperate wrestling for life.

In a second, Davis was in the room. Through the white blinds light enough penetrated to show Mr. Murray in the grip apparently of some invisible antagonist, who seemed to be strangling him.

To and fro from side to side the man and the unseen phantom went swaying in that awful struggle. Short and fast came Mr. Murray's breath, while, making one supreme effort, he flung his opponent from him and sank back across the bed exhausted.

Wiping the moisture from his forehead, Davis, trembling in every limb, advanced to where his master lay, and found *he was fast asleep!*

Mr. Murray's eyes were wide open, and he did not stir hand or foot while the man covered him up as well as he was able, and then looked timidly around, dreading to see the second actor in the scene just ended.

"I can't stand much more of this," Davis exclaimed, and the sound of his own voice made him start.

There was brandy in the room which had been left over-night, and the man poured himself out and swallowed a glass of the liquor. He ventured to lift the blind and look at the floor, which was wet, as though buckets of water had been thrown over it, while the prints of little feet were everywhere.

Mr. Davis took another glass of brandy. *That* had not been watered.

"Well, this is a start!" he said in his own simple phraseology. "I wonder what the governor has been up to?"

For it was now borne in upon the valet's understanding that this warning was no shadow of any event to come, but the tell-tale ghost of some tragedy which could never be undone.

CHAPTER SIX

Found Drowned

After such a dreadful experience it might have been imagined that Mr. Murray would be very ill indeed; but what we expect rarely comes to pass, and though during the whole of Sunday and Monday Davis felt, as he expressed the matter, "awfully shaky," his master appeared well and in fair spirits.

He went to the Cathedral, and no attendant footsteps dogged him. On Monday he accompanied his grandmother to Losdale Court, where he behaved so admirably as to please even the lady on whose favour his income depended. He removed to a furnished house Mrs. Murray had taken, and prepared to carry out her wishes. Day succeeded day and night to night, but neither by day nor night did Davis hear the sound of any ghostly voices or trace the print of any phantom foot.

Could it be that nothing more was to come of it—that the mystery was never to be elucidated but fade away as the marks of dainty feet had vanished from floor, pavement, steps, and platform?

The valet did not believe it; behind those signs made by nothing human lay some secret well worth knowing, but it had never been possible to know much about Mr. Murray.

"He was so little of a gentleman" that he had no pleasant, careless ways. He did not leave his letters lying loose for all the world to read. He did not tear up papers, and toss them into a waste-paper basket. He had the nastiest practice of locking up and burning; and though it was Mr. Davis' commendable custom to collect and preserve unconsidered odds and ends as his master occasionally left in his pockets, these, after all, were trifles light as air.

Nevertheless, as a straw shows how the wind blows, so that chance remark anent Chertsey Station made by Gage promised to provide a string on which to thread various little beads in Davis' possession.

The man took them out and looked at them: a woman's fall—white tulle, with black spots, smelling strongly of tobacco-smoke and musk; a receipt for a bracelet, purchased from an obscure jeweller; a Chertsey Lock ticket; and the return half of a first-class ticket from Shepperton to Waterloo, stamped with the date of the day before they left London.

At these treasures Davis looked long and earnestly.

"We shall see," he remarked as he put them up again; "there I think the scent lies hot."

It could not escape the notice of so astute a servant that his master was unduly anxious for a sight of the London papers, and that he glanced through them eagerly for something he apparently failed to find—more, that he always laid the print aside with a sigh of relief. Politics did not seem to trouble him, or any public burning question.

"He has some burning question of his own," thought the valet, though he mentally phrased his notion in different words.

Matters went on thus for a whole week. The doctor came and went and wrote prescriptions, for Mr. Murray either was still ailing or chose to appear so. Davis caught a word or two which had reference to the patient's heart, and some shock. Then he considered that awful night, and wondered how he, who "was in his sober senses, and wide awake, and staring," had lived through it.

"My heart, and a good many other things, will have to be considered," he said to himself. "No wages could pay for what has been put upon me this week past. I wonder whether I ought to speak to Mr. Murray now?"

Undecided on this point, he was still considering it when he called his master on the following Sunday morning. The first glance at the stained and polished floor decided him. Literally it was interlaced with footprints. The man's hand shook as he drew up the blind, but he kept his eyes turned on Mr. Murray while he waited for orders, and walked out of the room when dismissed as though such marks had been matters of customary occurrence in a nineteenth century bedroom.

No bell summoned him back on this occasion. Instead of asking for information, Mr. Murray dropped into a chair and nerved himself to defy the inevitable.

Once again there came a pause. For three days nothing occurred; but on the fourth a newspaper and a letter arrived, both of which Davis inspected curiously. They were addressed in Mr. Savill's hand-writing, and they bore the postmark "SHEPPERTON."

The newspaper was enclosed in an ungummed wrapper, tied round with a piece of string. After a moment's reflection Davis cut that string, spread out the print, and beheld a column marked at top with three blue crosses, containing the account of an inquest held at the King's Head on a body found on the previous Sunday morning, close by the "Tumbling Bay."

It was that of a young lady who had been missing since the previous Friday week, and could only be identified by the clothes.

Her mother, who, in giving evidence, frequently broke down, told how her daughter on the evening in question went out for a walk and never returned. She did not wish to go, because her boots were being mended, and her shoes were too large. No doubt they had dropped off. She had very small feet, and it was not always possible to get shoes to fit them. She was engaged to be married to the gentleman with whom she went out. He told her they had quarreled. She did not believe he could have anything to do with her child's death; but she did not know what to think. It had been said her girl was keeping company with somebody else, but that could not be true. Her girl was a good girl.

Yes; she had found a bracelet hidden away among her girl's clothes, and she could not say how she got the seven golden sovereigns that were in the purse, or the locket taken off the body; but her girl was a good girl, and she did not know whatever she would do without her, for Lucy was all she had.

Walter Grantley was next examined, after being warned that any-thing he said might be used against him.

Though evidently much affected, he gave his evidence in a clear and straightforward manner. He was a clerk in the War Office. He had, against the wishes of all his friends, engaged himself to the deceased, who, after having some time professed much affection, had latterly treated him with great coldness. On the evening in question she reluctantly came out with him for a walk; but after they passed the Ship she insisted he should take a boat. They turned and got into a boat. He wanted to go down the river, because there was no lock before Sunbury. She declared if he would not row her up the river, she would go home.

They went up the river, quarrelling all the way. There had been so much of this sort of thing that after they passed through Shepperton Lock he tried to bring matters to a conclusion, and asked her to name a day for their marriage. She scoffed at him and asked if he thought she meant to marry a man on such a trumpery salary. Then she insisted he should land her; and after a good deal of argument he did land her; and rowed back alone to Halliford. He knew no more.

Richard Savill deposed he took a boat at Lower Halliford directly after the last witness, with whom he was not acquainted, and rowed up towards Chertsey, passing Mr. Grantley and Miss Heath, who were evidently quarrelling. He went as far as Dumsey Deep, where, finding the stream most heavily against him, he turned, and on his way back saw the young lady walking slowly along the bank. At Shepperton Lock he and Mr. Grantley exchanged a few words, and rowed down to Halliford almost side by side. They bade each other good-evening, and Mr. Grantley walked off in the direction of Walton where it was proved by other witnesses he arrived at eight o'clock, and did not go out again till ten, when he went to bed.

All efforts to trace what had become of the unfortunate girl proved unavailing, till a young man named Lemson discovered the body on the previous Sunday morning close by the Tumbling Bay. The coroner wished to adjourn the inquest, in hopes some further light might be thrown on such a mysterious occurrence; but the jury protested so strongly against any proceeding of the sort, that they were directed to return an open verdict.

No one could dispute that the girl had been "found drowned," or that there was "no evidence to explain how she came to be drowned."

At the close of the proceedings, said the local paper, an affecting incident occurred. The mother wished the seven pounds to be given to the man "who brought her child home," but the man refused to accept a penny. The mother said she would never touch it, when a relation stepped forward and offered to take charge of it for her.

The local paper contained also a leader on the tragedy, in the course of which it remarked how exceedingly fortunate it was that Mr. Savill chanced to be staying at the Ship Hotel, so well known to boating-men, and that he happened to go up the river and see the poor young lady after Mr. Grantley left her, as otherwise the latter gentleman might have found himself in a most unpleasant position. He was much to be pitied, and the leader-writer felt confident that every one who read the evidence would sympathize with him. It was evident the in-quiry had failed to solve the mystery connected with Miss Heath's untimely fate, but it was still competent to pursue the matter if any fresh facts transpired.

"I must get to know more about all this," thought Davis as he re-folded and tied up the paper.

CHAPTER SEVEN
Davis Speaks

If there by any truth in old saws, Mr. Murray's wooing was a very happy one. Certainly it was very speedy. By the end of October he and Miss Ketterick were engaged, and before Christmas the family lawyers had their hands full drawing settlements and preparing deeds. Mrs. Murray disliked letting any money slip out of her own control, but she had gone too far to recede, and Mr. Ketterick was not a man who would have tolerated any proceeding of the sort.

Perfectly straightforward himself, he compelled straightforwardness in others, and Mrs. Murray was obliged to adhere to the terms pro-posed when nothing seemed to her less probable than that the marriage she wished ever would take place. As for the bridegroom, he won golden opinions from Mr. Ketterick. Beyond the income to be insured to his wife and himself, he asked for nothing. Further he objected to nothing. Never before, surely, had man been so easily satisfied.

"All I have ever wanted," he said, "was some settled income, so that I might not feel completely dependent on my grandmother. That will now be secured, and I am quite satisfied."

He deferred to Mr. Ketterick's opinions and wishes. He made no stipulations.

"You are giving me a great prize," he told the delighted father, "of which I am not worthy, but I will try to make her happy."

And the gentle girl was happy: no tenderer or more devoted lover could the proudest beauty have desired. With truth he told her he "counted the days till she should be his." For he felt secure when by her side. The footsteps had never followed him to Losdale Court. Just in the place that of all others he would have expected them to come, he failed to see that tiny print. There were times when he even forgot it for a season; when he did remember it, he believed, with the faith born of hope, that he should never see it again.

"I wonder he has the conscience," muttered Mr. Davis one morning, as he looked after the engaged pair. The valet had the strictest ideas concerning the rule conscience should hold over the doings of other folks, and some pleasingly lax notions about the sacrifices conscience had a right to demand from himself. "I suppose he thinks he is safe now that those feet are snugly tucked up in holy ground," proceeded Davis, who, being superstitious, faithfully subscribed to all the old formulæ. "Ah! he doesn't know what I know—yet;" which last word, uttered with much gusto, indicated a most unpleasant quarter of an hour in store at some future period for Mr. Murray.

It came one evening a week before his marriage. He was in London, in his grandmother's house, writing to the girl he had grown to love with the great, entire, remorseful love of his life, when Davis, respectful as ever, appeared, and asked if he might speak a word. Mr. Murray involuntarily put his letter beneath some blotting-paper, and, folding his hands over both, answered, unconscious of what was to follow, "Certainly."

Davis had come up with his statement at full-cock, and fired at once.

"I have been a faithful servant to you, sir."

Mr. Murray lifted his eyes and looked at him. Then he knew what was coming. "I have never found fault with you, Davis," he said, after an almost imperceptible pause.

"No, sir, you have been a good master—a master I am sure no servant who knew his place could find a fault with."

If he had owned an easy mind and the smallest sense of humour—neither of which possessions then belonged to Mr. Murray—he might have felt enchanted with such a complete turning of the tables; but as matters stood, he could only answer, "Good master as I have been, I suppose you wish to leave my service. Am I right, Davis?"

"Well, sir, you are right and you are wrong. I do not want to leave your service just yet. It may not be quite convenient to you for me to go now; only I want to come to an understanding."

"About what?" Mr. Murray asked, quite calmly, though he could feel his heart thumping hard against his ribs, and that peculiar choking sensation which is the warning of what in such cases must come some day.

"Will you cast your mind back, sir, to a morning in last August, when you called my attention to some extraordinary footprints on the floor of your room?"

"I remember the morning," said Mr. Murray, that choking sensation seeming to suffocate him. "Pray go on."

If Davis had not been master of the position, this indifference would have daunted him; as it was, he again touched the trigger, and fired this: "*I know all!*"

Mr. Murray's answer did not come so quick this time. The waters had gone over his head, and for a minute he felt as a man might if suddenly flung into a raging sea, and battling for his life. He was battling for his life with a wildly leaping heart. The noise of a hundred billows seemed dashing on his brain. Then the tempest lulled, the roaring torrent was stayed, and then he said interrogatively, "Yes?"

The prints of those phantom feet had not amazed Davis more than did his master's coolness.

"You might ha' knocked me down with a feather," he stated, when subsequently relating this interview. "I always knew he was a queer customer, but I never knew how queer till then."

"Yes?" said Mr. Murray, which reply quite disconcerted his valet.

"I wouldn't have seen what I have seen, sir," he remarked, "not for a king's ransom."

"No?"

"No, sir, and that is the truth. What we both saw has been with me at bed and at board, as the saying is, ever since. When I shut my eyes I still feel those wet feet dabbling about the room; and in the bright sunshine I can't help shuddering, because there seems to be a cold mist creeping over me."

"Are you not a little imaginative, Davis?" asked his master, himself repressing a shudder.

"No, sir, I am not; no man can be that about which his own eyes have seen and his own ears have heard; and I have heard and seen what I can never forget, and what nothing could pay me for going through."

"Nevertheless?" suggested Mr. Murray.

"I don't know whether I am doing right in holding my tongue, in being so faithful, sir; but I can't help it. I took to you from the first, and I wouldn't bring harm on you if any act of mine could keep it from you. When one made the remark to me awhile ago it was a strange thing to see a gentleman attended by a pair of wet footprints, I said they were a sign in your family that some great event was about to happen."

"Did you say so?"

"I did, sir, Lord forgive me!" answered Davis, with unblushing mendacity. "I have gone through more than will ever be known over this affair, which has shook me, Mr. Murray. I am not the man I was before ghosts took to following me, and getting into trains without paying any fare, and waking me in the middle of the night, and rousing me out of my own warm bed to see sights I would not have believed I could have seen if anybody had sworn it to me. I have aged twenty-five years since last August—my nerves are destroyed; and so, sir, before you got married, I thought I would make bold to ask what I am to do with a constitution broken in your service and hardly a penny put by;" and,

almost out of breath with his pathetic statement, Davis stopped and
waited for an answer.

With a curiously hunted expression in them, Mr. Murray raised his
eyes and looked at Davis.

"You have thought over all this," he said. "How much do you
assess them at?"

"I scarcely comprehend, sir—assess what at?"

"Your broken constitution and the five-and-twenty years you say
you have aged."

His master's face was so gravely serious that Davis could take the
question neither as a jest nor a sneer. It was a request to fix a price, and
he did so.

"Well, sir," he answered, "I have thought it all over. In the night-
watches, when I could get no rest, I lay and reflected what I ought to
do. I want to act fair. I have no wish to drive a hard bargain with you,
and, on the other hand, I don't think I would be doing justice by a
man that has worked hard if I let myself be sold for nothing. So, sir,
to cut a long story short, I am willing to take two thousand pounds."

"And where do you imagine I am to get two thousand pounds?"

Mr. Davis modestly intimated he knew his place better than to
presume to have any notion, but no doubt Mr. Murray could raise that
sum easily enough.

"If I could raise such a sum for you, do you not think I should have
raised it for myself long ago?"

Davis answered that he did; but, if he might make free to say so,
times were changed.

"They are, they are indeed," said Mr. Murray bitterly; and then
there was silence.

Davis knocked the conversational ball the next time.

"I am in no particular hurry, sir," he said. "So, long as we understand one another I can wait till you come back from Italy, and have
got the handling of some cash of your own. I daresay even then you
won't be able to pay me off all at once; but if you would insure your
life—"

"I can't insure my life: I have tried, and been refused."

Again there ensued a silence, which Davis broke once more.

"Well, sir," he began, "I'll chance that. If you will give me a line of
writing about what you owe me, and make a sort of a will, saying I am
to get two thousand, I'll hold my tongue about what's gone and past.
And I would not be fretting, sir, if I was you: things are quiet now,
and, please God, you might never have any more trouble."

Mr. Davis, in view of his two thousand pounds, his widow, and his wayside public, felt disposed to take an optimistic view of even his master's position; but Mr. Murray's thoughts were of a different hue. "If I do have any more," he considered, "I shall go mad;" a conclusion which seemed likely enough to follow upon even the memory of those phantom feet coming dabbling out of an unseen world to follow him with their accursed print in this.

Davis was not going abroad with the happy pair. For sufficient reason Mr. Murray had decided to leave him behind, and Mrs. Murray, ever alive to her own convenience, instantly engaged him to stay on with her as butler, her own being under notice to leave.

Thus, in a semi-official capacity, Davis witnessed the wedding, which people considered a splendid affair.

What Davis thought of it can never be known, because when he left Losdale Church his face was whiter than the bride's dress; and after the newly-wedded couple started on the first stage of their life-journey he went to his room, and stayed in it till his services were required.

"There is no money would pay me for what I've seen," he remarked to himself. "I went too cheap. But when once I handle the cash I'll try never to come anigh him or them again."

What was he referring to? Just this. As the bridal group moved to the vestry he saw, if no one else did, those wet, wet feet softly and swiftly threading their way round the bridesmaids and the groomsman, in front of the relations, before Mrs. Murray herself, and hurry on to keep step with the just wed pair.

For the last time the young wife signed her maiden name. Friends crowded around, uttering congratulations, and still through the throng those unnoticed feet kept walking in and out, round and round, back-ward and forward, as a dog threads its way through the people at a fair. Down the aisle, under the sweeping dresses of the ladies, past courtly gentlemen, Davis saw those awful feet running gleefully till they came up with bride and bridegroom.

"She is going abroad with them," thought the man; and then for a moment he felt as if he could endure the ghastly vision no longer, but must faint dead away. "It is a vile shame," he reflected, "to drag an innocent girl into such a whirlpool;" and all the time over the church step the feet were dancing merrily.

The clerk and the verger noticed them at last.

"I wonder who has been here with wet feet?" said the clerk; and the verger wonderingly answered he did not know.

Davis could have told him, had he been willing to speak or capable of speech.

CONCLUSION

He'd Have Seen Me Righted

It was August once again—August, fine, warm, and sunshiny—just one year after that damp afternoon on which Paul Murray and his friend stood in front of the Ship at Lower Halliford. No lack of visitors that season. Hotels were full, and furnished houses at a premium. The hearts of lodging-house keepers were glad. Ladies arrayed in rainbow hues flashed about the quiet village streets; boatmen reaped a golden harvest; all sorts of crafts swarmed on the river. Men in flannels gallantly towed their feminine belongings up against a languidly flowing stream. Pater and materfamilias, and all the olive branches, big and little, were to be met on the Thames, and on the banks of Thames, from Richmond to Staines, and even higher still. The lilies growing around Dockett Point floated with their pure cups wide open to the sun; no close folding of the white wax-leaves around the golden centre that season. Beside the water purple loosestrife grew in great clumps of brilliant colour dazzling to the sight. It was, in fact, a glorious August, in which pleasure-seekers could idle and sun themselves and get tanned to an almost perfect brown without the slightest trouble.

During the past twelvemonth local tradition had tried hard to add another ghost at Dumsey Deep to that already established in the adjoining Stabbery; but the unshrinking brightness of that glorious summer checked belief in it for the time. No doubts when the dull autumn days came again, and the long winter nights, full of awful possibilities, folded water and land in fog and darkness, a figure dressed in grey silk and black velvet fichu, with a natty grey hat trimmed with black and white feathers on its phantom head, with small feet covered by the thinnest of openwork stockings, from which the shoes, so much too large, had dropped long ago, would reappear once more, to the terror of all who heard, but for the time being, snugly tucked up in holy ground the girl whose heart had rejoiced in her beauty, her youth, her admirers, and her finery, was lying quite still and quiet, with closed eyes, and ears that heard neither the church bells nor the splash of oars nor the murmur of human voices.

Others, too, were missing from—though not missed by—Shepperton (the Thames villages miss no human being so long as other human beings, with plenty of money, come down by rail, boat, or carriage to supply his place). Paul Murray, Dick Savill, and Walter Grantley were absent. Mrs. Heath, too, had gone, a tottering, heartbroken woman, to

Mr. Pointer's, where she was most miserable, but where she and her small possessions were taken remarkably good care of.

"Only a year agone," she said one day, "my girl was with me. In the morning she wore her pretty cambric with pink spots; and in the afternoon, that grey silk in which she was buried—for we durst not change a thread, but just wrapped a winding-sheet round what was left. O! Lucy, Lucy, Lucy! to think I bore you for that!" and then she wept softly, and nobody heeded or tried to console her, for "what," as Mrs. Pointer wisely said, "was the use of fretting over a daughter dead a twelvemonth, and never much of a comfort neither?"

Mr. Richard Savill was still "grinding away," to quote his expression. Walter Grantley had departed, so reported his friends, for the diamond-fields; his enemies improved on this by carelessly answering,—

"Grantley! O, he's gone to the devil;" which latter statement could not have been quite true, since he has been back in England for a long time, and is now quite well to do and reconciled to his family.

As for Paul Murray, there had been all sorts of rumours floating about concerning him.

The honeymoon had been unduly protracted; from place to place the married pair wandered—never resting, never staying; alas! for him there was no rest—there could be none here.

It mattered not where he went—east, west, south, or north—those noiseless wet feet followed; no train was swift enough to outstrip them; no boat could cut the water fast enough to leave them behind; they tracked him with dogged persistence; they were with him sleeping, walking, eating, drinking, praying—for Paul Murray in those days often prayed after a desperate heathenish fashion—and yet the plague was not stayed; the accursed thing still dogged him like a Fate.

After a while people began to be shy of him, because the footsteps were no more intermittent; they were always where he was. Did he enter a cathedral, they accompanied him; did he walk solitary through the woods or pace the lake-side, or wander by the sea, they were ever and always with the unhappy man.

They were worse than any evil conscience, because conscience often sleeps, and they from the day of his marriage never did. They had waited for that—waited till he should raise the cup of happiness to his lips, in order to fill it with gall—waited till his wife's dream of bliss was perfect, and then wake her to the knowledge of some horror more agonizing than death.

There were times when he left his young wife for days and days, and went, like those possessed of old, into the wilderness, seeking rest and finding none; for no legion of demons could have cursed a man's life more than those wet feet, which printed marks on Paul Murray's heart that might have been branded by red-hot irons.

All that had gone before was as nothing to the trouble of having involved another in the horrible mystery of his own life—and that other a gentle, innocent, loving creature he might just as well have killed as married.

He did not know what to do. His brain was on fire; he had lost all hold upon himself, all grip over his mind. On the sea of life he tossed like a ship without a rudder, one minute taking a resolve to shoot himself, the next turing his steps to seek some priest, and confess the whole matter fully and freely, and, before he had walked a dozen yards, determining to go away into some savage and desolate land, where those horrible feet might, if they pleased, follow him to his grave.

By degrees this was the plan which took firm root in his dazed brain; and accordingly one morning he started for England, leaving a note in which he asked his wife to follow him. He never meant to see her sweet face again, and he never did. He had determined to go to his father-in-law and confess to him; and accordingly, on the anniversary of Lucy's death, he found himself at Losdale Court, where vague rumours of some unaccountable trouble had preceded him.

Mr. Ketterick was brooding over these rumours in his library, when, as if in answer to his thoughts, the servant announced Mr. Murray.

"Good God!" exclaimed the older man, shocked by the white, haggard face before him, "what is wrong?"

"I have been ill," was the reply.

"Where is your wife?"

"She is following me. She will be here in a day or so."

"Why did you not travel together?"

"That is what I have come to tell you."

Then he suddenly stopped and put his hand to his heart. He had voluntarily come up for execution, and now his courage failed him. His manhood was gone, his nerves unstrung. He was but a poor, weak, wasted creature, worn out by the ceaseless torment of those haunting feet, which, however, since he turned his steps to England had never followed him. Why had he travelled to Losdale Court? Might he not have crossed the ocean and effaced himself in the Far West, without telling his story at all?

Just as he had laid down the revolver, just as he had turned from the priest's door, so now he felt he could not say that which he had come determined to say.

"I have walked too far," he said, after a pause. "I cannot talk just yet. Will you leave me for half an hour? No; I don't want anything, thank you—except to be quiet." Quiet!—ah, heavens!

After a little he rose and passed out on to the terrace. Around there was beauty and peace and sunshine. He—he—was the only jarring element, and even on him there seemed falling a numbed sensation which for the time being simulated rest.

He left the terrace and crossed the lawn till he came to a great cedar tree, under which there was a seat, where he could sit a short time before leaving the Court.

Yes, he would go away and make no sign. Dreamily he thought of the wild lone lands beyond the sea, where there would be none to ask whence he came or marvel about the curse which followed him. Over the boundless prairie, up the mountain heights, let those feet pursue him if they would. Away from his fellows he could bear his burden. He would confess to no man—only to God, who knew his sin and sorrow; only to his Maker, who might have pity on the work of his hands, and some day bid that relentless avenger be still.

No, he would take no man into his confidence; and even as he so decided, the brightness of the day seemed to be clouded over, warmth was exchanged for a deadly chill, a horror of darkness seemed thrown like a pall over him, and a rushing sound as of many waters filled his ears.

An hour later, when Mr. Ketterick sought his son-in-law, he found him lying on the ground, which was wet and trampled, as though by hundreds of little feet.

His shouts brought help, and Paul Murray was carried into the house, where they laid him on a couch and piled rugs and blankets over his shivering body.

"Fetch a doctor at once," said Mr. Ketterick.

"And a clergyman," added the housekeeper.

"No, a magistrate," cried the sick man, in a loud voice.

They had thought him insensible, and, startled, looked at each other. After that he spoke no more, but turned his head away from them and lay quiet.

The doctor was the first to arrive. With quick alertness he stepped across the room, pulled aside the coverings, and took the patient's hand; then after gently moving the averted face, he said solemnly, like a man whose occupation has gone,—

"I can do nothing here; he is dead."

It was true. Whatever his secret, Paul Murray carried it with him to a country further distant than the lone land where he had thought to hide his misery.

"It is of no use talking to me," said Mr. Davis, when subsequently telling his story. "If Mr. Murray had been a gentleman as was a gentleman, he'd have seen me righted, dead or not. *She* was able to come back—at least, her feet were; and he could have done the same if he'd liked. It was as bad as swindling not making a fresh will after he was married. How was I to know that will would turn out so much waste paper? And then when I asked for my own, Mrs. Murray dismissed me without a character, and Mr. Ketterick's lawyers won't give me anything either; so a lot I've made by being a faithful servant, and I'd have all servants take warning by me."

Mr. Davis is his own servant now, and a very bad master he finds himself.

Anonymous

THE
OLD LADY IN BLACK

AN EPISODE OF MONTE CARLO.

There was not under the stars a happier man than I, Frederick
Luscombe, on a certain January evening in the year 1889, when, with
my young wife on my arm, I ascended the steps of the Casino at
Monte Carlo.

Young, healthy, and prosperous—my father was the head of an old-
established Midland banking-firm—married, just a week ago, to the
girl I adored, it really seemed that I had nothing left to wish for.

Georgie and I were spending our honeymoon at Nice, but had run
over to Monte Carlo for the day, and strolled into the Casino "just
to look at the tables."

We did not intend to play; we should be sure to lose, Georgie said,
quoting the proverb: "Happy in love, unlucky in play."

So for the first half hour we contented ourselves with looking on,
while a friend whom we had encountered at the hotel where we dined
pointed out the different celebrities for Georgie's benefit.

It was her first visit, and she looked about her with eager interest and curiosity.

"I am disappointed," she declared at last. "I expected it would be a scene of wild excitement; but all these people look as dull and decorous as if they were in church, and there are no 'types' among them."

"Look at that face opposite," I whispered—"the old lady in black. Isn't she 'typical' enough for you?"

She was a tall, gaunt old woman, spectrally thin, with haughty aquiline features which had once been handsome, and haggard dark eyes, unnaturally bright. Her face was calm and inscrutable as a mask, but her lips looked dry and feverish, and the withered claw-like hand she stretched out to deposit her stakes shook with suppressed agitation.

"What a weird old woman!" Georgie murmured. "Who is she, I wonder? Captain Fergusson, who is that old witch, opposite?"

"The old witch, my dear Mrs. Luscombe, is the Princess Vera Zaterinski."

" 'Princess'!"

"An authentic Russian Princess, widow of Prince Constantine Zaterinski, and one of the most inveterate gamblers in Europe. She has lost at play a princely fortune; has alienated children, relatives, and friends, and now is living miserably, Heaven knows how, with no companion or attendant but that ancient serving-man in shabby livery who is standing behind her chair."

"What a life! It ought to be a warning to us," my wife said solemnly; and almost in the same breath added inconsistently: "Frederick, I think I should like to stake a louis—just one, to see how it feels. Of course I shall lose, but never mind!"

But, in spite of the proverb, she did not lose, and, encouraged by her unexpected success, played on till she had accumulated a little heap of notes and gold, which she showed us in laughing triumph.

"There, you have gambled as much as is good for you," I said at last, drawing her away. "Look at your opposite neighbour, and be warned in time."

"Ah! poor thing, I wish I could have given her my luck," my wife answered, glancing compassionately at the old Princess, who had been losing heavily.

Though outwardly calm and unmoved as ever, her face was deadly pale, and her hand, on the forefinger of which gleamed a massive gold signet ring, closed convulsively on the worn leather pocket-book, from which she had just extracted a hundred-franc note.

"I believe that is her last stake," Georgie whispered. "Oh, I hope she will win this time!"

But again the Princess lost.

She watched as the croupier carelessly raked in her note with the other losings, then rose abruptly, with a look of such dumb despair as I trust I may never see on a human face again.

The other players made way for her; there was a tragic dignity in her figure which imposed respect, and the old man-servant, who had been anxiously watching her, came forward with a deferential bow. Accepting the proffered support of his arm, she moved away with the majesty of a fallen queen.

"Poor thing!" Georgie repeated, as we too moved away. "Yes, I know it is her own fault, but I can't help pitying her. Now I have played myself I understand how fierce the temptation must be—how one is drawn on in spite of one's self."

"She has dropped her pocket-book," I remarked, as we passed the place where she had been sitting.

"Is it empty?" my wife inquired. "I thought so—perhaps that note was all she had left in the world! I wish— Oh, Frederick," she broke off, with a sudden change of tone, clasping her hands on my arm, "I have such a lovely idea! Put my winnings in it and give it back to her."

"My dear child, she would be mortally offended," I objected. "She looks as proud as Lucifer."

"But she won't find it out till she gets home, and she will never see us again. Quick, before she is out of sight!"

I shrugged my shoulders, but without further protest placed a roll of notes in the inner pocket of the book, and, leaving Georgie in charge of my friend, hastened in pursuit of the Princess and her companion. They had left the gambling-rooms, and were passing through the outer hall.

"I beg your pardon, Madame," I said in French, "I think this is yours. You dropped it at the roulette table just now."

She looked at me vaguely a moment, as if the sense of my words had not reached her, then took it from my hand with a faint smile.

"Yes, it is mine. I thank you, sir," she answered, and bowing to me with high-bred courtesy, passed on.

A few moments later we too left the Casino by another entrance.

As we emerged from the heated rooms into the sweet, cool night air, Georgie drew a deep breath of relief.

"I am cured of gambling," she said, seriously. "The Princess Zaterinski's face is worth a hundred sermons. Frederick, let's go home."

II.

Three years passed before I saw Monte Carlo again—disastrous years for me!

The firm of which my father was the head had failed little more than a year after my marriage, in a financial crisis which brought many another house to ruin. My poor father did not long survive the blow, and I had to begin life afresh, hampered by a delicate wife and a young child.

For myself I was not afraid of poverty or hard work; I had courage, energy, and capacity enough to make my own way. It was for my wife I feared, my darling Georgie, who was so little fitted to endure the least hardship or privation. She had not been strong since the birth of our child, and the doctors pronounced it imperatively necessary for her to spend the winter in the south.

I had managed to bring her to Nice, but our slender "reserve fund" would soon be exhausted, and I should be compelled to take her back just at the bleakest period of the treacherous English spring.

My heart sank when I thought what might be the consequences.

She was always bright, hopeful, and unselfish, and if she had any fears about herself, never let me suspect them.

It was at her desire that I was at Monte Carlo this evening; it would "cheer me up" she said, though in fact it had quite an opposite effect. The happy memories the place brought back to me gave a keener edge to my present trouble.

However, I entered, and after wandering aimlessly for a time about the garish rooms, I found myself at the very table where Georgie and I had stood to watch the players.

Everything seemed exactly as it had been that night. The same motley crowd drifting to and fro, the same faces gathered round the tables; the same croupiers, with their monotonous cuckoo-cry. "*Faites vos jeux—le jeu est fait; rien ne va plus!*"

Almost unconsciously I took out my purse, and was about to place a twenty-franc piece on "Blanc," when a woman's voice behind me said quietly, in French: "Put it on the red."

I turned quickly, and found myself confronted by a face that seemed familiar to me, though I could not at first recall where I had seen it before; a face with thin, aquiline features, and deep-set dark eyes.

"On the red," she repeated, pointing to the table.

I recognised her then by that wasted hand with the gold seal-ring on the forefinger—it was the Princess Zaterinski.

Startlingly pale, and thinner if possible than ever, but otherwise unchanged.

Mechanically I complied—and won. I was about to take up my winnings when she interposed, in the same distinct, imperious under-tone, audible to me alone: "Leave them."

Again I obeyed, and again won.

The next time it was a number she indicated, and once more her forecast proved correct.

I played on automatically, in obedience to her whispered dictates, and always with success.

My strange run of luck began to attract attention, and other players timidly followed my lead.

I "plunged" recklessly; doubled and trebled my stakes; still my good fortune held.

My heart beat fast and my hands trembled as, time after time, I gathered in a handful of notes and gold to add to the growing heap at my side.

The croupiers began to look queerly at each other, and a whisper ran round the table that if this phenomenal luck continued long enough, I should break the bank.

My excitement rose to fever heat. I played on as one in a dream, seeing nothing but the table before me, hearing nothing but the low distinct voice of my monitress, whose prompting never once misled me. I forgot my troubles, I thought neither of the past nor the future; all was effaced in the delirium of the moment.

How long I played I know not, for I had lost all count of time, but at last the monitory voice said quietly: "You have won enough. Go now, and never enter this place again."

Her words broke the spell.

"Madame—" I began quickly, turning to accost her, but she was already moving away.

She looked at me over her shoulder with a grave smile—a smile which haunted me long afterwards.

"I have paid my debt," she murmured. "Adieu!"

The next moment she had disappeared in the crowd.

I drew a deep breath, and looked incredulously at the money so strangely won, half fearing it was but fairy-gold, which would turn to dead leaves in my grasp. But no, it was solid and tangible; and as I realized what it represented—a fresh start in life for me, care and comfort for my wife, a provision for my child, my heart swelled with gratitude towards my strange benefactress, and I felt that I could not let her go unthanked.

I thrust my winnings into my pockets and hastily buttoned my coat over them, looking eagerly round in search of her.

"That old lady who was standing behind me just now—did you notice in which direction she turned?" I asked my neighbour as I rose.

The Frenchman looked at me in surprise.

"I saw no lady near you, Monsieur," he replied.

"Yes, yes—a tall old lady in black; the Princess Zaterinski. You must have seen her," I persisted; "she was close to us a moment ago!"

One of the croupiers, near whom I stood, paused with his rake suspended, and looked up at me.

"*Whom* did you say, Monsieur?" he demanded, in a tone of emphatic astonishment.

"The Princess Zaterinski."

He shook his head.

"You are mistaken. It could not have been the Princess you saw!"

"But I assure you that it was! I know her by sight—I have seen her before!"

He shrugged his shoulders.

"It is quite impossible."

"Why impossible?" I demanded.

He paused to arrange the five-franc pieces in a neat little pile before him.

"Because, Monsieur, the Princess Zaterinski is dead," he answered deliberately. "She died at Nice a year ago, and is buried in the Russian cemetery there . . . Messieurs, *faites vos jeux!*"

Mrs. Margaret Oliphant

Mrs. Margaret Oliphant Oliphant (née Wilson) (1828–1897) was Scottish by birth, but spent most of her literary life in and around London. In one respect she was an exemplary British Victorian woman writer. Her husband died after a long illness while the Oliphants were in Italy, and Margaret Oliphant found herself penniless, with three small children to support. Their number was eventually increased when she was forced to take in her dead brother's children. She turned to writing for a livelihood and soon became known as one of the most prolific and versatile writers of quality: she wrote very capable domestic novels, adventure stories, historical novels, histories of the Italian cities, travel books, essays, biographies, a publishing history, and a history of Victorian literature. Her autobiography is still read for its description of hardships alternately seen through despair and faith.

Mrs. Oliphant's domestic novels were well-liked in the United States, but her greatest renown came from a series of supernatural fiction, the so-called "Little Pilgrim" stories, which told of the after-death experiences of a humble, self-sacrificing woman. While Mrs. Oliphant's heaven in these self-projective stories is too saccharine and too smug for modern tastes, her various hells and purgatories (which bear strong resemblances to British industrial cities) are vividly imagined. Equally popular in America was her short novel A Beleaguered City (1879), in which the dead rise in protest against the materialism and utilitarianism of a French city.

"The Library Window" (1896), one of Mrs. Oliphant's last works, lacks the religiosity of much of her other supernatural fiction. Set in a small Scottish town, it is believed to have autobiographical elements. Despite its late date of composition and publication, it is really a story that could have been written twenty years earlier.

THE LIBRARY WINDOW

I was not aware at first of the many discussions which had gone on about that window. It was almost opposite one of the windows of the large old-fashioned drawing-room of the house in which I spent that summer, which was of so much importance in my life. Our house and the library were on opposite sides of the broad High Street of St. Rule's, which is a fine street, wide and ample, and very quiet, as strangers think who come from noisier places; but in a summer evening there is much coming and going, and the stillness is full of sound—the sound of footsteps and pleasant voices, softened by the summer air. There are even exceptional moments when it is noisy: the time of the fair, and on Saturday night sometimes, and when there are excursion trains. Then even the softest sunny air of the evening will not smooth the harsh tones and the stumbling steps; but at these unlovely moments we shut the windows, and even I, who am so fond of that deep recess where I can take refuge from all that is going on inside, and make myself a spectator of all the varied story out of doors, withdraw from my watch-tower. To tell the truth, there never was very much going on inside. The house belonged to my aunt, to whom (she says, Thank God!) nothing ever happens. I believe that many things have happened to her in her time; but that was all over at the period of which I am speaking, and she was old, and very quiet. Her life went on in a routine never broken. She got up at the same hour every day, and did the same things in the same rotation, day by day the same. She said that this was the greatest support in the world, and that routine is a kind of salvation. It may be so; but it is a very dull salvation, and I used to feel that I would rather have incident, whatever kind of incident it might be. But then at that time I was not old, which makes all the difference.

At the time of which I speak the deep recess of the drawing-room window was a great comfort to me. Though she was an old lady (perhaps because she was so old) she was very tolerant, and had a kind of feeling for me. She never said a word, but often gave me a smile when she saw how I had built myself up, with my books and my basket of work. I did very little work, I fear—now and then a few stitches when the spirit moved me, or when I had got well afloat in a dream, and was more tempted to follow it out than to read my books, as sometimes happened. At other times, and if the book were interesting, I used to get through volume after volume sitting there, paying no attention to anybody. And yet I did pay a kind of attention. Aunt Mary's old ladies came in to call, and I heard them talk, though I very seldom listened; but for all that, if they had anything to say that was interesting, it is curious how I found it in my mind afterwards, as if the air had blown it to me. They came and went, and I had the sensation of their old bonnets gliding out and in, and their dresses rustling; and now and then had to jump up and shake hands with some one who knew me, and asked after my papa and mamma. Then Aunt Mary would give me a little smile again, and I slipped back to my window. She never seemed to mind. My mother would not have let me do it, I know. She would have remembered dozens of things there were to do. She would have sent me upstairs to fetch something which I was quite sure she did not want, or downstairs to carry some quite unnecessary message to the housemaid. She liked to keep me running about. Perhaps that was one reason why I was so fond of Aunt Mary's drawing-room, and the deep recess of the window, and the curtain that fell half over it, and the broad window-seat, where one could collect so many things without being found fault with for untidiness. Whenever we had anything the matter with us in these days, we were sent to St. Rule's to get up our strength. And this was my case at the time of which I am going to speak.

Everybody had said, since ever I learned to speak, that I was fantastic and fanciful and dreamy, and all the other words with which a girl who may happen to like poetry, and to be fond of thinking, is so often made uncomfortable. People don't know what they mean when they say fantastic. It sounds like Madge Wildfire or something of that sort. My mother thought I should always be busy, to keep nonsense out of my head. But really I was not at all fond of nonsense. I was rather serious than otherwise. I would have been no trouble to anybody if I had been left to myself. It was only that I had a sort of second-sight, and was conscious of things to which I paid no attention.

Even when reading the most interesting book, the things that were being talked about blew in to me; and I heard what the people were saying in the streets as they passed under the window. Aunt Mary always said I could do two or indeed three things at once—both read and listen, and see. I am sure that I did not listen much, and seldom looked out, of set purpose—as some people do who notice what bonnets the ladies in the street have on; but I did hear what I couldn't help hearing, even when I was reading my book, and I did see all sorts of things, though often for a whole half-hour I might never lift my eyes.

This does not explain what I said at the beginning, that there were many discussions about that window. It was, and still is, the last window in the row, of the College Library, which is opposite my aunt's house in the High Street. Yet it is not exactly opposite, but a little to the west, so that I could see it best from the left side of my recess. I took it calmly for granted that it was a window like any other till I first heard the talk about it which was going on in the drawing-room. "Have you never made up your mind, Mrs. Balcarres," said old Mr. Pitmilly, "whether that window opposite is a window or no?" He said Mistress Balcarres—and he was always called Mr. Pitmilly Morton: which was the name of his place.

"I am never sure of it, to tell the truth," said Aunt Mary, "all these years."

"Bless me!" said one of the old ladies, "and what window may that be?"

Mr. Pitmilly had a way of laughing as he spoke, which did not please me; but it was true that he was not perhaps desirous of pleasing me. He said, "Oh, just the window opposite," with his laugh running through his words; "our friend can never make up her mind about it, though she has been living opposite it since—"

"You need never mind the date," said another; "the Leebrary window! Dear me, what should it be but a window? up at that height it could not be a door."

"The question is," said my aunt, "if it is a real window with glass in it, or if it is merely painted, or if it once was a window, and has been built up. And the oftener people look at it, the less they are able to say."

"Let me see this window," said old Lady Carnbee, who was very active and strong-minded; and then they all came crowding upon me—three or four old ladies, very eager, and Mr. Pitmilly's white hair appearing over their heads, and my aunt sitting quiet and smiling behind.

"I mind the window very well," said Lady Carnbee; "ay: and so do more than me. But in its present appearance it is just like any other window; but has not been cleaned, I should say, in the memory of man."

"I see what ye mean," said one of the others. "It is just a very dead thing without any reflection in it; but I've seen as bad before."

"Ay, it's dead enough," said another, "but that's no rule; for these huzzies of women-servants in this ill age—"

"Nay, the women are well enough," said the softest voice of all, which was Aunt Mary's. "I will never let them risk their lives cleaning the outside of mine. And there are no women-servants in the Old Library: there is maybe something more in it than that."

They were all pressing into my recess, pressing upon me, a row of old faces, peering into something they could not understand. I had a sense in my mind how curious it was, the wall of old ladies in their old satin gowns all glazed with age, Lady Carnbee with her lace about her head. Nobody was looking at me or thinking of me; but I feel unconsciously the contrast of my youngness to their oldness, and stared at them as they stared over my head at the Library window. I had given it no attention up to this time. I was more taken up with the old ladies than with the thing they were looking at.

"The framework is all right at least, I can see that, and pented black—"

"And the panes are pented black too. It's no window, Mrs. Balcarres. It has been filled in, in the days of the window duties: you will mind, Leddy Carnbee."

"Mind!" said that oldest lady. "I mind when your mother was marriet, Jeanie: and that's neither the day nor yesterday. But as for the window, it's just a delusion: and that is my opinion of the matter, if you ask me."

"There's a great want of light in that muckle room at the college," said another. "If it was a window, the Leebrary would have more light."

"One thing is clear," said one of the younger ones, "it cannot be a window to see through. It may be filled in or it may be built up, but it is not a window to give light."

"And who ever heard of a window that was no to see through?" Lady Carnbee said. I was fascinated by the look on her face, which was a curious scornful look as of one who knew more than she chose to say: and then my wandering fancy was caught by her hand as she held it up, throwing back the lace that drooped over it. Lady Carnbee's lace was the chief thing about her—heavy black Spanish lace with large flowers. Everything she wore was trimmed with it. A large veil of it hung over her old bonnet. But her hand coming out of this heavy lace was a curious thing to see. She had very long fingers, very taper, which had been much admired in her youth; and her hand was very white, or rather more than white, pale, bleached, and bloodless, with large blue veins standing up upon the back; and she wore some fine rings, among others a big diamond in an ugly old claw setting. They were too big for her, and were wound round and round with yellow silk to make them keep on: and this little cushion of silk, turned brown with long wearing, had twisted round so that it was more conspicuous than the jewels; while the big diamond blazed underneath in the hollow of her hand, like some dangerous thing hiding and sending out darts of light. The hand, which seemed to come almost to a point, with this strange ornament underneath, clutched at my half-terrified imagination. It too seemed to mean far more than was said. I felt as if it might clutch me with sharp claws, and the lurking, dazzling creature bite—with a sting that would go to the heart.

Presently, however, the circle of the old faces broke up, the old ladies returned to their seats, and Mr. Pitmilly, small but very erect, stood up in the midst of them, talking with mild authority like a little oracle among the ladies. Only Lady Carnbee always contradicted the neat, little old gentleman. She gesticulated, when she talked, like a French-woman, and darted forth that hand of hers with the lace hanging over it, so that I always caught a glimpse of the lurking diamond. I thought she looked like a witch among the comfortable little group which gave such attention to everything Mr. Pitmilly said.

"For my part, it is my opinion there is no window there at all," he said. "It's very like the thing that's called in scienteefic language an optical illusion. It arises generally, if I may use such a word in the presence of ladies, from a liver that is not just in the perfitt order and balance that organ demands—and then you will see things—a blue dog, I remember, was the thing in one case, and in another—"

"The man has gane gyte," said Lady Carnbee; "I mind the windows in the Auld Leebrary as long as I mind anything. Is the Leebrary itself an optical illusion too?"

"Na, na," and "No, no," said the old ladies; "a blue dogue would be a strange vagary: but the Library we have all kent from our youth," said one. "And I mind when the Assemblies were held there one year when the Town Hall was building," another said.

"It is just a great divert to me," said Aunt Mary: but what was strange was that she paused there, and said in a low tone, "now": and then went on again, "for whoever comes to my house, there are aye discussions about that window. I have never just made up my mind about it myself. Sometimes I think it's a case of these wicked window duties, as you said, Miss Jeanie, when half the windows in our houses were blocked up to save the tax. And then, I think, it may be due to that blank kind of building like the great new buildings on the Earthen Mound in Edinburgh, where the windows are just ornaments. And then whiles I am sure I can see the glass shining when the sun catches it in the afternoon."

"You could so easily satisfy yourself, Mrs. Balcarres, if you were to—"

"Give a laddie a penny to cast a stone, and see what happens," said Lady Carnbee.

"But I am not sure that I have any desire to satisfy myself," Aunt Mary said. And then there was a stir in the room, and I had to come out from my recess and open the door for the old ladies and see them downstairs, as they all went away following one another. Mr. Pitmilly gave his arm to Lady Carnbee, though she was always contradicting him; and so the tea-party dispersed. Aunt Mary came to the head of the stairs with her guests in an old-fashioned gracious way, while I went down with them to see that the maid was ready at the door. When I came back Aunt Mary was still standing in the recess looking out. Returning to my seat she said, with a kind of wistful look, "Well, honey: and what is your opinion?"

"I have no opinion. I was reading my book all the time," I said.

"And so you were, honey, and no' very civil; but all the same I ken well you heard every word we said."

II

It was a night in June; dinner was long over, and had it been winter the maids would have been shutting up the house, and my Aunt Mary preparing to go upstairs to her room. But it was still clear daylight, that daylight out of which the sun has been long gone, and which has no longer any rose reflections, but all has sunk into a pearly neutral tint —a light which is daylight yet is not day. We had taken a turn in the garden after dinner, and now we had returned to what we called our usual occupations. My aunt was reading. The English post had come in, and she had got her *Times*, which was her great diversion. The *Scotsman* was her morning reading, but she liked her *Times* at night.

As for me, I too was at my usual occupation, which at that time was doing nothing. I had a book as usual, and was absorbed in it; but I was conscious of all that was going on all the same. The people strolled along the broad pavement, making remarks as they passed under the open window which came up into my story or my dream, and some-times made me laugh. The tone and the faint sing-song, or rather chant, of the accent, which was "a wee Fifish," was novel to me, and associated with holiday, and pleasant; and sometimes they said to each other something that was amusing, and often something that suggested a whole story; but presently they began to drop off, the footsteps slackened, the voices died away. It was getting late, though the clear soft daylight went on and on. All through the lingering evening, which seemed to consist of interminable hours, long but not weary, drawn out as if the spell of the light and the outdoor life might never end, I had now and then, quite unawares, cast a glance at the mysterious window which my aunt and her friends had discussed, as I felt, though I dared not say it even to myself, rather foolishly. It caught my eye without any intention on my part, as I paused, as it were, to take breath, in the flowing and current of undistinguishable thoughts and things from without and within which carried me along. First it occurred to me, with a little sensation of discovery, how absurd to say it was not a window, a living window, one to see through! Why, then, had they never *seen* it, these old folk? I saw as I looked up suddenly the faint greyness as of visible space within—a room behind, certainly—dim, as it was natural a room should be on the other side of the street— quite indefinite: yet so clear that if some one were to come to the window there would be nothing surprising in it. For certainly there was a feeling of space behind the panes which these old half-blind ladies had disputed about whether they were glass or only fictitious panes marked on the wall. How silly! when eyes that could see could make it out in a minute. It was only a greyness at present, but it was unmistakable, a space that went back into gloom, as every room does when you look into it across a street. There were no curtains to show whether it was inhabited or not; but a room—oh, as distinctly as ever room was! I was pleased with myself, but said nothing, while Aunt Mary rustled her paper, waiting for a favourable moment to announce a discovery which settled her problem at once. Then I was carried away upon the stream again, and forgot the window, till somebody threw unawares a word from the outer world, "I'm goin' hame; it'll soon be dark." Dark! what was the fool thinking of? it never would be dark if one waited out, wandering in the soft air for hours longer; and then my eyes, acquiring easily that new habit, looked across the way again.

Ah, now! nobody indeed had come to the window; and no light had been lighted, seeing it was still beautiful to read by—a still, clear, colourless light; but the room inside had certainly widened. I could see the grey space and air a little deeper, and a sort of vision, very dim, of a wall, and something against it; something dark, with the blackness that a solid article, however indistinctly seen, takes in the lighter dark- ness that is only space—a large, black, dark thing coming out into the grey. I looked more intently, and made sure it was a piece of furniture, either a writing-table or perhaps a large bookcase. No doubt it must be the last, since this was part of the old library. I never visited the old College Library, but I had seen such places before, and I could well imagine it to myself. How curious that for all the time these old people had looked at it, they had never seen this before!

It was more silent now, and my eyes, I suppose, had grown dim with gazing, doing my best to make it out, when suddenly Aunt Mary said, "Will you ring the bell, my dear? I must have my lamp."

"Your lamp?" I cried, "when it is still daylight." But then I gave another look at my window, and perceived with a start that the light had indeed changed: for now I saw nothing. It was still light, but there was so much more change in the light that my room, with the grey space and the large shadowy bookcase, had gone out, and I saw them no more: for even a Scotch night in June, though it looks as if it would never end, does darken at the last. I had almost cried out, but checked myself, and rang the bell for Aunt Mary, and made up my mind I would say nothing till next morning, when to be sure naturally it would be more clear.

Next morning I rather think I forgot all about it—or was busy: or was more idle than usual: the two things meant nearly the same. At all events I thought no more of the window, though I still sat in my own, opposite to it, but occupied with some other fancy. Aunt Mary's visitors came as usual in the afternoon; but their talk was of other things, and for a day or two nothing at all happened to bring back my thoughts into this channel. It might be nearly a week before the subject came back, and once more it was old Lady Carnbee who set me thinking; not that she said anything upon that particular theme. But she was the last of my aunt's afternoon guests to go away, and when she rose to leave she threw up her hands, with those lively gesticulations which so many old Scotch ladies have. "My faith!" said she, "there is that bairn there still like a dream. Is the creature bewitched, Mary Balcarres? and is she bound to sit there by night and by day for the rest of her days? You should mind that there's things about, uncanny for women of our blood."

I was too much startled at first to recognise that it was of me she was speaking. She was like a figure in a picture, with her pale face the colour of ashes, and the big pattern of the Spanish lace hanging half over it, and her hand held up, with the big diamond blazing at me from the inside of her uplifted palm. It was held up in surprise, but it looked as if it were raised in malediction; and the diamond threw out darts of light and glared and twinkled at me. If it had been in its right place it would not have mattered; but there, in the open of the hand! I started up, half in terror, half in wrath. And then the old lady laughed, and her hand dropped. "I've wakened you to life, and broke the spell," she said, nodding her old head at me, while the large black silk flowers of the lace waved and threatened. And she took my arm to go downstairs, laughing and bidding me be steady, and no' tremble and shake like a broken reed. "You should be as steady as a rock at your age. I was like a young tree," she said, leaning so heavily that my willowy girlish frame quivered—"I was a support to virtue, like Pamela, in my time."

"Aunt Mary, Lady Carnbee is a witch!" I cried, when I came back.

"Is that what you think, honey? well: maybe she once was," said Aunt Mary, whom nothing surprised.

And it was that night once more after dinner, and after the post came in, and *The Times*, that I suddenly saw the Library window again. I had seen it every day—and noticed nothing; but to-night, still in a little tumult of mind over Lady Carnbee and her wicked diamond which wished me harm, and her lace which waved threats and warnings at me, I looked across the street, and there I saw quite plainly the room opposite, far more clear than before. I saw dimly that it must be a large room, and that the big piece of furniture against the wall was a writing-desk. That in a moment, when first my eyes rested upon it, was quite clear: a large old-fashioned escritoire, standing out into the room: and I knew by the shape of it that it had a great many pigeon-holes and little drawers in the back, and a large table for writing. There was one just like it in my father's library at home. It was such a surprise to see it all so clearly that I closed my eyes, for the moment almost giddy, wondering how papa's desk could have come here—and then when I reminded myself that this was nonsense, and that there were many such writing-tables besides papa's, and looked again—lo! it had all become quite vague and indistinct as it was at first; and I saw nothing but the blank window, of which the old ladies could never be certain whether it was filled up to avoid the window-tax, or whether it had ever been a window at all.

This occupied my mind very much, and yet I did not say anything to Aunt Mary. For one thing, I rarely saw anything at all in the early part of the day; but then that is natural: you can never see into a place from outside, whether it is an empty room or a looking-glass, or people's eyes, or anything else that is mysterious, in the day. It has, I suppose, something to do with the light. But in the evening in June in Scotland—then is the time to see. For it is daylight, yet it is not day, and there is a quality in it which I cannot describe, it is so clear, as if every object was a reflection of itself.

I used to see more and more of the room as the days went on. The large escritoire stood out more and more into the space: with sometimes white glimmering things, which looked like papers lying on it: and once or twice I was sure I saw a pile of books on the floor close to the writing-table, as if they had gilding upon them in broken specks, like old books. It was always about the time when the lads in the street began to call to each other that they were going home, and sometimes a shriller voice would come from one of the doors, bidding somebody to "cry upon the laddies" to come back to their suppers. That was always the time I saw best, though it was close upon the moment when the veil seemed to fall and the clear radiance became less living, and all the sounds died out of the street, and Aunt Mary said in her soft voice, "Honey! will you ring for the lamp?" She said honey as people say darling: and I think it is a prettier word.

Then finally, while I sat one evening with my book in my hand, looking straight across the street, not distracted by anything, I saw a little movement within. It was not any one visible—but everybody must know what it is to see the stir in the air, the little disturbance— you cannot tell what it is, but that it indicates some one there, even though you can see no one. Perhaps it is a shadow making just one flicker in the still place. You may look at an empty room and the furniture in it for hours, and then suddenly there will be the flicker, and you know that something has come into it. It might only be a dog or a cat; it might be, if that were possible, a bird flying across; but it is some one, something living, which is so different, so completely different, in a moment from the things that are not living. It seemed to strike right through me, and I gave a little cry. Then Aunt Mary stirred a little, and put down the huge newspaper that almost covered her from sight, and said, "What is it, honey?" I cried "Nothing," with a little gasp, quickly, for I did not want to be disturbed just at this moment when somebody was coming! But I suppose she was not satisfied, for she got up and stood behind to see what it was, putting her hand on my shoulder. It was the softest touch in the world, but I could have flung it off angrily: for that moment everything was still again, and the place grew grey and I saw no more.

"Nothing," I repeated, but I was so vexed I could have cried. "I told you it was nothing, Aunt Mary. Don't you believe me, that you come to look—and spoil it all!"

I did not mean of course to say these last words; they were forced out of me. I was so much annoyed to see it all melt away like a dream: for it was no dream, but as real as—as real as—myself or anything I ever saw.

She gave my shoulder a little pat with her hand. "Honey," she said, "were you looking at something? Is't that? is't that?" "Is it what?" I wanted to say, shaking off her hand, but something in me stopped me: for I said nothing at all, and she went quietly back to her place. I suppose she must have rung the bell herself, for immediately I felt the soft flood of the light behind me and the evening outside dimmed down, as it did every night, and I saw nothing more.

It was next day, I think, in the afternoon that I spoke. It was brought on by something she said about her fine work. "I get a mist before my eyes," she said; "you will have to learn my old lace stitches, honey—for I soon will not see to draw the threads."

"Oh, I hope you will keep your sight," I cried, without thinking what I was saying. I was then young and very matter-of-fact. I had not found out that one may mean something, yet not half or a hundredth part of what one seems to mean: and even then probably hoping to be contradicted if it is anyhow against one's self.

"My sight!" she said, looking up at me with a look that was almost angry; "there is no question of losing my sight—on the contrary, my eyes are very strong. I may not see to draw fine threads, but I see at a distance as well as ever I did—as well as you do."

"I did not mean any harm. Aunt Mary," I said. "I thought you said— But how can your sight be as good as ever when you are in doubt about that window? I can see into the room as clear as—" My voice wavered, for I had just looked up and across the street, and I could have sworn that there was no window at all, but only a false image of one painted on the wall.

"Ah!" she said, with a little tone of keenness and of surprise: and she half rose up, throwing down her work hastily, as if she meant to come to me: then, perhaps seeing the bewildered look on my face, she paused and hesitated— "Ay, honey!" she said, "have you got so far ben as that?"

What did she mean? Of course I knew all the old Scotch phrases as well as I knew myself; but it is a comfort to take refuge in a little ignorance, and I know I pretended not to understand whenever I was put out. "I don't know what you mean by 'far ben,'" I cried out, very impatient. I don't know what might have followed, but some one just then came to call, and she could only give me a look before she went forward, putting out her hand to her visitor. It was a very soft look, but anxious, and as if she did not know what to do: and she shook her head a very little, and I thought, though there was a smile on her face, there was something wet about her eyes. I retired into my recess, and nothing more was said.

But it was very tantalising that it should fluctuate so; for sometimes I saw that room quite plain and clear—quite as clear as I could see

papa's library, for example, when I shut my eyes. I compared it
naturally to my father's study, because of the shape of the writing-
table, which, as I tell you, was the same as his. At times I saw the
papers on the table quite plain, just as I had seen his papers many a day.
And the little pile of books on the floor at the foot—not ranged
regularly in order, but put down one above the other, with all their
angles going different ways, and a speck of the old gilding shining
here and there. And then again at other times I saw nothing, absolutely
nothing, and was no better than the old ladies who had peered over my
head, drawing their eyelids together, and arguing that the window had
been shut up because of the old long-abolished window tax, or else
that it had never been a window at all. It annoyed me very much at
those dull moments to feel that I too puckered up my eyelids and saw
no better than they.

Aunt Mary's old ladies came and went day after day while June
went on. I was to go back in July, and I felt that I should be very
unwilling indeed to leave until I had quite cleared up—as I was indeed
in the way of doing—the mystery of that window which changed so
strangely and appeared quite a different thing, not only to different
people, but to the same eyes at different times. Of course I said to
myself it must simply be an effect of the light. And yet I did not quite
like that explanation either, but would have been better pleased to
make out to myself that it was some superiority in me which made it
so clear to me, if it were only the great superiority of young eyes over
old—though that was not quite enough to satisfy me, seeing it was a
superiority which I shared with every little lass and lad in the street. I
rather wanted, I believe, to think that there was some particular insight
in me which gave clearness to my sight—which was a most impertinent
assumption, but really did not mean half the harm it seems to mean
when it is put down here in black and white. I had several times again,
however, seen the room quite plain, and made out that it was a large
room, with a great picture in a dim gilded frame hanging on the farther
wall, and many other pieces of solid furniture making a blackness here
and there, besides the great escritoire against the wall, which had
evidently been placed near the window for the sake of the light. One
thing became visible to me after another, till I almost thought I should
end by being able to read the old lettering on one of the big volumes
which projected from the others and caught the light; but this was
all preliminary to the great event which happened about Midsummer
Day—the day of St. John, which was once so much thought of as a
festival, but now means nothing at all in Scotland any more than any
other of the saints' days: which I shall always think a great pity and
loss to Scotland, whatever Aunt Mary may say.

III

It was about midsummer, I cannot say exactly to a day when, but near that time, when the great event happened. I had grown very well acquainted by this time with that large dim room. Not only the escritoire, which was very plain to me now, with the papers upon it, and the books at its foot, but the great picture that hung against the farther wall, and various other shadowy pieces of furniture, especially a chair which one evening I saw had been moved into the space before the escritoire,—a little change which made my heart beat, for it spoke so distinctly of some one who must have been there, the some one who had already made me start, two or three times before, by some vague shadow of him or thrill of him which made a sort of movement in the silent space: a movement which made me sure that next minute I must see something or hear something which would explain the whole—if it were not that something always happened outside to stop it, at the very moment of its accomplishment. I had no warning this time of movement or shadow. I had been looking into the room very attentively a little while before, and had made out everything almost clearer than ever; and then had bent my attention again on my book, and read a chapter or two at a most exciting period of the story: and consequently had quite left St. Rule's, and the High Street, and the College Library, and was really in a South American forest, almost throttled by the flowery creepers, and treading softly lest I should put my foot on a scorpion or a dangerous snake. At this moment something suddenly calling my attention to the outside, I looked across, and then, with a start, sprang up, for I could not contain myself. I don't know what I said, but enough to startle the people in the room, one of whom was old Mr. Pitmilly. They all looked round upon me to ask what was the matter. And when I gave my usual answer of "Nothing," sitting down again shamefaced but very much excited, Mr. Pitmilly got up and came forward, and looked out, apparently to see what was the cause. He saw nothing, for he went back again, and I could hear him telling Aunt Mary not to be alarmed, for Missy had fallen into a doze with the heat, and had startled herself waking up, at which they all laughed: another time I could have killed him for his impertinence, but my mind was too much taken up now to pay any attention. My head was throbbing and my heart beating. I was in such high excitement, however, that to restrain myself completely, to be perfectly silent, was more easy to me then than at any other time of my life. I waited until the old gentleman had taken his seat again, and then I looked back. Yes, there he was! I had not been deceived. I knew then, when I looked across, that this was what I had been looking for all the time—that I had known he was there, and had been waiting for him, every time there was that flicker of movement in the room—him and no one else. And there at last, just as I had expected, he was. I don't know that in reality I ever had expected him, or any one: but this was what I felt when, suddenly looking into that curious dim room, I saw him there.

He was sitting in the chair, which he must have placed for himself, or which some one else in the dead of night when nobody was looking must have set for him, in front of the escritoire—with the back of his head towards me, writing. The light fell upon him from the left hand, and therefore upon his shoulders and the side of his head, which, however, was too much turned away to show anything of his face. Oh, how strange that there should be some one staring at him as I was doing, and he never to turn his head, to make a movement! If any one stood and looked at me, were I in the soundest sleep that ever was, I would wake, I would jump up, I would feel it through everything. But there he sat and never moved. You are not to suppose, though I said the light fell upon him from the left hand, that there was very much light. There never is in a room you are looking into like that across the street; but there was enough to see him by—the outline of his figure dark and solid, seated in the chair, and the fairness of his head visible faintly, a clear spot against the dimness. I saw this outline against the dim gilding of the frame of the large picture which hung on the farther wall.

I sat all the time the visitors were there, in a sort of rapture, gazing at this figure. I knew no reason why I should be so much moved. In an ordinary way, to see a student at an opposite window quietly doing his work might have interested me a little, but certainly it would not have moved me in any such way. It is always interesting to have a glimpse like this of an unknown life—to see so much and yet know so little, and to wonder, perhaps, what the man is doing, and why he never turns his head. One would go to the window—but not too close, lest he should see you and think you were spying upon him— and one would ask, Is he still there? is he writing, writing always? I wonder what he is writing! And it would be a great amusement: but no more. This was not my feeling at all in the present case. It was a sort of breathless watch, an absorption. I did not feel that I had eyes for anything else, or any room in my mind for another thought. I no longer heard, as I generally did, the stories and the wise remarks (or foolish) of Aunt Mary's old ladies or Mr. Pitmilly. I heard only a murmur behind me, the interchange of voices, one softer, one sharper; but it was not as in the time when I sat reading and heard every word, till the story in my book and the stories they were telling (what they said almost always shaped into stories), were all mingled into each other, and the hero in the novel became somehow the hero (or more likely heroine) of them all. But I took no notice of what they were saying now. And it was not that there was anything very interesting to look at, except the fact that he was there. He did nothing to keep up the absorption of my thoughts. He moved just so much as a man will do when he is very busily writing, thinking of nothing else. There was a faint turn of his head as he went from one side to another of the page he was writing; but it appeared to be a long page which never wanted turning. Just a little inclination when he was at the end of the line, outward, and then a little inclination inward when he began the next. That was little enough to keep one gazing. But I suppose it was the gradual course of events leading up to this, the finding out of one thing after another as the eyes got accustomed to the vague light: first the room itself, and then the writing-table, and then the other furniture, and last of all the human inhabitant who gave it all meaning. This was all so interesting that it was like a country which one had discovered. And then the extraordinary blindness of the other people who disputed among themselves whether it was a window at all! I did not, I am sure, wish to be disrespectful, and I was very fond of my Aunt Mary, and I liked Mr. Pitmilly well enough, and I was afraid of Lady Carnbee. But yet to think of the—I know I ought not to say stupidity—the blindness of them, the foolishness, the insensibility! discussing it as if a thing that your eyes could see was a thing to discuss! It would have been unkind to think it was because they were old and their faculties dimmed. It is so sad to think that the faculties grow dim, that such a woman as my Aunt Mary should fail in seeing, or hearing, or feeling, that I would not have dwelt on it for a moment, it would have seemed so cruel! And then such a clever old lady as Lady Carnbee, who could see through a millstone, people said—and Mr. Pitmilly, such an old man of the world. It did indeed bring tears to my eyes to think that all those clever people, solely by reason of being no longer young as I was, should have the simplest things shut out from them; and for all their wisdom and their knowledge be unable to see what a girl like me could see so easily. I was too much grieved for them to dwell upon that thought, and half ashamed, though perhaps half proud too, to be so much better off than they.

All those thoughts flitted through my mind as I sat and gazed across the street. And I felt there was so much going on in that room across the street! He was so absorbed in his writing, never looked up, never paused for a word, never turned round in his chair, or got up and walked about the room as my father did. Papa is a great writer, everybody says: but he would have come to the window and looked out, he would have drummed with his fingers on the pane, he would have watched a fly and helped it over a difficulty, and played with the fringe of the curtain, and done a dozen other nice, pleasant, foolish things, till the next sentence took shape. "My dear, I am waiting for a word," he would say to my mother when she looked at him, with a question why he was so idle, in her eyes; and then he would laugh, and go back again to his writing-table. But He over there never stopped at all. It was like a fascination. I could not take my eyes from him and that little scarcely perceptible movement he made, turning his head. I trembled with impatience to see him turn the page, or perhaps throw down his finished sheet on the floor, as somebody looking into a window like me once saw Sir Walter do, sheet after sheet. I should have cried out if this Unknown had done that. I should not have been able to help myself, whoever had been present; and gradually I got into such a state of suspense waiting for it to be done that my head grew hot and my hands cold. And then, just when there was a little movement of his elbow, as if he were about to do this, to be called away by Aunt Mary to see Lady Carnbee to the door! I believe I did not hear her till she had called me three times, and then I stumbled up, all flushed and hot, and nearly crying. When I came out from the recess to give the old lady my arm (Mr. Pitmilly had gone away some time before), she put up her hand and stroked my cheek. "What ails the bairn?" she said; "she's fevered. You must not let her sit her lane in the window, Mary Balcarres. You and me know what comes of that." Her old fingers had a strange touch, cold like something not living, and I felt that dreadful diamond sting me on the cheek.

I do not say that this was not just a part of my excitement and suspense; and I know it is enough to make any one laugh when the excitement was all about an unknown man writing in a room on the other side of the way, and my impatience because he never came to an end of the page. If you think I was not quite as well aware of this as any one could be! but the worst was that this dreadful old lady felt my heart beating against her arm that was within mine. "You are just in a dream," she said to me, with her old voice close at my ear as we went downstairs. "I don't know who it is about, but it's bound to be some man that is not worth it. If you were wise you would think of him no more."

"I am thinking of no man!" I said, half crying. "It is very unkind and dreadful of you to say so, Lady Carnbee. I never thought of—any man, in all my life!" I cried in a passion of indignation. The old lady clung tighter to my arm, and pressed it to her, not unkindly.

"Poor little bird," she said, "how it's strugglin' and flutterin'! I'm not saying but what it's more dangerous when it's all for a dream."

She was not at all unkind; but I was very angry and excited, and would scarcely shake that old pale hand which she put out to me from her carriage window when I had helped her in. I was angry with her, and I was afraid of the diamond, which looked up from under her finger as if it saw through and through me; and whether you believe me or not, I am certain that it stung me again—a sharp malignant prick, oh full of meaning! She never wore gloves, but only black lace mittens, through which that horrible diamond gleamed. I ran upstairs—she had been the last to go—and Aunt Mary too had gone to get ready for dinner, for it was late. I hurried to my place, and looked across, with my heart beating more than ever. I made quite sure I should see the finished sheet lying white upon the floor. But what I gazed at was only the dim blank of that window which they said was no window. The light had changed in some wonderful way during that five minutes I had been gone, and there was nothing, nothing, not a reflection, not a glimmer. It looked exactly as they all said, the blank form of a window painted on the wall. It was too much: I sat down in my excitement and cried as if my heart would break. I felt that they had done something to it, that it was not natural, that I could not bear their unkindness—even Aunt Mary. They thought it not good for me! not good for me! and they had done something—even Aunt Mary herself —and that wicked diamond that hid itself in Lady Carnbee's hand. Of course I knew all this was ridiculous as well as you could tell me; but I was exasperated by the disappointment and the sudden stop to all my excited feelings, and I could not bear it. It was more strong than I.

I was late for dinner, and naturally there were some traces in my eyes that I had been crying when I came into the full light in the dining-room, where Aunt Mary could look at me at her pleasure, and I could not run away. She said, "Honey, you have been shedding tears. I'm loth, loth that a bairn of your mother's should be made to shed tears in my house."

"I have not been made to shed tears," cried I; and then, to save myself another fit of crying, I burst out laughing and said, "I am afraid of that dreadful diamond on old Lady Carnbee's hand. It bites— I am sure it bites! Aunt Mary, look here."

"You foolish lassie," Aunt Mary said; but she looked at my cheek under the light of the lamp, and then she gave it a little pat with her soft hand. "Go away with you, you silly bairn. There is no bite; but a flushed cheek, my honey, and a wet eye. You must just read out my paper to me after dinner when the post is in: and we'll have no more thinking and no more dreaming for to-night."

"Yes, Aunt Mary," said I. But I knew what would happen; for when she opens up her *Times*, all full of the news of the world, and the speeches and things which she takes an interest in, though I cannot tell why—she forgets. And as I kept very quiet and made not a sound, she forgot to-night what she had said, and the curtain hung a little more over me than usual, and I sat down in my recess as if I had been a hundred miles away. And my heart gave a great jump, as if it would have come out of my breast; for he was there. But not as he had been in the morning—I suppose the light, perhaps, was not good enough to go on with his work without a lamp or candles—for he had turned away from the table and was fronting the window, sitting leaning back in his chair, and turning his head to me. Not to me—he knew nothing about me. I thought he was not looking at anything; but with his face turned my way, My heart was in my mouth: it was so unexpected, so strange! though why it should have seemed strange I know not, for there was no communication between him and me that it should have moved me; and what could be more natural than that a man, wearied of his work, and feeling the want perhaps of more light, and yet that it was not dark enough to light a lamp, should turn round in his own chair, and rest a little, and think—perhaps of nothing at all? Papa always says he is thinking of nothing at all. He says things blow through his mind as if the doors were open, and he has no responsibility. What sort of things were blowing through this man's mind? or was he thinking, still thinking, of what he had been writing and going on with it still? The thing that troubled me most was that I could not make out his face. It is very difficult to do so when you see a person only through two windows, your own and his. I wanted very much to recognise him afterwards if I should chance to meet him in the street. If he had only stood up and moved about the room, I should have made out the rest of his figure, and then I should have known him again; or if he had only come to the window (as papa always did), then I should have seen his face clearly enough to have recognised him. But, to be sure, he did not see any need to do anything in order that I might recognise him, for he did not know I existed; and probably if he had known I was watching him, he would have been annoyed and gone away.

But he was as immovable there facing the window as he had been seated at the desk. Sometimes he made a little faint stir with a hand or a foot, and I held my breath, hoping he was about to rise from his chair—but he never did it. And with all the efforts I made I could not be sure of his face. I puckered my eyelids together as old Miss Jeanie did who was shortsighted, and I put my hands on each side of my face to concentrate the light on him: but it was all in vain. Either the face changed as I sat staring, or else it was the light that was not good enough, or I don't know what it was. His hair seemed to me light— certainly there was no dark line about his head, as there would have been had it been very dark—and I saw, where it came across the old gilt frame on the wall behind, that it must be fair: and I am almost sure he had no beard. Indeed I am sure that he had no beard, for the outline of his face was distinct enough; and the daylight was still quite clear out of doors, so that I recognised perfectly a baker's boy who was on the pavement opposite, and whom I should have known again whenever I had met him: as if it was of the least importance to recognise a baker's boy! There was one thing, however, rather curious about this boy. He had been throwing stones at something or somebody. In St. Rule's they have a great way of throwing stones at each other, and I suppose there had been a battle. I suppose also that he had one stone in his hand left over from the battle, and his roving eye took in all the incidents of the street to judge where he could throw it with most effect and mischief. But apparently he found nothing worthy of it in the street, for he suddenly turned round with a flick under his leg to show his cleverness and aimed it straight at the window. I remarked without remarking that it struck with a hard sound and without any breaking of glass, and fell straight down on the pavement. But I took no notice of this even in my mind, so intently was I watching the figure within, which moved not nor took the slightest notice, and remained just as dimly clear, as perfectly seen, yet as indistinguishable, as before. And then the light began to fail a little, not diminishing the prospect within, but making it still less distinct than it had been.

Then I jumped up, feeling Aunt Mary's hand upon my shoulder. "Honey," she said, "I asked you twice to ring the bell; but you did not hear me."

"Oh, Aunt Mary!" I cried in great penitence, but turning again to the window in spite of myself.

"You must come away from there: you must come away from there," she said, almost as if she were angry: and then her soft voice grew softer, and she gave me a kiss: "never mind about the lamp, honey; I have rung myself, and it is coming; but, silly bairn, you must not aye be dreaming—your little head will turn."

All the answer I made, for I could scarcely speak, was to give a little wave with my hand to the window on the other side of the street.

She stood there patting me softly on the shoulder for a whole minute or more, murmuring something that sounded like, "She must go away, she must go away." Then she said, always with her hand soft on my shoulder, "Like a dream when one awaketh." And when I looked again, I saw the blank of an opaque surface and nothing more.

Aunt Mary asked me no more questions. She made me come into the room and sit in the light and read something to her. But I did not know what I was reading, for there suddenly came into my mind and took possession of it, the thud of the stone upon the window, and its descent straight down, as if from some hard substance that threw it off: though I had myself seen it strike upon the glass of the panes across the way.

IV

I am afraid I continued in a state of great exaltation and commotion of mind for some time. I used to hurry through the day till the evening came, when I could watch my neighbour through the window opposite. I did not talk much to any one, and I never said a word about my own questions and wonderings. I wondered who he was, what he was doing, and why he never came till the evening (or very rarely); and I also wondered much to what house the room belonged in which he sat. It seemed to form a portion of the old College Library, as I have often said. The window was one of the line of windows which I understood lighted the large hall; but whether this room belonged to the library itself, or how its occupant gained access to it, I could not tell. I made up my mind that it must open out of the hall, and that the gentleman must be the Librarian or one of his assistants, perhaps kept busy all the day in his official duties, and only able to get to his desk and do his own private work in the evening. One had heard of so many things like that—a man who had to take up some other kind of work for his living, and then when his leisure-time came, gave it all up to something he really loved—some study or some book he was writing. My father himself at one time had been like that. He had been in the Treasury all day, and then in the evening wrote his books, which made him famous. His daughter, however little she might know of other things, could not but know that! But it discouraged me very much when somebody pointed out to me one day in the street an old gentleman who wore a wig and took a great deal of snuff, and said, That's the Librarian of the old College. It gave me a great shock for a moment; but then I remembered that an old gentleman has generally assistants, and that it must be one of them.

Gradually I became quite sure of this. There was another small window above, which twinkled very much when the sun shone, and looked a very kindly bright little window, above that dullness of the other which hid so much. I made up my mind this was the window of his other room, and that these two chambers at the end of the beautiful hall were really beautiful for him to live in, so near all the books, and so retired and quiet, that nobody knew of them. What a fine thing for him; and you could see what use he made of his good fortune as he sat there, so constant at his writing for hours together. Was it a book he was writing, or could it be perhaps Poems? This was a thought which made my heart beat; but I concluded with much regret that it could not be Poems, because no one could possibly write Poems like that, straight off, without pausing for a word or a rhyme. Had they been Poems he must have risen up, he must have paced about the room or come to the window as papa did—not that papa wrote Poems: he always said, "I am not worthy even to speak of such prevailing mysteries," shaking his head—which gave me a wonderful admiration and almost awe of a Poet, who was thus much greater even than papa. But I could not believe that a poet could have kept still for hours and hours like that. What could it be then? perhaps it was history; that is a great thing to work at, but you would not perhaps need to move nor to stride up and down, or look out upon the sky and the wonderful light.

He did move now and then, however, though he never came to the window. Sometimes, as I have said, he would turn round in his chair and turn his face towards it, and sit there for a long time musing when the light had begun to fail, and the world was full of that strange day which was night, that light without colour, in which everything was so clearly visible, and there were no shadows. "It was between the night and the day, when the fairy folk have power." This was the after-light of the wonderful, long, long summer evening, the light without shadows. It had a spell in it, and sometimes it made me afraid: and all manner of strange thoughts seemed to come in, and I always felt that if only we had a little more vision in our eyes we might see beautiful folk walking about in it, who were not of our world. I thought most likely he saw them, from the way he sat there looking out: and this made my heart expand with the most curious sensation, as if of pride that, though I could not see, he did, and did not even require to come to the window, as I did, sitting close in the depth of the recess, with my eyes upon him, and almost seeing things through his eyes.

I was so much absorbed in these thoughts and in watching him every evening—for now he never missed an evening, but was always there—that people began to remark that I was looking pale and that I could not be well, for I paid no attention when they talked to me, and did not care to go out, nor to join the other girls for their tennis, nor to do anything that others did; and some said to Aunt Mary that I was quickly losing all the ground I had gained, and that she could never send me back to my mother with a white face like that. Aunt Mary had begun to look at me anxiously for some time before that, and, I am sure, held secret consultations over me, sometimes with the doctor, and sometimes with her old ladies, who thought they knew more about young girls than even the doctors. And I could hear them saying to her that I wanted diversion, that I must be diverted, and that she must take me out more, and give a party, and that when the summer visitors began to come there would perhaps be a ball or two, or Lady Carnbee would get up a picnic. "And there's my young lord coming home," said the old lady whom they called Miss Jeanie, "and I never knew the young lassie yet that would not cock up her bonnet at the sight of a young lord."

But Aunt Mary shook her head. "I would not lippen much to the young lord," she said. "His mother is sore set upon siller for him; and my poor bit honey has no fortune to speak of. No, we must not fly so high as the young lord; but I will gladly take her about the country to see the old castles and towers. It will perhaps rouse her up a little."

"And if that does not answer we must think of something else," the old lady said.

I heard them perhaps that day because they were talking of me, which is always so effective a way of making you hear—for latterly I had not been paying any attention to what they were saying; and I thought to myself how little they knew, and how little I cared about even the old castles and curious houses, having something else in my mind. But just about that time Mr. Pitmilly came in, who was always a friend to me, and, when he heard them talking, he managed to stop them and turn the conversation into another channel. And after a while, when the ladies were gone away, he came up to my recess, and gave a glance right over my head. And then he asked my Aunt Mary if ever she had settled her question about the window opposite "that you thought was a window sometimes, and then not a window, and many curious things," the old gentleman said.

My Aunt Mary gave me another very wistful look; and then she said, "Indeed, Mr. Pitmilly, we are just where we were, and I am quite as unsettled as ever; and I think my niece she has taken up my views, for I see her many a time looking across and wondering, and I am not clear now what her opinion is."

"My opinion!" I said, "Aunt Mary." I could not help being a little scornful, as one is when one is very young. "I have no opinion. There is not only a window but there is a room, and I could show you—" I was going to say, "show you the gentleman who sits and writes in it," but I stopped, not knowing what they might say, and looked from one to another. "I could tell you—all the furniture that is in it," I said. And then I felt something like a flame that went over my face, and that all at once my cheeks were burning. I thought they gave a little glance at each other, but that may have been folly. "There is a great picture, in a big dim frame," I said, feeling a little breathless, "on the wall opposite the window—"

"Is there so?" said Mr. Pitmilly, with a little laugh. And he said, "Now I will tell you what we'll do. You know that there is a conversation party, or whatever they call it, in the big room to-night, and it will be all open and lighted up. And it is a handsome room, and two-three things well worth looking at. I will just step along after we have all got our dinner, and take you over to the pairty, madam—Missy and you—"

"Dear me!" said Aunt Mary. "I have not gone to a a pairty for more years than I would like to say—and never once to the Library Hall." Then she gave a little shiver, and said quite low, "I could not go there."

"Then you will just begin again to-night, madam," said Mr. Pitmilly, taking no notice of this, "and a proud man will I be leading in Mistress Balcarres that was once the pride of the ball."

"Ah, once!" said Aunt Mary, with a low little laugh and then a sigh. "And we'll not say how long ago"; and after that she made a pause, looking always at me; and then she said, "I accept your offer, and we'll put on our braws; and I hope you will have no occasion to think shame of us. But why not take your dinner here?"

That was how it was settled, and the old gentleman went away to dress, looking quite pleased. But I came to Aunt Mary as soon as he was gone, and besought her not to make me go. "I like the long bonnie night and the light that lasts so long. And I cannot bear to dress up and go out, wasting it all in a stupid party. I hate parties, Aunt Mary!" I cried, "and I would far rather stay here."

"My honey," she said, taking both my hands, "I know it will maybe be a blow to you,—but it's better so."

"How could it be a blow to me?" I cried; "but I would far rather not go."

"You'll just go with me, honey, just this once: it is not often I go out. You will go with me this one night, just this one night, my honey sweet."

I am sure there were tears in Aunt Mary's eyes, and she kissed me between the words. There was nothing more that I could say; but how I grudged the evening! A mere party, a conversazione (when all the College was away, too, and nobody to make conversation!), instead of my enchanted hour at my window and the soft strange light, and the dim face looking out, which kept me wondering and wondering what was he thinking of, what was he looking for, who was he? all one wonder and mystery and question, through the long, long slowly fading night!

It occurred to me, however, when I was dressing—though I was so sure that he would prefer his solitude to everything—that he might perhaps, it was just possible, be there. And when I thought of that, I took out my white frock—though Janet had laid out my blue one—and my little pearl necklace which I had thought was too good to wear. They were not very large pearls, but they were real pearls, and very even and lustrous though they were small; and though I did not think much of my appearance then, there must have been something about me—pale as I was but apt to colour in a moment, with my dress so white, and my pearls so white, and my hair all shadowy—perhaps, that was pleasant to look at: for even old Mr. Pitmilly had a strange look in his eyes, as if he was not only pleased but sorry too, perhaps thinking me a creature that would have troubles in this life, though I was so young and knew them not. And when Aunt Mary looked at me, there was a little quiver about her mouth. She herself had on her pretty lace and her white hair very nicely done, and looking her best. As for Mr. Pitmilly, he had a beautiful fine French cambric frill to his shirt, plaited in the most minute plaits, and with a diamond pin in it which sparkled as much as Lady Carnbee's ring; but this was a fine frank kindly stone, that looked you straight in the face and sparkled, with the light dancing in it as if it were pleased to see you, and to be shining on that old gentleman's honest and faithful breast: for he had been one of Aunt Mary's lovers in their early days, and still thought there was nobody like her in the world.

I had got into quite a happy commotion of mind by the time we set out across the street in the soft light of the evening to the Library Hall. Perhaps, after all, I should see him, and see the room which I was so well acquainted with, and find out why he sat there so constantly and never was seen abroad. I thought I might even hear what he was working at, which would be such a pleasant thing to tell papa when I went home. A friend of mine at St. Rule's—oh, far, far more busy than you ever were, papa!—and then my father would laugh as he always did, and say he was but an idler and never busy at all.

The room was all light and bright, flowers wherever flowers could be, and the long lines of the books that went along the walls on each side, lighting up wherever there was a line of gilding or an ornament, with a little response. It dazzled me at first all that light: but I was very eager, though I kept very quiet, looking round to see if perhaps in any corner, in the middle of any group, he would be there. I did not expect to see him among the ladies. He would not be with them—he was too studious, too silent: but perhaps among that circle of grey heads at the upper end of the room—perhaps—

No: I am not sure that it was not half a pleasure to me to make quite sure that there was not one whom I could take for him, who was at all like my vague image of him. No: it was absurd to think that he would be here, amid all that sound of voices, under the glare of that light. I felt a little proud to think that he was in his room as usual, doing his work, or thinking so deeply over it, as when he turned round in his chair with his face to the light.

I was thus getting a little composed and quiet in my mind, for now that the expectation of seeing him was over, though it was a disappointment, it was a satisfaction too—when Mr. Pitmilly came up to me, holding out his arm. "Now," he said, "I am going to take you to see the curiosities." I thought to myself that after I had seen them and spoken to everybody I knew, Aunt Mary would let me go home, so I went very willingly, though I did not care for the curiosities. Something, however, struck me strangely as we walked up the room. It was the air, rather fresh and strong, from an open window at the east end of the hall. How should there be a window there? I hardly saw what it meant for the first moment, but it blew in my face as if there was some meaning in it, and I felt very uneasy without seeing why.

Then there was another thing that startled me. On that side of the wall which was to the street there seemed no windows at all. A long line of bookcases filled it from end to end. I could not see what that meant either, but it confused me. I was altogether confused. I felt as if I was in a strange country, not knowing where I was going, not knowing what I might find out next. If there were no windows on the wall to the street, where was my window? My heart, which had been jumping up and calming down again all the time, gave a great leap at this, as if it would have come out of me—but I did not know what it could mean.

Then we stopped before a glass case, and Mr. Pitmilly showed me some things in it. I could not pay much attention to them. My head was going round and round. I heard his voice going on, and then myself speaking with a queer sound that was hollow in my ears; but I did not know what I was saying or what he was saying. Then he took me to the very end of the room, the east end, saying something that I caught —that I was pale, that the air would do me good. The air was blowing full on me, lifting the lace of my dress, lifting my hair, almost chilly. The window opened into the pale daylight, into the little lane that ran by the end of the building. Mr. Pitmilly went on talking, but I could not make out a word he said. Then I heard my own voice speaking through it, though I did not seem to be aware that I was speaking. "Where is my window?—where, then, is my window?" I seemed to be saying, and I turned right round, dragging him with me, still holding his arm. As I did this my eyes fell upon something at last which I knew. It was a large picture in a broad frame, hanging against the farther wall.

What did it mean? Oh, what did it mean? I turned round again to the open window at the east end, and to the daylight, the strange light without any shadow, that was all round about this lighted hall, holding it like a bubble that would burst, like something that was not real. The real place was the room I knew, in which that picture was hanging, where the writing-table was, and where he sat with his face to the light. But where was the light and the window through which it came? I think my senses must have left me. I went up to the picture which I knew, and then I walked straight across the room, always dragging Mr. Pitmilly, whose face was pale, but who did not struggle but allowed me to lead him straight across to where the window was— where the window was not;—where there was no sign of it. "Where is my window?—where is my window?" I said. And all the time I was sure that I was in a dream, and these lights were all some theatrical illusion, and the people talking; and nothing real but the pale, pale, watching, lingering day standing by to wait until that foolish bubble should burst.

"My dear," said Mr. Pitmilly, "my dear! Mind that you are in public. Mind where you are. You must not make an outcry and frighten your Aunt Mary. Come away with me. Come away, my dear young lady! and you'll take a seat for a minute or two and compose yourself; and I'll get you an ice or a little wine." He kept patting my hand, which was on his arm, and looking at me very anxiously. "Bless me! bless me! I never thought it would have this effect," he said.

But I would not allow him to take me away in that direction. I went to the picture again and looked at it without seeing it: and then I went across the room again, with some kind of wild thought that if I insisted I should find it. "My window—my window!" I said.

There was one of the professors standing there, and he heard me. "The window!" said he. "Ah, you've been taken in with what appears outside. It was put there to be in uniformity with the window on the stair. But it never was a real window. It is just behind that bookcase. Many people are taken in by it," he said.

His voice seemed to sound from somewhere far away, and as if it would go on for ever; and the hall swam in a dazzle of shining and of noises round me; and the daylight through the open window grew greyer, waiting till it should be over, and the bubble burst.

V

It was Mr. Pitmilly who took me home; or rather it was I who took him, pushing him on a little in front of me, holding fast by his arm, not waiting for Aunt Mary or any one. We came out into the daylight again outside, I, without even a cloak or a shawl, with my bare arms, and uncovered head, and the pearls round my neck. There was a rush of the people about, and a baker's boy, that baker's boy, stood right in my way and cried, "Here's a braw ane!" shouting to the others: the words struck me somehow, as his stone had struck the window, without any reason. But I did not mind the people staring, and hurried across the street, with Mr. Pitmilly half a step in advance. The door was open, and Janet standing at it, looking out to see what she could see of the ladies in their grand dresses. She gave a shriek when she saw me hurrying across the street; but I brushed past her, and pushed Mr. Pitmilly up the stairs, and took him breathless to the recess, where I threw myself down on the seat, feeling as if I could not have gone another step farther, and waved my hand across to the window. "There! there!" I cried. Ah! there it was—not that senseless mob— not the theatre and the gas, and the people all in a murmur and clang of talking. Never in all these days had I seen that room so clearly. There was a faint tone of light behind, as if it might have been a reflection from some of those vulgar lights in the hall, and he sat against it, calm, wrapped in his thoughts, with his face turned to the window. Nobody but must have seen him. Janet could have seen him had I called her upstairs. It was like a picture, all the things I knew, and the same attitude, and the atmosphere, full of quietness, not disturbed by anything. I pulled Mr. Pitmilly's arm before I let him go,— "You see, you see!" I cried. He gave me the most bewildered look, as if he would have liked to cry. He saw nothing! I was sure of that from his eyes. He was an old man, and there was no vision in him. If I had called up Janet, she would have seen it all. "My dear!" he said. "My dear!" waving his hands in a helpless way.

"He has been there all these nights," I cried, "and I thought you could tell me who he was and what he was doing; and that he might have taken me in to that room and showed me, that I might tell papa. Papa would understand, he would like to hear. Oh, can't you tell me what work he is doing, Mr. Pitmilly? He never lifts his head as long as the light throws a shadow, and then when it is like this he turns round and thinks, and takes a rest!"

Mr. Pitmilly was trembling, whether it was with cold or I know not what. He said, with a shake in his voice, "My dear young lady— my dear—" and then stopped and looked at me as if he were going to cry. "It's peetiful, it's peetiful," he said; and then in another voice, "I am going across there again to bring your Aunt Mary home; do you understand, my poor little thing, my— I am going to bring her home— you will be better when she is here." I was glad when he went away, as he could not see anything: and I sat alone in the dark which was not dark, but quite clear light—a light like nothing I ever saw. How clear it was in that room! not glaring like the gas and the voices, but so quiet, everything so visible, as if it were in another world. I heard a little rustle behind me, and there was Janet, standing staring at me with two big eyes wide open. She was only a little older than I was. I called to her, "Janet, come here, come here, and you will see him—come here and see him!" impatient that she should be so shy and keep behind. "Oh, my bonnie young leddy!" she said, and burst out crying. I stamped my foot at her, in my indignation that she would not come, and she fled before me with a rustle and swing of haste, as if she were afraid. None of them, none of them! not even a girl like myself, with the sight in her eyes, would understand. I turned back again, and held out my hands to him sitting there, who was the only one that knew. "Oh," I said, "say something to me! I don't know who you are, or what you are: but you're lonely and so am I; and I only—feel for you. Say something to me!" I neither hoped that he would hear, nor expected any answer. How could he hear, with the street between us, and his window shut, and all the murmuring of the voices and the people standing about? But for one moment it seemed to me that there was only him and me in the whole world.

But I gasped with my breath, that had almost gone from me, when I saw him move in his chair! He had heard me, though I knew not how. He rose up, and I rose too, speechless, incapable of anything but this mechanical movement. He seemed to draw me as if I were a puppet moved by his will. He came forward to the window, and stood looking across at me. I was sure that he looked at me. At last he had seen me: at last he had found out that somebody, though only a girl, was watching him, looking for him, believing in him. I was in such trouble and commotion of mind and trembling, that I could not keep on my feet, but dropped kneeling on the window-seat, supporting myself against the window, feeling as if my heart were being drawn out of me. I cannot describe his face. It was all dim, yet there was a light on it: I think it must have been a smile; and as closely as I looked at him he looked at me. His hair was fair, and there was a little quiver about his lips. Then he put his hands upon the window to open it. It was stiff and hard to move; but at last he forced it open with a sound that echoed all along the street. I saw that the people heard it, and several looked up. As for me, I put my hands together, leaning with my face against the glass, drawn to him as if I could have gone out of myself, my heart out of my bosom, my eyes out of my head. He opened the window with a noise that was heard from the West Port to the Abbey. Could any one doubt that?

And then he leaned forward out of the window, looking out. There was not one in the street but must have seen him. He looked at me first, with a little wave of his hand, as if it were a salutation—yet not exactly that either, for I thought he waved me away; and then he looked up and down in the dim shining of the ending day, first to the east, to the old Abbey towers, and then to the west, along the broad line of the street where so many people were coming and going, but so little noise, all like enchanted folk in an enchanted place. I watched him with such a melting heart, with such a deep satisfaction as words could not say; for nobody could tell me now that he was not there,— nobody could say I was dreaming any more. I watched him as if I could not breathe—my heart in my throat, my eyes upon him. He looked up and down, and then he looked back to me. I was the first, and I was the last, though it was not for long: he did know, he did see, who it was that had recognised him and sympathised with him all the time. I was in a kind of rapture, yet stupor too; my look went with his look, following it as if I were his shadow; and then suddenly he was gone, and I saw him no more.

I dropped back again upon my seat, seeking something to support me, something to lean upon. He had lifted his hand and waved it once again to me. How he went I cannot tell, nor where he went I cannot tell; but in a moment he was away, and the windows standing open, and the room fading into stillness and dimness, yet so clear, with all its space, and the great picture in its gilded frame upon the wall. It gave me no pain to see him go away. My heart was so content, and I was so worn out and satisfied—for what doubt or question could there be about him now? As I was lying back as weak as water, Aunt Mary came in behind me and flew to me with a little rustle as if she had come on wings, and put her arms round me, and drew my head on to her breast. I had begun to cry a little, with sobs like a child. "You saw him, you saw him!" I said. To lean upon her, and feel her so soft, so kind, gave me a pleasure I cannot describe, and her arms round me, and her voice saying "Honey, my honey!"—as if she were nearly crying too. Lying there I came back to myself, quite sweetly, glad of everything. But I wanted some assurance from them that they had seen him too. I waved my hand to the window that was still standing open, and the room that was stealing away into the faint dark. "This time you saw it all!" I said, getting more eager. "My honey!" said Aunt Mary, giving me a kiss: and Mr. Pitmilly began to walk about the room with short little steps behind, as if he were out of patience. I sat straight up and put away Aunt Mary's arms. "You cannot be so blind, so blind!" I cried. "Oh, not to-night, at least not to-night!" But neither the one nor the other made any reply. I shook myself quite free, and raised myself up. And there, in the middle of the street, stood the baker's boy like a statue, staring up at the open window, with his mouth open and his face full of wonder—breathless, as if he could not believe what he saw. I darted forward, calling to him, and beckoned him to come to me. "Oh, bring him up; bring him, bring him to me!" I cried.

Mr. Pitmilly went out directly, and got the boy by the shoulder. He did not want to come. It was strange to see the little old gentleman, with his beautiful frill and his diamond pin, standing out in the street, with his hand upon the boy's shoulder, and the other boys round, all in a little crowd. And presently they came towards the house, the others all following, gaping and wondering. He came in unwilling, almost resisting, looking as if we meant him some harm. "Come away, my laddie, come and speak to the young lady," Mr. Pitmilly was saying. And Aunt Mary took my hands to keep me back. But I would not be kept back.

"Boy," I cried, "you saw it too: you saw it: tell them you saw it! It is that I want, and no more."

He looked at me as they all did, as if he thought I was mad. "What's she wantin' wi' me?" he said; and then, "I did nae harm, even if I did throw a bit stane at it—and it's nae sin to throw a stane."

"You rascal!" said Mr. Pitmilly, giving him a shake; "have you been throwing stones? You'll kill somebody some of these days with your stones." The old gentleman was confused and troubled, for he did not understand what I wanted, nor anything that had happened. And then Aunt Mary, holding my hands and drawing me close to her, spoke. "Laddie," she said, "answer the young lady, like a good lad. There's no intention of finding fault with you. Answer her, my man, and then Janet will give ye your supper before you go."

"Oh speak, speak!" I cried; "answer them and tell them! you saw that window opened, and the gentleman look out and wave his hand?"

"I saw nae gentleman," he said, with his head down, "except this wee gentleman here."

"Listen, laddie," said Aunt Mary. "I saw ye standing in the middle of the street staring. What were ye looking at?"

"It was naething to make a wark about. It was just yon windy yonder in the library that is nae windy. And it was open—as sure's death. You may laugh if you like. Is that a' she's wantin' wi' me?"

"You are telling a pack of lies, laddie," Mr. Pitmilly said.

"I'm tellin' nae lees—it was standin' open just like ony ither windy. It's as sure's death. I couldna believe it mysel'; but it's true."

"And there it is," I cried, turning round and pointing it out to them with great triumph in my heart. But the light was all grey, it had faded, it had changed. The window was just as it had always been, a sombre break upon the wall.

I was treated like an invalid all that evening, and taken upstairs to bed, and Aunt Mary sat up in my room the whole night through. Whenever I opened my eyes she was always sitting there close to me, watching. And there never was in all my life so strange a night. When I would talk in my excitement, she kissed me and hushed me like a child. "Oh, honey, you are not the only one!" she said. "Oh whisht, whisht, bairn! I should never have let you be there!"

"Aunt Mary, Aunt Mary, you have seen him too?"

"Oh whisht, whisht, honey!" Aunt Mary said: her eyes were shining —there were tears in them. "Oh whisht, whisht! Put it out of your mind, and try to sleep. I will not speak another word," she cried.

But I had my arms round her, and my mouth at her ear. "Who is he there?—tell me that and I will ask no more—"

"Oh honey, rest, and try to sleep! It is just—how can I tell you?— a dream, a dream! Did you not hear what Lady Carnbee said?—the women of our blood—"

"What? what? Aunt Mary, oh Aunt Mary—"

"I canna tell you," she cried in her agitation, "I canna tell you! How can I tell you, when I know just what you know and no more? It is a longing all your life after—it is a looking—for what never comes."

"He will come," I cried. "I shall see him to-morrow—that I know, I know!"

She kissed me and cried over me, her cheek hot and wet like mine. "My honey, try if you can sleep—try if you can sleep: and we'll wait to see what to-morrow brings."

"I have no fear," said I; and then I suppose, though it is strange to think of, I must have fallen asleep—I was so worn-out, and young, and not used to lying in my bed awake. From time to time I opened my eyes, and sometimes jumped up remembering everything; but Aunt Mary was always there to soothe me, and I lay down again in her shelter like a bird in its nest.

But I would not let them keep me in bed next day. I was in a kind of fever, not knowing what I did. The window was quite opaque, without the least glimmer in it, flat and blank like a piece of wood. Never from the first day had I seen it so little like a window. "It cannot be wondered at," I said to myself, "that seeing it like that, and with eyes that are old, not so clear as mine, they should think what they do." And then I smiled to myself to think of the evening and the long light, and whether he would look out again, or only give me a signal with his hand. I decided I would like that best: not that he should take the trouble to come forward and open it again, but just a turn of his head and a wave of his hand. It would be more friendly and show more confidence—not as if I wanted that kind of demonstration every night.

I did not come down in the afternoon, but kept at my own window upstairs alone, till the tea-party should be over. I could hear them making a great talk; and I was sure they were all in the recess staring at the window, and laughing at the silly lassie. Let them laugh! I felt above all that now. At dinner I was very restless, hurrying to get it over; and I think Aunt Mary was restless too. I doubt whether she read her *Times* when it came; she opened it up so as to shield her, and watched from a corner. And I settled myself in the recess, with my heart full of expectation. I wanted nothing more than to see him writing at his table, and to turn his head and give me a little wave of his hand, just to show that he knew I was there. I sat from half-past seven o'clock to ten o'clock: and the daylight grew softer and softer, till at last it was as if it was shining through a pearl, and not a shadow to be seen. But the window all the time was as black as night, and there was nothing, nothing there.

Well: but other nights it had been like that; he would not be there every night only to please me. There are other things in a man's life, a great learned man like that. I said to myself I was not disappointed. Why should I be disappointed? There had been other nights when he was not there. Aunt Mary watched me, every movement I made, her eyes shining, often wet, with a pity in them that almost made me cry: but I felt as if I were more sorry for her than for myself. And then I flung myself upon her, and asked her, again and again, what it was, and who it was, imploring her to tell me if she knew? and when she had seen him, and what had happened? and what it meant about the women of our blood? She told me that how it was she could not tell, nor when: it was just at the time it had to be; and that we all saw him in our time —"that is," she said, "the ones that are like you and me." What was it that made her and me different from the rest? but she only shook her head and would not tell me. "They say," she said, and then stopped short. "Oh, honey, try and forget all about it—if I had but known you were of that kind! They say—that once there was one that was a Scholar, and liked his books more than any lady's love. Honey, do not look at me like that. To think I should have brought all this on you!"

"He was a Scholar?" I cried.

"And one of us, that must have been a light woman, not like you and me— But may be it was just in innocence; for who can tell? She waved to him and waved to him to come over: and yon ring was the token: but he would not come. But still she sat at her window and waved and waved—till at last her brothers heard of it, that were stirring men; and then—oh, my honey, let us speak of it no more!"

"They killed him!" I cried, carried away. And then I grasped her with my hands, and gave her a shake, and flung away from her. "You tell me that to throw dust in my eyes—when I saw him only last night: and he as living as I am, and as young!"

"My honey, my honey!" Aunt Mary said.

After that I would not speak to her for a long time; but she kept close to me, never leaving me when she could help it, and always with that pity in her eyes. For the next night it was the same: and the third night. That third night I thought I could not bear it any longer. I would have to do something—if only I knew what to do! If it would ever get dark, quite dark, there might be something to be done. I had wild dreams of stealing out of the house and getting a ladder, and mounting up to try if I could not open that window, in the middle of the night—if perhaps I could get the baker's boy to help me; and then my mind got into a whirl, and it was as if I had done it; and I could almost see the boy put the ladder to the window, and hear him cry out that there was nothing there. Oh, how slow it was, the night! and how light it was, and everything so clear—no darkness to cover you, no shadow, whether on one side of the street or on the other side! I could not sleep, though I was forced to go to bed. And in the deep midnight, when it is dark dark in every other place, I slipped very softly downstairs, though there was one board on the landing-place that creaked—and opened the door and stepped out. There was not a soul to be seen, up or down, from the Abbey to the West Port: and the trees stood like ghosts, and the silence was terrible, and everything as clear as day. You don't know what silence is till you find it in the light like that, not morning but night, no sun-rising, no shadow, but everything as clear as the day.

It did not make any difference as the slow minutes went on: one o'clock, two o'clock. How strange it was to hear the clocks striking in that dead light when there was nobody to hear them! But it made no difference. The window was quite blank; even the marking of the panes seemed to have melted away. I stole up again after a long time, through the silent house, in the clear light, cold and trembling, with despair in my heart.

I am sure Aunt Mary must have watched and seen me coming back, for after a while I heard faint sounds in the house; and very early, when there had come a little sunshine into the air, she came to my bedside with a cup of tea in her hand; and she, too, was looking like a ghost. "Are you warm, honey—are you comfortable?" she said. "It doesn't matter," said I. I did not feel as if anything mattered; unless if one could get into the dark somewhere—the soft, deep dark that would cover you over and hide you—but I could not tell from what. The dreadful thing was that there was nothing, nothing to look for, nothing to hide from—only the silence and the light.

That day my mother came and took me home. I had not heard she was coming; she arrived quite unexpectedly, and said she had no time to stay, but must start the same evening so as to be in London next day, papa having settled to go abroad. At first I had a wild thought I would not go. But how can a girl say I will not, when her mother has come for her, and there is no reason, no reason in the world, to resist, and no right! I had to go, whatever I might wish or any one might say. Aunt Mary's dear eyes were wet; she went about the house drying them quietly with her handkerchief, but she always said, "It is the best thing for you, honey—the best thing for you!" Oh, how I hated to hear it said that it was the best thing, as if anything mattered, one more than another! The old ladies were all there in the afternoon, Lady Carnbee looking at me from under her black lace, and the diamond lurking, sending out darts from under her finger. She patted me on the shoulder, and told me to be a good bairn. "And never lippen to what you see from the window," she said. "The eye is deceitful as well as the heart." She kept patting me on the shoulder, and I felt again as if that sharp wicked stone stung me. Was that what Aunt Mary meant when she said yon ring was the token? I thought afterwards I saw the mark on my shoulder. You will say why? How can I tell why? If I had known, I should have been contented, and it would not have mattered any more.

I never went back to St. Rule's, and for years of my life I never again looked out of a window when any other window was in sight. You ask me did I ever see him again? I cannot tell: the imagination is a great deceiver, as Lady Carnbee said: and if he stayed there so long, only to punish the race that had wronged him, why should I ever have seen him again? for I had received my share. But who can tell what happens in a heart that often, often, and so long as that, comes back to do its errand? If it was he whom I have seen again, the anger is gone from him, and he means good and no longer harm to the house of the woman that loved him. I have seen his face looking at me from a crowd. There was one time when I came home a widow from India, very sad, with my little children: I am certain I saw him there among all the people coming to welcome their friends. There was nobody to welcome me—for I was not expected: and very sad was I, without a face I knew: when all at once I saw him, and he waved his hand to me. My heart leaped up again: I had forgotten who he was, but only that it was a face I knew, and I landed almost cheerfully, thinking here was some one who would help me. But he had disappeared, as he did from the window, with that one wave of his hand.

And again I was reminded of it all when old Lady Carnbee died—an old, old woman—and it was found in her will that she had left me that diamond ring. I am afraid of it still. It is locked up in an old sandal-wood box in the lumber-room in the little old country-house which belongs to me, but where I never live. If any one would steal it, it would be a relief to my mind. Yet I never knew what Aunt Mary meant when she said, "Yon ring was the token," nor what it could have to do with that strange window in the old College Library of St. Rule's.

Mrs. Alfred Baldwin

Mrs. Alfred Baldwin (née Louisa MacDonald) (1845–1925) was a minor British author who flourished from the 1880s to 1910; her last book was Afterglow (1911), a collection of lyric poetry. Nothing is known of her life, beyond the fact that she was an occasional contributor to such periodicals as Longmans magazine and Cornhill and that much of her fiction was first published anonymously. Her best-known work was The Story of a Marriage (1889), a sentimental novel that went through several editions.

"The Empty Picture Frame" has been taken from The Shadow on the Blind (1895), Mrs. Baldwin's only collection of ghost stories. The other stories in the volume involve supernatural reenactment of ancient crimes, second sight, deathbed apparitions, and ghosts; this one, with its female center of interest and the magical aspects of portraits, harks back to Gothic prototypes. Since the days of Horace Walpole's The Castle of Otranto (1764) Gothic novelists have been fascinated with pictures that step out of their frames.

THE
EMPTY PICTURE
FRAME

It was a wild day in September. An equinoctial gale had raged since dawn, shaking doors and windows, and battering the walls of Eastwick Court. The orchards were strewed with bruised fruit plucked by the rude hand of the wind. The gardens that yesterday, neat and trim, basked in autumn sunshine, to-day were littered with branches stript from the trees, and melancholy with uprooted flowers. The paths were cut into channels by torrents of rain, that washed the loose sand on the grass, where, as the water subsided, it lay in red patches. At sunset there came a sudden lull. The gale fell to a whisper, and the rain ceased. But no flush of light overspread the grey sky. No western glow shone on the sombre walls, or reflected its red light on the rain-washed windows of the old house.

Within doors it was too dark to read or work, and in the enforced idleness of twilight, Miss Swinford laid down her book, and seated herself on a low chair by the fire.

Katherine Swinford was alone in the great drawing-room. As she leaned forward with hands clasped in her lap, watching the bickering flames that played about the logs on the hearth, there was something pathetic as well as dignified in her appearance. The mistress of Eastwick Court was no longer young. Her thick hair was streaked with white, and sundry lines on her brow, and about her clear grey eyes, showed where time's finger had touched her and left its mark. Her features were large but finely formed, her expression firm and self-reliant. Miss Swinford had lived so long alone, mistress of a large property, and a law unto herself in her own domain, that she had acquired the somewhat imperious manner of one who exercises a benevolent tyranny, and has an unquestioned right to be obeyed. She was the only child and heiress of Sir John Swinford who had been dead some twelve years, and she had lost her mother in her infancy.

No one could have supposed that Miss Swinford, like Queen Eliza-beth, was destined to reign alone. She had had as many suitors as the Virgin Queen herself, and they might be classed in three orders. The first, and most numerous, was attracted by the estate to which the lady seemed but the necessary appendage. The second felt the charm of the heiress, and the still greater charm of her wealth, while the third order of suitor was represented by one man only, who loved Katherine for her own sake, and would have sought her for his wife if she had been penniless. No need to tell the story—"es ist ein altes Liedchen"—the true love died long ago, and his fever-worn body lay buried in the hot sand of a tropic shore, and Katherine Swinford was still and would always remain Katherine Swinford.

Perhaps as she sat by her lonely hearth in the gathering dusk, she was thinking of what might have been, of the strong arm she might have leaned on, of the children that might have called her mother. She sighed, and rising abruptly, rang for lights. "This will never do! I shall grow melancholy if I sit by myself in the twilight. It is peopled with ghosts, and with might-have-beens, the worst of all ghosts. I have been too much alone lately. I ought to keep up a succession of visitors. By the way, I wonder why I have not heard from Sir Piers Hammersley. It is ten days since I wrote to him inviting his daughter to come and stay with me." And an air of bright energy succeeded to her mo-mentary depression, and when the lamps were brought into the room Miss Swinford was looking ten years younger than she had done a short time before.

Sir Piers Hammersley was a cousin of the late Sir John Swinford, and both descended from a common ancestor, Sir Miles Swinford, who lived at Eastwick Court in the time of Charles the First. The Hammers-leys were originally Swinfords. But Sir Miles' second son Adam had married an heiress in Cumberland, Anne Hammersley, on the condition that he should bear her name as well as share her fortune. When Adam went to live in the north he took with him his sister Joceline, whose lover Colonel Dacres had been wounded fighting for his king, and died in her father's house, since when she had pined and drooped at Eastwick Court. Joceline was only three-and-twenty years old, and her family thought that absence from home and its tragic associations would restore her to health and cheerfulness. And in this hope she made what was then the long wild journey out of Herefordshire into Cumberland. But no change of air or scene could arrest the decline into which she had fallen. Before the spring came she was laid in the vault of the Hammersleys.

Her sad story and the tradition of her beauty, confirmed by a por-trait still preserved at Eastwick Court, had caused her to be remembered both by the Swinfords and Hammersleys, and the name of Joceline had not been allowed to die out in the family. The very reason why Miss Swinford had bestirred herself to write to her father's cousin whom she had not seen since she was a girl, was that his only daughter was named Joceline. Her heart had warmed towards her unknown kinswoman in her loneliness, and she had written asking Sir Piers to allow his daughter to visit her at the house that was the birthplace of the original Joceline. The Hammersleys still lived in Cumberland, and Miss Swinford's letter must have reached its destination the day after it was posted. But she had received no answer to her friendly invitation. She was astonished and almost affronted by chilling silence where she had hoped to meet with a cordial response.

"My cousin Joceline is so much younger than I that perhaps she does not feel very eager about spending a few weeks alone with me," she argued with herself. "But at least she should be wishful to see the home of her ancestors, and the portrait of Joceline Swinford, whom she is fortunate if she resembles in personal appearance."

Here Miss Swinford's soliloquy was cut short by an unexpected interruption. A sound of heavy wheels driving slowly up the avenue by which the house was approached from the high road, and the carriage, waggon, or whatever it was that could be so ponderous, came to a standstill at the front door. "The storm must have cut the gravel up terribly," thought Miss Swinford; "I never heard wheels sound so heavy in the avenue before. Who can be paying an afternoon call so late, just when I am about to dress for dinner!" and the heavy carriage drove slowly away. Immediately afterwards the drawing-room door was thrown open, and Bennet the old butler announced "Miss Hammersley." Miss Swinford started with surprise, and advanced to welcome a young and tall lady dressed in black, some fifteen years her junior. She was of a mortal pallor of complexion, with dreamy brown eyes and fair hair, and bearing the most extraordinary resemblance to the portrait of Joceline Swinford.

"My dear cousin! You have dropped upon me from the clouds! I have received no intimation that I should have the pleasure of seeing you to-day, or I would have driven to the station to meet you myself," and she kissed her young kinswoman's pale cheek.

"How cold you are, my dear! Come and sit near the fire before you take off your cloak." And she led Joceline to a low chair, and she sat down by the flickering fire, with her back to the lamp.

"What sort of a journey have you had this stormy day? I'm afraid you had to change trains rather often between Cumberland and our little village station."

Joceline Hammersley raised her eyes with a strange uncomprehending gaze, as though she were listening to a language she did not under-stand, and instead of replying to her question merely said, "I have come a long way, I am very tired."

"You are not strong, my dear, I am afraid, you look so pale and weary. It is a pity I cannot give you a little of my superfluous strength," and Miss Swinford smiled kindly on her young cousin. She could not take her eyes from the white oval face with its high marble brow, large dark eyes and heavy eyelids, delicate nose and small mouth with lips too pale for health. "It is astounding, perfectly astounding!" at length she said. "Do you know that you are the living image of our common ancestress Joceline Swinford! You are exactly like the Van Dyke portrait in the library! I must show it to you!"

"Oh, not to-night! not to-night!" pleaded her cousin.

"Very well then, not to-night, but first thing in the morning. By candle-light it might startle you, it would be like looking at the reflec-tion of your face in a mirror. But let me unfasten your cloak for you, my dear." For her guest was enveloped in a long black silk cloak, with a hood drawn over her fair curls, a quaint garment becoming her so well as to suggest the idea, that the pale silent lady was an artist in dress, and studied effects very successfully.

"Do not let me trouble you," she replied, throwing her hood back upon her shoulders, "my waiting woman will give me the help I re-quire."

"Your waiting woman! Dear child, what an antiquated phrase! But I suppose odd words and expressions still linger in the wilds of Cumber-land. Your maid, yes, I will ring for her, and I will show you to your room, where I am afraid the fire can hardly be lighted yet. It should have been burning all day if you had only done me the honour to an-nounce your arrival beforehand." And Miss Swinford opened the draw-ing room door, when to her amazement her guest with unhesitating step as though she knew her way perfectly, turned towards the old part of the house, that was full of empty rooms.

"Not that way, my dear! You are going to the disused part of the building, that has not been inhabited since my grandfather's time, and belongs now-a-days entirely to ghosts and rats. Let me lead you to our comfortable modern rooms, less historically interesting, but better suited to the requirements of a tired traveller like yourself." And her guest turned to follow her with an expression of disappointment on her pale face.

"May I not see the old rooms?"

"Certainly. I will show you everything, beginning with your own portrait, to-morrow morning. But here is your maid and this is your room, as we dine in half an hour I will leave you now to dress." And mistress and maid were left together.

Miss Hammersley's maid was no less remarkable looking than her mistress, with the same extreme pallor, though here the resemblance ended, for the mistress was beautiful and the maid distinctly ugly. Her grey hair was drawn away from her dark bony forehead under a close fitting white cap. Her eyes were small and black, and her mouth large, with thin compressed lips. Like her mistress, she was dressed in entire disregard of existing fashion, in a dark woollen material, with a deep linen collar and long white apron. At first the sight of a maid wearing a cap that a modern cook would scorn, and an apron suitable in size for a scullion, occasioned rude mirth among Miss Swinford's servants. But their laughter was brief, and succeeded by uneasy fear, for Mistress Galt (as Miss Hammersley called her maid) had queer unaccountable ways, in harmony with her strange and repellant appearance.

The morning after Miss Hammersley's arrival at Eastwick Court, the sun shone brightly on the destruction caused by the storm of the previous day, and the gardeners were busy repairing damage done by the wind and rain.

When Miss Swinford entered the breakfast room, her guest was walking on the terrace, dressed in a white close-fitting gown low and open at the front, and her bare neck exposed to the chilly morning air. Miss Swinford hastened to her from the open window, exclaiming, "My dear child, you will catch your death of cold! Come back and put a shawl over your neck. Is it still the fashion to come down to breakfast in a low dress as my grandmother used to do!" and she led her into the house, and wrapped a soft shawl about her shoulders.

"How cold you are! And the morning air has brought no colour to your face! My dear child, are you always as cold as this?"

"Yes, always," she replied quietly. Then adding as though speaking to herself, "yet I am clothed in woollen and sheltered from wind and rain."

"Drink your coffee, you make me cold to look at you! And after breakfast I will take you upstairs to the library to show you the portrait of your namesake, and you shall tell me if you see the resemblance to yourself which I think so striking. It is an odd coincidence, the dress you are wearing might have been copied from that in the picture. But you shall see for yourself," and Miss Swinford, pleased to have someone to talk to, continued chatting, and did not notice how silent her cousin remained.

After breakfast she took Joceline's cold hand in hers, and led her upstairs.

"The library was my father's favourite room, and I have made no alteration in it since his time. It was there that I last saw your father, and I remember how greatly he admired Joceline Swinford's portrait. He said he should like to have a copy of it, but he does not need that as long as he has you to look at, my dear." And Miss Swinford flung the door of the library wide open with a triumphant "there!"

But she started with astonishment, for over the fireplace, where the portrait of Joceline Swinford had been, hung only the empty frame, its tarnished gilding in sombre harmony with the square of blackened wall that had been covered by the canvas.

Miss Swinford rang the bell impetuously, and ran into the corridor to second its summons with her voice.

"Bennet, Bennet! there is the most extraordinary thing! The old portrait of Miss Joceline Swinford has been taken out of the frame, and carried away bodily! The house has been broken into during the night! Search everywhere, and find out by what door or window it has been entered."

The servants gathered in a cluster round the library door, looking up at the empty frame with awe-stricken faces, and Miss Swinford sat down and fairly burst into tears. Joceline gently laid her hand on her shoulder, and said in a low voice, "Do not weep, the picture will be restored to you!" and raising her eyes her cousin beheld the very embodiment of Joceline Swinford's portrait standing beside her. The shawl had slipped from her shoulders, leaving her neck uncovered, and in face, attitude, and costume, she was so amazingly like the figure in the missing picture that Miss Swinford started. And the servants, still peering in at the door, looked from the empty frame to the pale lady, and then at each other with indefinable fear.

No trace of the thieves could be discovered. No lock, bolt or bar on door or window had been tampered with, and the picture was hung so high that whoever had stolen it, must have accomplished the theft by the help of a ladder. The local superintendent of police came to examine the house, and to take down a description of the missing picture from Miss Swinford's lips, and she advertised a large reward for its discovery or for such information as should lead to the detection of the thief.

"The picture will be restored to you," repeated Joceline.

"I am afraid not, my dear. The stolen portrait of the beautiful Duchess of Devonshire has never been recovered, and how can I hope to get my picture back again, and to unravel the mystery of its disappearance?" Miss Swinford telegraphed tidings of her loss to her lawyer in London, and followed it up by a long letter of instructions. He was to send a description of the missing portrait to all the picture dealers, and an advertisement was put in the papers warning pawn-brokers to detain the bearer, as well as the picture, if it was offered to them. And having done everything in her power to recover her treasure, Miss Swinford remained inconsolable under her loss.

The excitement in the servants' hall was intense, and the physical difficulty of abstracting from its frame, a picture hung at such a height was dilated upon at great length. Finally they all agreed with old Bennet when he gave it as his opinion, "that it was like as if it had been sperited away!"

Only one person in the house appeared indifferent to the prevailing distress and anxiety, and this was Mistress Galt, who went about chuckling to herself with eldrich laughter.

Several days passed in which Miss Swinford did little but lament her loss, and exhaust conjecture as to how the picture could have been so mysteriously removed. But neither search nor enquiry threw any light on the matter. The portrait had vanished, leaving no more trace than if it had melted into thin air.

Her distraction of mind at first prevented Miss Swinford from notic-ing her guest, as she otherwise would have done. But as she became less preoccupied, she observed in Joceline Hammersley numberless little peculiarities, that, taken all together, convinced her she was unlike anyone she had ever met before. She had none of the ardour and im-petuosity of youth, she was silent and reticent. She was ignorant of everyday matters that a child would know, and yet surprised her by considerable out of the way knowledge, and acquaintance with by-gone times, though she knew nothing of contemporary history. Her phraseology was often amusingly antiquated. Sometimes too she would misunderstand the plainest language, and require it to be translated into another form before she appeared to grasp its meaning.

"Does your father never take you to London, my dear?" asked Miss Swinford, thinking it a pity that so lovely a young creature should not see more society than her country home afforded.

"He took me thither once on a time when I was but a child, and I call to mind that while we were at our lodging in Whitehall the Queen was brought to bed of a son, and the rejoicing thereat."

"My dear Joceline, you positively must not make use of such an old-fashioned, countrified expression as 'brought to bed!'" said Miss Swin-ford, "it is only fit for an old nurse! Ladies may have spoken in that way a century ago, but it is purely rustic now. If you must date your visit to London by royal domestic events, you should say you were there when the Queen was confined."

"But that would not be the truth," replied Joceline, raising her dark eyes and folding her hands in her lap, "for it was not the Queen's but the King's majesty that was confined in Carisbrook Castle," and she sighed heavily.

Miss Swinford was confounded. Could it be that her beautiful young kinswoman was mildly deranged? She looked into the dreamy brown eyes fixed upon her, and merely saying, "I think you have lived too much alone in the country," lapsed into thoughtful silence.

That night when Miss Swinford was retiring to rest and her maid was about to leave the room, she lingered at the door and said, "There's something I want to speak to you about, miss, but I hardly know how to, for it's about Miss Hammersley."

"What is it, Dapper? What can you have to say that concerns my cousin?"

"There's something strange about the young lady, miss, and about Mistress Galt too, as she calls her. They walk in their sleep or something as bad. Last night when I was lying awake I heard footsteps, and I got up and opened my door, and crossed the gallery and looked over the bannisters, and there below if there wasn't Miss Hammersley and her maid going into the empty rooms in the old part of the house. I saw them quite plain in the moonlight through the big window. They were in their day dresses, they hadn't undressed for bed though it was past two o'clock, and Miss Hammersley was crying and sobbing. They seemed to know their way about the house in the dark as well as we do by daylight! I felt frightened and went back to bed, and it would be a good half hour before I heard them creep back to their rooms again. I thought I'd better tell you about it, miss."

"You amaze me, Dapper! It's impossible that they both walk in their sleep. But perhaps my cousin does, and her maid follows her lest she should meet with some accident, or wake suddenly and be alarmed."

"I hope, miss, that if you hear anything to-night you'll please to get up and see for yourself. I'll put your dressing-gown by the candle and matches, and if you want me I'm a light sleeper, I should wake if you only scratched on the door." And Dapper retired, leaving her mistress profoundly uneasy.

Many uncomfortable thoughts were suggested to Miss Swinford's mind by what she had heard. She rose and locked the door, that if Joceline walked in her sleep, at all events she would not be startled by her entering the room in the night with wide unseeing eyes. She thought over all her cousin's peculiarities, her strange inanimate expression, her deadly pallor and coldness, her silence and dreamy look, and decided that she was a very likely subject to be a somnambulist. Having settled this painful matter to her satisfaction, Miss Swinford's mind reverted to its favourite theme—the inexplicable loss of the portrait. And she fell asleep to dream that her cousin stood in the tarnished frame over the library mantel-shelf, saying, "I told you that Joceline Swinford's portrait would come back to you!" when she woke suddenly, the clock struck two, and she heard gentle steps in the carpeted gallery.

In a moment she had put on her dressing-gown and opened the door. Dapper had left a lamp burning, and by its light she saw Joceline Hammersley in the gallery on the opposite side of the hall, followed by her maid, walking towards the door leading to the old part of the house.

Miss Swinford hastened along the gallery that ran round the four sides of the hall, till she was close behind the dim figures that had now past beyond the light of the lamp. Mistress Galt was silent and rigid, but Joceline, pale as death, walked with clasped hands, moaning to herself. They left the door open as they entered the deserted rooms, and Miss Swinford followed unperceived. They passed quickly across stretches of pallid moonlight falling through the dusty windows, alternating with breadths of blackest shadow, opening door after door till they came to a corner room, looking out to the front and end of the house. Then they paused, and Joceline lifted up her face that no moonlight could bleach whiter, and cried, "It was here that he died! On this spot my love died! Here he lay till they bore him to his last resting place, but far from me! I lie alone in my narrow bed!" and Miss Swinford, terrified, and convinced that her cousin was either a mad woman or a somnambulist, turned and fled.

She did not pause or look behind her till she had locked herself in her room, when she fell half fainting upon the bed. "My poor cousin is insane! She has heard the story of the death of Joceline Swinford's lover in this house, and has brooded over it, till with her peculiar temperament it has turned her brain. And that strange woman Galt is her keeper, I see it all now! How shall I get rid of her? I shall become mad myself if we stay together much longer in this old house. How could she know the room in which Colonel Dacres died? I have not told her, and she has not been at Eastwick Court before. It is hateful, it is uncanny!" and Miss Swinford shuddered.

Presently she heard light footsteps once more, and opening the door saw the dim figures of her cousin and her maid returning to their room. They had made a complete circuit of the house, and regained the gallery by means of a disused staircase, the door leading to which was kept locked. When all was once more silent, Miss Swinford crossed the gallery, candle in hand, to examine for herself if the lock had been tampered with. But the door was fastened as it had been for many years, and the paper pasted round it to prevent draughts was undisturbed. Yet there was no other means of reaching the side of the

gallery by which Joceline Hammersley and Mistress Galt had returned
to their rooms, except by this staircase.

Miss Swinford slept no more that night, and when she closed her
eyes, it was only to open them and assure herself that the pale-faced
Joceline was not standing by her side.

At length when morning light filled the room, she drew aside the
curtain and looked into the garden. She was startled to see Joceline
and Mistress Galt standing together under the window. Neither of
them wore hood or kerchief in the keen morning air, and Joceline's
bare neck looked white and cold as marble. "She is as like the old portrait as though she were the original Joceline come back from the
dead!" exclaimed Miss Swinford.

Mistress and maid were looking fixedly at a spot in the garden, towards which first one pointed and then another, and in the silence of
the early morning Miss Swinford could hear every word.

"And I say, Mistress Joceline, that the bowling green lay yonder!"

"Nay, be not so confident. You were here but for a few months
when all was sorrow and confusion, while I dwelt here for three-and-
twenty years, and till the cruel wars came had great joy and pleasure
in my home. The bowling green was by the sundial, and lay to the
north of the maze. But that is gone too. All is changed, the very flowers
wear strange faces."

"Shall you not rest, Mistress, since you have seen that which you
prayed to see once more?"

"Yes, I shall rest. I shall sleep till we all wake together."

"Mad! Stark mad!" ejaculated her cousin as she dropped the curtain
and turned from the window.

The day proved wet and stormy, and Miss Swinford had to pass the
heavy hours indoors with her uncanny guest. She was now so fully convinced of her cousin's insanity that she felt nervous in her presence, and
unable to question her about her mysterious conduct. Joceline was, if
possible, quieter and more reserved than ever. She looked fearfully ill,
at times scarcely conscious, and as though her dark eyes moved with
difficulty from one object to another.

"I am afraid you did not rest well last night, you seem so tired,"
Miss Swinford ventured to say.

"I have not slept of late, but soon I shall rest again." And she seemed
almost to fall asleep as she spoke. Only once did she show spontaneous
interest in anything, when turning over the leaves of a book, she came
upon an engraving of the celebrated portrait of Strafford. Then her
pale face seemed to radiate light. "My Lord Strafford!" she exclaimed,
"and yet how unlike, for no picture can give the dark fire of his eye!

O noble soul, that gave thy life for thy king, and yet wast powerless to avert his doom!"

At length the tedious day drew to an end. The two ladies were sitting in silence in the drawing-room, Miss Swinford wondering when her strange cousin would depart. She was resolved that she would write to Sir Piers to say that the change back to the bracing air of the north would be beneficial to his daughter's health, when Joceline rose noiselessly and left the room. "How shall I get through another night with that unaccountable being wandering about the house, asleep or insane!" she thought looking after her with a troubled expression. "I cannot bear the strain of her company! It will be long indeed before I invite a stranger again to pay me a visit!" when the door opened and her cousin stood before her pale as a lily, dressed in her black travelling cloak and hood. Miss Swinford rose in amazement. "My dear, what is the meaning of this! You came unannounced, you cannot surely be leaving me as abruptly as your arrived!"

"I must go, I am wanted" she said. And as she spoke the sound of heavy wheels was heard approaching the house. An inexplicable fear fell upon Miss Swinford.

"But how shall you travel? You are too late for any train to-night."

"I go as I came. I shall soon be at my journey's end. Farewell, cousin Katherine, and be of good cheer, the portrait of Joceline Swinford will be restored to you!" Miss Swinford mechanically followed her downstairs, where Mistress Galt was already waiting, and the servants peering over the bannisters to watch the departure. Miss Swinford stept into the porch with her guest, and there stood waiting a huge coach, drawn by four black horses. By the light of the moon, issuing from beneath a cloud, she saw that the coachman was dressed in as antique a style as his mistress, and that his face like hers was deadly pale.

"Farewell, cousin, farewell!" said Joceline, touching Miss Swinford's cheek with her cold lips, "the missing picture will be restored to its place." And followed by Mistress Galt she stepped into the coach, in which six persons could have seated themselves with ease. She leaned out of the window, and bowed to her hostess with solemn formality. Then the horses moving at a heavy trot drew the lumbering vehicle down the avenue towards the high road. Miss Swinford, Bennet, Dapper and a couple of grooms attracted by the extraordinary sound of the heavy carriage approaching the house, stood awestruck watching it depart. Not one of them could have expressed his fear in words, and the terror each felt was the greater for being unspoken. The huge coach rumbled along the avenue, when it turned into the high road, and still they could hear the heavy waggon-like sound of its wheels.

"They have taken the turning to the left!" cried Miss Swinford, the first to break silence. "That great carriage and four horses can never cross the Brook Bridge. They should have turned to the right. See if you can overtake them before the road is too narrow for them to turn!" and the grooms ran down a side path that was used as a short cut to the road. The heavy sound of wheels grew duller and more distant, and suddenly ceased. "Thank goodness they are stopped in time, they will turn now!" said Miss Swinford. But still no sound was heard. Presently the grooms came back breathless with running, the younger of them looking ready to faint.

"You stopped them in time, Landon, I hope?" asked Miss Swinford of the elder of the two men.

"O Lord, O Lord, ma'am, there's no coach nor nothing to stop! As I'm a living sinner there's nothing but a three mile stretch o' road clear as day in the moonlight, and not so much as a wheelbarrow on it, and neither man nor beast to be seen! That big coach and four's clean gone, same as if it had sunk into the ground!"

"Come into the house, madam," said Dapper, supporting her mistress, for she staggered as though she would fall "and thank God, however they're gone, those white-faced witches are out of the place at last!" And sick with amazement Miss Swinford suffered herself to be led indoors.

When she had recovered herself, she said with her usual determination, "Dapper and Bennet, come with me into the library, I want you both!" And they followed their mistress in silence. Miss Swinford paused for an instant on the threshold, then opening wide the door all three entered the room. The lamp stood on the table, a cheerful fire burned on the hearth. Everything was in its accustomed order, and Dapper and Bennet looked vaguely about them wondering why they were wanted. But their mistress pointed to the wall above the mantel-shelf. From its tarnished frame the portrait of Joceline Swinford looked down on them once more, as though it had never been missing from its place. Dapper screamed shrilly, Bennet gazed open mouthed, Miss Swinford buried her face in her hands and said in a tremulous voice, "This is dreadful! What does it mean, what can it mean!"

The next morning's post brought Miss Swinford a letter from Sir Piers Hammersley, at Carlsbad, where he and his daughter were staying, apologising for her letter remaining so long unanswered, but it had been carelessly overlooked and only forwarded to him that day. He was exceedingly annoyed to think how uncourteous he must have appeared. Joceline, too, was as sorry as himself. She hoped that her cousin would renew her kind invitation some future time, to give her the pleasure of making her acquaintance, and of visiting the old home of the family.

Then the strange beautiful girl who had come and gone so mysteriously, whose visit had corresponded with the absence of the portrait of Joceline Swinford, was not her cousin after all! Who then was she, or *what* was she? Miss Swinford believed that she knew who her strange guest had been. But she dared not express her conviction in words. Her friends would have thought her mad. She kept her secret locked in her breast. But she was a changed woman from that time forward, and within twelve months the last of the Swinfords was laid to rest in the family burial place. The old servants still tell the story of the pale lady's visit, and her weird ways, and how their mistress fell into pining health from the very night of her mysterious departure.

Elia W. Peattie

Mrs. Elia Peattie (née Wilkinson) (1862–1935) was born in Kalamazoo, Michigan, but spent most of her adult life in Chicago and Omaha. She was a newspaperwoman by profession, working as an editorial writer for the Omaha World-Herald *and as a literary critic for the Chicago* Tribune. *She was also a free-lance writer, with several novels to her credit and a book about Alaska,* A Trip through Wonderland.

Mrs. Peattie's contribution to supernatural fiction is to be found in the very rare little collection The Shape of Fear *(1898), which was assembled in part at least from earlier, anonymous newspaper publications. It contains thirteen stories, which display varied styles of writing. Some are written in the decorated style of the 1890s and have symbolic overtones; others are composed in the homely, simple style that is usually associated with the work of Mary Wilkins Freeman. There is no reason to think that the supernatural was ever more than a literary device to Mrs. Peattie, a clever way of presenting a good idea. In "A Grammatical Ghost" the influence of Charles Dickens can be seen.*

A
GRAMMATICAL GHOST

There was only one possible objection to the drawing-room, and that was the occasional presence of Miss Carew; and only one possible objection to Miss Carew. And that was, that she was dead.

She had been dead twenty years, as a matter of fact and record, and to the last of her life sacredly preserved the treasures and traditions of her family, a family bound up—as it is quite unnecessary to explain to any one in good society—with all that is most venerable and heroic in the history of the Republic. Miss Carew never relaxed the proverbial hospitality of her house, even when she remained its sole representative. She continued to preside at her table with dignity and state, and to set an example of excessive modesty and gentle decorum to a generation of restless young women.

It is not likely that having lived a life of such irreproachable gentility as this, Miss Carew would have the bad taste to die in any way not pleasant to mention in fastidious society. She could be trusted to the last, not to outrage those friends who quoted her as an exemplar of propriety. She died very unobtrusively of an affection of the heart, one June morning, while trimming her rose trellis, and her lavender-colored print was not even rumpled when she fell, nor were more than the tips of her little bronze slippers visible.

"Isn't it dreadful," said the Philadelphians, "that the property should go to a very, very distant cousin in Iowa or somewhere else on the frontier, about whom nobody knows anything at all?"

The Carew treasures were packed in boxes and sent away into the Iowa wilderness; the Carew traditions were preserved by the Historical Society; the Carew property, standing in one of the most umbrageous and aristocratic suburbs of Philadelphia, was rented to all manner of

259

folk—anybody who had money enough to pay the rental—and society entered its doors no more.

But at last, after twenty years, and when all save the oldest Philadelphians had forgotten Miss Lydia Carew, the very, very distant cousin appeared. He was quite in the prime of life, and so agreeable and unassuming that nothing could be urged against him save his patronymic, which, being Boggs, did not commend itself to the euphemists. With him were two maiden sisters, ladies of excellent taste and manners, who restored the Carew china to its ancient cabinets, and replaced the Carew pictures upon the walls, with additions not out of keeping with the elegance of these heirlooms. Society, with a magnanimity almost dramatic, overlooked the name of Boggs—and called.

All was well. At least, to an outsider all seemed to be well. But, in truth, there was a certain distress in the old mansion, and in the hearts of the well-behaved Misses Boggs. It came about most unexpectedly. The sisters had been sitting upstairs, looking out at the beautiful grounds of the old place, and marvelling at the violets, which lifted their heads from every possible cranny about the house, and talking over the cordiality which they had been receiving by those upon whom they had no claim, and they were filled with amiable satisfaction. Life looked attractive. They had often been grateful to Miss Lydia Carew for leaving their brother her fortune. Now they felt even more grateful to her. She had left them a Social Position—one, which even after twenty years of desuetude, was fit for use.

They descended the stairs together, with arms clasped about each other's waists, and as they did so presented a placid and pleasing sight. They entered their drawing room with the intention of brewing a cup of tea, and drinking it in calm sociability in the twilight. But as they entered the room they became aware of the presence of a lady, who was already seated at their tea-table, regarding their old Wedgwood with the air of a connoisseur.

There were a number of peculiarities about this intruder. To begin with, she was hatless, quite as if she were a habitué of the house, and was costumed in a prim lilac-colored lawn of the style of two decades past. But a greater peculiarity was the resemblance this lady bore to a faded Daguerrotype. If looked at one way, she was perfectly discernible; if looked at another, she went out in a sort of blur. Notwithstanding this comparative invisibility, she exhaled a delicate perfume of sweet lavender, very pleasing to the nostrils of the Misses Boggs, who stood looking at her in gentle and unprotesting surprise.

"I beg your pardon," began Miss Prudence, the younger of the Misses Boggs, "but—"

But at this moment the Daguerrotype became a blur, and Miss Prudence found herself addressing space. The Misses Boggs were irritated. They had never encountered any mysteries in Iowa. They began an impatient search behind doors and portières, and even under sofas, though it was quite absurd to suppose that a lady recognizing the merits of the Carew Wedgwood would so far forget herself as to crawl under a sofa.

When they had given up all hope of discovering the intruder, they saw her standing at the far end of the drawing-room critically examining a water-color marine. The elder Miss Boggs started toward her with stern decision, but the little Daguerrotype turned with a shadowy smile, became a blur and an imperceptibility.

Miss Boggs looked at Miss Prudence Boggs.

"If there were ghosts," she said, "this would be one."

"If there were ghosts," said Miss Prudence Boggs, "this would be the ghost of Lydia Carew."

The twilight was settling into blackness, and Miss Boggs nervously lit the gas while Miss Prudence ran for other tea-cups, preferring, for reasons superfluous to mention, not to drink out of the Carew china that evening.

The next day, on taking up her embroidery frame, Miss Boggs found a number of old-fashioned cross-stitches added to her Kensington. Prudence, she knew, would never have degraded herself by taking a cross-stitch, and the parlor-maid was above taking such a liberty. Miss Boggs mentioned the incident that night at a dinner given by an ancient friend of the Carews.

"Oh, that's the work of Lydia Carew, without a doubt!" cried the hostess. "She visits every new family that moves to the house, but she never remains more than a week or two with any one."

"It must be that she disapproves of them," suggested Miss Boggs.

"I think that's it," said the hostess. "She doesn't like their china, or their fiction."

"I hope she'll disapprove of us," added Miss Prudence.

The hostess belonged to a very old Philadelphian family, and she shook her head.

"I should say it was a compliment for even the ghost of Miss Lydia Carew to approve of one," she said severely.

The next morning, when the sisters entered their drawing-room there were numerous evidences of an occupant during their absence. The sofa pillows had been rearranged so that the effect of their grouping was less bizarre than that favored by the Western women; a horrid little Buddhist idol with its eyes fixed on its abdomen, had been chastely hidden behind a Dresden shepherdess, as unfit for the scrutiny of polite eyes; and on the table where Miss Prudence did work in water colors, after the fashion of the impressionists, lay a prim and impossible composition representing a moss-rose and a number of heartsease, colored with that caution which modest spinster artists instinctively exercise.

"Oh, there's no doubt it's the work of Miss Lydia Carew," said Miss Prudence, contemptuously. "There's no mistaking the drawing of that rigid little rose. Don't you remember those wreaths and bouquets framed, among the pictures we got when the Carew pictures were sent to us? I gave some of them to an orphan asylum and burned up the rest."

"Hush!" cried Miss Boggs, involuntarily. "If she heard you, it would hurt her feelings terribly. Of course, I mean—" and she blushed. "It might hurt her feelings—but how perfectly ridiculous! It's impossible!"

Miss Prudence held up the sketch of the moss-rose.

"*That* may be impossible in an artistic sense, but it is a palpable thing."

"Bosh!" cried Miss Boggs.

"But," protested Miss Prudence, "how do you explain it?"

"I don't," said Miss Boggs, and left the room.

That evening the sisters made a point of being in the drawing-room before the dusk came on, and of lighting the gas at the first hint of twilight. They didn't believe in Miss Lydia Carew—but still they meant to be beforehand with her. They talked with unwonted vivacity and in a louder tone than was their custom. But as they drank their tea even their utmost verbosity could not make them oblivious to the fact that the perfume of sweet lavender was stealing insidiously through the room. They tacitly refused to recognize this odor and all that it indicated, when suddenly, with a sharp crash, one of the old Carew teacups fell from the tea-table to the floor and was broken. The disaster was followed by what sounded like a sigh of pain and dismay.

"I didn't suppose Miss Lydia Carew would ever be as awkward as that," cried the younger Miss Boggs, petulantly.

"Prudence," said her sister with a stern accent, "please try not to be a fool. You brushed the cup off with the sleeve of your dress."

"Your theory wouldn't be so bad," said Miss Prudence, half laughing and half crying, "if there were any sleeves to my dress, but, as you see, there aren't," and then Miss Prudence had something as near hysterics as a healthy young woman from the West can have.

"I wouldn't think such a perfect lady as Lydia Carew," she ejaculated between her sobs, "would make herself so disagreeable! You may talk about good-breeding all you please, but I call such intrusion exceedingly bad taste. I have a horrible idea that she likes us and means to stay with us. She left those other people because she did not approve of their habits or their grammar. It would be just our luck to please her."

"Well, I like your egotism," said Miss Boggs.

However, the view Miss Prudence took of the case appeared to be the right one. Time went by and Miss Lydia Carew still remained. When the ladies entered their drawing-room they would see the little lady-like Daguerrotype revolving itself into a blur before one of the family portraits. Or they noticed that the yellow sofa cushion, toward which she appeared to feel a peculiar antipathy, had been dropped behind the sofa upon the floor; or that one of Jane Austen's novels, which none of the family ever read, had been removed from the book shelves and left open upon the table.

"I cannot become reconciled to it," complained Miss Boggs to Miss Prudence. "I wish we had remained in Iowa where we belong. Of course I don't believe in the thing! No sensible person would. But still I cannot become reconciled."

But their liberation was to come, and in a most unexpected manner.

A relative by marriage visited them from the West. He was a friendly man and had much to say, so he talked all through dinner, and afterward followed the ladies to the drawing-room to finish his gossip. The gas in the room was turned very low, and as they entered Miss Prudence caught sight of Miss Carew, in company attire, sitting in upright propriety in a stiff-backed chair at the extremity of the apartment.

Miss Prudence had a sudden idea.

"We will not turn up the gas," she said, with an emphasis intended to convey private information to her sister. "It will be more agreeable to sit here and talk in this soft light."

Neither her brother nor the man from the West made any objection. Miss Boggs and Miss Prudence, clasping each other's hands, divided their attention between their corporeal and their incorporeal guests. Miss Boggs was confident that her sister had an idea, and was willing to await its development. As the guest from Iowa spoke, Miss Carew bent a politely attentive ear to what he said.

"Ever since Richards took sick that time," he said briskly, "it seemed like he shed all responsibility." (The Misses Boggs saw the Daguerrotype put up her shadowy head with a movement of doubt and apprehension.) "The fact of the matter was, Richards didn't seem to scarcely get on the way he might have been expected to." (At this conscienceless split to the infinitive and misplacing of the preposition, Miss Carew arose trembling perceptibly.) "I saw it wasn't no use for him to count on a quick recovery—"

The Misses Boggs lost the rest of the sentence, for at the utterance of the double negative Miss Lydia Carew had flashed out, not in a blur, but with mortal haste, as when life goes out at a pistol shot!

The man from the West wondered why Miss Prudence should have cried at so pathetic a part of his story:

"Thank Goodness!"

And their brother was amazed to see Miss Boggs kiss Miss Prudence with passion and energy.

It was the end. Miss Carew returned no more.

E. Nesbit

Edith Nesbit (*1858–1924*) was a favorite writer of children's books two or three generations ago. She wrote under both her maiden name, E. Nesbit, and her married name, Mrs. Hubert Bland. Her books, which were often serialized in periodicals before book publication, dealt in a fantastic vein with the experiences of upper-middle-class children in adventurous circumstances. Best known are The Story of the Treasure-Seekers (*1899*), The Wouldbegoods (*1901*), and The Railway Children (*1904*). She was also one of the founders of the Fabian Society and was associated with most of the literary figures of the day.

In addition to being a children's writer, E. Nesbit wrote in many other areas—articles and essays, poetry, and some adult supernatural fiction, most of which appeared in the periodicals. Her better ghost stories were assembled in a rare little volume called Grim Tales (*1893*). She was also the author of Dormant (*1911*), a story of suspended animation, partly supernatural, partly early science fiction.

THE MYSTERY
OF THE
SEMI-DETACHED

He was waiting for her; he had been waiting an hour and a half in a dusty suburban lane, with a row of big elms on one side and some eligible building sites on the other—and far away to the south-west the twinkling yellow lights of the Crystal Palace. It was not quite like a country lane, for it had a pavement and lamp-posts, but it was not a bad place for a meeting all the same; and farther up, towards the cemetery, it was really quite rural, and almost pretty, especially in twilight. But twilight had long deepened into night, and still he waited. He loved her, and he was engaged to be married to her, with the complete disapproval of every reasonable person who had been consulted. And this half-clandestine meeting was to-night to take the place of the grudgingly sanctioned weekly interview—because a certain rich uncle was visiting at her house, and her mother was not the woman to acknowledge to a moneyed uncle, who might "go off" any day, a match so deeply ineligible as hers with him.

So he waited for her, and the chill of an unusually severe May evening entered into his bones.

The policeman passed him with but a surly response to his "Good night." The bicyclists went by him like grey ghosts with fog-horns; and it was nearly ten o'clock, and she had not come.

He shrugged his shoulders and turned towards his lodgings. His road led him by her house—desirable, commodious, semi-detached—and he walked slowly as he neared it. She might, even now, be coming out. But she was not. There was no sign of movement about the house, no sign of life, no lights even in the windows. And her people were not early people.

He paused by the gate, wondering.

Then he noticed that the front door was open—wide open—and the

266

street lamp shone a little way into the dark hall. There was something about all this that did not please him—that scared him a little, indeed. The house had a gloomy and deserted air. It was obviously impossible that it harboured a rich uncle. The old man must have left early. In which case—

He walked up the path of patent-glazed tiles, and listened. No sign of life. He passed into the hall. There was no light anywhere. Where was everybody, and why was the front door open? There was no one in the drawing-room, the dining-room and the study (nine feet by seven) were equally blank. Every one was out, evidently. But the unpleasant sense that he was, perhaps, not the first casual visitor to walk through that open door impelled him to look through the house before he went away and closed it after him. So he went upstairs, and at the door of the first bedroom he came to he struck a wax match, as he had done in the sitting-rooms. Even as he did so he felt that he was not alone. And he was prepared to see *something;* but for what he saw he was not prepared. For what he saw lay on the bed, in a white loose gown—and it was his sweetheart, and its throat was cut from ear to ear. He doesn't know what happened then, nor how he got downstairs and into the street; but he got out somehow, and the policeman found him in a fit, under the lamp-post at the corner of the street. He couldn't speak when they picked him up, and he passed the night in the police-cells, because the policeman had seen plenty of drunken men before, but never one in a fit.

The next morning he was better, though still very white and shaky. But the tale he told the magistrate was convincing, and they sent a couple of constables with him to her house.

There was no crowd about it as he had fancied there would be, and the blinds were not down.

As he stood, dazed, in front of the door, it opened, and she came out.

He held on to the door-post for support.

"*She's* all right, you see," said the constable, who had found him under the lamp. "I told you you was drunk, but you *would* know best—"

When he was alone with her he told her—not all—for that would not bear telling—but how he had come into the commodious semi-detached, and how he had found the door open and the lights out, and that he had been into that long back room facing the stairs, and had seen something—in even trying to hint at which he turned sick and broke down and had to have brandy given him.

"But, my dearest," she said, "I dare say the house was dark, for we were all at the Crystal Palace with my uncle, and no doubt the door was open, for the maids *will* run out if they're left. But you could not have been in that room, because I locked it when I came away, and the key was in my pocket. I dressed in a hurry and I left all my odds and ends lying about."

"I know," he said; "I saw a green scarf on a chair, and some long brown gloves, and a lot of hairpins and ribbons, and a prayer-book, and a lace handkerchief on the dressing-table. Why, I even noticed the almanac on the mantelpiece—October 21. At least it couldn't be that, because this is May. And yet it was. Your almanac is at October 21, isn't it?"

"No, of course it isn't," she said, smiling rather anxiously; "but all the other things were just as you say. You must have had a dream, or a vision, or something."

He was a very ordinary, commonplace, City young man, and he didn't believe in visions, but he never rested day or night till he got his sweetheart and her mother away from that commodious semi-detached, and settled them in a quite distant suburb. In the course of the removal he incidentally married her, and the mother went on living with them.

His nerves must have been a good bit shaken, because he was very queer for a long time, and was always inquiring if any one had taken the desirable semi-detached; and when an old stockbroker with a family took it, he went the length of calling on the old gentleman and imploring him by all that he held dear, not to live in that fatal house.

"Why?" said the stockbroker, not unnaturally.

And then he got so vague and confused, between trying to tell why and trying not to tell why, that the stockbroker showed him out, and thanked his God he was not such a fool as to allow a lunatic to stand in the way of his taking that really remarkably cheap and desirable semi-detached residence.

Now the curious and quite inexplicable part of this story is that when she came down to breakfast on the morning of the 22nd of October she found him looking like death, with the morning paper in his hand. He caught hers—he couldn't speak, and pointed to the paper. And there she read that on the night of the 21st a young lady, the stockbroker's daughter, had been found, with her throat cut from ear to ear, on the bed in the long back bedroom facing the stairs of that desirable semi-detached.

Vincent O'Sullivan

Vincent O'Sullivan (1868–1940), the son of a Civil War profiteer who made millions by selling coffee to the Union army, was born in New York. He was educated in England, attending Oscott at the time that Frederick Rolfe (Baron Corvo) was a master there. After leaving school O'Sullivan remained in England, gravitating toward the Aesthetic Movement. Aubrey Beardsley was his closest friend, and Oscar Wilde, George Moore, Max Beerbohm, Frank Harris, and Ernest Dowson were among his associates. He contributed the introductory text to Beardsley's edition of Volpone *and the cash to finance Wilde's trip to Italy after Wilde left prison.*

O'Sullivan was a fairly frequent contributor of both short stories and essays to the periodicals of the time. His novel The Good Girl *(1912) was a minor cause célèbre, some critics calling it a work of great originality; others, a sordid, unpleasant story. At some time after World War I O'Sullivan lost his fortune under circumstances that have not been revealed, and he moved to France, where he lived in great poverty for the remainder of his life. Not long before his death he wrote* Aspects of Wilde *(1935), which offered reminiscences and impressions of literary notables in Wilde's circle. O'Sullivan was supported by charity from the American colony at Biarritz, and when he died, he was buried in a pauper's grave.*

Today, O'Sullivan is remembered for A Book of Bargains *(1896), which is collected as much for the frontispiece by Beardsley as for the stories in it. It contains four supernatural stories, original in subject matter, written in the decorated style of the period. After a few years O'Sullivan abandoned this style and wrote plainly, an evolution in which he was not alone.*

MY ENEMY
AND MYSELF

In the garden, when I was a child, I used to stare for hours at the white roses. In these there was for me a certain strangeness, which was yet quite human; for I know that I was full of sorrow if I found the petals strewn over the hushed grass. I had a terror of great waters, wild and lonely; I saw an austere dignity in the moon shining on a flat sea; things, cordage and broken spars, cast ashore by the ocean, told me wonderful, sad tales. And because my head was thick with thoughts, I had little speech; and for this I was laughed at and called stupid: "He was always a dull child," murmured my mother, bending over me, when I, in the crisis of a fever, was on the point of embarking for a vague land. As I grew older, I still dwelt within my soul, a satisfied prisoner: the complaint of huge trees in a storm; the lash and surge of breakers on an iron coast; the sound of certain words; the sight of dim colours which blend sometimes in gray sunsets; the heavy scent of some ex- quisite poisonous flower; a contemplation of youthful forms engaged in an unruly game;—ah! in these things also I found perfect sensation and ecstacy. Still, my tongue held to its old stubbornness: I was ever delayed by a habit of commonplace speech, a shame at exposing my thoughts. In time I won a cloud of easy acquaintance; but my awk- wardness in conversation, my tendency to be maladroit,—call it what you like! always stepped between when I was about to make a friend. Then, at last, came Jacquette.

I remember that she was playing a composition by Chopin, a curious black-coloured thing, when I first came into her company; and now, even as I write, when our love is over, I hear that sombre music again. But the important matter is, that here was the person I had been seek- ing so long; here was the mind to meet with my mind; with her I could, at length, get out of myself (as we now say); become free. All the dear thoughts which had for years dwelt with me in close privateness, I gave to her; all my desires, all my mean hopes. Ah! the merry airs we had then: her bright laughter which, as wind, drove glumness, as foam, before it! I think I tired her of my enthusiasms and decisions; but it was so sweet to have some one to listen and understand, and she never would admit that she was tired. Nay! one morning in the apple-orchard, when the wind was turning her hair to the sunshine, she kissed me very prettily on the mouth.

After that, I forget how long it was till I came in one night and found my enemy sitting with her at the fireside. He was not my enemy then, mind you: indeed, I thought him a nice, pleasant creature, with a mighty handsome face. We became familiar: he seemed to like me, and I was sure I had gained another friend. The months glided by, and we three came to sitting together late of nights: he and Jacquette, the wise people, silent, gazing at each other; I, the fool, in the middle, talking in a youthful, impassioned way. Once I paused suddenly, and looked up, and caught a somewhat contemptuous smile peeping from the corners of Jacquette's mouth and dancing in her eyes; while he, for an answer, fell a-laughing into her face. Of course, I must have wearied them both, *bored them* (as we say) to desperation; but I was a very young man, with all the warmth and admiration of the young; and in the time of youth, a woman is always older than a man. Besides, I loved her so much, and I had such strange pleasure in loving her, that I think it was rather cruel of her to laugh.

"Why did you laugh at me?" I asked, when I was twisting a garland of wild roses for her hair.

"Oh, I didn't laugh!" she exclaimed. "Or if I did," she added, looking down with a tooth on her lip, "it must have been because I was so pleased to hear you saying beautiful words to us—poor ignorant things!"

The next day I had an affair of great importance in the town where I lived, so I told Jacquette that on account of this affair I could not go down, as my custom was, to her cottage by the sea, that night. But as the day waned, and the night closed in, I became the thrall of a longing to hear her singing voice, to play fantastic music with her delightfully. Thus it came about that it was nearly eleven o'clock when I reached the shore, and hearkened to the calling sea. There was a note of melancholy, almost a sob, in the noise of it to-night: and that, taken with a monstrous depression, filled me strangely with a desire to die—to give up life at this point! I saw a light in Jacquette's bedroom, but the rest of the little house was dark; and I was turning away, when my hand chanced to strike the door-handle, which I pushed, and found the door not locked. Let me go in! (thinks I): I shall sit awhile and dream of Jacquette, and a few chords touched softly on the piano will tell my love I am dreaming of her. Here (perhaps you will say!) I was wrong: but I was ready to welcome a servant's company, or, in spite of his growing offensiveness, my enemy's, should I find him there, rather than be alone with my saddening thoughts. The room I chose to sit in, because there was a dying fire in it, was just under Jacquette's bedroom; and ere I had sat a minute, I became conscious of voices in the room above. As soon as I made out the man's voice, a thousand serpents seemed literally to eat their way into my brain, turning my vision red; and I lay for an hour, may-be, on the carpet, fainting, and stricken, and dazed. Now, at last, after an hour I was myself, or rather more than myself, with every nerve tight as a fiddle-string, still seeing red, as I unclasped the long jack-knife, which the Greek sailor had given me, and laid it in the hollow of my hand.

I knew that it would dawn by three o'clock, so I stood quite still, only moving my tongue over my dry lips, and shaking my head to keep a sweat from running into my eyes. A cat cried in the road, and the breakers thundered against the rocks.

A little before dawn, while it was yet dark, I heard a murmur of low voices—her voice and my enemy's; and then the man came down the stairs.

"Good night, my sweet love!" said Jacquette.

"O my darling, good night!" came from my enemy, and so he banged the door behind him.

One moment I paused to peer through the window, and make sure of my man. Then I fetched a run, and was on him like a panther, holding him close, with his hot breath scorching my face. Coming on him from behind, as I did, the middle finger of my left hand struck his eye, and now, as I pressed, the eye bulged out.

"My friend," he groaned, "for Christ's sake, have pity!"

"To hell with your friendship!" I said. "Much pity you had for my honour!" says I, and with that I let him have the knife in his throat, and the blood spurted over my hands hot and sticky. As soon as I could get free of his clutch, I looked up at Jacquette's bedroom window, and there she was, sure enough! in her nightdress, with the blind in her hand, gazing out. Straight up to her room I went, and flung open the door. She turned to me gray and whingeing.

"My little love—," she began.

I put my hands on my hips and spat hard into her face. Then I tramped down stairs and out of the lonely cottage.

I had not the least fear of detection: the servants slept in an outhouse, and the place was too desolate for any chance passenger. I stood triumphing by the corpse of my enemy; but even as I looked the moon shewed from a rift of cloud, lighting the blood, and the hue left by violent death in the features, and I ran for my life from that hideous one-eyed thing.

I came to the town, and to a house where I lay constantly, about four o'clock, in a curious trembling fit. I bathed my head and hands, however, in a heavy perfume, and then became strangely calm, and fell to thinking of the rightness of the deed. Just there was the consoling thought: certainly I had done a murder, but in doing it I had delivered punishment to a traitress and her paramour. Now that the thing was over, it was clearly my duty to forget all about it as soon as possible; and this I set myself to do, aided by a cigarette and a novel of the ingenious Miss Jane Austen. I had succeeded in my aim, I was clear-minded and very serene, when of a sudden something heavy fell against the door of my room.

"At this hour?" I murmured in surprise, and went to the door.

A body that nearly knocked me down, the dead body of a man, fell into the room, and lay, face downward, on the carpet. Then I did the one act I shall never cease to regret: From a movement of kindness, pity, curiosity, what you will! I bent down and turned over the corpse. Slowly the thing got to its feet; and my enemy, with a dry gaping wound in his throat, and his eye hanging from its socket by a bit of skin, stood before me, face to face.

"O God, have mercy!" I screamed, and beat on the wall with my hands; and again and again:—"God, have mercy!"

"You do well to ask God for mercy," says my enemy; "for you will not get much from men." He stood by the fire-place.

"I beg of you," I said, in a low, passionate voice, "I beg of you, by all you find dear, for the sake of our old friendship, to leave this place, to let me go free."

He shook his head. "For Jacquette's sake?" He laughed harshly.

"My friend," I said to my enemy, "for Christ's sake, have pity!"

"Pity you?" says he, in a jeer. "You!"

As I looked at him, I was stung into strong fury. My eyes clung to the wound in his throat, and my fingers ached to close in it—to misuse it, to maul it.

But as I sprang at him, he gave a shriek that woke the town; a shriek of fear too, let me think it at this last, like to that of a lost soul when the gates of hell have closed behind for ever: and when the people of the house rushed in, they found me kneeling by his dead body, with my knife in my enemy's throat, and his new blood, bright and wet, on my hands.

They will hang me because I loved Jacquette.

Paul Heyse

Paul Heyse (*1830–1914*), although almost unknown in the English-speaking world, was a dominant figure in late nineteenth-century German literature. The leading writer in the so-called Munich School, he excelled in nouvelles of psychological interest, the most famous of which is L'Arrabbiata (*1855*). He was also a fine lyric poet and did excellent translations of Shakespeare's plays into German. In *1910* he received the Nobel Prize for literature.

"Midday Magic" ("Mittagszauber") is one of a series of ghost stories told by a circle of acquaintances in Heyse's In der Geisterstunde (*1892*). The other stories range from a grotesque tale in the mode of E. T. A. Hoffmann to the story of a child ghost that worried about its pets, to a story about a classical vampire. The present tale of a pathetic suicide from Napoleonic times is based on the English translation by Mrs. F. A. Van Santford, which has been slightly corrected and heavily edited by the editor of this volume.

MIDDAY MAGIC

I can tell you not only the year, but even the day of which my adventure took place. It was the 16th of July, 1868. On the 10th I had taken my doctorate in history at Leipzig, and immediately afterward I went to visit my uncle and aunt, who had taken me in as a son on the death of my parents. Under their roof I hoped to recover from the strain of my examinations. They lived in Dresden, in a small house in the new section of the city, and I do not have to say that they received me with the honors of a conquering hero. But despite their care I continued to be pale, thin, and nervous. On the morning of the sixth day my aunt declared that something drastic had to be done to reawaken my vital powers. "There is nothing better in cases like yours," she said, "than to spend some time in the open air up in the mountains." My uncle agreed with her, and they decided to pack me off to the Saxon Switzerland.

I could agree about the open air, but the place was simply impossible. It was the middle of summer and every road and path would be swarming with tourists and vacationers, and there would be no hope of peace and quiet.

But while my aunt was explaining her plans to me, there rose before me the memory of a much closer, quiet little spot, which I had often visited during holidays when I was a student in Dresden. This was a small inn on the right bank of the Elbe. It was situated fairly high and was surrounded by gardens. It was only about half a mile from Loschwitz. Unfortunately, it no longer exists, for it had to give way to a large villa, as I saw to my sorrow when I happened to be there not too long ago. At that time the inn was owned by a young married couple with whom I was on fairly friendly terms. I liked their wine, and most of all I liked the quiet on a balcony that hung out over the shore road.

It was an old-fashioned sort of inn, patronized by well-to-do towns-men who came to drink Blümchenkaffee, and by occasional people on walking tours. The owners did well enough that they could scoff at the idea of enlarging their business by going stylish and modern.

It is true that I did not know whether my friends were taking lodgers, but I felt sure that they would not refuse me a bed in one room or another of their old house.

And so, with my knapsack on my back, I made my way that hot afternoon along the road by the river. Nothing had changed very much in the couple of years since I had been there. Except that one of the farm houses, which I knew so well, had been newly white-washed and that there was a new arbor among the bushes that thrust their blossoming branches over the garden hedge. The road by the river was still little travelled, for most of the traffic moved along the highway on the other side of the houses. In the deep silence the only sound that accompanied me was the soft plash of the waves as they lapped up on the pebble-covered river bank. At the house, too, every-thing seemed exactly as it used to be.

I climbed the same weathered stone steps up to the little grilled gate, which, if one knew the technique, could be opened from the outside. The narrow path that led through the inn garden was as overgrown and neglected as before. Only the members of the house-hold and a few regular patrons knew of this entrance. The general public came in from above. Since I recognized a familiar face among the guests who were sitting inside and did not wish to jeopardize my privacy, I carefully went around to the back of the house.

There I met old Ursel, who was practically a fixture in the house and an old favorite of mine. She greeted me like a long-lost friend, and when I told her that my first want was not food and drink, but a few words with the landlord, she took me into the livingroom on the top floor and then ran down to fetch the landlord and his wife, who were working in the farm buildings, which were off to one side.

I had some time to look around the room, which I had never seen before. The furniture was old, but everything was neat and attractive. There were potted plants on the window sills, roses in a vase on the table in front of the black horsehair sofa, a twittering canary in a cage by the open window, and outside, the dark foliage of a chestnut tree, waving gently in the morning breeze. On the wall above the sofa hung three large family portraits. On the left was the picture of an imposing man in the costume of the 'twenties; across from him, dressed in the high fashion of the day, was a plump woman with a small child wrapped in embroidered swaddling clothes on her arm. Between them was a young woman clad in the fashion of the First Empire. I found her more attractive than the other two. It was not that she was remarkably beautiful. Her face, which was turned fully to the viewer, was a little too round, and her turned-up, small nose and pouting lips did not correspond to my concept of beauty. But her eyes, large and dark, with long lashes, had such an odd combination of touching innocence and suspicious melancholy that they enchanted me. She was clad in a white gown, ornamented on the hems with blue embroidery, with a girdle high under her young bosom. Her slender neck was bare, as were her arms, and she wore a narrow red shawl across her shoulders. Her head was covered with short brown curls. In her hand she held an open white rose and on her fourth finger she had a gold ring with a blue heart-shaped stone.

I must have been staring for a full ten minutes at this interesting young woman, probably now long dead, when the door opened and the landlord entered. Behind him came his wife, who had become somewhat plumper since I last saw her; the reason for this was to be seen in the year-old child that she carried in her arms.

They both greeted me warmly and scolded me for having stayed away so long. With great pride they showed me their child. They told me that everything had gone very nicely over the past couple of years. Their wine business, that used to be small, had grown to such an extent that they had been compelled to build a large wine garden, in which weddings and family festivities were celebrated.

I did not begrudge these fine people their small worldly success, but it really destroyed my plans, since the quiet and seclusion that I had hoped for was no longer to be found here. I asked them, nevertheless, if I might have a quiet room for a week or two, but the landlady replied that unfortunately it could not be done. The room under the roof they had set up as a nursery and the other two rooms were occupied by a couple from the city with a sick child, who was supposed to be recuperating in the country air. But his coughing and crying meant that there would be no rest in the single remaining room.

They were sorry, extremely sorry, and if they could have guessed that I would be coming, they would not have accepted these strangers. Her husband corroborated this, but seemed to be considering a way around these difficulties. As I, with suppressed sigh, picked up my hat and walking stick, he said, "No, Riekchen. We can't let the Herr Doctor go away and take unpleasant lodgings with strangers. There is Great Aunt Blandine's garden house. It hasn't been occupied for many years, but if it is swept out and clean drapes put up—the Herr Doctor is only concerned about peace and quiet—if he doesn't want to leave the garden house, we can bring his meals over to the sitting room. He could sleep in the rear room. And he would have the whole garden to himself. I would say . . ."

"What are you saying, husband," interrupted his wife, making a reproachful gesture while she seemed to signal to him with her eyes.

Her husband only laughed good humoredly, gave her a little slap on her plump shoulders, and then turned to me.

"These women! They're all alike. Even the sensible ones, like Riekchen here, can be taken in by foolish talk. You see, Doctor, the old people say that there is something queer about the garden house, and the young ones pick it up. But no one has ever seen anything. And even if Blandine's ghost does walk, what of it? The Herr Doctor can decide for himself if a visit from a nice young woman is so unpleasant. That's her hanging above our sofa. Does she look as if she would find it amusing to chase people around? Herr Doctor, you see, Great Aunt Blandine . . ."

At this point Ursel came with the message that the masons needed the landlord about the new bathhouse. The landlord and his wife left, after giving instructions about my accommodations, and I was alone with the old woman.

I asked her if she knew anything about Blandine. No, she didn't know anything much, except that the young Mademoiselle used to live over there in the little garden house, and people say that she still appears every now and then. But she had never met anyone who had seen her, and she didn't believe the story. Blandine had a good, pious face, and she wouldn't have committed the crime that would make her rest uneasy in her grave.

We both descended the steps and went through the garden to a side gate that opened on a narrow alley sloping gradually up from the road by the river. The gate was usually kept locked. Almost exactly across the alley was a similar little gate, which opened to the same key. Beyond the gate was an overgrown garden, which had gone wild. I had never paid any attention to it before, since I usually did not spend much time outside in this area. Also, you could not look into it from the street below. The hedge that bordered the garden had grown too thick and too high, and the lower entrance, a barred doorway, atop a couple of steps, was so overgrown by thick lilac bushes that one could easily pass by it without noticing it.

As I now entered this quiet enclosure, which was something less than two hundred feet square and sloped gently up toward the highway, I saw a remarkable sight.

Here, as if human foot had not entered for the past ten years or so, was an incredible profusion of the most beautiful roses, mostly centi-

folia roses, together with carnations, wallflowers, jasmine, and helio-
trope, all growing together helterskelter. Amid them, like white islands
emerging from a sea of blossom, were clusters of unusually tall lilies,
whose strong scent overpowered all the rest. This paradise was aglow
with the reddish radiance of the setting sun. Since the trees and shrubs
enclosing the garden on all four sides were so dense that the neighboring houses could not be seen, the impression that I received of the
garden was of something enchanted, as in a fairytale, yet, also, a little
oppressive.

"The mistress lets it all grow as God wills," said the old woman,
bending the branches of overgrown rose bushes aside to let me pass.
"There hasn't been time to clean it out proper and keep it in order. It
wouldn't pay to hire a gardener. Twice a week they cut flowers and
send them to a dealer in the city. If the paths get too overgrown, the
master clears them with his hedge clippers. Years ago the master's
father used to come out here evenings and smoke a pipe in front of the
garden house. But then he stopped. Perhaps some night ghost came
and soured it for him. But it certainly couldn't have been Fräulein
Blandine."

Now I saw the little garden house where I was to stay. It was a small,
square, gray wooden building with a peaked roof and overhanging
eaves. There was a door in the front and a single window, covered
by a shutter that had once been painted green. There was also a
shuttered window on each side of the house. It was all weatherbeaten.
Under the eaves were a couple of sparrow nests, whose occupants flew
away with indignant twitterings when the old woman pushed the door
open on its rusty hinges and we stepped over the threshold.

A clammy smell of mold met us. But when we put up the shutters on
all three sides, the room did not look out of the ordinary. There was
a rococo commode against one wall, a garden bench, a couple of odd
chairs, and a table with a faded, patterned tablecloth. At the window
stood a nice little inlaid table, on which was an embroidery basket with
what looked like a piece of started needlework. Most attractive, however, were six large floral drawings on the walls, framed in unfinished
wood. They were mostly of roses and lilies, drawn very carefully if a
little stiffly, but with a fine sense of form. They were on light gray
paper and were painstakingly colored. Among these modest pictures
I was surprised to see a large map of Europe, on which a heavy red
line led from Dresden to Moscow. Beneath this rather odd decoration
for a summerhouse was a small miniature portrait set in a golden frame.
It was the portrait of a young man in a uniform of the turn of the
century. The face was so faded that except for brown dots for eyes
and a fine black moustache, the features were lost.

The old woman opened the door to the inner room and I stepped into a dark chamber into which no light penetrated until I threw open the shutters of a small window. Then I saw a narrow bedstead in the corner, then a washstand with a Meissen toilet set, and on the opposite wall an engraving of Carlo Dolce's "Ecce Homo."

"Here is where the Herr Doctor will have to sleep," said Ursel, "if it is not too narrow and uncomfortable. The mattresses are in good condition, and we will bring over the rest of the bedding and whatever else a good Christian may need. The Herr Doctor will not have to worry about being disturbed, if he is ghost-proof. But that's all stupid superstition, though I know many who wouldn't spend a night here for all the gold in the world, just because Fräulein Blandine used to sleep in that bed. But that was a long time ago, when her young man was at Moscow, with Napoleon. And the Lord God, that she prayed to every night wouldn't send her poor soul out wandering to frighten us poor mortals, no matter what she did. No, he wouldn't do that. Why should he?"

This sensible old woman finally left me, to get whatever else I needed and about a half hour later I was completely settled. The bed was made up freshly with pillow and spread; water was fetched from a little well that lay hidden near the garden house, under a lilac bush; and the simple meal that I had ordered was served on the table in the front room. I was so delighted with my wonderful lodgings that I couldn't persuade myself, this first night, to go over to the inn, which was alive with guests, as could be seen from the lights and lanterns.

The old woman came once more, to wish me good night in the name of the landlord and landlady, who apologized for not coming over in person. The landlady could not leave the kitchen, and the master had to help the waiter, things were so busy.

The old woman cleared the table and left me with my bottle of Moselle.

Now for the first time I roamed through the narrow, overgrown paths, over my tiny domain, and worked my way through the flowering bushes over to an arbor which stood in a corner of the garden, at about the same height as the garden house. It was completely covered with honeysuckle, which was in full bloom, so that inside the arbor it was very dark, while the odor of the flowers was almost overpowering. I fetched out a chair that was inside the arbor, lit my pipe, and sat, I don't know how long, in peaceful contemplation of the clear heaven and the stars. The perfume of the flowers grew stronger and fireflies flashed now and then above the bushes.

I could see the broad, quiet river behind the bushes at the lower end of the garden. An occasional small ship or boat glided by, throwing up dark waves that distorted the reflection of the lantern on the prow. Once a steam vessel, with music aboard, passed by and disappeared like a dream image behind the willows, on its way to the city. Not until later did the crescent of the waning moon hover over the broad landscape. The flat land on the other side of the river, with houses on it, was veiled by mist and only an occasional light could be seen.

The air gradually became cooler, and after the hot day I drank it in with such a feeling of delight that I just sat there. The clock in the church tower at Loschwitz struck first eleven, then twelve, before I could make up my mind to go to bed. Of the horrors of the ghost-hour I found not the slightest trace, and even when I lay down on the young lady's bed, my thoughts were far away from anything supernatural. I left the little window open, and the branches of the tall shrubs swayed lightly in the night breezes. In a neighboring garden a nightingale sang. I listened to it for a short time, then fell asleep. I slept fitfully, awakened by noises of the summer night—birds in search of their prey, the scratching and snuffling of a cat or marten prowling on the roof for sparrows; the groaning of wheels and crackling of whips in early morning along the nearby highway. There was still nothing from the world of the supersensual.

And so it happened that I did not awake until late the next morning, when the old woman put her head into my room. She asked if I had met anyone during the night. I assured her, laughingly, that the young lady had not visited me, and that she could ease the Frau's mind on that point. After breakfast, the garden, shining with dew, beckoned to me, especially while most of it was still in the shade. But I resisted the temptation long enough to write letters to my aunt and uncle in Dresden and to friends in Leipzig, and to the printer who was setting my dissertation.

By this time the morning chill had disappeared and over the flowers, which were now in full sun, lay such a glow of heat that I thought it best not to leave the little house, but to pass the heat of the day in the golden twilight afforded by the half-closed shutters.

I took up a book that I had brought along with me, Hermann Lingg's poems. It had just come out, and despite an introduction by Geibel, it was still little known in Northern Germany. A South German student friend of mine had recommended it and had given me his copy as a parting present. That morning I opened the little book at random and read in it. I was especially delighted with his sonnet "Midday Magic." You must permit me to quote it, although I am sure that you know it. But it expressed my mood at the time so completely.

In the tremble of air the swelling midday heat
In silence globes the meadow and the hill.
There is no sound save the woodpecker's knocking beat,
And from downstream the wedging whirr of the mill.
In search of coolth the brown brook twists in flight.
The flowers, agape with thirst, all limply lie,
And butterflies with throbbing wings alight
Then flutter drunken from the daisy's eye.

A boatsman at the sluggish river weaves
A boatshade from willows growing at the wall,
And watches the cloudway in the glaring flow.
It is high noon: a click of reed sword leaves,
The fisherman wakes; the hunter hears a call,
And the herdsman sees the cliff in golden glow.

After I had finished reading this, I closed my eyes and abandoned myself for a while to the sweet sense of a lyric enchantment that poured through my veins like a strong wine. Then I arose and went to the threshold of my little house. There lay the world, my own green and peaceful world, quivering in the same sultry brightness that the verses pictured. The butterflies, that hung as if drunken on the lilies and roses; the soft bird voices all around me; the waves in the river down below, that looked as if they were trying to escape from the sun into the shade—it was all indeed magical. After a time I walked slowly, repeating the verse to myself, to the honeysuckle-covered arbor.

There was a bench inside the arbor. I sat down, book of poetry still in my hand, but I could not read, for it was dark inside.

I can still envision, quite clearly, how wonderful it seemed to look out from my dark green hiding place into the shimmering midday glare. It was as if the ether above me was a crystal-clear sea and I sat deep in its depths, so that the lightly moving waves wove and swirled over me and trickled down in bright pearls over the plants at the bottom of the sea. I myself, was imprisoned in a deep grotto, in which it was as heavy to breathe as in a diving bell. And yet this confinement did not cause me any pain; on the contrary, I was suffused with a secret sense of well being, such as I had experienced when a child, when we played hide and seek, and I would crouch down in some corner where I was sure that I could not be found.

My eyes ached when I stared too long into the pulsing light. I had to shut them for a few minutes. In the purple darkness around me I listened to the humming, whirring noises which pierced through the vines on the arbor. There were the rustling and whispering of insects and other mysterious voices that are perceptible only when all human sounds are departed and the day, at its height, seems to stand still for a moment and hold its breath.

When I opened my eyes again I beheld a strange sight.

At the other end of the garden, as if she had just entered through the lower gate, a bright, slender female figure was walking slowly, as if absorbed in herself. Her face was hidden under a large straw bonnet of old-fashioned shape. She obviously was not a stranger here, for she knew where to find the narrow path, even though it was almost swallowed up by the overhanging shrubs, and she passed along it, bending the sprays lightly back, without haste or effort. Every now and then she stooped gracefully down to the flowers on her right and left, as if she were examining them to see how it fared with individual plants. As soon as she came to the end of the path, she moved over to the next one parallel, but she kept facing away from me, so that I could catch only slight glimpses of her profile and a lock of her brown hair, which peeped from beneath the edge of her straw hat. The sight of this youthful garden-lover among the flow of roses and lilies was so lovely that I stood stock still, lest I should frighten her away by stepping out too suddenly.

The figure paused for a moment before a spray of centifolia roses. I watched her stoop and bury her face in the full, open flowers. Then she raised her head and broke off a half-open bud. Her hand was half-covered by a black lace palm glove. Since all this took place fairly close to my arbor, I was able to see more exactly what she was wearing. No, I had not been deceived. She wore a gown, girdled high, below the bosom, like the one I had seen yesterday on the young woman whose picture hung in my host's living room. And along the edge, bordering the low neckline, ran the blue embroidery. The same red scarf was thrown about her shoulders, and her white sleeves reached only to her elbows. And now, as she turned and looked up toward the garden house, I admit that for a moment a shudder passed over me. It was the same rather round face, under the broad forehead with its shadowing brown curls, and large black eyes that held the same look of intense melancholy.

The strange sensation did not last long. I did not know why, but even though this unknown young woman seemed at the height of youth and health, a deep feeling of sympathy for her stirred in my breast. I also felt a certain curiosity, too, as to why she should walk about in the daylight in the costume of her grandmother's day, as though she had just run away from a masquerade. And the likeness to the portrait! And how had she entered the garden? Old Ursel had told me that the key to the shore road gate had been lost.

I did not have much time to consider these puzzles, for the slender figure had already reached the top of the garden, and was coming, though with dallying step, along the upper walk, right up to my arbor. At this point I thought it would be the proper thing for me to step out and introduce myself as the temporary lord of the land. But when I arose from my bench, I saw her start, stare for a moment into the gloom of the arbor, and fly toward me with a half-stifled cry, "Edward! Edward! You've finally come!"

Her arms were outstretched, her curls fluttered, her bosom heaved—and then she suddenly stopped still as if turned to stone. Her arms sank down to her side; an expressibly sad expression came over her face, from which color had departed, and tears ran down from her long lashes.

"Pardon me, sir," she murmured, almost inaudibly. "I've let myself be deceived by the light—once again. I beg you to excuse me. I shall not disturb you any further."

I stepped to the entrance of the arbor, and she involuntarily drew back a step.

"It is not you, Fräulein, but I who should ask pardon," I said. "I have been quartered here as a guest, and I only came yesterday. But you obviously belong to the house, and if you wish to be alone in the garden I shall leave at once."

She looked at me unmoved while I was speaking. Her features had regained their composure, but a strange, restless look in her eyes made me wonder whether this pleasant young lady might not be entirely in her right mind. Her strange mode of dress would seem to confirm my suspicion.

"How could I drive you away?" she answered, in a soft, lovely voice. "I have no more right to be here. I must be content if they let me come back now and then to look at the flowers that I loved so much. But I've forfeited the right to tend them. Not that they need any care. Look at the way they are growing, without me. Heaven must watch over them."

She sighed and pressed the rosebud to her snub nose. Then, after a moment of silence, "So you live here now? It is beautiful, isn't it? I used to enjoy living here, until I couldn't any longer. But we must not talk of that. Everyone has his own fate, and that fate comes to every-one—out of his own heart."

We were silent for a while. Our meeting seemed stranger and stranger, and although what she said was rational enough, the thought again flashed through my mind that she was not quite right.

"Wouldn't you like to step into the arbor, Fräulein?" I finally said. But she waved a refusal with a hasty movement of her hand. "No, no," she whispered. "There are too many memories in there. It is not good to awaken them. Some time in the future it will be different, and I won't have to sit there alone any more. Then I'll be laughing and crying in the darkness there. It cannot last much longer. It has already lasted far too long, and sometimes I think that I have waited in vain.

"But you believe, don't you, that faithfulness is not an empty delusion? You can be faithful during life. And if I've been faithful, do you think someone else would be bored and tired of it? Yes, bored and tired . . . I am, often enough. Long sleep and sad dreams . . . If you permit, I will sit down here for a moment. Then I must leave right away."

The chair was still in front of the arbor. The young lady sank down on it, crossing her little feet, which, in white satin shoes, peeped out from beneath the tucks of her cambric gown. She drew a deep breath, as if the walk had tired her. She seemed to have forgotten my presence, for she busied herself with her toilet. She took off her hat, pushed her sleeves back to her shoulders. All the while she inhaled the fragrance of her rose, with an expression of longing.

For the sake of saying something, for the silence embarrassed me, I asked her whether the drawings in the garden house were her work. She nodded abstractedly, and suddenly looked at me again, and asked, "Have you ever been in Russia?"

I said that I had not.

"Too bad," she said. "I would like to know if it is as cold there as people say. Oh, warmth, warmth! Doesn't everyone want to be back in the warmth. And to snuggle up to a warm heart— But this is no way for a young lady who should be cool and dignified to talk. Well, it is all the same to me. I am old enough that no one has any right to criticize me.

"Now you, sir, I can tell, find my clothing odd. What does it matter how you dress as long as you don't reveal your innermost thoughts? No, don't ask me any questions. He promised me he would return, and when he does, I'll step right up to all of them and tell them to be ashamed of themselves. And now— Dieu vous bénisse."

She rose quietly, nodded slightly to me, and made as if to leave.

"May I ask a favor of you, Fräulein?" I cried. "Give me the flowers you have in your hand. I would like to keep them in memory of this delightful meeting."

A swift look of suspicion flashed at me from her black eyes.

"I regret," she said, "that I cannot grant you that. Giving a rose has a significance. Do you understand the language of flowers? No matter. One must be careful. That is the way it begins, and who knows how it will end? First a flower, then a wreath. And even if you told *no one* about it, *he* would know about it, for how could I conceal it from him when he returns?

"And you, too, think that he will come back, don't you? No matter how long the way is?"

"Certainly, most certainly," I said, fully convinced that my suspicion had been correct. Once again I felt a painful feeling of sympathy for the poor young woman, whose face shone with joy when I assured her that vanished happiness would return.

"I thank you," she said with some emotion. "You have helped me quite a bit. The others all avoid me. They think there is something wrong with my mind. But it is only the fever of longing which makes me fantasize at times. I must go and cool my head, and then I shall be entirely reasonable again. Good bye."

"No," she said quickly, as I made a move to accompany her. "You must not walk with me. If they saw us together, they might misjudge me. Do you intend to stay here much longer? Perhaps I can come back again, about this time, if I am allowed. Oh, the world is wonderful for those with good fortune. But I shall be fortunate again. 'They who endure shall be crowned.' "

She nodded to me in friendly fashion, put on her hat again, and went softly away through the tangled paths between the flowerbeds. I saw her white neck above the tall rosebushes and would have followed her, despite her prohibition, but an inexplicable force held me bound to the spot. For an instant my attention was diverted by a noise that seemed to come from the alley between the garden and the inn. When I turned my eyes back to the place where she had disappeared among the rosebushes, there was nothing to be seen, except the tall lilies swaying, as if a passing bird had brushed them lightly with his wings.

I told no one of my wonderful experience, for I felt that if I remained silent about it, she might visit me again. But on the evening of that day a heavy thunderstorm broke, followed the next day by gray weather and a steady drizzle of rain. When the air cleared again, the weather remained raw and uncomfortable. During the two weeks that I spent at my garden house I never again experienced midday magic.

R. Murray Gilchrist

Robert Murray Gilchrist (1868–1917) is now remembered mostly as a British regionalistic writer who concentrated on the moors and mountains of Derbyshire. His naturalistic stories of life among the people of the small towns and farms of the Peaks area, told in dialect, have been highly regarded. His best-known work in this area is probably A Peakland Faggot (1897), which is occasionally reissued.

Gilchrist's earlier work lay in a different range. This was a series of highly individual, slightly cryptic short stories that combined aspects of the Victorian fable with fin de siècle interest in the outré and outlandish. Such are the stories of The Stone Dragon (1897), from which the following one is taken; these stories are told in a decorated style and often have a semiallegorical point.

WITCH
IN-GRAIN

Of late Michal had been much engrossed in the reading of the black-letter books that Philosopher Bale brought from France. As you know I am no Latinist—though one while she was earnest in her desire to instruct me; but the open air had ever greater charms for me than had the dry precincts of a library. So I grudged the time she spent apart, and throughout the spring I would have been all day at her side, talking such foolery as lovers use. But ever she must steal away and hide herself amongst dead volumes.

Yestereven I crossed the Roods, and entered the garden, to find the girl sitting under a yew-tree. Her face was haggard and her eyes sunken: for the time it seemed as if many years had passed over her head, but somehow the change had only added to her beauty. And I marvelled greatly, but ere I could speak a huge bird, whose plumage was as the brightest gold, fluttered out of her lap from under the silken apron; and looking on her uncovered bosom I saw that his beak had pierced her tender flesh. I cried aloud, and would have caught the thing, but it rose slowly, laughing like a man, and, beating upwards, passed out of sight in the quincunx. Then Michal drew long breaths, and her youth came back in some measure. But she frowned, and said, "What is it, sweetheart? Why hast awakened me? I dreamed that I fed the Dragon of the Hesperidean Garden." Meanwhile, her gaze set on the place whither the bird had flown.

"Thou hast chosen a filthy mammet," I said. "Tell me how came it hither?"

She rose without reply, and kissed her hands to the gaudy wings, which were nearing through the trees. Then, lifting up a great tome that had lain at her feet, she turned towards the house. But ere she had reached the end of the maze she stopped, and smiled with strange subtlety.

"How camest *thou* hither, O satyr?" she cried. "Even when the Dragon slept, and the fruit hung naked to my touch. . . . The gates fell to."

Perplexed and sore adread, I followed to the hall; and found in the herb garden the men struggling with an ancient woman—a foul crone, brown and puckered as a rotten costard. At sight of Michal she thrust out her hands, crying, "Save me, mistress!" The girl cowered, and ran up the perron and indoors. But for me, I questioned Simon, who stood well out of reach of the wretch's nails, as to the wherefore of this hurly-burly.

His underlings bound the runnion with cords, and haled her to the closet in the banqueting gallery. Then, her beldering being stilled, Simon entreated me to compel Michal to prick her arm. So I went down to the library, and found my sweetheart sitting by the window, tranced with seeing that goblin fowl go tumbling on the lawn.

My heart was full of terror and anguish. "Dearest Michal," I prayed, "for the sake of our passion let me command. Here is a knife." I took a poniard from Sir Roger's stand of arms. "Come with me now; I will tell you all."

Her gaze still shed her heart upon the popinjay; and when I took her hand and drew her from the room, she strove hard to escape. In the gallery I pressed her fingers round the haft, and knowing that the witch was bound, flung open the door so that they faced each other. But Mother Benmusk's eyes glared like fire, so that Michal was withered up, and sank swooning into my arms. And a chuckle of disdain leaped from the hag's ragged lips. Simon and the others came hurrying, and when Michal had found her life, we begged her to cut into one of those knotted arms. Yet she would none of it, but turned her face and signed no—no—she would not. And as we strove to prevail with her, word came that one of the Bishop's horses had cast a shoe in the village, and that his lordship craved the hospitality of Ford, until the smith had mended the mishap. Nigh at the heels of his message came the divine, and having heard and pondered our tale, he would fain speak with her.

I took her to the withdrawing-room, where at the sight of him she burst into such a loud fit of laughter that the old man rose in fear and went away.

"Surely it is an obsession," he cried; "nought can be done until the witch takes back her spells!"

So I bade the servants carry Benmusk to the mere, and cast her in the muddy part thereof where her head would lie above water. That was

fifteen hours ago, but methinks I still hear her screams clanging through
the stagnant air. Never was hag so fierce and full of strength! All along
the garden I saw a track of uprooted flowers. Amongst the sedges the
turmoil grew and grew till every heron fled. They threw her in, and
the whole mere seethed as if the floor of it were hell. For full an hour
she cursed us fearsomely: then, finding that every time she neared the
land the men thrust her back again, her spirit waxed abject, and she
fell to whimpering. Two hours before twelve she cried that she would
tell all she knew. So we landed her, and she was loosened of her bonds
and she mumbled in my ear: "I swear by Satan that I am innocent of
this harm! I ha' none but pawtry secrets. Go at midnight to the lows
and watch Baldus's tomb. There thou shalt find all."

The beldam tottered away, her bemired petticoats clapping her legs;
and I bade them let her rest in peace until I had certainly proved her
guilt. With this I returned to the house; but, finding that Michal had
retired for the night, I sat by the fire, waiting for the time to pass. A
clock struck the half before eleven, and I set out for King Baldus's
grave, whither, had not such a great matter been at stake, I dared not
have ventured after dark. I stole from the garden and through the first
copse. The moon lay against a brazen curtain; little snail-like clouds
were crawling underneath, and the horns of them pricked her face.

As I neared the lane to the waste, a most unholy dawn broke behind
the fringe of pines, looping the boles with strings of grey-golden light.
Surely a figure moved there? I ran. A curious motley and a noisy
swarmed forth at me. Another moment, and I was in the midst of a
host of weasels and hares and such-like creatures, all flying from the
precincts of the tomb. I quaked with dread, and the hair of my flesh
stood upright. But I thrust on, and parted the thorn boughs, and looked
up at the mound.

On the summit thereof sat Michal, triumphing, invested with flames.
And the Shape approached, and wrapped her in his blackness.

Emma Dawson

Emma Frances Dawson (1851–1926) was one of the notable figures in the small literary renaissance in late nineteenth-century San Francisco. Born in Massachusetts, she went to California with her family sometime in the 1870s. Little is known of her life other than that she taught school for a time, gave music lessons, and contributed to the local periodicals, notably the Overland Monthly. *She was a protégée of Ambrose Bierce, who praised her highly romantic stories and lush Swinburnean verse in his newspaper column. Her later years were spent in poverty as a semirecluse and she is said to have died of starvation.*

Emma Dawson's supernatural fiction was influenced more by Continental (particularly French) fantasies than by British Victorian ghost stories, but her works were usually set in California surroundings. Her California, however, was not the mining camp or hill country of Bret Harte and Bierce, but a San Francisco of culture and sophistication. Much of her work is experimental in style. She inserts poetry at dramatic moments, writes her plots elliptically, and on one occasion shifts suddenly from adventure narrative to a symbolic play. Her work is always unusual.

Her only significant book is the rare An Itinerant House *(1897), most copies of which were destroyed in the great San Francisco earthquake of 1906. It is possible that additional fiction remains uncollected in the unstudied periodicals of the Bay area.*

A STRAY REVELER

"Who hath known the ways and the wrath,
The sleepless spirit, the root
And blossom of evil will?"

"Which is the room, and which is the picture?" I asked my friend Aura, when she received me after my long absence abroad, during which I heard she had fallen heir to a fortune, but found her looking pinched and wan.

The picture filled nearly one side of the room, which was arranged as an exact copy of it, even having a lattice-window opening lengthwise, put in to match the painted one. Carpet, Navajo rugs, chairs, tables, draperies were alike. A strip of carpet hid the lower part of the frame, so that one might fancy he saw double parlors instead of one room and a painting. The screen in the room stood at just such an angle as just such a screen stood in the painted scene. Tall Japanese vases, low bookcase, hanging shelves filled with rare, odd trifles, were all thus doubled.

"Yes," she said, seeing me glance to and fro, "I felt impelled to copy everything painted there, and to banish all my room held before. That knotted rope under glass on the mantel? Well, no; that was neither in the picture nor here, till now; the fact is, I hold the property Penniel left me only by keeping that there. Two of his friends, Dacre and Chartram, received bequests on condition of calling here unexpectedly at irregular intervals to see that I let it remain always in my sight."

"I don't like it there."

"Nor I; but there is nothing puzzling about it as about the picture, finished just before he—he died. *That* is a legacy I have often pondered over. Why did he call it prophetic? I always wonder where the window in it looks, and that inner door ajar, showing a banquet-scene. Is it a Christmas revel?"

"One of the female figures resembles you—why, it is meant for you!"

"Don't, don't say so! It makes me uneasy, and angry, too; for I will *not* believe in the 'mystic' nonsense of his scribbling, painting, and acting tribe."

"Yet you always let them hang round you."

"Because they are amusing, often handsome, and sometimes have money. But few come now, except Chartram and Dacre, in their uncertain visits. I am no longer gay enough company."

"Pshaw! as if the influence of one who is dead could thus last!"

"If not, how could there be so many true tales of curses which have followed individuals or families through generation after generation. I never used to believe any such thing. I am forced to keep the picture under the terms of Penniel's will, and I cannot help studying it."

"Did Penniel paint it?"

"Yes. He put me in that festive scene because I am yet alive. He once spoke of ghosts as stray revelers after life's banquet. The vacant seat beside me was to signify his absence. 'Not eternal,' he wrote; 'I shall come back when you least expect it.' "

"You make me shiver. Let us talk of other things. What a pretty inlaid table—wild-fowl flying over a marsh—isn't it? Ah! it is just like that one in the picture, even to a manuscript lying upon it spread open under a horseshoe paper-weight."

"You see," said Aura, "one drifts inevitably to that painting. What the manuscript there represents I have often asked myself. The one beside you, Dacre wrote. Read it."

It was:

A FLIGHT OF FANCY.

"In single file wild-ducks drift by.
Dyed red by western glow.
Belated swallows lonely fly,
And strange birds trooping go.

"Though flown from forest-pine remote,
Or from near orchard-pear,
Along the water-depths they float,
As on the heights of air.

"The lake, with mirror-surface spread,
Bronzed by the day's bright close,
To each wayfarer overhead,
A shadowy double shows.

"Ah! thus reflected in my soul
What flitting thoughts will stray
From hidden source—ancestors' dole,
Or sunshine of my day.

"Fantastic shapes that, circling, throng,
Some charming, some unblest;
I snare one in this fragile song,
I cannot count the rest."

I made another effort to divert her mind. "What is behind your lovely screen?" I asked.

"Nothing. What is behind that one?" she asked, pointing to the pictured one. "That question haunts me like the indefinite meaning of some passage in Browning or Rossetti."

"What have you learned by your study of it?"

"What do you discover by examining that screen near you?"

"Masses of interwoven flowers with trailing vines and lights and shadows athwart the whole. Who painted it?"

"Chartram; and while he was doing it he and I suddenly detected amid those apparently random dashes of color eleven letters. Look again—begin at the lower left-hand corner and cross diagonally—here are lilies of the valley, then eschscholtzias, a branch of *xanthoxylum fraxineum*, tuberoses, azalias, lobelia, iris-lilies, oleander blossoms, Neapolitan violets, ixia-lilies, and stephanotis flowers."

"Well?"

"Don't you see? Two words not merely spelled by the first letter of the plants' names, as the old-fashioned 'regard' rings were set with ruby, emerald, garnet, amethyst, ruby, and diamond, but by looking carefully you can discern, in the seemingly careless spray or cluster, the letter in indistinct and fanciful form."

As she spoke and I gazed at the screen, I was surprised to distinguish so plainly now the words, *Lex talionis!* so skillfully placed as to elude a careless glance. "The law of revenge!" I cried. "Was this more of your old coquetries?"

"No; I did not tire of Penniel as usual. He had one charm all my other lovers had lacked: a stronger will than mine."

I looked at her inquiringly.

"When you went away you remember I was starving—genteelly starving. I met Penniel; he was engaged to an heiress. I reasoned with myself that she did not need his money as I did. I used every art to win him from her."

"Oh, Aura!"

"I did, I did! I may own it now, since both are dead."

"Both?"

"Yes; he broke the engagement on account of something I told him about her. She died soon after, some say broken-hearted; but, of course, we know that is a mere phrase. I presume she got a cold, or something."

"And your refusal of him killed him?"

"No; I accepted him. All went well until one night we went on horseback with a party of friends, on a moonlight trip to the Cliff House. While there, he overheard me own my worship for money. '*Not* marry for it?' I said. 'It is a woman's duty.' And he met there that night some old friend who completely disproved all I had told him about Helen Rothsay, the girl who died. Oh, how angry he was!—his eyes were lurid, he never spoke to me again. Next day he sent back to me these verses he had found that Dacre had written for me to give him as mine, though you know there is nothing nonsensical about me."

She gave me to read a

VILLANELLE.

"*What clouds of laughing little Loves arise—
    On buoyant wing are all about me blown!
I dream within the night of his dark eyes.*

"*How blest to be, though but in flower guise,
    Worn on his heart until my life were flown!
What clouds of laughing little Loves arise!*

"*Forgotten is the sun, to-day's blue skies,
    I know nor time nor space nor any zone;
I dream within the night of his dark eyes—*

"*By fancied blisses borne to Paradise,
    Like some translated saint that Art has shown.
What clouds of laughing little Loves arise!*

"*Such lotos-eating lures until one dies,
    No poppy-petals such nepenthe own;
I dream within the night of his dark eyes.*

"*For him my passion waxes crescent-wise;
    Will wind and tide of Fate its sway disown?
What clouds of laughing little Loves arise!
I dream within the night of his dark eyes.*"

"He also sent me a letter telling me of these discoveries and taking leave. 'I shall avenge Helen's wrongs,' he wrote, 'I shall avenge my own wrongs, but in my own time and in my own way. You shall suffer for what you have done, if I have to come back from the next world to make you. Poor or rich, old or young, sad or gay, remember that *I have not forgotten.*' "

"He died soon after?"

"Yes; in a year and a day from the time we first met, which was Christmas Eve."

Company came, and I could hear no more.

Two weeks later, on Christmas Eve, Aura sent for me. I found her in the same room, looking thinner and more depressed, and studying the painting.

"Don't!" I said; "you will dream of it."

"I did. I have been in the picture, gathered a leaf from that graceful clump of ferns growing in the odd jar, sat in that antique chair, and looked from that open window."

I could not understand my hitherto matter-of-fact friend. "What did you see?" I asked.

"The same grand sunrise that thrilled us, Penniel, Dacre, Chartram, and I, as we returned from a New Year's Eve ball. A sunrise Penniel wrote about."

She showed me these lines:

A NEW-YEAR'S DAWN.

"*Through fog that veils both sky and bay there gleam*
The sun and wraith, red glowing;
So interblended that one flame they seem
As if dread portent showing.

"*Where will it lead us through the year untried,*
Through what vast desert places,
Vague tracts of time whose misty margins glide
Within eternal spaces?

"*I, weary, pilgrim in Life's caravan,*
That pillared fire must follow
Past pyramid and sphinx of Doubt and Ban,
Mirage of Hope, how hollow!

"*Palm-shaded wells of joy, too far apart,*
Long leagues through changeful weather,
Unless that foe in ambush, my own heart,
Leaps, and we fall together!"

"What else happened?" I asked.

"Nothing. I was dimly conscious of coming from that room into this. I want to stay here. Tell me about your travels, and divert me."

I talked to her a long while; then she brewed rich chocolate, which we sipped as we sat silently listening to the sounds of mirth from a party given by boarders in the opposite room, listening to the fog-horn and the wind, till drowsiness stole over us insensibly as the fog crept round the house, as if forming an impalpable barrier around a region enchanted.

Suddenly Aura started out of her doze with a piercing cry, and sat trembling from head to foot. "I have been there again," she said.

"You have not left your chair." I murmured, half-awake; "you dropped asleep."

"Perhaps you think so; but I have been in the picture." She shuddered as she turned her head to look at it. "There were *two* vacant places at the table. I no longer sat there, but wandered about the outer room while the guests at supper were watching and whispering and pointing, and a murmur of '*Lex talionis!*' ran from mouth to mouth. I felt that some horror waited for me and drew me to that screen, but I tried not to go. I went to the window, but the view was changed to the blackness of midnight. I looked in the mirror, yet saw nothing reflected but the room behind me. I was not to be seen. I noticed the perfume of the flowers in the bouquet on the table. I saw this room, with our figures sitting before the fire, with our chocolate-tray between us, as a picture on the wall of that room. I took the manuscript from the table, and found it to be verses, as we thought. I can repeat them:

BALLADE OF THE SEA OF SLEEP.

When from far headland of the Night I slip,
  What potent force within the rising tide
Bears me resistless as the billows dip,
  To meet their shifting wonders, eager-eyed,
Or float, half-conscious what stars watch me glide,
  To fear when nightmare monster's weight o'erpowers,
Or laugh with nymphs and mermen in their bowers—
  Through blinding tempest toss on breakers steep,
Or fall for countless fathoms past what lowers
  Below the dream waves of the sea of Sleep!

I trace, with sails all set, the unbuilt ship,
  And sunken treasure, ere the waves subside;
Find here the wrecked craft making phantom trip;
  Define the misty bounds: upon this side,
The mighty mountains of the Dark abide;
  On that, the realms of Light expand like flowers;
There, 'tis the rocky coast of Death that towers;
  Here, on the shoals, Life must its lighthouse keep.
Who is it that vague terror thus empowers
  Below the dream-waves of the sea of Sleep?

On shore all day I find slight fellowship,
  But in those surges fain would plunge and hide.
Those depths hold joys that none above outstrip.
  Perchance—I cannot choose what shall betide—
Friend flown afar I clasp, dread foe deride,
  Forget that sorrow all my heart devours,
Avenge the wrongs that Fate upon me showers.
  Not my control can lift the tide at neap,
Nor quell its rise. Who thus my will deflours
  Below the dream-waves of the sea of Sleep?

ENVOY.

Archangels, princes, thrones, dominions, powers!
Which of ye dwarf the centuries to hours,
  Or swell the moments into eons' sweep?
Is it the Prince of Darkness, then, who cowers
  Below the dream-waves of the sea of Sleep?

"I was full of indecision and fear about looking behind the screen, but, at last, I did look—"

Her voice failed. I gave her some wine.

"What did you think you saw?"

"Think! I *saw* it."

"What?"

"Don't ask me!" she cried, shuddering. "I cannot describe it. Can you imagine the aspect of a corpse, long dead, mouldering, luminous, all blue light, and threads and tatters of its burial robe? O God, save us!" Her glance rested on the mantel. "I will not keep that rope. I will *not!* I *will* not! Curses on him and his memory!"

She snatched down the glass case, broke it, and flung the rope in the grate. We watched it as the fire consumed it and for a few moments held its charred outlines as it had fallen in a distinct semblance of a closed hand with index-finger pointing toward the screen! Our eyes met above it. "Do poets and artists possess an extra sense?" she muttered, grasping my arm in awe.

"But the property!" I stammered in sudden alarm. "What will you do without that?"

"No one need know at present of this conflagration. I will lock up and go abroad. I will start to-morrow!"

Just then we heard the voices of Dacre and Chartram in the hall. We stared at each other in dismay. "They must not come here!" she cried, and hurrying toward the next room disappeared behind the screen. The next instant a blood-curdling shriek rang through the room, rooting me to the spot where I stood. Before I knew anything more, Dacre and

Chartram were standing by me, asking what was the matter. I could not speak. Weighed down by a sense of dread, I could only point to the screen. As they turned it aside, throwing another part of the room into shadow, the picture vanished in gloom, but the room took a more picturesque aspect. The door ajar showed, across the narrow hall, the open door where the merry-makers paused, leaning forward with startled faces and anxious gestures. Aura was lying full length on the carpet, dead! Her face was full of terror. Was it only a shadow, that livid line around her neck as if she had been strangled? As we turned away in horror, Dacre uttered a cry of surprise, and touching Chartram, pointed to the vacant space on the mantel.

"The rope?" they cried with one voice, like the chorus to a tragic opera.

"She had just burned it," I stammered.

They looked at each other. "Did she furnish Penniel with the means to destroy her?" Dacre asked Chartram.

"Tell me," I begged, "what is the mystery of that rope?"

There was a moment's delay. Then Chartram gave the startling reply: "It was the one with which Penniel hung himself."

Bernard Capes

Bernard Edward Joseph Capes (c. 1860–1918) was a British professional writer. Very little is known about his personal life beyond the fact that he was married to Harriet Capes, herself a popular writer of women's fiction, and that he was possibly a friend of G. K. Chesterton, who wrote an obituary notice on him in the posthumous detective novel The Skeleton Key.

During his lifetime Capes was a fairly popular writer of romantic historical fiction and detective stories, including a little-known pastiche of Sherlock Holmes. He wrote, altogether, about forty stories that are supernatural in one way or another, ranging from elaborately styled horror stories to romantic fiction, like that of Arthur Quiller-Couch, in which supernaturalism emerges from a reasonably scholarly historical setting. Many of his stories introduced new motifs to the genre, and his work, at its best, shows a poetic touch and crystallinity of image that are unusual.

Chesterton provided what is still the best characterization of Capes's work: "He always gave a touch of distinction to [a story, but] gave it where it was not valued, because it was not expected . . . We might put this truth flippantly, and therefore falsely, by saying that he put superior work into inferior works. I should not admit the distinction, for I deny that there is necessarily anything inferior in sensationalism . . . Men may well go back to find the poems thus embedded in his prose."

"My grandfather," said the banjo, "drank 'dog's-nose,' my father drank 'dog's-nose,' and I drink 'dog's-nose.' If that ain't heredity, there's no virtue in the board schools."

"Ah!" said the piccolo, "you're always a-boasting of your science. And so, I suppose, your son'll drink 'dog's-nose,' too?"

"No," retorted the banjo, with a rumbling laugh, like wind in the bung-hole of an empty cask; "for I ain't got none. The family ends with me; which is a pity, for I'm a full-stop to be proud on."

He was an enormous, tun-bellied person—a mere mound of expressionless flesh, whose size alone was an investment that paid a perpetual dividend of laughter. When, as with the rest of his company, his face was blackened, it looked like a specimen coal on a pedestal in a museum.

There was Christmas company in the Good Intent, and the sanded tap-room, with its trestle tables and sprigs of holly stuck under sooty beams reeked with smoke and the steam of hot gin and water.

"How much could you put down of a night, Jack?" said a little grinning man by the door.

"Why," said the banjo, "enough to lay the dustiest ghost as ever walked."

"*Could* you, now?" said the little man.

"Ah!" said the banjo, chuckling. "There's nothing like settin' one sperit to lay another; and there I could give you proof number two of heredity."

"What! Don't you go for to say you ever see'd a ghost!"

"Haven't I? What are you whisperin' about, you blushful chap there by the winder?"

"I was only remarkin', sir, 'twere snawin' like the devil."

"*Is* it? Then the devil has been misjudged these eighteen hundred and ninety odd years."

"But *did* you ever see a ghost?" said the little grinning man, pursuing his subject.

"No, I didn't, sir," mimicked the banjo, "saving in coffee grounds. But my grandfather in *his* cups see'd one; which brings us to number three in the matter of heredity."

"Gives us the story, Jack," said the "bones," whose agued shins were extemporizing a rattle on their own account before the fire.

"Well, I don't mind," said the fat man. "It's seasonable; and I'm seasonable, like the blessed plum-pudden, I am; and the more burnt brandy you set about me, the richer and headier I'll go down."

"You'd be a jolly old pudden to digest," said the piccolo.

"You blow your aggrawation into your pipe and sealing-wax the stops," said his friend.

He drew critically at his "churchwarden" a moment or so, leaned forward, emptied his glass into his capacious receptacles, and, giving his stomach a shift, as if to accommodate it to its new burden, proceeded as follows:—

"Music and malt is my nat'ral inheritance. My grandfather blew his 'dog's-nose,' and drank his clarinet like a artist; and my father—"

"What did you say your grandfather did?" asked the piccolo.

"He played the clarinet."

"You said he blew his 'dog's-nose.'"

"Don't be a ass, Fred!" said the banjo, aggrieved. "How the blazes could a man blow his dog's nose, unless he muzzled it with a handkercher, and then twisted its tail? He played the clarinet, I say; and my father played the musical glasses, which was a form of harmony pertiklerly genial to him. Amongst us we've piped out a good long century—ah! we have, for all I look sich a babby bursting on sops and spoon meat."

"What!" said the little man by the door. "You don't include them cockt hatses in your expeerunce?"

"My grandfather wore 'em, sir. He wore a play-actin' coat, too, and buckles to his shoes, when he'd got any; and he and a friend or two made a permanency of 'waits' (only they called 'em according to the season), and got their profit goin' from house to house, principally in the country, and discoursin' music at the low rate of whatever they could get for it."

"Ain't you comin' to the ghost, Jack?" said the little man hungrily.

"All in course, sir. Well, gentlemen, it was hard times pretty often with my grandfather and his friends, as you may suppose; and never so much as when they had to trudge it across country, with the nor'-

easter buzzin' in their teeth and the snow piled on their cockt hats like
lemon sponge on entry dishes. The rewards, I've heard him say—for
he lived to be ninety, nevertheless—was poor compensation for the
drifts, and the inflienza, and the broken chilblains; but now and again
they'd get a fair skinful of liquor from a jolly squire, as 'd set 'em up
like boggarts mended wi' new broomsticks."

"Ho-haw!" broke in a hurdle-maker in a corner; and then, regretting
the publicity of his merriment, put his fingers bashfully to his stubble
lips.

"Now," said the banjo, "it's of a pertikler night and a pertikler skinful that I'm a-going to tell you; and that night fell dark, and that
skinful were took a hundred years ago this December, as I'm a Jack-
pudden!"

He paused a moment for effect, before he went on:—

"They were down in the sou'-west country, which they little knew;
and were anighing Winchester city, or should 'a' been. But they got
muzzed on the ungodly downs, and before they guessed, they was off
the track. My good hat! there they was, as lost in the snow as three
nut-shells a-sinkin' into a hasty pudden. Well, they wandered round;
pretty confident at first, but getting madder and madder as every
sense of their bearings slipped from them. And the bitter cold took their
vitals, so as they saw nothing but a great winding sheet stretched
abroad for to wrap their dead carcases in.

"At last my grandfather he stopt and pulled hisself together with an
awful face, and says he: 'We're Christmas pie for the carrying-on
crows if we don't prove ourselves human. Let's fetch out our pipes
and blow our trouble into 'em.' So they stood together, like as if they
was before a house, and they played 'Kate of Aberdare' mighty dismal
and flat, for their fingers froze to the keys.

"Now, I tell you, they hadn't climbed over the first stave, when
there come a skirl of wind and spindrift of snow as almost took them
off of their feet; and, on the going down of it, Jem Sloke, as played
the hautboy, dropped the reed from his mouth, and called out, 'Sakes
alive! if we fools ain't been standin' outside a gentleman's gate all the
time, and not knowin' it!'

"You might 'a' knocked the three of 'em down wi' a barley straw,
as they stared and stared, and then fell into a low, enjoyin' laugh. For
they was standin' not six fut from a tall iron gate in a stone wall, and
behind these was a great house showin' out dim, with the winders all
lighted up.

"'Lord!' chuckled my grandfather, 'to think o' the tricks o' this
vagarious country! But, as we're here, we'll go on and give 'em a taste
of our quality.'

"They put new heart into the next movement, as you may guess; and they hadn't fair started on it, when the door of the house swung open, and down the shaft of light that shot out as far as the gate there come a smiling young gal, with a tray of glasses in her hands.

"Now she come to the bars; and she took and put a glass through, not sayin' nothin', but invitin' some one to drink with a silent laugh.

"Did any one take that glass? Of course he did, you'll be thinkin'; and you'll be thinkin' wrong. Not a man of the three moved. They was struck like as stone, and their lips was gone the colour of sloe berries. Not a man took the glass. For why? The moment the gal presented it, each saw the face of a thing lookin' out of the winder over the porch, and the face was hidjus beyond words, and the shadder of it, with the light behind, stretched out and reached to the gal, and made her hidjus, too.

"At last my grandfather give a groan and put out his hand; and, as he did it, the face went, and the gal was beautiful to see agen.

" 'Death and the devil!' said he. 'It's one or both, either way; and I prefer 'em hot to cold!'

"He drank off half the glass, smacked his lips, and stood staring a moment.

" 'Dear, dear!' said the gal, in a voice like falling water, 'you've drunk blood, sir!'

"My grandfather gave a yell, slapped the rest of the liquor in the faces of his friends, and threw the cup agen the bars. It broke with a noise like thunder, and at that he up'd with his hands and fell full length into the snow."

There was a pause. The little man by the door was twisting nervously in his chair.

"He came to—of course, he came to?" said he at length.

"He come to," said the banjo solemnly, "in the bitter break of dawn; that is, he come to as much of hisself as he ever was after. He give a squiggle and lifted his head; and there was he and his friends a-lyin' on the snow of the high downs."

"And the house and the gal?"

"Narry a sign of either, sir, but just the sky and the white stretch; and one other thing."

"And what was that?"

"A stain of red sunk in where the cup had spilt."

There was a second pause, and the banjo blew into the bowl of his pipe.

"They cleared out of that neighborhood double quick, you'll bet," said he. "But my grandfather was never the same man agen. His face took purple, while his friends' only remained splashed with red, same as birth marks; and, I tell you, if he ever ventur'd upon 'Kate of Aberdare,' his cheeks swelled up to the reed of his clarinet, like as a blue plum on a stalk. And forty year after, he died of what they call solution of blood to the brain."

"And you can't have better proof than that," said the little man.

"That's what *I* say," said the banjo. "Next player, gentlemen, please."

Ambrose Bierce

Ambrose Gwinnett Bierce (1842–1914?) was a native of Ohio. The tenth of thirteen children, all of whose names began with A, he suffered through a miserable childhood of poverty, violent sibling hatred, parental eccentricity and madness, and religious fanaticism that left its marks on him. His escape came with the Civil War. He enlisted in Indiana and served with distinction, rising to the rank of captain. After his discharge Bierce settled in San Francisco and soon entered journalism, where his remarkable polemic gifts brought him fame in the rough-and-tumble West Coast newspaper world. He became associated with William Randolph Hearst, and his column "Prattle" was considered one of the great newspaper features of the day. In his old age he quarreled with Hearst, moved to Washington, and in 1913, even though he was obviously physically unfit for the assignment, announced that he was going to Mexico to serve as a war correspondent with Pancho Villa's forces. He disappeared in Mexico, and to this day the circumstances or place of his death and burial are unknown.

Although Ambrose Bierce's working range was narrow, he could do certain things very well. His collection of sardonic definitions, The Devil's Dictionary, is a monument of American black humor and satire, and his Civil War stories are generally considered the finest written by a combatant. His supernatural fiction is highly original, what with experimental form, narration by suggestion, multiple narratives, and its preoccupation with psychological rather than material or spiritual horror, sexual elements, and the humor of the grotesque.

This is the only modern printing of the following pieces. They first appeared in the Cassell edition of Can Such Things Be? (1893) and were last printed in the Neale edition of 1903. They demonstrate a persistent interest of Bierce's later years: strange disappearances and inexplicable happenings, related as if journalism.

BODIES
OF THE DEAD

About ten miles to the southeast of Whitesburg, Ky., in a little "cove" of the Cumberland mountains, lived for many years an old woman named Sarah (or Mary) Magone. Her house, built of logs and containing but two rooms, was a mile and a half distant from any other, in the wildest part of the "cove," entirely surrounded by forest except on one side, where a little field, or "patch," of about a half-acre served her for a vegetable garden. How she subsisted nobody exactly knew; she was reputed to be a miser with a concealed hoard; she certainly paid for what few articles she procured on her rare visits to the village store. Many of her ignorant neighbors believed her to be a witch, or thought, at least, that she possessed some kind of supernatural powers. In November, 1881, she died, and fortunately enough, the body was found while yet warm by a passing hunter, who locked the door of the cabin and conveyed the news to the nearest settlement.

Several persons living in the vicinity at once went to the cabin to prepare for her burial; others were to follow the next day with a coffin and whatever else was needful. Among those who first went was the Rev. Elias Atney, a Methodist minister of Whitesburg, who happened to be in the neighborhood visiting a relation. He was to conduct the funeral services on the following day. Mr. Atney is, or was, well known in Whitesburg and all that country as a good and pious man of good birth and education. He was closely related to the Marshalls and several other families of distinction. It is from him that the particulars here related were learned; and the account is confirmed by the affidavits of John Hershaw, William C. Wrightman, and Catharine Doub, residents of the vicinity and eye-witnesses.

The body of "Granny" Magone had been "laid out" on a wide plank supported by two chairs at the end of the principal room, opposite the fireplace, and the persons mentioned were acting as "watchers," according to the local custom. A bright fire on the hearth lighted one end of the room brilliantly, the other dimly. The watchers sat about the fire, talking in subdued tones, when a sudden noise in the direction of the corpse caused them all to turn and look. In a black shadow near the remains, they saw two glowing eyes staring fixedly; and before they could do more than rise, uttering exclamations of alarm, a large black cat leaped upon the body and fastened its teeth into the cloth covering the face. Instantly the right hand of the dead was violently raised from the side, seized the cat, and hurled it against the wall, whence it fell to the floor, and then dashed wildly through an open window into the outer darkness, and was seen no more.

Inconceivably horrified, the watchers stood a moment speechless; but finally, with returning courage, approached the body. The face-cloth lay upon the floor; the cheek was terribly torn; the right arm hung stiffly over the side of the plank. There was not a sign of life. They chafed the forehead, the withered cheeks and neck. They carried the body to the heat of the fire and worked upon it for hours: all in vain. But the funeral was postponed until the fourth day brought unmistakable evidence of dissolution, and poor Granny was buried.

"Ah, but your eyes deceived you," said he to whom the reverend gentleman related the occurrence. "The arm was disturbed by the efforts of the cat, which, taking sudden fright, leaped blindly against the wall."

"No," he answered, "the clenched right hand, with its long nails, was full of black fur."

A LIGHT SLEEPER.

John Hoskin, living in San Francisco, had a beautiful wife, to whom he was devotedly attached. In the spring of 1871 Mrs. Hoskin went East to visit her relations in Springfield, Ill., where, a week after her arrival, she suddenly died of some disease of the heart; at least the physician said so. Mr. Hoskin was at once apprised of his loss, by telegraph, and he directed that the body be sent to San Francisco. On arrival there the metallic case containing the remains was opened. The body was lying on the right side, the right hand under the cheek, the other on the breast. The posture was the perfectly natural one of a sleeping child, and in a letter to the deceased lady's father, Mr. Martin L. Whitney of Springfield, Mr. Hoskin expressed a grateful sense of the thoughtfulness that had so composed the remains as to soften the suggestion of death. To his surprise he learned from the father that nothing of the kind had been done: the body had been put in the casket in the customary way, lying on the back, with the arms extended along the sides. In the meantime the casket had been deposited in the receiving vault at Laurel Hill Cemetery, awaiting the completion of a tomb.

Greatly disquieted by this revelation, Hoskin did not at once reflect that the easy and natural posture and placid expression precluded the idea of suspended animation, subsequent revival, and eventual death by suffocation. He insisted that his wife had been murdered by medical incompetency and heedless haste. Under the influence of this feeling he wrote to Mr. Whitney again, expressing in passionate terms his horror and renewed grief. Some days afterward, someone having suggested that the casket had been opened *en route*, probably in the hope of plunder, and pointing out the impossibility of the change having occurred in the straitened space of the confining metal, it was resolved to reopen it.

Removal of the lid disclosed a new horror: the body now lay upon its *left* side. The position was cramped, and to a living person would have been uncomfortable. The face wore an expression of pain. Some costly rings on the fingers were undisturbed. Overcome by his emotions, to which was now added a sharp, if mistaken remorse, Mr. Hoskin lost his reason, dying years afterward in the asylum at Stockton.

A physician having been summoned, to assist in clearing up the mystery, viewed the body of the dead woman, pronounced life obviously extinct, and ordered the casket closed for the third and last time. "Obviously extinct," indeed: the corpse had, in fact, been embalmed at Springfield.

THE MYSTERY OF CHARLES FARQUHARSON.

One night in the summer of 1843 William Hayner Gordon, of Philadelphia, lay in his bed reading Goldsmith's "Traveler," by the light of a candle. It was about eleven o'clock. The room was in the third story of the house and had two windows looking out upon Chestnut Street; there was no balcony, nothing below the windows but other windows in a smooth brick wall.

Becoming drowsy, Gordon laid away his book, extinguished his candle, and composed himself to sleep. A moment later (as he afterward averred) he remembered that he had neglected to place his watch within reach, and rose in the dark to get it from the pocket of his waistcoat, which he had hung on the back of a chair on the opposite side of the room, near one of the windows. In crossing, his foot came in contact with some heavy object and he was thrown to the floor. Rising, he struck a match and lighted his candle. In the center of the room lay the corpse of a man.

Gordon was no coward, as he afterward proved by his gallant death upon the enemy's parapet at Chapultepec, but this strange apparition of a human corpse where but a moment before, as he believed, there had been nothing, was too much for his nerves, and he cried aloud. Henri Granier, who occupied an adjoining room, but had not retired, came instantly to Gordon's door and attempted to enter. The door being bolted, and Gordon too greatly agitated to open it, Granier burst it in.

Gordon was taken into custody and an inquest held, but what has been related was all that could be ascertained. The most diligent efforts on the part of the police and the press failed to identify the dead. Physicians testifying at the inquest agreed that death had occurred but a few hours before the discovery, but none was able to divine the cause; all the organs of the body were in an apparently healthy condition; there were no traces of either violence or poison.

Eight or ten months later Gordon received a letter from Charles Ritcher in Bombay, relating the death in that city of Charles Farquharson, whom both Gordon and Ritcher had known when all were boys. Enclosed in the letter was a daguerreotype of the deceased, found among his effects. As nearly as the living can look like the dead it was an exact likeness of the mysterious body found in Gordon's bedroom, and it was with a strange feeling that Gordon observed that the death, making allowance for the difference of time, was said to have occurred on the very night of the adventure. He wrote for further particulars, with especial reference to what disposition had been made of Farquharson's body.

"You know he turned Parsee," wrote Ritcher in reply; "so his naked remains were exposed on the grating of the Tower of Silence, as those of all good Parsees are. I saw the buzzards fighting for them and gorging themselves helpless on his fragments."

On some pretense Gordon and his friends obtained authority to open the dead man's grave. The coffin had evidently not been disturbed. They unscrewed the lid. The shroud was a trifle moldy. There was no body nor any vestige of one.

DEAD AND "GONE."

On the morning of the 14th day of August, 1872, George J. Reid, a young man of twenty-one years, living at Xenia, O., fell while walking across the dining room in his father's house. The family consisted of his father, mother, two sisters, and a cousin, a boy of fifteen. All were present at the breakfast table. George entered the room, but instead of taking his accustomed seat near the door by which he had entered, passed it and went obliquely toward one of the windows—with what purpose no one knows. He had passed the table but a few steps when he fell heavily to the floor and did not again breathe. The body was carried into a bedroom and, after vain efforts at resuscitation by the stricken family, left lying on the bed with composed limbs and covered face.

In the meantime the boy had been hastily dispatched for a physician, who arrived some twenty minutes after the death. He afterward remembered as an uncommon circumstance that when he arrived the weeping relations—father, mother, and two sisters—were all in the room out of which the bedroom door opened, and that the door was closed. There was no other door to the bedroom. This door was at once opened by the father of the deceased, and as the physician passed through it he observed the dead man's clothing lying in a heap on the floor. He saw, too, the outlines of the body under the sheet that had been thrown over it; and the profile was plainly discernible under the face-cloth, clear-cut and sharp, as profiles of the dead seem always to be. He approached and lifted the cloth. There was nothing there. He pulled away the sheet. Nothing.

The family had followed him into the room. At this astonishing discovery—if so it may be called—they looked at one another, at the physician, at the bed, in speechless amazement, forgetting to weep. A moment later the three ladies required the physician's care. The father's condition was but little better; he stood in a stupor, muttering inarticulately and staring like an idiot.

Having restored the ladies to a sense of their surroundings, the physician went to the window—the only one the room had, opening upon a garden. It was locked on the inside with the usual fastening attached to the bottom bar of the upper sash and engaging with the lower.

No inquest was held—there was nothing to hold it on; but the physician and many others who were curious as to this occurrence made the most searching investigation into all the circumstances; all without result. George Reid was dead and "gone," and that is all that is known to this day.

A COLD NIGHT.

The first day's battle at Stone River had been fought, resulting in disaster to the Federal army, which had been driven from its original ground at every point except its extreme left. The weary troops at this point lay behind a railway embankment to which they had retired, and which had served them during the last hours of the fight as a breastwork to repel repeated charges of the enemy. Behind the line the ground was open and rocky. Great bowlders lay about everywhere, and among them lay many of the Federal dead, where they had been carried out of the way. Before the embankment the dead of both armies lay more thickly, but they had not been disturbed.

Among the dead in the bowlders lay one whom nobody seemed to know—a Federal sergeant, shot directly in the center of the forehead. One of our surgeons, from idle curiosity, or possibly with a view to the amusement of a group of officers during a lull in the engagement (we needed something to divert our minds), had pushed his probe clean through the head. The body lay on its back, its chin in the air, and with straightened limbs, as rigid as steel; frost on its white face and in its beard and hair. Some Christian soul had covered it with a blanket, but when the night became pretty sharp a companion of the writer removed this, and we lay beneath it ourselves.

With the exception of our pickets, who had been posted well out in front of the embankment, every man lay silent. Conversation was forbidden; to have made a fire, or even struck a match to light a pipe would have been a grave offense. Stamping horses, moaning wounded —everything that made a noise had been sent to the rear; the silence was absolute. Those whom the chill prevented from sleeping nevertheless reclined as they shivered, or sat with their hands on their arms, suffering but making no sign. Everyone had lost friends, and all expected death on the morrow. These matters are mentioned to show the improbability of anyone going about during these solemn hours to commit a ghastly practical joke.

When the dawn broke the sky was still clear. "We shall have a warm day," the writer's companion whispered as we rose in the gray light; "let's give back the poor devil his blanket."

The sergeant's body lay in the same place, two yards away. But not in the same attitude. It was upon its right side. The knees were drawn up nearly to the breast, both hands thrust to the wrist between the buttons of the jacket, the collar of which was turned up, concealing the ears. The shoulders were elevated, the head was retracted, the chin rested on the collar bone. The posture was that of one suffering from intense cold. But for what had been previously observed—but for the ghastly evidence of the bullet-hole—one might have thought the man had died of cold.

A CREATURE OF HABIT.

At Hawley's Bar, a mining camp near Virginia City, Mont., a gambler named Henry Graham, but commonly known as "Gray Hank," met a miner named Dreyfuss one day, with whom he had had a dispute the previous night about a game of cards, and asked him into a barroom to have a drink. The unfortunate miner, taking this as an overture of peace, gladly accepted. They stood at the counter, and while Dreyfuss was in the act of drinking Graham shot him dead. This was in 1865. Within an hour after the murder Graham was in the hands of the vigilantes, and that evening at sunset, after a fair, if informal, trial, he was hanged to the limb of a tree which grew upon a little eminence within sight of the whole camp. The original intention had been to "string him up," as is customary in such affairs; and with a view to that operation the long rope had been thrown over the limb, while a dozen pairs of hands were ready to hoist away. For some reason this plan was abandoned; the free end of the rope was made fast to a bush and the victim compelled to stand on the back of a horse, which at the cut of a whip sprang from under him, leaving him swinging. When steadied, his feet were about eighteen inches from the earth.

The body remained suspended for exactly half an hour, the greater part of the crowd remaining about it: then the "judge" ordered it taken down. The rope was untied from the bush, and two men stood by to lower away. The moment the feet came squarely upon the ground the men engaged in lowering, thinking doubtless that those standing about the body had hold of it to support it, let go the rope. The body at once ran quickly forward toward the main part of the crowd, the rope paying out as it went. The head rolled from side to side, the eyes and tongue protruding, the face ghastly purple, the lips covered with bloody froth. With cries of horror the crowd ran hither and thither, stumbling, falling over one another, cursing. In and out among them—over the fallen, coming into collision with others, the horrible dead man "pranced," his feet lifted so high at each step that his knees struck his breast, his tongue swinging like that of a panting dog, the foam flying in flakes from his swollen lips. The deepening twilight added its terror to the scene, and men fled from the spot, not daring to look behind.

Straight into this confusion from the outskirts of the crowd walked with rapid steps the tall figure of a man whom all who saw instantly recognized as a master spirit. This was Dr. Arnold Spier, who with two other physicians had pronounced the man dead and had been retiring to the camp. He moved as directly toward the dead man as the now somewhat less rapid and erratic movements of the latter would permit, and seized him in his arms. Encouraged by this, a score of men sprang shouting to the free end of the rope, which had not been drawn entirely over the limb, and laid hold of it, intending to make a finish of their work. They ran with it toward the bush to which it had been fastened, but there was no resistance; the physician had cut it from the murderer's neck. In a moment the body was lying on its back, with composed limbs and face upturned to the kindling stars, in the motionless rigidity appropriate to death. The hanging had been done well enough—the neck was broken.

"The dead are creatures of habit," said Dr. Spier. "A corpse which when on its feet will walk and run will lie still when placed on its back."

Gertrude Atherton

Gertrude Franklin Atherton (née Horn) (1857–1948) was a well-known California romantic novelist, historian, folklorist, and miscellaneous writer. Her mainstream novels, based on Edwardian aesthetics, often were regionalistic and were concerned with cultural clashes and social response. Among her better-known books are The Californians *(1898);* The Aristocrats *(1901); and* The Conqueror *(1902), which is a fictionalized but accurate life of Alexander Hamilton, some of whose letters she later edited. When she was almost ninety she wrote an excellent volume of reminiscences and local lore,* My San Francisco *(1947).*

Mrs. Atherton was not a prolific author of supernatural fiction. She wrote only a half-dozen or so stories which were collected in The Bell in the Fog *(1905) and* The Foghorn *(1934). Her work in this area was greatly influenced by Henry James both in theme and technique, as evidenced by her fascination with the past, dislocations of time and merging of past and present, and calculated ambiguities of interpretation. The present story, "Death and the Woman" (1892), is simpler than her later work.*

DEATH
AND THE
WOMAN

Her husband was dying, and she was alone with him. Nothing could exceed the desolation of her surroundings. She and the man who was going from her were in the third-floor-back of a New York boarding-house. It was summer, and the other boarders were in the country; all the servants except the cook had been dismissed, and she, when not working, slept profoundly on the fifth floor. The landlady also was out of town on a brief holiday.

The window was open to admit the thick unstirring air; no sound rose from the row of long narrow yards, nor from the tall deep houses annexed. The latter deadened the rattle of the streets. At intervals the distant elevated lumbered protestingly along, its grunts and screams muffled by the hot suspended ocean.

She sat there plunged in the profoundest grief that can come to the human soul, for in all other agony hope flickers, however forlornly. She gazed dully at the unconscious breathing form of the man who had been friend, and companion, and lover, during five years of youth too vigorous and hopeful to be warped by uneven fortune. It was wasted by disease; the face was shrunken; the night-garment hung loosely about a body which had never been disfigured by flesh, but had been muscular with exercise and full-blooded with health. She was glad that the body was changed; glad that its beauty, too, had gone some other-where than into the coffin. She had loved his hands as apart from himself; loved their strong warm magnetism. They lay limp and yellow on the quilt: she knew that they were already cold, and that moisture was gathering on them. For a moment something convulsed within her. *They* had gone too. She repeated the words twice, and, after them, "*forever.*" And the while the sweetness of their pressure came back to her.

She leaned suddenly over him. HE was in there still, somewhere. *Where?* If he had not ceased to breathe, the Ego, the Soul, the Personality was still in the sodden clay which had shaped to give it speech. Why could it not manifest itself to her? Was it still conscious in there, unable to project itself through the disintegrating matter which was the only medium its Creator had vouchsafed it? Did it struggle there, seeing her agony, sharing it, longing for the complete disintegration which should put an end to its torment? She called his name, she even shook him slightly, mad to tear the body apart and find her mate, yet even in that tortured moment realizing that violence would hasten his going.

The dying man took no notice of her, and she opened his gown and put her cheek to his heart, calling him again. There had never been more perfect union; how could the bind still be so strong if he were not at the other end of it? He was there, her other part; until dead he must be living. There was no intermediate state. Why should he be as entombed and unresponding as if the screws were in the lid? But the faintly beating heart did not quicken beneath her lips. She extended her arms suddenly, describing eccentric lines, above, about him, rapidly opening and closing her hands as if to clutch some escaping object; then sprang to her feet, and went to the window. She feared insanity. She had asked to be left alone with her dying husband, and she did not wish to lose her reason and shriek a crowd of people about her.

The green plots in the yards were not apparent, she noticed. Something heavy, like a pall, rested upon them. Then she understood that the day was over and that night was coming.

She returned swiftly to the bedside, wondering if she had remained away hours or seconds, and if he were dead. His face was still discernible, and Death had not relaxed it. She laid her own against it, then withdrew it with shuddering flesh, her teeth smiting each other as if an icy wind had passed.

She let herself fall back in the chair, clasping her hands against her heart, watching with expanding eyes the white sculptured face which, in the glittering dark, was becoming less defined of outline. Did she light the gas it would draw mosquitoes, and she could not shut from him the little air he must be mechanically grateful for. And she did not want to see the opening eye—the falling jaw.

Her vision became so fixed that at length she saw nothing, and closed her eyes and waited for the moisture to rise and relieve the strain. When she opened them his face had disappeared; the humid waves above the house-tops put out even the light of the stars, and night was come.

Fearfully, she approached her ear to his lips; he still breathed. She

made a motion to kiss him, then threw herself back in a quiver of agony
—they were not the lips she had known, and she would have nothing
less.

His breathing was so faint that in her half-reclining position she
could not hear it, could not be aware of the moment of his death.
She extended her arm resolutely and laid her hand on his heart. Not
only must she feel his going, but, so strong had been the comradeship
between them, it was a matter of loving honor to stand by him to
the last.

She sat there in the hot heavy night, pressing her hand hard against
the ebbing heart of the unseen, and awaited Death. Suddenly an odd
fancy possessed her. Where was Death? Why was he tarrying? Who
was detaining him? From what quarter would he come? He was taking
his leisure, drawing near with footsteps as measured as those of men
keeping time to a funeral march. By a wayward deflection she thought
of the slow music that was always turned on in the theatre when the
heroine was about to appear, or something eventful to happen. She
had always thought that sort of thing ridiculous and inartistic. So
had He.

She drew her brows together angrily, wondering at her levity, and
pressed her relaxed palm against the heart it kept guard over. For a
moment the sweat stood on her face; then the pent-up breath burst
from her lungs. He still lived.

Once more the fancy wantoned above the stunned heart. Death—
where was he? What a curious experience: to be sitting alone in a big
house—she knew that the cook had stolen out—waiting for Death to
come and snatch her husband from her. No; he would not snatch, he
would steal upon his prey as noiselessly as the approach of Sin to
Innocence—an invisible, unfair, sneaking enemy, with whom no man's
strength could grapple. If he would only come like a man, and take
his chances like a man! Women had been known to reach the hearts
of giants with the dagger's point. But he would creep upon her.

She gave an exclamation of horror. Something was creeping over the
window-sill. Her limbs palsied, but she struggled to her feet and looked
back, her eyes dragged about against her own volition. Two small
green stars glared menacingly at her just above the sill; then the cat
possessing them leaped downward, and the stars disappeared.

She realized that she was horribly frightened. "Is it possible?" she
thought. "Am I afraid of Death, and of Death that has not yet come?
I have always been rather a brave woman; *He* used to call me heroic;
but then with him it was impossible to fear anything. And I begged
them to leave me alone with him as the last of earthly boons. Oh,
shame!"

But she was still quaking as she resumed her seat, and laid her hand again on his heart. She wished that she had asked Mary to sit outside the door; there was no bell in the room. To call would be worse than desecrating the house of God, and she would not leave him for one moment. To return and find him dead—gone alone!

Her knees smote each other. It was idle to deny it; she was in a state of unreasoning terror. Her eyes rolled apprehensively about; she wondered if she should see It when It came; wondered how far off It was now. Not very far; the heart was barely pulsing. She had heard of the power of the corpse to drive brave men to frenzy, and had wondered, having no morbid horror of the dead. But this! To wait— and wait—and wait—perhaps for hours—past the midnight—on to the small hours—while that awful, determined, leisurely Something stole nearer and nearer.

She bent to him who had been her protector with a spasm of anger. Where was the indomitable spirit that had held her all these years with such strong and loving clasp? How could he leave her? How could he desert her? Her head fell back and moved restlessly against the cushion; moaning with the agony of loss, she recalled him as he had been. Then fear once more took possession of her, and she sat erect, rigid, breathless, awaiting the approach of Death.

Suddenly, far down in the house, on the first floor, her strained hearing took note of a sound—a wary, muffled sound, as if some one were creeping up the stair, fearful of being heard. Slowly! It seemed to count a hundred between the laying down of each foot. She gave a hysterical gasp. Where was the slow music?

Her face, her body, were wet—as if a wave of death-sweat had broken over them. There was a stiff feeling at the roots of her hair; she wondered if it were really standing erect. But she could not raise her hand to ascertain. Possibly it was only the coloring matter freezing and bleaching. Her muscles were flabby, her nerves twitched helplessly.

She knew that it was Death who was coming to her through the silent deserted house; knew that it was the sensitive ear of her intelligence that heard him, not the dull, coarse-grained ear of the body.

He toiled up the stair painfully, as if he were old and tired with much work. But *how* could he afford to loiter, with all the work he had to do? Every minute, every second, he must be in demand to hook his cold, hard finger about a soul struggling to escape from its putrefying tenement. But probably he had his emissaries, his minions: for only those worthy of the honor did he come in person.

He reached the first landing and crept like a cat down the hall to the next stair, then crawled slowly up as before. Light as the footfalls were, they were squarely planted, unfaltering; slow, they never halted.

Mechanically she pressed her jerking hand closer against the heart; its beats were almost done. They would finish, she calculated, just as those footfalls paused beside the bed.

She was no longer a human being; she was an Intelligence and an EAR. Not a sound came from without, even the Elevated appeared to be temporarily off duty; but inside the big quiet house that footfall was waxing louder, louder, until iron feet crashed on iron stairs and echo thundered.

She had counted the steps—one—two—three—irritated beyond endurance at the long deliberate pauses between. As they climbed and clanged with slow precision she continued to count, audibly and with equal precision, noting their hollow reverberation. How many steps had the stair? She wished she knew. No need! The colossal trampling announced the lessening distance in an increasing volume of sound not to be misunderstood. It turned the curve; it reached the landing; it advanced—slowly—down the hall; it paused before her door. Then knuckles of iron shook the frail panels. Her nerveless tongue gave no invitation. The knocking became more imperious; the very walls vibrated. The handle turned, swiftly and firmly. With a wild instinctive movement she flung herself into the arms of her husband.

When Mary opened the door and entered the room she found a dead woman lying across a dead man.

Arthur Quiller-Couch

Sir Arthur Quiller-Couch (1863–1940) first became known to the British reading public as "Q," the author of romantic historical fiction in the manner of Robert Louis Stevenson, usually set in Cornwall. He was also associated with the publishing house of Cassell, and was active in politics. In 1910 he received a knighthood, and in 1912 he was appointed Edward VII Professor of English Literature at Cambridge University. The appointment was criticized since it was obviously political, but Quiller-Couch proved to be an excellent choice. He was a fine lecturer, a tasteful critic, and an inspirational figure to students rebelling against the traditional philological approach to literature. The books On the Art of Writing (1916) and On the Art of Reading (1920) were based on his lectures. The first contains the fine essay "On Jargon" that used to be (and perhaps still is, in a few places?) required reading for students of English.

Quiller-Couch wrote many supernatural stories that are scattered among his collections of short stories and essays. Twenty-seven have appeared in book form under his name, and it is possible that others may lurk among his unpublished periodical work.

Most of "Q's" ghost stories are regionalistic or historical in setting. His early work was heavily Stevensonian, but he soon evolved to a more personal style. Some stories, like "A Blue Pantomime," involve the unquiet dead; others are based on Cornish folklore. In still others he was caught up in the Hellenophilia of the day and accomplished the strange feat of bringing the Greek gods to Cornwall.

THE
LAIRD'S LUCK

[In a General Order issued from the Horse-Guards on New Year's Day, 1836, His Majesty King William IV was pleased to direct, through the Commander-in-Chief, Lord Hill, that "with the view of doing the fullest justice to Regiments, as well as to Individuals who had distinguished themselves in action against the enemy," an account of the services of every Regiment in the British Army should be published, under the supervision of the Adjutant-General.

With fair promptitude this scheme was put in hand, under the editorship of Mr. Richard Cannon, Principal Clerk of the Adjutant-General's Office. The duty of examining, sifting, and preparing the records of that distinguished Regiment which I shall here call the Moray Highlanders (concealing its real name for reasons which the narrative will make apparent) fell to a certain Major Reginald Sparkes; who in the course of his researches came upon a number of pages in manuscript sealed under one cover and docketed "Memoranda concerning Ensign D. M. J. Mackenzie, J. R., Jan. 3rd, 1816"— the initials being those of Lieut.-Colonel Sir James Ross, who had commanded the 2nd Battalion of the Morays through the campaign of Waterloo. The cover also bore, in the same handwriting, the word "Private," twice underlined.

Of the occurrences related in the enclosed papers—of the private ones, that is—it so happened that of the four eye-witnesses none survived at the date of Major Sparkes' discovery. They had, moreover, so carefully taken their secret with them that the Regiment preserved not a rumour of it. Major Sparkes' own commission was considerably more recent than the Waterloo year, and he at least had heard no whisper of the story. It lay outside the purpose of his inquiry, and he judiciously omitted it from his report. But the time is past when its publication might conceivably have been injurious; and with some alterations in the names—to carry out the disguise of the Regiment—it is here given. The reader will understand that I use the IPSISSIMA VERBA of Colonel Ross.—Q.]

I had the honour of commanding my Regiment, the Moray High-landers, on the 16th of June 1815, when the late Ensign David Marie Joseph Mackenzie met his end in the bloody struggle of Quatre Bras (his first engagement). He fell beside the colours, and I gladly bear witness that he had not only borne himself with extreme gallantry, but maintained, under circumstances of severest trial, a coolness which might well have rewarded me for my help in procuring the lad's commission. And yet at the moment I could scarcely regret his death, for he went into action under a suspicion so dishonouring that, had it been proved, no amount of gallantry could have restored him to the respect of his fellows. So at least I believed, with three of his brother officers who shared the secret. These were Major William Ross (my half-brother), Captain Malcolm Murray, and Mr. Ronald Braintree Urquhart, then our senior ensign. Of these, Mr. Urquhart fell two days later, at Waterloo, while steadying his men to face that heroic shock in which Pack's skeleton regiments were enveloped yet not over-whelmed by four brigades of the French infantry. From the others I received at the time a promise that the accusation against young Mackenzie should be wiped off the slate by his death, and the affair kept secret between us. Since then, however, there has come to me an explanation which—though hard indeed to credit—may, if true, exculpate the lad. I laid it before the others, and they agreed that if, in spite of precautions, the affair should ever come to light, the explanation ought also in justice to be forthcoming; and hence I am writing this memorandum.

It was in the late September of 1814 that I first made acquaintance with David Mackenzie. A wound received in the battle of Salamanca—a shattered ankle—had sent me home invalided, and on my partial recovery I was appointed to command the 2nd Battalion of my Regiment, then being formed at Inverness. To this duty I was equal; but my ankle still gave trouble (the splinters from time to time working through the flesh), and in the late summer of 1814 I obtained leave of absence with my step-brother, and spent some pleasant weeks in cruising and fishing about the Moray Firth. Finding that my leg bettered by this idleness, we hired a smaller boat and embarked on a longer excursion, which took us almost to the south-western end of Loch Ness.

Here, on September 18th, and pretty late in the afternoon, we were overtaken by a sudden squall, which carried away our mast (we found afterwards that it had rotted in the step), and put us for some minutes in no little danger; for my brother and I, being inexpert seamen, did not cut the tangle away, as we should have done, but made a bungling attempt to get the mast on board, with the rigging and drenched sail; and thereby managed to knock a hole in the side of the boat, which at once began to take in water. This compelled us to desist and fall to baling with might and main, leaving the raffle and jagged end of the mast to bump against us at the will of the waves. In short, we were in a highly unpleasant predicament, when a coble or row-boat, carrying one small lug-sail, hove out of the dusk to our assistance. It was manned by a crew of three, of whom the master (though we had scarce light enough to distinguish features) hailed us in a voice which was patently a gentleman's. He rounded up, lowered sail, and ran his boat alongside; and while his two hands were cutting us free of our tangle, inquired very civilly if we were strangers. We answered that we were, and desired him to tell us of the nearest place alongside where we might land and find a lodging for the night, as well as a carpenter to repair our damage.

"In any ordinary case," said he, "I should ask you to come aboard and home with me. But my house lies five miles up the lake; your boat is sinking, and the first thing is to beach her. It happens that you are but half a mile from Ardlaugh and a decent carpenter who can answer all requirements. I think, if I stand by you, the thing can be done; and afterwards we will talk of supper."

By diligent baling we were able, under his direction, to bring our boat to a shingly beach, over which a light shone warm in a cottage window. Our hail was quickly answered by a second light. A lantern issued from the building, and we heard the sound of footsteps.

"Is that you, Donald?" cried our rescuer (as I may be permitted to call him).

Before an answer could be returned, we saw that two men were approaching; of whom the one bearing the lantern was a grizzled old carlin with bent knees and a stoop of the shoulders. His companion carried himself with a lighter step. It was he who advanced to salute us, the old man holding the light obediently; and the rays revealed to us a slight, up-standing youth, poorly dressed, but handsome, and with a touch of pride in his bearing.

"Good evening, gentlemen." He lifted his bonnet politely, and turned to our rescuer. "Good evening, Mr. Gillespie," he said—I thought more coldly. "Can I be of any service to your friends?"

Mr. Gillespie's manner had changed suddenly at sight of the young man, whose salutation he acknowledged more coldly and even more curtly than it had been given. "I can scarcely claim them as my friends," he answered. "They are two gentlemen, strangers in these parts, who have met with an accident to their boat: one so serious that I brought them to the nearest landing, which happened to be Donald's."

He shortly explained our mishap, while the young man took the lantern in hand and inspected the damage with Donald.

"There is nothing," he announced, "which cannot be set right in a couple of hours; but we must wait till morning. Meanwhile if, as I gather, you have no claim on these gentlemen, I shall beg them to be my guests for the night."

We glanced at Mr. Gillespie, whose manners seemed to have deserted him. He shrugged his shoulders. "Your house is the nearer," said he, "and the sooner they reach a warm fire the better for them after their drenching." And with that he lifted his cap to us, turned abruptly, and pushed off his own boat, scarcely regarding our thanks.

A somewhat awkward pause followed as we stood on the beach, listening to the creak of the thole-pins in the departing boat. After a minute our new acquaintance turned to us with a slightly constrained laugh.

"Mr. Gillespie omitted some of the formalities," said he. "My name is Mackenzie—David Mackenzie; and I live at Ardlaugh Castle, scarcely half a mile up the glen behind us. I warn you that its hospitality is rude, but to what it affords you are heartily welcome."

He spoke with a high, precise courtliness which contrasted oddly with his boyish face (I guessed his age at nineteen or twenty), and still more oddly with his clothes, which were threadbare and patched in many places, yet with a deftness which told of a woman's care. We introduced ourselves by name, and thanked him, with some expressions of regret at inconveniencing (as I put it, at hazard) the family at the Castle.

"Oh!" he interrupted, "I am sole master there. I have no parents living, no family, and," he added, with a slight sullenness which I afterwards recognized as habitual, "I may almost say, no friends: though to be sure, you are lucky enough to have one fellow-guest to-night—the minister of the parish, a Mr. Saul, and a very worthy man."

He broke off to give Donald some instructions about the boat, watched us while we found our plaids and soaked valises, and then took the lantern from the old man's hand. "I ought to have explained," said he," that we have neither cart here nor carriage: indeed, there is no carriage-road. But Donald has a pony."

He led the way a few steps up the beach, and then halted, perceiving my lameness for the first time, "Donald, fetch out the sheltie. Can you ride bareback?" he asked: "I fear there's no saddle but an old piece of sacking." In spite of my protestations the pony was led forth; a starved little beast, on whose over-sharp ridge I must have cut a sufficiently ludicrous figure when hoisted into place with the valises slung behind me.

The procession set out, and I soon began to feel thankful for my seat, though I took no ease in it. For the road climbed steeply from the cottage, and at once began to twist up the bottom of a ravine so narrow that we lost all help of the young moon. The path, indeed, resembled the bed of a torrent, shrunk now to a trickle of water, the voice of which ran in my ears while our host led the way, springing from boulder to boulder, avoiding pools, and pausing now and then to hold his lantern over some slippery place. The pony followed with admirable caution, and my brother trudged in the rear and took his cue from us. After five minutes of this the ground grew easier and at the same time steeper, and I guessed that we were slanting up the hillside and away from the torrent at an acute angle. The many twists and angles, and the utter darkness (for we were now moving between trees) had completely baffled my reckoning when—at the end of twenty minutes, perhaps—Mr. Mackenzie halted and allowed me to come up with him.

I was about to ask the reason of this halt when a ray of his lantern fell on a wall of masonry; and with a start almost laughable I knew we had arrived. To come to an entirely strange house at night is an experience which holds some taste of mystery even for the oldest campaigner; but I have never in my life received such a shock as this building gave me—naked, unlit, presented to me out of a darkness in which I had imagined a steep mountain scaur dotted with dwarfed trees—a sudden abomination of desolation standing, like the prophet's, where it ought not. No light showed on the side where we stood—the side over the ravine; only one pointed turret stood out against the faint moonlight glow in the upper sky: but feeling our way around the gaunt side of the building, we came to a back court-yard and two windows lit. Our host whistled, and helped me to dismount.

In an angle of the court a creaking door opened. A woman's voice cried: "That will be you, Ardlaugh, and none too early! The minister—"

She broke off, catching sight of us. Our host stepped hastily to the door and began a whispered conversation. We could hear that she was protesting, and began to feel awkward enough. But whatever her objections were, her master cut them short.

"Come in, sirs," he invited us: "I warned you that the fare would be hard, but I repeat that you are welcome."

To our surprise and, I must own, our amusement, the woman caught up his words with new protestations, uttered this time at the top of her voice.

"The fare hard? Well, it might not please folks accustomed to city feasts; but Ardlaugh was not yet without a joint of venison in the larder and a bottle of wine, maybe two, maybe three, for any guest its master chose to make welcome. It was an ill bird that 'filed his own nest' "—with more to this effect, which our host tried in vain to interrupt.

"Then I will lead you to your rooms," he said, turning to us as soon as she paused to draw breath.

"Indeed, Ardlaugh, you will do nothing of the kind." She ran into the kitchen, and returned holding high a lighted torch—a grey-haired woman, with traces of past comeliness, overlaid now by an air of worry, almost of fear. But her manner showed only a defiant pride as she led us up the uncarpeted stairs, past old portraits sagging and rotting in their frames, through bleak corridors, where the windows were parched and the plastered walls discoloured by fungus. Once only she halted. "It will be a long way to your ap-partments. A grand house!" She had faced round on us, and her eyes seemed to ask a question of ours. "I have known it filled," she added—"filled with guests, and the drink and fiddles never stopping for a week. You will see it better to-morrow. A grand house!"

I will confess that, as I limped after this barbaric woman and her torch, I felt some reasonable apprehensions of the bedchamber towards which they were escorting me. But here came another surprise. The room was of moderate size, poorly furnished indeed, but comfortable and something more. It bore traces of many petty attentions, even— in its white dimity curtains and valances—of an attempt at daintiness. The sight of it brought quite a pleasant shock after the dirt and disarray of the corridor. Nor was the room assigned to my brother one whit less habitable. But if surprised by all this, I was fairly astounded to find in each room a pair of candles lit—and quite recently lit—beside the looking-glass and an ewer of hot water standing, with a clean towel upon it, in each washhand basin. No sooner had the woman departed than I visited my brother and begged him (while he unstrapped his valise) to explain this apparent miracle. He could only guess with me that the woman had been warned of our arrival by the noise of footsteps in the courtyard, and had dispatched a servant by some back-stairs to make ready for us.

Our valises were, fortunately, waterproof. We quickly exchanged our damp clothes for dry ones, and groped our way together along the corridors, helped by the moon which shone through their uncurtained windows, to the main staircase. Here we came on a scent of roasting meat—appetizing to us after our day in the open air—and at the foot found our host waiting for us. He had donned his Highland dress of ceremony—velvet jacket, filibeg and kilt, with the tartan of his clan— and looked (I must own) extremely well in it, though the garments had long since lost their original gloss. An apology for our rough touring suits led to some few questions and replies about the regimental tartan of the Morays, in the history of which he was passably well informed.

Thus chatting, we entered the great hall of Ardlaugh Castle—a tall but narrow and ill-proportioned apartment, having an open timber roof, a stone-paved floor, and walls sparsely decorated with antlers and round targes—where a very small man stood warming his back at an immense fireplace. This was the Reverend Samuel Saul, whose acquaintance we had scarce time to make before a cracked gong summoned us to dinner in the adjoining room.

The young Laird of Ardlaugh took his seat in a roughly carved chair of state at the head of the table; but before doing so treated me to another surprise by muttering a Latin grace and crossing himself. Up to now I had taken it for granted he was a member of the Scottish Kirk. I glanced at the minister in some mystification; but he, good man, appeared to have fallen into a brown study, with his eyes fastened upon a dish of apples which adorned the centre of our promiscuously furnished board.

Of the furniture of our meal I can only say that poverty and decent appearance kept up a brave fight throughout. The table-cloth was ragged, but spotlessly clean; the silver-ware scanty and worn with high polishing. The plates and glasses displayed a noble range of patterns, but were for the most part chipped or cracked. Each knife had been worn to a point, and a few of them joggled in their handles. In a lull of the talk I caught myself idly counting the darns in my table-napkin. They were—if I remember—fourteen, and all exquisitely stitched. The dinner, on the other hand, would have tempted men far less hungry than we—grilled steaks of salmon, a roast haunch of venison, grouse, a milk-pudding, and, for dessert, the dish of apples already mentioned; the meats washed down with one wine only, but that wine was claret, and beautifully sound. I should mention that we were served by a grey-haired retainer, almost stone deaf, and as hopelessly cracked as the gong with which he had beaten us to dinner. In the long waits between the courses we heard him quarrelling outside with the woman who had admitted us; and gradually—I know not how—the conviction grew on me that they were man and wife, and the only servants of our host's establishment. To cover the noise of one of their altercations I began to congratulate the Laird on the quality of his venison, and put some idle question about his care for his deer.

"I have no deer-forest," he answered. "Elspeth is my only housekeeper."

I had some reply on my lips, when my attention was distracted by a sudden movement by the Rev. Samuel Saul. This honest man had, as we shook hands in the great hall, broken into a flood of small talk. On our way to the dining-room he took me, so to speak, by the button-hole, and within the minute so drenched me with gossip about Ardlaugh, its climate, its scenery, its crops, and the dimensions of the parish, that I feared a whole evening of boredom lay before us. But from the moment we seated ourselves at table he dropped to an absolute silence. There are men, living much alone, who by habit talk little during their meals; and the minister might be reserving himself. But I had almost forgotten his presence when I heard a sharp exclamation, and, looking across, saw him take from his lips his wine-glass of claret and set it down with a shaking hand. The Laird, too, had heard, and bent a darkly questioning glance on him. At once the little man—whose face had turned to a sickly white—began to stammer and excuse himself.

"It was nothing—a spasm. He would be better of it in a moment. No, he would take no wine: a glass of water would set him right—he was more used to drinking water," he explained, with a small, nervous laugh.

Perceiving that our solicitude embarrassed him, we resumed our talk, which now turned upon the last Peninsular campaign and certain engagements in which the Morays had borne part; upon the stability of the French Monarchy, and the career (as we believed, at an end) of Napoleon. On all these topics the Laird showed himself well informed, and while preferring the part of listener (as became his youth) from time to time put in a question which convinced me of his intelligence, especially in military affairs.

The minister, though silent as before, had regained his colour; and we were somewhat astonished when, the cloth being drawn and the company left to its wine and one dish of dessert, he rose and announced that he must be going. He was decidedly better, but (so he excused himself) would feel easier at home in his own manse; and so, declining our host's offer of a bed, he shook hands and bade us good night. The Laird accompanied him to the door, and in his absence I fell to peeling an apple, while my brother drummed with his fingers on the table and eyed the faded hangings. I suppose that ten minutes elapsed before we heard the young man's footsteps returning through the flagged hall and a woman's voice uplifted.

"But had the minister any complaint, whatever—to ride off without a word? She could answer for the collops—"

"Whist, woman! Have done with your clashin', ye doited old fool!" He slammed the door upon her, stepped to the table, and with a sullen frown poured himself a glass of wine. His brow cleared as he drank it.

"I beg your pardon, gentlemen; but this indisposition of Mr. Saul has annoyed me. He lives at the far end of the parish—a good seven miles away—and I had invited him expressly to talk of parish affairs."

"I believe," said I, "you and he are not of the same religion?"

"Eh?" He seemed to be wondering how I had guessed. "No, I was bred a Catholic. In our branch we have always held to the Old Profession. But that doesn't prevent my wishing to stand well with my neighbours and do my duty towards them. What disheartens me is, they won't see it." He pushed the wine aside, and for a while, leaning his elbows on the table and resting his chin on his knuckles, stared gloomily before him. Then, with sudden boyish indignation, he burst out: "It's an infernal shame; that's it—an infernal shame! I haven't been home here a twelve-month, and the people avoid me like the plague. What have I done? My father wasn't popular—in fact, they hated him. But so did I. And he hated me, God knows: misused my mother, and wouldn't endure me in his presence. All my miserable youth I've been mewed up in a school in England—a private seminary. Ugh, what a den it was, too! My mother died calling for me—I was not allowed to come: I hadn't seen her for three years. And now, when the old tyrant is dead, and I come home meaning—so help me!—to straighten things out and make friends—come home, to the poverty you pretend not to notice, though it stares you in the face from every wall—come home, only asking to make the best of it, live on good terms with my fellows, and be happy for the first time in my life—damn them, they won't fling me a kind look! What have I *done*?—that's what I want to know. The queer thing is, they behaved more decently at first. There's that Gillespie, who brought you ashore: he came over the first week, offered me shooting, was altogether as pleasant as could be. I quite took to the fellow. Now, when we meet, he looks the other way! If he has anything against me, he might at least explain: it's all I ask. What have I done?"

Throughout this outburst I sat slicing my apple and taking now and then a glance at the speaker. It was all so hotly and honestly boyish! He only wanted justice. I know something of youngsters, and recognized the cry. Justice! It's the one thing every boy claims confidently as his right, and probably the last thing on earth he will ever get. And this boy looked so handsome, too, sitting in his father's chair, petulant, restive under a weight too heavy (as any one could see) for his age. I couldn't help liking him.

My brother told me afterwards that I pounced like any recruiting-sergeant. This I do not believe. But what, after a long pause, I said was this: "If you are innocent or unconscious of offending, you can only wait for your neighbours to explain themselves. Meanwhile, why not leave them? Why not travel, for instance?"

"Travel!" he echoed, as much as to say, "You ought to know, without my telling, that I cannot afford it."

"Travel," I repeated; "see the world, rub against men of your age. You might by the way do some fighting."

He opened his eyes wide. I saw the sudden idea take hold of him, and again I liked what I saw.

"If I thought—" He broke off. "You don't mean—" he began, and broke off again.

"I mean the Morays," I said. "There may be difficulties; but at this moment I cannot see any real ones."

By this time he was gripping the arms of his chair. "If I thought—" he harked back, and for the third time broke off. "What a fool I am! It's the last thing they ever put in a boy's head at that infernal school. If you will believe it, they wanted to make a priest of me!"

He sprang up, pushing back his chair. We carried our wine into the great hall, and sat there talking the question over before the fire. Before we parted for the night I had engaged to use all my interest to get him a commission in the Morays; and I left him pacing the hall, his mind in a whirl, but his heart (as was plain to see) exulting in his new prospects.

And certainly, when I came to inspect the castle by the next morning's light, I could understand his longing to leave it. A gloomier, more pretentious, or worse-devised structure I never set eyes on. The Mackenzie who erected it may well have been (as the saying is) his own architect, and had either come to the end of his purse or left his heirs to decide against planting gardens, laying out approaches, or even maintaining the pile in decent repair. In place of a drive a grassy cart-track, scored deep with old ruts, led through a gateless entrance into a courtyard where the slates had dropped from the roof and lay strewn like autumn leaves. On this road I encountered the young Laird returning from an early tramp with his gun; and he stood still and pointed to the castle with a grimace.

"A white elephant," said I.

"Call it rather the corpse of one," he answered. "Cannot you imagine some *genie* of the Oriental Tales dragging the beast across Europe and dumping it down here in a sudden fit of disgust? As a matter of fact my grandfather built it, and cursed us with poverty thereby. It soured my father's life. I believe the only soul honestly proud of it is Elspeth."

"And I suppose," said I, "you will leave her in charge of it when you join the Morays?"

"Ah!" he broke in, with a voice which betrayed his relief: "you are in earnest about that? Yes, Elspeth will look after the castle, as she does already. I am just a child in her hands. When a man has one only servant it's well to have her devoted." Seeing my look of surprise, he added, "I don't count old Duncan, her husband; for he's half-witted, and only serves to break the plates. Does it surprise you to learn that, barring him, Elspeth is my only retainer."

"H'm," said I, considerably puzzled—I must explain why.

I am by training an extraordinary light sleeper; yet nothing had disturbed me during the night until at dawn my brother knocked at the door and entered, ready dressed.

"Hallo!" he exclaimed, "are you responsible for this?" and he pointed to a chair at the foot of the bed where lay, folded in a neat pile, not only the clothes I had tossed down carelessly overnight, but the suit in which I had arrived. He picked up this latter, felt it, and handed it to me. It was dry, and had been carefully brushed.

"Our friend keeps a good valet," said I; "but the queer thing is that, in a strange room, I didn't wake. I see he has brought hot water too."

"Look here," my brother asked: "did you lock your door?"

"Why, of course not—the more by token that it hasn't a key."

"Well," said he, "mine has, and I'll swear I used it; but the same thing has happened to me!"

This, I tried to persuade him, was impossible; and for the while he seemed convinced. "It *must* be," he owned; but if I didn't lock that door I'll never swear to a thing again in all my life."

The young Laird's remark set me thinking of this, and I answered after a pause: "In one of the pair, then, you possess a remarkably clever valet."

It so happened that, while I said it, my eyes rested, without the least intention, on the sleeve of his shooting-coat; and the words were scarcely out before he flushed hotly and made a motion as if to hide a neatly mended rent in its cuff. In another moment he would have retorted, and was indeed drawing himself up in anger, when I prevented him by adding:

"I mean that I am indebted to him or to her this morning for a neatly brushed suit; and I suppose to your freeness in plying me with wine last night that it arrived in my room without waking me. But for that I could almost set it down to the supernatural."

I said this in all simplicity, and was quite unprepared for its effect upon him, or for his extraordinary reply. He turned as white in the face as, a moment before, he had been red. "Good God!" he said eagerly, "you haven't missed anything, have you?"

"Certainly not," I assured him. "My dear sir—"

"I know, I know. But you see," he stammered, "I am new to these servants. I know them to be faithful, and that's all. Forgive me; I feared from your tone one of them—Duncan perhaps . . ."

He did not finish his sentence, but broke into a hurried walk and led me towards the house. A minute later, as we approached it, he began to discourse half-humorously on its more glaring features, and had apparently forgotten his perturbation.

I too attached small importance to it, and recall it now merely through unwillingness to omit any circumstance which may throw light on a story sufficiently dark to me. After breakfast our host walked down with us to the loch-side, where we found old Donald putting the last touches on his job. With thanks for our entertainment we shook hands and pushed off: and my last word at parting was a promise to remember his ambition and write any news of my success.

II

I anticipated no difficulty, and encountered none. The *Gazette* of January, 1815, announced that David Marie Joseph Mackenzie, gentleman, had been appointed to an ensigncy in the ——th Regiment of Infantry (Moray Highlanders); and I timed my letter of congratulation to reach him with the news. Within a week he had joined us at Inverness, and was made welcome.

I may say at once that during his brief period of service I could find no possible fault with his bearing as a soldier. From the first he took seriously to the calling of arms, and not only showed himself punctual on parade and in all the small duties of barracks, but displayed, in his reserved way, a zealous resolve to master whatever by book or conversation could be learned of the higher business of war. My junior officers—though when the test came, as it soon did, they acquitted themselves most creditably—showed, as a whole, just then no great promise. For the most part they were young lairds, like Mr. Mackenzie, or cadets of good Highland families; but, unlike him, they had been allowed to run wild, and chafed under harness. One or two of them had the true Highland addiction to card-playing; and though I set a pretty stern face against this curse—as I dare to call it—its effects were to be traced in late hours, more than one case of shirking "rounds," and a general slovenliness at morning parade.

In such company Mr. Mackenzie showed to advantage, and I soon began to value him as a likely officer. Nor, in my dissatisfaction with them, did it give me any uneasiness—as it gave me no surprise—to find that his brother-officers took less kindly to him. He kept a certain reticence of manner, which either came of a natural shyness or had been ingrained in him at the Roman Catholic seminary. He was poor, too; but poverty did not prevent his joining in all the regimental amusements, figuring modestly but sufficiently on the subscription lists, and even taking a hand at cards for moderate stakes. Yet he made no headway, and his popularity diminished instead of growing. All this I noted, but without discovering any definite reason. Of his professional promise, on the other hand, there could be no question; and the men liked and respected him.

Our senior ensign at this date was a Mr. Urquhart, the eldest son of a West Highland laird, and heir to a considerable estate. He had been in barracks when Mr. Mackenzie joined; but a week later his father's sudden illness called for his presence at home, and I granted him a leave of absence, which was afterwards extended. I regretted this, not only for the sad occasion, but because it deprived the battalion for a time of one of its steadiest officers, and Mr. Mackenzie in particular of the chance to form a very useful friendship. For the two young men had (I thought) several qualities which might well attract them each to the other, and a common gravity of mind in contrast with their companions' prevalent and somewhat tiresome frivolity. Of the two I judged Mr. Urquhart (the elder by a year) to have the more stable character. He was a good-looking, dark-complexioned young Highlander, with a serious expression which, without being gloomy, did not escape a touch of melancholy. I should judge this melancholy of Mr. Urquhart's constitutional, and the boyish sullenness which lingered on Mr. Mackenzie's equally handsome face to have been imposed rather by circumstances.

Mr. Urquhart rejoined us on the 24th of February. Two days later, as all the world knows, Napoleon made his escape from Elba; and the next week or two made it certain not only that the Allies must fight, but that the British contingent must be drawn largely, if not in the main, from the second battalions then drilling up and down the country. The 29th of March brought us our marching orders; and I will own that, while feeling no uneasiness about the great issue, I mistrusted the share my raw youngsters were to take in it.

On the 12th of April we were landed at Ostend, and at once marched up to Brussels, where we remained until the middle of June, having been assigned to the 5th (Picton's) Division of the Reserve. For some reason the Highland regiments had been massed into the Reserve, and were billeted about the capital, our own quarters lying between the 92nd (Gordons) and General Kruse's Nassauers, whose lodgings stretched out along the Louvain road; and although I could have wished some harder and more responsible service to get the Morays into training, I felt what advantage they derived from rubbing shoulders with the fine fellows of the 42nd, 79th, and 92nd, all First Battalions toughened by Peninsular work. The gaieties of life in Brussels during these two months have been described often enough; but among the military they were chiefly confined to those officers whose means allowed them to keep the pace set by rich civilians, and the Morays played the part of amused spectators. Yet the work and the few gaieties which fell to our share, while adding to our experiences, broke up to some degree the old domestic habits of the battalion. Excepting on duty I saw less of Mr. Mackenzie and thought less about him; he might be left now to be shaped by active service. But I was glad to find him often in company with Mr. Urquhart.

I come now to the memorable night of June 15th, concerning which and the end it brought upon the festivities of Brussels so much has been written. All the world has heard of the Duchess of Richmond's ball, and seems to conspire in decking it out with pretty romantic fables. To contradict the most of these were waste of time; but I may point out (1) that the ball was over and, I believe, all the company dispersed, before the actual alarm awoke the capital; and (2) that all responsible officers gathered there shared the knowledge that such an alarm was impending, might arrive at any moment, and would almost certainly arrive within a few hours. News of the French advance across the frontier and attack on General Zieten's outposts had reached Wellington at three o'clock that afternoon. It should have been brought five hours earlier; but he gave his orders at once, and quietly, and already our troops were massing for defence upon Nivelles. We of the Reserve had secret orders to hold ourselves prepared. Obedient to a hint from their Commander-in-Chief, the generals of division and brigade who attended the Duchess's ball withdrew themselves early on various pleas. Her Grace had honoured me with an invitation, probably because I represented a Highland regiment; and Highlanders (especially the Gordons, her brother's regiment) were much to the fore that night with reels, flings, and strathspeys. The many withdrawals warned me that something was in the wind, and after remaining just so long as seemed respectful I took leave of my hostess and walked homewards across the city as the clocks were striking eleven.

We of the Morays had our headquarters in a fairly large building— the Hôtel de Liège—in time of peace a resort of *commis-voyageurs* of the better class. It boasted a roomy hall, out of which opened two coffee-rooms, converted by us into guard- and mess-room. A large drawing-room on the first floor overlooking the street served me for sleeping as well as working quarters, and to reach it I must pass the *entresol,* where a small apartment had been set aside for occasional uses. We made it, for instance, our ante-room, and assembled there before mess; a few would retire there for smoking or card-playing; during the day it served as a waiting-room for messengers or any one whose business could not be for the moment attended to.

I had paused at the entrance to put some small question to the sentry, when I heard the crash of a chair in this room, and two voices broke out in fierce altercation. An instant after, the mess-room door opened, and Captain Murray, without observing me, ran past me and up the stairs. As he reached the *entresol,* a voice—my brother's—called down from an upper landing, and demanded: "What's wrong there?"

"I don't know, Major," Captain Murray answered, and at the same moment flung the door open. I was quick on his heels, and he wheeled round in some surprise at my voice, and to see me interposed between him and my brother, who had come running downstairs, and now stood behind my shoulder in the entrance.

"Shut the door," I commanded quickly. "Shut the door, and send away any one you may hear outside. Now, gentleman, explain yourselves, please."

Mr. Urquhart and Mr. Mackenzie faced each other across a small table, from which the cloth had been dragged and lay on the floor with a scattered pack of cards. The elder lad held a couple of cards in his hand; he was white in the face.

"He cheated!" He swung round upon me in a kind of indignant fury, and tapped the cards with his forefinger.

I looked from him to the accused. Mackenzie's face was dark, almost purple, rather with rage (as it struck me) than with shame.

"It's a lie." He let out the words slowly, as if holding rein on his passion. "Twice he's said so, and twice I've called him a liar." He drew back for an instant, and then lost control of himself. "If that's not enough—" He leapt forward, and almost before Captain Murray could interpose had hurled himself upon Urquhart. The table between them went down with a crash, and Urquhart went staggering back from a blow which just missed his face and took him on the collarbone before Murray threw both arms around the assailant.

"Mr. Mackenzie," said I, "you will consider yourself under arrest. Mr. Urquhart, you will hold yourself ready to give me a full explanation. Whichever of you may be in the right, this is a disgraceful business, and dishonouring to your regiment and the cloth you wear: so disgraceful, that I hesitate to call up the guard and expose it to more eyes than ours. If Mr. Mackenzie"—I turned to him again—"can behave himself like a gentleman, and accept the fact of his arrest without further trouble, the scandal can at least be postponed until I discover how much it is necessary to face. For the moment, sir, you are in charge of Captain Murray. Do you understand?"

He bent his head sullenly. "He shall fight me, whatever happens," he muttered.

I found it wise to pay no heed to this. "It will be best," I said to Murray, "to remain here with Mr. Mackenzie until I am ready for him. Mr. Urquhart may retire to his quarters, if he will—I advise it, indeed—but I shall require his attendance in a few minutes. You understand," I added significantly, "that for the present this affair remains strictly between ourselves." I knew well enough that, for all the King's regulations, a meeting would inevitably follow sooner or later, and will own I looked upon it as the proper outcome, between gentlemen, of such a quarrel. But it was not for me, their Colonel, to betray this knowledge or my feelings, and by imposing secrecy I put off for the time all the business of a formal challenge with seconds. So I left them, and requesting my brother to follow me, mounted to my own room. The door was no sooner shut than I turned on him.

"Surely," I said, "this is a bad mistake of Urquhart's? It's an incredible charge. From all I've seen of him, the lad would never be guilty . . ." I paused, expecting his assent. To my surprise he did not give it, but stood fingering his chin and looking serious.

"I don't know," he answered unwillingly. "There are stories against him."

"What stories?"

"Nothing definite." My brother hesitated. "It doesn't seem fair to him to repeat mere whispers. But the others don't like him."

"Hence the whispers, perhaps. They have not reached me."

"They would not. He is known to be a favourite of yours. But they don't care to play with him." My brother stopped, met my look, and answered it with a shrug of the shoulders, adding: "He wins pretty constantly."

"Any definite charge before to-night's?"

"No: at least, I think not. But Urquhart may have been put up to watch."

"Fetch him up, please," said I promptly; and seating myself at the writing-table I lit candles (for the lamp was dim), made ready the writing materials and prepared to take notes of the evidence.

Mr. Urquhart presently entered, and I wheeled round in my chair to confront him. He was still exceedingly pale—paler, I thought, than I had left him. He seemed decidedly ill at ease, though not on his own account. His answer to my first question made me fairly leap in my chair.

"I wish," he said, "to qualify my accusation of Mr. Mackenzie. That he cheated I have the evidence of my own eyes; but I am not sure how far he knew he was cheating."

"Good heavens, sir!" I cried. "Do you know you have accused that young man of a villainy which must damn him for life? And now you tell me—" I broke off in sheer indignation.

"I know," he answered quietly. "The noise fetched you in upon us on the instant, and the mischief was done."

"Indeed, sir," I could not avoid sneering, "to most of us it would seem that the mischief was done when you accused a brother-officer of fraud to his face."

He seemed to reflect. "Yes, sir," he assented slowly; "it is done. I saw him cheat: that I must persist in; but I cannot say how far he was conscious of it. And since I cannot, I must take the consequences."

"Will you kindly inform us how it is possible for a player to cheat and not know that he is cheating?"

He bent his eyes on the carpet as if seeking an answer. It was long in coming. "No," he said at last, in a slow, dragging tone, "I cannot."

"Then you will at least tell us exactly what Mr. Mackenzie did."

Again there was a long pause. He looked at me straight, but with hopelessness in his eyes. "I fear you would not believe me. It would not be worth while. If you can grant it, sir, I would ask time to decide."

"Mr. Urquhart," said I sternly, "are you aware you have brought against Mr. Mackenzie a charge under which no man of honour can live easily for a moment? You ask me without a word of evidence in substantiation to keep *him* in torture while I give *you* time. It is monstrous, and I beg to remind you that, unless your charge is proved, you can— and will—be broken for making it."

"I know it, sir," he answered firmly enough; "and because I knew it, I asked—perhaps selfishly—for time. If you refuse, I will at least ask permission to see a priest before telling a story which I scarcely expect you to believe." Mr. Urquhart too was a Roman Catholic.

But my temper for the moment was gone. "I see little chance," said I, "of keeping this scandal secret, and regret it the less if the consequences are to fall on a rash accuser. But just now I will have no meddling priest share the secret. For the present, one word more. Had you heard before this evening of any hints against Mr. Mackenzie's play?"

He answered reluctantly: "Yes."

"And you set yourself to lay a trap for him?"

"No, sir; I did not. Unconsciously I may have been set on the watch: no, that is wrong—I *did* watch. But I swear it was in every hope and expectation of clearing him. He was my friend. Even when I *saw*, I had at first no intention to expose him until—"

"That is enough, sir," I broke in, and turned to my brother. "I have no option but to put Mr. Urquhart too under arrest. Kindly convey him back to his room, and send Captain Murray to me. He may leave Mr. Mackenzie in the *entresol*."

My brother led Urquhart out, and in a minute Captain Murray tapped at my door. He was an honest Scot, not too sharp-witted, but straight as a die. I am to show him this description, and he will cheerfully agree with it.

"This is a hideous business, Murray," said I as he entered. "There's something wrong with Urquhart's story. Indeed, between ourselves it has the fatal weakness that he won't tell it."

Murray took half a minute to digest this: then he answered: "I don't know anything about Urquhart's story, sir. But there's something wrong about Urquhart." Here he hesitated.

"Speak out, man," said I: "in confidence. That's understood."

"Well, sir," said he, "Urquhart won't fight."

"Ah! so that question came up, did it?" I asked, looking at him sharply.

He was abashed, but answered, with a twinkle in his eye: "I believe, sir, you gave me no orders to stop their talking, and in a case like this—between youngsters—some question of a meeting would naturally come up. You see, I know both the lads. Urquhart I really like; but he didn't show up well, I must own—to be fair to the other, who is in the worse fix."

He seemed surprised. "Indeed, Colonel? Well," he resumed, "I being the sort of fellow they could talk before, a meeting *was* discussed. The question was how to arrange it without seconds—that is, without breaking your orders and dragging in outsiders. For Mackenzie wanted blood at once, and for a while Urquhart seemed just as eager. All of a sudden, when . . ." here he broke off suddenly, not wishing to commit himself.

"Tell me only what you think necessary," said I.

He thanked me. "That is what I wanted," he said. "Well, all of a sudden, when we had found out a way and Urquhart was discussing it, he pulled himself up in the middle of a sentence, and with his eyes fixed on the other—a most curious look it was—he waited while you could count ten, and, "No," says he, "I'll not fight you at once"—for we had been arranging something of the sort—"not to-night, anyway, nor to-morrow," he says. "I'll fight you; but I won't have your blood on my head *in that way*." Those were his words. I have no notion what he meant; but he kept repeating them, and would not explain, though Mackenzie tried him hard and was for shooting across the table. He was repeating them when the Major interrupted us and called him up.

"He has behaved ill from the first," said I. "To me the whole affair begins to look like an abominable plot against Mackenzie. Certainly I cannot entertain a suspicion of his guilt upon a bare assertion which Urquhart declines to back with a tittle of evidence."

"The devil he does!" mused Captain Murray. "That looks bad for him. And yet, sir, I'd sooner trust Urquhart than Mackenzie, and if the case lies against Urquhart—"

"It will assuredly break him," I put in, "unless he can prove the charge, or that he was honestly mistaken."

"Then, sir," said the Captain, "I'll have to show you this. It's ugly, but it's only justice."

He pulled a sovereign from his pocket and pushed it on the writing-table under my nose.

"What does this mean?"

"It is a marked one," said he.

"So I perceive." I had picked up the coin and was examining it.

"I found it just now," he continued, "in the room below. The upsetting of the table had scattered Mackenzie's stakes about the floor."

"You seem to have a pretty notion of evidence!" I observed sharply. "I don't know what accusation this coin may carry; but why need it be Mackenzie's? He might have won it from Urquhart."

"I thought of that," was the answer. "But no money had changed hands. I inquired. The quarrel arose over the second deal, and as a matter of fact Urquhart had laid no money on the table, but made a pencil-note of the few shillings he lost by the first hand. You may remember, sir, how the table stood when you entered."

I reflected. "Yes, my recollection bears you out. Do I gather that you have confronted Mackenzie with this?"

"No. I found it and slipped it quietly into my pocket. I thought we had trouble enough on hand for the moment."

"Who marked this coin?"

"Young Fraser, sir, in my presence. He has been losing small sums, he declares, by pilfering. We suspected one of the orderlies."

"In this connection you had no suspicion of Mr. Mackenzie?"

"None, sir." He considered for a moment, and added: "There was a curious thing happened three weeks ago over my watch. It found its way one night to Mr. Mackenzie's quarters. He brought it to me in the morning; said it was lying, when he awoke, on the table beside his bed. He seemed utterly puzzled. He had been to one or two already to discover the owner. We joked him about it, the more by token that his own watch had broken down the day before and was away at the mender's. The whole thing was queer, and has not been explained. Of course in that instance he was innocent: everything proves it. It just occurred to me as worth mentioning, because in both instances the lad may have been the victim of a trick."

"I am glad you did so," I said; "though just now it does not throw any light that I can see." I rose and paced the room. "Mr. Mackenzie had better be confronted with this, too, and hear your evidence. It's best he should know the worst against him; and if he be guilty it may move him to confession."

"Certainly, sir," Captain Murray assented. "Shall I fetch him?"

"No, remain where you are," I said; "I will go for him myself."

I understood that Mr. Urquhart had retired to his own quarters or to my brother's, and that Mr. Mackenzie had been left in the *entresol* alone. But as I descended the stairs quietly I heard within that room a voice which at first persuaded me he had company, and next that, left to himself, he had broken down and given way to the most childish wailing. The voice was so unlike his, or any grown man's, that it arrested me on the lowermost stair against my will. It resembled rather the sobbing of an infant mingled with short strangled cries of contrition and despair.

"What shall I do? What shall I do? I didn't mean it—I meant to do good! What shall I do?"

So much I heard (as I say) against my will, before my astonishment gave room to a sense of shame at playing, even for a moment, the eavesdropper upon the lad I was to judge. I stepped quickly to the door, and with a warning rattle (to give him time to recover himself) turned the handle and entered.

He was alone, lying back in an easy chair—not writhing there in anguish of mind, as I had fully expected, but sunk rather in a state of dull and hopeless apathy. To reconcile his attitude with the sounds I had just heard was merely impossible; and it bewildered me worse than any in the long chain of bewildering incidents. For five seconds or so he appeared not to see me; but when he grew aware his look changed suddenly to one of utter terror, and his eyes, shifting from me, shot a glance about the room as if he expected some new accusation to dart at him from the corners. His indignation and passionate defiance were gone: his eyes seemed to ask me: "How much do you know?" before he dropped them and stood before me, sullenly submissive.

"I want you upstairs," said I: "not to hear your defence on this charge, for Mr. Urquhart has not yet specified it. But there is another matter."

"Another?" he echoed dully, and, I observed, without surprise.

I led the way back to the room where Captain Murray waited. "Can you tell me anything about this?" I asked, pointing to the sovereign on the writing-table.

He shook his head, clearly puzzled, but anticipating mischief.

"The coin is marked, you see. I have reason to know that it was marked by its owner in order to detect a thief. Captain Murray found it just now among your stakes."

Somehow—for I liked the lad—I had not the heart to watch his face as I delivered this. I kept my eyes upon the coin, and waited, expecting an explosion—a furious denial, or at least a cry that he was the victim of a conspiracy. None came. I heard him breathing hard. After a long and very dreadful pause some words broke from him, so lowly uttered that my ears only just caught them.

"This too? O my God!"

I seated myself, the lad before me, and Captain Murray erect and rigid at the end of the table. "Listen, my lad," said I. "This wears an ugly look, but that a stolen coin has been found in your possession does not prove that you've stolen it."

"I did not. Sir, I swear to you on my honour, and before Heaven, that I did not."

"Very well," said I: "Captain Murray asserts that he found this among the moneys you had been staking at cards. Do you question that assertion?"

He answered almost without pondering. "No, sir. Captain Murray is a gentleman, and incapable of falsehood. If he says so, it was so."

"Very well again. Now, can you explain how this coin came into your possession?"

At this he seemed to hesitate; but answered at length: "No, I cannot explain."

"Have you any idea? Or can you form any guess?"

Again there was a long pause before the answer came in low and strained tones: "I can guess."

"What is your guess?"

He lifted a hand and dropped it hopelessly. "You would not believe," he said.

I will own a suspicion flashed across my mind on hearing these words —the very excuse given a while ago by Mr. Urquhart—that the whole affair was a hoax and the two young men were in conspiracy to befool me. I dismissed it at once: the sight of Mr. Mackenzie's face was convincing. But my temper was gone.

"Believe you?" I exclaimed. "You seem to think the one thing I can swallow as credible, even probable, is that an officer in the Morays has been pilfering and cheating at cards. Oddly enough, it's the last thing

I'm going to believe without proof, and the last charge I shall pass without clearing it up to my satisfaction. Captain Murray, will you go and bring me Mr. Urquhart and the Major?"

As Captain Murray closed the door I rose, and with my hands behind me took a turn across the room to the fireplace, then back to the writing-table.

"Mr. Mackenzie," I said, "before we go any further I wish you to believe that I am your friend as well as your Colonel. I did something to start you upon your career, and I take a warm interest in it. To believe you guilty of these charges will give me the keenest grief. However unlikely your defence may sound—and you seem to fear it—I will give it the best consideration I can. If you are innocent, you shall not find me prejudiced because many are against you and you are alone. Now, this coin—" I turned to the table.

The coin was gone.

I stared at the place where it had lain; then at the young man. He had not moved. My back had been turned for less than two seconds, and I could have sworn he had not budged from the square of carpet on which he had first taken his stand, and on which his feet were still planted. On the other hand, I was equally positive the incriminating coin had lain on the table at the moment I turned my back.

"It is gone!" cried I.

"Gone?" he echoed, staring at the spot to which my finger pointed. In the silence our glances were still crossing when my brother tapped at the door and brought in Mr. Urquhart, Captain Murray following.

Dismissing for a moment this latest mystery, I addressed Mr. Urquhart. "I have sent for you, sir, to request in the first place that here in Mr. Mackenzie's presence and in colder blood you will either withdraw or repeat and at least attempt to substantiate the charge you brought against him."

"I adhere to it, sir, that there was cheating. To withdraw would be to utter a lie. Does he deny it?"

I glanced at Mr. Mackenzie. "I deny that I cheated," said he sullenly.

"Further," pursued Mr. Urquhart, "I repeat what I told you, sir. He *may*, while profiting by it, have been unaware of the cheat. At the moment I thought it impossible; but I am willing to believe—"

"*You* are willing!" I broke in. "And pray, sir, what about me, his Colonel, and the rest of his brother-officers? Have you the coolness to suggest—"

But the full question was never put, and in this world it will never be answered. A bugle call, distant but clear, cut my sentence in half. It came from the direction of the Place d'Armes. A second bugle echoed it from the height of the Montagne du Parc, and within a minute its note was taken up and answered across the darkness from quarter after quarter of the city.

We looked at one another in silence. "Business," said my brother at length, curtly and quietly.

Already the rooms above us were astir. I heard windows thrown open, voices calling questions, feet running.

"Yes," said I, "it is business at length, and for the while this inquiry must end. Captain Murray, look to your company. You, Major, see that the lads tumble out quick to the alarm-post. One moment!"—and Captain Murray halted with his hand on the door—"It is understood that for the present no word of to-night's affair passes our lips." I turned to Mr. Mackenzie and answered the question I read in the lad's eyes. "Yes, sir; for the present I take off your arrest. Get your sword. It shall be your good fortune to answer the enemy before answering me."

To my amazement Mr. Urquhart interposed. He was, if possible, paler and more deeply agitated than before. "Sir, I entreat you not to allow Mr. Mackenzie to go. I have reasons—I was mistaken just now—"

"Mistaken, sir?"

"Not in what I saw. I refused to fight him—under a mistake. I thought—"

But I cut his stammering short. "As for you," I said, "the most charitable construction I can put on your behaviour is to believe you mad. For the present you, too, are free to go and do your duty. Now leave me. Business presses, and I am sick and angry at the sight of you."

It was just two in the morning when I reached the alarm-post. Brussels by this time was full of the rolling of drums and screaming of pipes; and the regiment formed up in darkness rendered tenfold more confusing by a mob of citizens, some wildly excited, others paralysed by terror, and all intractable. We had, moreover, no small trouble to disengage from our ranks the wives and families who had most unwisely followed many officers abroad, and now clung to their dear ones bidding them farewell. To end this most distressing scene I had in some instances to use a roughness which it still afflicts me to remember. Yet in actual time it was soon over, and dawn scarcely breaking when the Morays with the other regiments of Pack's brigade filed out of the park and fell into stride on the road which leads southward to Charleroi.

In this record it would be immaterial to describe either our march or the since-famous engagement which terminated it. Very early we began to hear the sound of heavy guns far ahead and to make guesses at their distance; but it was close upon two in the afternoon before we reached the high ground above Quatre Bras, and saw the battle spread below us like a picture. The Prince of Orange had been fighting his ground stubbornly since seven in the morning. Ney's superior artillery and far superior cavalry had forced him back, it is true; but he still covered the cross-roads which were the key of his defence, and his position, remained sound, though it was fast becoming critical. Just as we arrived, the French, who had already mastered the farm of Pier-mont on the left of the Charleroi road, began to push their skirmishers into a thicket below it and commanding the road running east to Namur. Indeed, for a short space they had this road at their mercy, and the chance within grasp of doubling up our left by means of it.

This happened, I say, just as we arrived; and Wellington, who had reached Quatre Bras a short while ahead of us (having fetched a cir-cuit from Brussels through Ligny, where he paused to inspect Field-Marshal Blücher's dispositions for battle), at once saw the danger, and detached one of our regiments, the 95th Rifles, to drive back the tirailleurs from the thicket; which, albeit scarcely breathed after their march, they did with a will, and so regained the Allies' hold upon the Namur road. The rest of us meanwhile defiled down this same road, formed line in front of it, and under a brisk cannonade from the French heights waited for the next move.

It was not long in coming. Ney, finding that our artillery made poor play against his, prepared to launch a column against us. Warned by a cloud of skirmishers, our light companies leapt forward, chose their shelter, and began a very pretty exchange of musketry. But this was preliminary work only, and soon the head of a large French column appeared on the slope to our right, driving the Brunswickers slowly before it. It descended a little way, and suddenly broke into three or four columns of attack. The mischief no sooner threatened than Picton came galloping along our line and roaring that our division would advance and engage with all speed. For a raw regiment like the Morays this was no light test; but, supported by a veteran regiment on either hand, they bore it admirably. Dropping the Gordons to protect the road in case of mishap, the two brigades swung forward in the prettiest style, their skirmishers running in and forming on their flank as they advanced. Then for a while the work was hot; but, as will al-ways happen when column is boldly met by line, the French quickly had enough of our enveloping fire, and wavered. A short charge with the bayonet finished it, and drove them in confusion up the slope: nor had I an easy task to resume a hold on my youngsters and restrain them from pursuing too far. The brush had been sharp, but I had the satis-faction of knowing that the Morays had behaved well. They also knew it, and fell to jesting in high good-humour as General Pack withdrew the brigade from the ground of its exploit and posted us in line with the 42nd and 44th Regiments on the left of the main road to Charleroi.

To the right of the Charleroi road, and some way in advance of our position, the Brunswickers were holding ground as best they could under a hot and accurate artillery fire. Except for this, the battle had come to a lull, when a second mass of the enemy began to move down the slopes: a battalion in line heading two columns of infantry direct upon the Brunswickers, while squadron after squadron of lancers crowded down along the road into which by weight of numbers they must be driven. The Duke of Brunswick, perceiving his peril, headed a charge of his lancers upon the advancing infantry, but without the least effect. His horsemen broke. He rode back and called on his infantry to retire in good order. They also broke, and in the attempt to rally them he fell mortally wounded.

The line taken by these flying Brunswickers would have brought them diagonally across the Charleroi road into our arms, had not the French lancers seized this moment to charge straight down it in a body. They encountered, and the indiscriminate mass was hurled on to us, choking and overflowing the causeway. In a minute we were swamped —the two Highland regiments and the 44th bending against a sheer weight of French horsemen. So suddenly came the shock that the 42nd had no time to form square, until two companies were cut off and well-nigh destroyed; *then* that noble regiment formed around the horsemen who could boast of having broken it, and left not one to bear back the tale. The 44th behaved more cleverly, but not more intrepidly: it did not attempt to form square, but faced its rear rank round and gave the Frenchmen a volley; before they could check their impetus the front rank poured in a second; and the light company, which had held its fire, delivered a third, breaking the crowd in two, and driving the hinder-part back in disorder and up the Charleroi road. But already the fore-part had fallen upon the Morays, fortunately the last of the three regiments to receive the shock. Though most fortunate, they had least experience, and were consequently slow in answering my shout. A wedge of lancers broke through us as we formed around the two standards, and I saw Mr. Urquhart with the King's colours hurled back in the rush. The pole fell with him, after swaying within a yard of a French lancer, who thrust out an arm to grasp it. And with that I saw Mackenzie divide the rush and stand—it may have been for five seconds —erect, with his foot upon the standard. Then three lances pierced him, and he fell. But the lateral pressure of their own troopers broke off the head of the wedge which the French had pushed into us. Their leading squadrons were pressed down the road and afterwards accounted for by the Gordons. Of the seven-and-twenty assailants around whom the Morays now closed, not one survived.

Towards nightfall, as Ney weakened and the Allies were reinforced, our troops pushed forward and recaptured every important position taken by the French that morning. The Morays, with the rest of Picton's division, bivouacked for the night in and around the farmstead of Gemiancourt.

So obstinately had the field been contested that darkness fell before the wounded could be collected with any thoroughness; and the comfort of the men around many a camp-fire was disturbed by groans (often quite near at hand) of some poor comrade or enemy lying helpless and undiscovered, or exerting his shattered limbs to crawl towards the blaze. And these interruptions at length became so distressing to the Morays, that two or three officers sought me and demanded leave to form a fatigue party of volunteers and explore the hedges and thickets with lanterns. Among them was Mr. Urquhart; and having readily given leave and accompanied them some little way on their search, I was bidding them good night and good speed when I found him standing at my elbow.

"May I have a word with you, Colonel?" he asked.

His voice was low and serious. Of course I knew what subject filled his thoughts. "Is it worth while, sir?" I answered. "I have lost to-day a brave lad for whom I had a great affection. For him the account is closed; but not for those who liked him and are still concerned in his good name. If you have anything further against him, or if you have any confession to make, I warn you that this is a bad moment to choose."

"I have only to ask," said he, "that you will grant me the first convenient hour for explaining; and to remind you that when I besought you not to send him into action to-day, I had no time to give you reasons."

"This is extraordinary talk, sir. I am not used to command the Morays under advice from my subalterns. And in this instance I had reasons for not even listening to you." He was silent. "Moreover," I continued, "you may as well know, though I am under no obligation to tell you, that I do most certainly not regret having given that permission to one who justified it by a signal service to his king and country."

"But would you have sent him *knowing* that he must die? Colonel," he went on rapidly, before I could interrupt, "I beseech you to listen. I *knew* he had only a few hours to live. I saw his wraith last night. It stood behind his shoulder in the room when in Captain Murray's presence he challenged me to fight him. You are a Highlander, sir: you may be sceptical about the second sight; but at least you must have heard many claim it. I swear positively that I saw Mr. Mackenzie's wraith last night, and for that reason, and no other, tried to defer the meeting. To fight him, knowing he must die, seemed to me as bad as murder. Afterwards, when the alarm sounded and you took off his arrest, I knew that his fate must overtake him—that my refusal had done no good. I tried to interfere again, and you would not hear. Naturally you would not hear; and very likely, if you had, his fate would have found him in some other way. That is what I try to believe. I hope it is not selfish, sir; but the doubt tortures me."

"Mr. Urquhart," I asked, "is this the only occasion on which you have possessed the second sight, or had reason to think so?"

"No, sir."

"Was it the first or only time last night you believed you were granted it?"

"It was the *second* time last night," he said steadily.

We had been walking back to my bivouac fire, and in the light of it I turned and said: "I will hear your story at the first opportunity. I will not promise to believe, but I will hear and weigh it. Go now and join the others in their search."

He saluted, and strode away into the darkness. The opportunity I promised him never came. At eleven o'clock next morning we began our withdrawal, and within twenty-four hours the battle of Waterloo had begun. In one of the most heroic feats of that day—the famous resistance of Pack's brigade—Mr. Urquhart was among the first to fall.

III

Thus it happened that an affair which so nearly touched the honour of the Morays, and which had been agitating me at the very moment when the bugle sounded in the Place d'Armes, became a secret shared by three only. The regiment joined in the occupation of Paris, and did not return to Scotland until the middle of December.

I had ceased to mourn for Mr. Mackenzie, but neither to regret him nor to speculate on the mystery which closed his career, and which, now that death had sealed Mr. Urquhart's lips, I could no longer hope to penetrate, when, on the day of my return to Inverness, I was reminded of him by finding, among the letters and papers awaiting me, a visiting-card neatly indited with the name of the Reverend Samuel Saul. On inquiry I learnt that the minister had paid at least three visits to Inverness during the past fortnight, and had, on each occasion, shown much anxiety to learn when the battalion might be expected. He had also left word that he wished to see me on a matter of much importance.

Sure enough, at ten o'clock next morning the little man presented himself. He was clearly bursting to disclose his business, and our salutations were scarce over when he ran to the door and called to someone in the passage outside.

"Elspeth! Step inside, woman. The housekeeper, sir, to the late Mr. Mackenzie of Ardlaugh," he explained, as he held the door to admit her.

She was dressed in ragged mourning, and wore a grotesque and fearful bonnet. As she saluted me respectfully I saw that her eyes indeed were dry and even hard, but her features set in an expression of quiet and hopeless misery. She did not speak, but left explanation to the minister.

"You will guess, sir," began Mr. Saul, "that we have called to learn more of the poor lad." And he paused.

"He died most gallantly," said I: "died in the act of saving the colours. No soldier could have wished for a better end."

"To be sure, to be sure. So it was reported to us. He died, as one might say, without a stain on his character?" said Mr. Saul, with a sort of question in his tone.

"He died," I answered, "in a way which could only do credit to his name."

A somewhat constrained silence followed. The woman broke it. "You are not telling us all," she said, in a slow, harsh voice.

It took me aback. "I am telling all that needs to be known," I assured her.

"No doubt, sir, no doubt," Mr. Saul interjected. "Hold your tongue, woman. I am going to tell Colonel Ross a tale which may or may not bear upon anything he knows. If not, he will interrupt me before I go far; but if he says nothing I shall take it I have his leave to continue. Now, sir, on the 16th day of June last, and at six in the morning—that would be the day of Quatre Bras—"

He paused for me to nod assent, and continued. "At six in the morning or a little earlier, this woman, Elspeth Mackenzie, came to me at the Manse in great perturbation. She had walked all the way from Ardlaugh. It had come to her (she said) that the young Laird abroad was in great trouble since the previous evening. I asked: 'What trouble? Was it danger of life, for instance?'—asking it not seriously, but rather to compose her; for at first I set down her fears to an old woman's whimsies. Not that I would call Elspeth *old* precisely—"

Here he broke off and glanced at her; but, perceiving she paid little attention, went on again at a gallop. "She answered that it was worse—that the young Laird stood very near disgrace, and (the worst of all was) at a distance she could not help him. Now, sir, for reasons I shall hereafter tell you, Mr. Mackenzie's being in disgrace would have little surprised me; but that she should know of it, he being in Belgium, was incredible. So I pressed her, and she being distraught and (I verily believe) in something like anguish, came out with a most extraordinary story: to wit, that the Laird of Ardlaugh had in his service, unbeknown to him (but, as she protested, well known to her), a familiar spirit—or, as we should say commonly, a "brownie"—which in general served him most faithfully but at times erratically, having no conscience nor any Christian principle to direct him. I cautioned her, but she persisted, in a kind of wild terror, and added that at times the spirit would, in all good faith, do things which no Christian allowed to be permissible, and further, that she had profited by such actions. I asked her: 'Was thieving one of them?' She answered that it was, and indeed the chief.

"Now, this was an admission which gave me some eagerness to hear more. For to my knowledge there were charges lying against young Mr. Mackenzie—though not pronounced—which pointed to a thief in his employment and presumably in his confidence. You will remember, sir, that when I had the honour of meeting you at Mr. Mackenzie's table, I took my leave with much abruptness. You remarked upon it, no doubt. But you will no longer think it strange when I tell you that there—under my nose—were a dozen apples of a sort which grows nowhere within twenty miles of Ardlaugh but in my own Manse garden. The tree was a new one, obtained from Herefordshire, and planted three seasons before as an experiment. I had watched it, therefore, particularly; and on that very morning had counted the fruit, and been dismayed to find twelve apples missing. Further, I am a pretty good judge of wine (though I taste it rarely), and could there and then have taken my oath that the claret our host set before us was the very wine I had tasted at the table of his neighbour Mr. Gillespie. As for the venison—I had already heard whispers that deer and all game were not safe within a mile or two of Ardlaugh. These were injurious tales, sir, which I had no mind to believe; for, bating his religion, I saw everything in Mr. Mackenzie which disposed me to like him. But I knew (as neighbours must) of the shortness of his purse; and the multiplied evidence (particularly my own Goodrich pippins staring me in the face) overwhelmed me for a moment.

"So then, I listened to this woman's tale with more patience—or, let

me say, more curiosity—than you, sir, might have given it. She persisted, I say, that her master was in trouble; and that the trouble had
something to do with a game of cards, but that Mr. Mackenzie had
been innocent of deceit, and the real culprit was this spirit I tell of—"

Here the women herself broke in upon Mr. Saul. "He had nae conscience—he had nae conscience. He was just a poor luck-child, born
by mischance and put away without baptism. He had nae conscience.
How should he?"

I looked from her to Mr. Saul in perplexity.

"Whilst!" said he; "we'll talk of that anon."

"We will not," said she. "We will talk of it now. He was my own
child, sir, by the young Laird's own father. That was before he was
married upon the wife he took later—"

Here Mr. Saul nudged me, and whispered: "The old Laird had her
married to that daunderin' old half-wit Duncan, to cover things up.
This part of the tale is true enough, to my knowledge."

"My bairn was overlaid, sir," the woman went on; "not by purpose,
I will swear before you and God. They buried his poor body without
baptism; but not his poor soul. Only when the young Laird came, and
my own bairn clave to him as Mackenzie to Mackenzie, and wrought
and hunted and mended for him—it was not to be thought that the
poor innocent, without knowledge of God's ways—"

She ran on incoherently, while my thoughts harked back to the
voice I had heard wailing behind the door of the *entresol* at Brussels;
to the young Laird's face, his furious indignation, followed by hopeless apathy, as of one who in the interval had learnt what he could
never explain; to the marked coin so mysteriously spirited from sight;
to Mr. Urquhart's words before he left me on the night of Quatre
Bras.

"But he was sorry," the woman ran on; "he was sorry—sorry. He
came wailing to me that night; yes, and sobbing. He meant no wrong;
it was just that he loved his own father's son, and knew no better.
There was no priest living within thirty miles; so I dressed, and ran to
the minister here. *He* gave me no rest until I started."

I addressed Mr. Saul. "Is there reason to suppose that, besides this
woman and (let us say) her accomplice, any one shared the secret of
these pilferings?"

"Ardlaugh never knew," put in the woman quickly. "He may have
guessed we were helping him; but the lad knew nothing, and may the
saints in heaven love him as they ought? He trusted me with his purse,
and slight it was to maintain him. But until too late he never knew—
no, never, sir!"

I thought again of that voice behind the door of the *entresol*.

"Elspeth Mackenzie," I said, "I and two other living men alone know of what your master was accused. It cannot affect him; but these two shall hear your exculpation of him. And I will write the whole story down, so that the world, if it ever hears the charge, may also hear your testimony, which of the two (though both are strange) I believe to be not the less credible."

Sources

[Anonymous], "Le Vert Galant." From *Belgravia Annual*, London, 1871.

[Anonymous], "The Old Lady in Black." From *Argosy*, London, 1894.

GERTRUDE ATHERTON, "Death and the Woman." From *The Bell in the Fog*, New York, 1905. First published in 1892.

MRS. ALFRED BALDWIN, "The Empty Picture Frame." From *The Shadow on the Blind*, London, 1895.

AMBROSE BIERCE, "Bodies of the Dead." From *Can Such Things Be?*, New York, 1893.

MARY E. BRADDON, "At Chrighton Abbey." From *Belgravia Annual*, London, 1871.

RHODA BROUGHTON, "The Man with the Nose." From *Tales for Christmas Eve*, London, 1873. As reprinted London, 1947.

BERNARD CAPES, "The Vanishing House." From *At a Winter's Fire*, London, 1899.

WILKIE COLLINS, "Nine O'Clock!" From *Bentley's Miscellany*, London, 1852.

MRS. CATHERINE CROWE, "The Dutch Officer's Story." From *Ghosts and Family Legends*, London, 1848. As reprinted in *The Eerie Book*, edited by Margaret Armour, London, 1898.

EMMA DAWSON, "A Stray Reveler." From *An Itinerant House and Other Stories*, San Francisco, 1897.

CHARLES DICKENS, "To Be Read at Dusk." From *The Keepsake*, London, 1852.

———, "The Ghost in the Bride's Chamber." From *Household Words*, London, 1857. As reprinted in *The Lazy Tour of Two Lazy Apprentices and Other Stories* by Charles Dickens and Wilkie Collins, London, 1890.

353

R. MURRAY GILCHRIST, "Witch In-grain." From *The Stone Dragon and Other Tragic Romances*, London, 1894.

JULIAN HAWTHORNE, "Ken's Mystery." From *David Poindexter's Disappearance*, New York, 1888.

PAUL HEYSE, "Midday Magic." Edited from *At the Ghost Hour: Midday Magic*, New York, 1894.

J. S. LE FANU, "Wicked Captain Walshawe of Wauling." From *Dublin University Magazine*, Dublin, 1864.

E. NESBIT, "The Mystery of the Semi-detached." From *Grim Tales*, London, 1893.

MRS. MARGARET OLIPHANT, "The Library Window." From *Blackwood's Magazine*, Edinburgh, 1896. As reprinted in *Stories of the Seen and Unseen*, Edinburgh, 1902.

VINCENT O'SULLIVAN, "My Enemy and Myself." From *A Book of Bargains*, London, 1896.

ELIA W. PEATTIE, "A Grammatical Ghost." From *The Shape of Fear*, New York, 1898.

ARTHUR QUILLER-COUCH, "The Laird's Luck." From *The Laird's Luck*, London, 1901. As reprinted in *Q's Mystery Stories*, London, 1937.

MRS. J. H. RIDDELL, "A Terrible Vengeance." From *Princess Sunshine and Other Stories*, London, 1889.

MRS. HENRY WOOD, "A Curious Experience." From *Argosy*, London, 1874. As reprinted in *Johnny Ludlow, Fourth Series*, London, 1890.

A Suggested Chronological Reading List in Victorian Supernatural Fiction

MEINHOLD, WILHELM. *The Amber Witch* (1844 in English translation) and *Sidonia the Sorceress* (1847 in English translation). German origin. Chronicle novels of seventeenth-century Germany, with witchcraft and magic described with a verisimilitude worthy of Daniel Defoe. *The Amber Witch* was taken to be a historical document when it was first published.

LE FANU, JOSEPH SHERIDAN. *Ghost Stories and Tales of Mystery* (1851), *In a Glass Darkly* (1872), *Madam Crowl's Ghost* (1923, edited by M. R. James). Le Fanu, all in all, is probably the most important nineteenth-century author of supernatural fiction. Since the original collections are extremely rare books, the reader should consult two modern collections that gather together all Le Fanu's supernatural fiction: *Best Ghost Stories of J. S. Le Fanu* (New York, 1964) and *Ghost Stories and Mysteries of J. S. Le Fanu* (New York, 1975).

DICKENS, CHARLES. *The Christmas Stories of Charles Dickens* (1852). Often reprinted under this title, or variants, or in his collected works, including *A Christmas Carol in Prose* (1843), *The Chimes* (1844), and *The Haunted Man and the Ghost's Bargain* (1848). Available in many collections are "The Bagman's Story," "The Story of the Bagman's Uncle," and "The Story of the Goblins Who Stole a Sexton" from *Posthumous Papers of the Pickwick Club* (1836–37) as well as the stories "To Be Taken with a Grain of Salt" (1865) and "No. 1 Branch Line, The Signalman (1866)."

MACDONALD, GEORGE. *Phantastes* (1858). Allegorical fantastic adventure, with an odd mixture of erotic and somewhat heretical Christian religious symbolism. Ultimately a story of redemption

355

through self-sacrifice. *The Portent* (1864) is a highly colored neo-Gothic fiction based ultimately on psychopathology.

BULWER-LYTTON, EDWARD GEORGE. "The Haunted and the Haunters" (1859). Very often anthologized, it is probably the most lurid and most influential haunted house in the literature. *A Strange Story* (1861) is a long occult novel about the magical quest, partly allegorical. Muddled and inconsequential at times, but historically probably the most important nineteenth-century supernatural novel with influence on later developments as far separated as Robert Louis Stevenson's *Dr. Jekyll and Mr. Hyde* and the stories of W. H. Hodgson.

COLLINS, WILKIE. *Armadale* (1866). A long novel about crime, mystery, a prophetic dream, and fate; on the same level as his *The Moonstone* and *The Woman in White*. *Little Novels* (1887) is a collection of short stories, some of which are supernatural. The earlier short stories "Mad Monkton" and "The Dream Woman" are very often anthologized.

BROUGHTON, RHODA. *Tales for Christmas Eve* (1873). Also reprinted under the title *Twilight Tales*. The original edition is nearly impossible to find, but there is a modern reprinting edited by Herbert Van Thal (London, 1947).

RIDDELL, MRS. J. H. *Weird Stories* (1882). She is probably second to Le Fanu among the middle Victorian writers. The original publication is impossibly rare, but all her shorter supernatural fiction has been reprinted in *The Collected Ghost Stories of Mrs. J. H. Riddell* (New York, 1977). The best of her supernatural novels, *The Uninhabited House* (1875), has been reprinted in *Five Victorian Ghost Novels*, edited by E. F. Bleiler (New York, 1971).

PRAED, ROSA C. *Affinities* (1885) and *The Brother of the Shadow* (1886). Mrs. Praed was primarily a society novelist, but was greatly interested in occultism, and these two novels, the best of her work, provide a good picture of Theosophical interests in the 1880s.

LEE, VERNON (pseudonym of VIOLET PAGET). *Hauntings* (1890). The author was one of the pioneers in the study of eighteenth-century Italian culture and her fiction often incorporated antiquarian lore about music and art. The book is difficult to find, but individual stories are often anthologized.

DOYLE, ARTHUR CONAN. *The Captain of the "Polestar"* (1890) and *The Great Keinplatz Experiment* (1895). There is no point in going to the rare original editions. *The Conan Doyle Stories Omnibus* (London, 1929) contains most of Doyle's supernatural fiction, as does *Best Supernatural Fiction of A. C. Doyle* (New York, 1979).

BIERCE, AMBROSE. *Tales of Men and Ghosts* (1891) and *Can Such Things Be?* (1893). Original editions are rare, and the bibliography of reprints and secondary collections is very complex. A modern edition that contains almost all Bierce's supernatural stories (not including "Bodies of the Dead") is *Ghost and Horror Stories of Ambrose Bierce* (New York, 1964).

WILDE, OSCAR. *The Picture of Dorian Gray* (1891) and *Lord Arthur Savile's Crime* (1891). The second contains the amusing parody "The Canterville Ghost," which is often anthologized.

MACHEN, ARTHUR. *The Great God Pan* (1894) and *The Three Impostors* (1895). Probably the outstanding British writer of fin de siècle supernatural fiction, highly important historically. Original editions are rare, but individual stories are often anthologized.

CHAMBERS, ROBERT W. *The King in Yellow* (1895). Superior to Chambers's later work, very important in the development of American supernatural fiction. His stories are often anthologized, and a reprint edition, *The King in Yellow and Other Horror Stories* (New York, 1970), contains the better stories.

FALKNER, JOHN MEADE. *The Lost Stradivarius* (1895). Usually available in reprint editions.

SHIEL, M. P. *Shapes in the Fire* (1896). The eccentric Shiel was probably the most extreme of the fin de siècle writers, and his stories are a welter of stylistic sound effects, not to everyone's taste. The book is rare, but individual stories are often anthologized.

STOKER, BRAM. *Dracula* (1897). A listing would not be complete without this crude but powerful vampire novel. Stoker's later work, beyond the Victorian era, is much weaker.

JAMES, MONTAGUE RHODES. *Ghost Stories of an Antiquary* (1904). Although the book publication date is outside the Victorian period, several of the stories were written before 1900.

QUILLER-COUCH, SIR ARTHUR. *Q's Mystery Stories* (1937). This reprints some of "Q"'s earlier stories, but many more are scattered in his early collections of short stories.

JAMES, HENRY. All James's supernatural fiction and several borderline stories are reprinted in Leon Edel's excellent collection *The Ghostly Tales of Henry James* (1948). Individual stories, such as "The Turn of the Screw," are often anthologized.

While Victorian humorous supernatural fiction is weak as a subgenre, the following volumes are recommended:

ANSTEY, F. (pseudonym of THOMAS S. GUTHRIE). *Vice Versa* (1882). A full, Dickensian school story of personality interchange and adjustment. *A Fallen Idol* (1886) is a spoof on Theosophy and Wisdom of the East. Both are reprinted in the collection *Humour and Fantasy* (1931).

GARNETT, RICHARD. *The Twilight of the Gods* (1888; enlarged edition, 1903). Heavily ironic short stories based on antiquarian lore.

A treasury of Victorian ghost stories